CARRIER P9-EJK-734

These are the stories of the Carrier Battle Group Fourteen—a force including a supercarrier, amphibious unit, guided missile cruiser, and destroyer. And these are the novels that capture the blistering reality of international combat. Exciting. Authentic. Explosive.

CARRIER . . . The smash debut thriller about the ultimate military nightmare: the takeover of a U.S. Intelligence ship.

VIPER STRIKE . . . A renegade Chinese fighter group penetrates Thai airspace—and launches a full-scale invasion.

ARMAGEDDON MODE . . . With India and Pakistan on the verge of nuclear destruction, the Carrier Battle Group Fourteen must prevent a final showdown.

FLAME-OUT . . . The Soviet Union is reborn in a military takeover—and their strike force shows no mercy.

MAELSTROM . . . The Soviet occupation of Scandinavia leads the Carrier Battle Group Fourteen into conventional weapons combat—and possibly all-out war.

COUNTDOWN . . . Carrier Battle Group Fourteen must prevent the deployment of Russian submarines. The problem: They have nukes.

AFTERBURN . . . Carrier Battle Group Fourteen receives orders to enter the Black Sea—in the middle of a Russian civil war.

continued on next page . . .

ALPHA STRIKE . . . When American and Chinese interests collide in the South China Sea, the superpowers risk waging a third world war.

ARCTIC FIRE . . . A Russian splinter group has occupied the Aleutian Islands off the coast of Alaska—in the ultimate invasion of U.S. soil.

ARSENAL . . . Magruder and his crew are trapped between Cuban revolutionaries . . . and a U.S. power play that's spun wildly out of control.

NUKE ZONE . . . When a nuclear missile is launched against the U.S. Sixth Fleet, Magruder must face a frightening question: In an age of computer warfare, how do you tell friends from enemies?

CHAIN OF COMMAND . . . Magruder enters the jungles of Vietnam, looking for answers about his missing father. Little does he know that another bloody war is about to be unleashed—with his fleet caught in the crosshairs.

BRINK OF WAR . . . Friendly war games with the Russians take a deadly turn, and Carrier Battle Group Fourteen must prevent war from erupting in the skies. Little do they know that's just what someone wants.

TYPHOON . . . An American yacht is attacked by a Chinese helicopter in international waters, and the Carrier team is called to the front lines of what may be the start of a war between the superpowers.

ENEMY OF MY ENEMY . . . A Greek pilot unwittingly downs a news chopper, and Magruder must keep the peace between Greece and the breakaway republic of Macedonia. But what no one knows is that it wasn't an accident at all.

JOINT OPERATIONS . . . China launches a surprise attack on Hawaii—and the Carrier team can't handle it alone. As Tombstone and his fleet take charge of the air, Lieutenant Murdock and his SEALs are called in to work ashore.

THE ART OF WAR . . . When Iranian militants take the first bloody step toward toppling the decadent West, the Carrier group are the only ones who can stop the madmen.

ISLAND WARRIORS . . . China launches a full-scale invasion on their tiny capitalist island neighbor—and Carrier Battle Group Fourteen is the only hope to stop it.

FIRST STRIKE . . . A group of radical Russian military officers are planning a nuclear attack on the United States, but Carrier Battle Group Fourteen has been called in to make sure the Cold War ends without a bang.

HELLFIRE . . . A top-secret missile defense system being tested aboard the *USS Jefferson* accidentally targets Russia, igniting Cold War tensions once more—leaving Carrier Battle Group Fourteen to defend itself.

TERROR AT DAWN . . . Even as a raid on an Idaho militia compound goes horribly wrong—with deadly consequences—Carrier Battle Group Fourteen must face attacks from both Iran and North Korea, which may spark all-out war.

FINAL JUSTICE . . . The United States is under siege as vengeful militants plan to bomb the Super Bowl, and a deranged Kim Jong Il moves his troops to the 38th Parallel. Now only Carrier Battle Group Fourteen can prevent the outbreak of World War III.

book twenty-three

CARRIER

Last Stand

KEITH DOUGLASS

JOVE BOOKS, NEW YORK

THE BERKLEY PUBLISHING GROUP
Published by the Penguin Group
Penguin Group (USA) Inc.
375 Hudson Street, New York, New York 10014, USA
Penguin Group (Canada), 90 Eglinton Avenue East, Suite 700, Toronto, Ontario M4P 2Y3, Canada
(a division of Pearson Penguin Canada Inc.)
Penguin Books Ltd., 80 Strand, London WC2R 0RL, England
Penguin Group Ireland, 25 St. Stephen's Green, Dublin 2, Ireland (a division of Penguin Books Ltd.)
Penguin Group (Australia), 250 Camberwell Road, Camberwell, Victoria 3124, Australia
(a division of Pearson Australia Group Pty. Ltd.)
Penguin Books India Pvt. Ltd., 11 Community Centre, Panchsheel Park, New Delhi—110 017, India
Penguin Group (NZ), Cnr. Airborne and Rosedale Roads, Albany, Auckland 1310, New Zealand
(a division of Pearson New Zealand Ltd.)
Penguin Books (South Africa) (Pty.) Ltd., 24 Sturdee Avenue, Rosebank, Johannesburg 2196, South
Africa

Penguin Books Ltd., Registered Offices: 80 Strand, London WC2R 0RL, England

This is a work of fiction. Names, characters, places, and incidents either are the product of the author's
imagination or are used fictitiously, and any resemblance to actual persons, living or dead, business establishments, events, or locales is entirely coincidental. The publisher does not have any control over
and does not assume any responsibility for author or third-party websites or their content.

CARRIER: LAST STAND

A Jove Book / published by arrangement with the author.

PRINTING HISTORY
Jove mass market edition / January 2006

Copyright © 2006 by The Berkley Publishing Group.

ISBN: 0-515-14053-8

JOVE®
Jove Books are published by The Berkley Publishing Group,
a division of Penguin Group (USA) Inc.,
375 Hudson Street, New York, New York 10014.
JOVE is a registered trademark of Penguin Group (USA) Inc.
The "J" design is a trademark belonging to Penguin Group (USA) Inc.

PRINTED IN THE UNITED STATES OF AMERICA

10 9 8 7 6 5 4 3 2 1

*To Darrell Shelor
Major, USMC, Retired*

*Special Acknowledgment to
Patrick E. Andrews*

CHAPTER ONE

***The Container Ship* Edvard Grieg**
East China Sea
27 May
1640 Hours

The *Edvard Grieg* was a month out of Stavanger after stops in Liverpool, Lisbon, Taiwan, and Singapore to discharge and take on cargo. This state-of-the-art Norwegian vessel was now bound for Osaka with machinery and parts needed at various Japanese industrial centers. The ship would pick up finished products there for transport to the port of Long Beach, California.

The bridge officer on the first dog watch was Second Officer Lars Stensland. He was a slim blond man with an angular clean-shaven face that portrayed the blue-eyed, tanned look of a Scandinavian seafarer. His only companion was *Kadett* Sven Bjornson who was on summer assignment to the ship from Stensland's old alma mater, the Norwegian Maritime Academy. Stensland was amused by Bjornson's constant and unnecessary monitoring of the vessel's instrumentation, but he appreciated the youngster's keenness.

The second officer felt almost useless on the bridge that seemed so clinical and antiseptic even to a clean freak like a

Scandinavian. Computers performed the functions that
ancient sailors had once done with sextants, wheels, sails,
and dead reckoning. A quick glance at any of the cathode
ray tubes gave exact position, course, ETA, weather, hazards, and other vital information necessary to maintain a
safe and timely voyage. In addition to being able to check
their exact position by the GPS, they could electronically
plot and computerize the vessel to run on automatic pilot.
This was done when the captain or navigator moved a computer mouse on the map display, being careful to avoid indicated navigational hazards. The information was stored
on a 3.5-inch disc, which was then loaded into a guidance
computer console. This instrumentation piloted the vessel
along the selected course from that data.

Stensland's eyes swept the state-of-the-art bridge, thinking about his Viking ancestors who first ventured away from
the sight of land. Those daring seafarers used crude navigational methods such as observing the color of water or the
direction of waves to determine the course they must follow. As innumerable decades rolled by, they mastered the
use of the sun, moon, and stars to determine direction. It
was amazing that they could accurately move from point **A**
to point **B**, but somehow they did. Of course, those were
the successful ones. He wondered about the failures. How
many bones lay scattered across the ocean floor because
mistakes were made? One never heard of their fates in history books. The percentage of losses must have been great.
But, as more time passed, the direction-finding efforts improved with the sun compasses, astrolabes, cross staffs,
magnetic compasses, sextants, and chronometers right up to
the state-of-the-art bridge of the *Edvard Grieg.*

Yet, in spite of that impersonal automation, Stensland
was as proud of his ship as any of his Viking ancestors had
been of their sail-and-oar-propelled boats. Of course those
old Vikings weren't always hauling cargo; sometimes they
took to the ocean on raiding and plundering cruises. The
goods they brought back to their homeland were loot taken
from victims, not merchandise acquired through peaceful
trade.

The *Edvard Grieg* had been 100 percent Norwegian designed and manufactured five years earlier at the Olson Maritimfabrikk shipyard in Ålesund. She displaced 51,000 tons as her single-screw 50,000 horsepower Lynstråle diesel engine drove her through the water at speeds up to twenty-five knots. At this time the good ship's maximum cargo capacity of 4,500 TEU was filled, and the resultant weight kept her solid on the ocean as she plowed the waves toward Japan.

Stensland glanced forward over the deck. The containers there were stacked five high as symmetrically and solid as a regiment of marines on parade. Belowdecks, in the cells of the holds, additional containers were securely nestled together. The size of those devices had been standardized for fitting on any make of truck or railroad car anywhere in the world.

The only thing that marred the sight of the containers on deck was the varied colors and conditions. Reds and yellows were the most common with a few blues and greens scattered through the group. Some seemed brand-new, but the majority were faded and rust-streaked.

Stensland wondered if everything inside them matched the cargo manifest. He recalled a time in the port of Vancouver during unloading when an unexpected noise was heard coming from a container. When it was opened, a famished young Chinaman staggered out, half mad with thirst. He and two companions had paid some stevedores in Hong Kong to let them conceal themselves in the interior. The kid's buddies were dead, and the incident caused a myriad of paperwork and court appearances for the ship's captain. At least Canadian law was liberal about aliens appearing on their shores, no matter the circumstances. That made things easier.

Stensland was used to the vagaries of international law. He was a veteran in his country's merchant marine with a dozen years of experience. When he finished his studies at the academy and earned an officer's certificate, he sought the adventurous life offered in Norway's fishing fleet rather than the mostly mundane routine of cargo shipping. He had kept his choice of assignments from his parents and his fiancée, Kristina Olson, during the school year, but he had to reveal his duty destination to all three on the day of his graduation. He broke the news to them immediately following the ceremony. It was not surprising that his mother, herself descended from one of Norway's most prestigious seafaring families, had been extremely disappointed with his choice.

"Lars!" she cried. "You are an honor graduate! Your grandfather, Commodore Brundtland, will turn over in his grave! Several shipping lines have sent letters offering you excellent positions in their organizations. Why do you want to go—well, *fishing*?"

"It is difficult to explain, Mother," he replied. "But I have made up my mind."

Kristina chimed in. "*Elskling!* The fishing fleet will not pay you as much as the shipping lines."

"Actually I might make more money when the fishing goes well," Stensland countered.

His father was more understanding. "Julia! Kristina! Let Lars get it out of his system. He is a robust young man. He will yearn for a more desirable position after a few seasons with the fishing fleet. Trust me on that."

Mrs. Stensland sighed and nodded a reluctant acquiescence. "Oh, very well, Henrik." Kristina knew better than to argue with her future father-in-law, but she expressed her disagreement with a cold glare at the young officer.

Henrik Stensland was very much aware his son Lars wanted adventure, danger, and a manly experience after the years of study and books that afforded only brief episodes of sea duty. The father was secretly proud that the adventurous spirit of Viking warriors burned in his only son's soul.

Out in the fishing fleet, the navigation and steerage was done with brain and muscle. Of course they used GPS, loran, and Decca navigational systems, but they followed no set courses while out seeking the abundant fish that schooled in the North and Norwegian Seas. It was a wild, unpredictable life, and the men who lived it had a fierce pride in their collective disregard of the peril and hardship. Their work was done on sleet-swept decks where the wind-chill factor dropped far below 0° Fahrenheit.

Unfortunately, Kristina's love faded during the long separations, and she broke off the engagement to marry a banker in Oslo. Stensland took the loss stoically, knowing it was probably better than marrying and later divorcing after a long period of unhappiness. He smothered his hurt, returning to continue his career.

Stensland spent a full five years in that thunderous environment aboard the seiner *Heldig,* and no less than a half-dozen times the unpredictable weather flared up into tempestuous furies without warning. The fishermen were propelled by nature's wrath into harm's way as they fought like hell to save life, limb, and their boats. Waves with crests whipped into froth rose so high during the tempests that even nearby vessels were lost to view, and the decks beneath the crewmen's feet vibrated with a solid thumping as the structures creaked with the natural torque applied by the attacks of both wind and water.

These were frightening experiences, but young Stensland reveled in the danger, proud that he possessed instinctive physical courage in the face of the pounding peril. But in the fifth season of the job, the black hand of death gripped down hard on the *Heldig* after thirty-six hours of brutal pounding. The captain fought the wheel, riding with the wind that blew them farther out onto the open ocean. Everyone had gotten into their survival suits as per regulations. These hooded garments that could also be classified as dry suits, were made of a neoprene and titanium combination fabric. Each suit contained a built-in PFD along with a harness. The latter was handy for somebody to grab when pulling the wearer aboard a vessel or lifeboat. If the rescue was by helicopter, the fasteners at the end of the lifting cable could be hooked onto an eyelet there as well. All this, along with neoprene gloves and nonslip booties guaranteed a lost soul in the sea several hours of survival in even the coldest water.

As the crew huddled below, Stensland stood by the skipper, helping him when the rudder refused the pressure from the wheel. They worked at the shoulder-cramping chore, their thigh muscles aching from the constant need to balance themselves against the erratic maneuverings of the deck. Then the wheel suddenly whirled to one side and came to a stop with such force that both Stensland and his captain were thrown to the wheelhouse deck. They quickly struggled back to their feet, but even their combined strength could not budge the wheel.

A quick look out the aft window at the stern revealed the problem. The lines holding the auxiliary seine had broken loose from the securing pad eyes, and the net had slid abaft to the stern. A large portion had gone over the side and ended up jammed around the rudder and propeller. The *Heldig* was completely powerless and without steerage.

Stensland acted instinctively without orders. He wrenched the fire ax from its place on the bulkhead and charged through the door to the outside. The wind was so cold that it burned hot against his face as his skin reacted to the first onslaught of frostbite. He staggered across the pitching deck toward the stern, ready to begin chopping the net loose. Suddenly the bow pitched up under a climbing wave, causing Stensland to fall and slide. The last thing he remembered was hitting the aft rail hard, then being picked up by the wind and blown upward under the uplifting gusts.

It was impossible to determine how long he had been tossed across the gray green mountains of the raging sea. His survival suit did not keep him warm, but it kept him afloat while providing enough protection to delay the onslaught of hypothermia. His mind sank into a deep blankness as the ordeal continued.

When he regained consciousness, he was in a comfortable rack aboard an unknown ship. He lay there sore and exhausted, and looked up when the figure of a man loomed over him. It was a Norwegian navy medical *kapteinløtnant* who assured Stensland that he was all right. No frozen fingers or toes to be amputated. Even his nose had escaped gangrene. But the doctor had bad news, too. The *Heldig* had been lost at sea with all hands. The last contact with her stated she was taking on water and sinking fast. It was the worst timing possible. All *Krigsflåte* helicopters were grounded because of the weather, and no ship was close enough to render aid. No trace was ever found of her or the crew. *Heldig* translated as "lucky" in English, and she had not lived up to her name.

When Stensland was released from the hospital, he was healthy physically but devastated spiritually. He would lie awake at nights trying to figure out how to deal with this dilemma. The main problem was being unable to recall the long hours of being all alone in the pitching expanse of the ocean, while held on the water's surface by the buoyancy of the survival suit. If he could remember details, he could deal with them in his conscious mind. It was his subconscious that engendered those feelings of dread that plagued him so relentlessly.

Many times as he slept, he would have nightmares of huge undulating mountains of water that rose up, curled over, then crashed down on him. He would be pushed under the crushing ocean, holding his breath until he thought his lungs would burst before he suddenly surfaced in a violent upheaval. He would no sooner begin to breathe again than another of the gigantic cascades of green foaming seawater slammed down on him until he was once again submerged in the bubbly cold and wet deepness. He would wake up from the recurring dream gasping for breath. These were moments of hurtful truth that forced him to admit to himself that he didn't have the guts to go out fishing again.

When Stensland returned to duty, he did not seek a berth on a fishing boat. Instead, he applied for the first available position on board any cruise ship that sailed the tropical waters in the winter season. Those vessels seemed even farther removed from the fishing fleet than cargo freighters. He needed a change, and he need it badly.

Within a month he was sailing as the third officer aboard the *Happy Vagabond* of the Halverson Cruise Lines. They used Port Canaveral, Florida, as their home port and made biweekly winter cruises to the Bahamas,

Puerto Rico, and various other ports farther south into the Lesser Antilles. Everything was predictable and safe. The area's hurricane warning system meant no storms would unexpectedly erupt from sea and sky to sweep over the large vessel. The only problem for Stensland was that he hated to deal with any of the 2,000 passengers that boarded the ship for each voyage. Most came from America's northeast or Canada's southeast. They arrived on board, almost frantic for even a temporary escape from the cold, wet misery of their homes to bask for a short time in the warmth of the Caribbean sun.

The first days on deck they appeared as pale-skinned creatures arrayed in colorful clothing. As a ship's officer Stensland was expected to be polite, helpful, and courteous to the vacationers. He soon discovered that while people might be well-educated, well-off, and well-behaved at home, the moment they became tourists, they turned into demanding idiots. The offspring of these seasonal dolts were noisy, spoiled, and petulant during the days confined aboard. Stensland put up with them as best he could during his hours on duty.

Single women passengers were attracted to the handsome ship's officer, and several made bold advances toward him. But company regulations and his undying love for the lost Katrina precluded any shipboard romance. But it made him realize how lonely he was. He did have several brief affairs on shore during respites between cruises, but none ever turned serious.

After a year and a half on the *Happy Vagabond,* Stensland had had enough with tourists and resigned his position. But he still could not make himself go back to fishing. When he returned to Norway, he hid his private shame and sought a berth in the merchant fleet. Thus, Lars Stensland was appointed second officer on the *Edvard Grieg.*

Now, as the container ship moved toward Japan, Stensland walked to the starboard side of the bridge and took a disinterested glance out toward the watery horizon. Suddenly he stiffened and spoke tersely to the cadet.

"Bjornson! Why didn't you report that warship closing in on us?"

Bjornson frowned in puzzlement and looked at the radarscope. "There is no vessel within our detection range, sir."

Stensland angrily hurried over to the radar. It was blank. He rushed back and took another glance outside to make sure he wasn't going crazy. He noticed the warship was a destroyer, and it showed no national ensign. Stensland went back and checked the radar to make sure it was operating properly. Everything checked out, but the stranger's image did not appear in the green and yellow tube. Then a voice speaking heavily accented English came over the radio loudspeaker.

"Attention, Norwegian ship. Attention, Norwegian ship. Heave to and prepare to be boarded. Over."

Stensland turned to Bjornson. "Fetch the captain quickly!" As the cadet rushed off, the second officer picked up the microphone, pushing the Transmit button. "This is the Norwegian container ship *Edvard Grieg*. Identify yourself and your nationality. Over."

The accented voice responded. "I say again. Heave to and prepare to be boarded. You will do so immediately or suffer consequences. Over."

"I am not authorized to break this voyage," Stensland replied. "Wait for the captain. He will be here presently."

Captain Trim Bokkerson came up on the bridge. "What the hell is going on, Number Two?"

"An unidentified warship has ordered us to heave to and prepare to be boarded, *Keptein*," Stensland reported. Then he added, "Sir, she does not show up on the radar."

"*Umulig*—impossible!" Captain Bokkerson scoffed. He walked over to the scope, then to the window. He returned for another glance at the radar. "What the hell is she? A *spøelseskip*—a ghost ship?" He picked up the microphone. "This is the captain. What is your message for me? Over."

"You are to heave to immediately. Prepare to be boarded. If you do not comply, we will fire on you. Over."

"What is your nationality?" Captain Bokkerson demanded to know. "Over."

The speaker ignored the question. "Heave to immediately and prepare to be boarded. If you do not begin the procedure within five minutes, we will fire on you. Over."

The captain's jaw tightened, then relaxed. "I will comply. Over." He turned to Stensland. "Bring the ship to a halt, Number Two."

Stensland walked to the large console to send a signal to the engine room as he switched to manual control. The slowdown began gradually, then the engine was reversed. A half hour passed before the *Edvard Grieg* was relatively still in the water. The destroyer drew closer as its crew lowered an MWB for transport to the Norwegian vessel. An officer and a dozen sailors were in the boat. All were armed with automatic shoulder weapons. Stensland was puzzled by the officer's appearance. He carried a pistol and sword. Two more sailors boarded the small craft, carrying a bulky item between them that was covered by an opaque plastic cover.

Stensland went to the chart desk and pulled out his digital camera. He took it over to the bridge window and took several shots. Captain Bokkerson nodded his approval, saying, "Good thinking, Number Two. These fellows are going to have to answer for this."

After Stensland returned the camera to its place, Bokkerson sent him and Bjornson down to the third deck where a door and the accommodation ladder were located. This position was mostly used to take on board the harbor pilots required to guide the ship into various ports. When the pair arrived, they opened the door and stepped out onto the platform just as the MWB pulled up. It was at that point that Stensland noted the unexpected visitors were Japanese.

The coxswain skillfully maneuvered the small craft into position as a sailor jumped aboard with a line. The officer immediately followed and clambered up the ladder, holding onto what appeared to be a traditional samurai sword. When he reached the top, he turned to Stensland and saluted.

"*Konnichi wa!*" he said briskly. "I am Lieutenant Gentaro Oyama of the Imperial Japanese Navy!"

1750 Hours

Lars Stensland, Captain Bokkerson, Cadet Bjornson, the two other ship's officers, and fifteen crewmen were locked in the wardroom of the *Edvard Grieg*.

The only portholes were in the aft bulkhead, but these had been covered by blankets. Two tough-looking young Japanese sailors stood at the door, staring impassively at the men who were now prisoners in their own vessel. Captain Bokkerson sat hunched over the table, angrily tapping his fingers on the can of Coca-Cola that sat in front of him. He glanced over at Stensland, speaking in a low voice.

"You are sure that officer said he was from the Japanese *Imperial* Navy, not the Japanese Maritime Self Defense Forces?"

"Positive, sir," Stensland replied. "They haven't been imperial since World War Two, have they?"

"Of course not," Bokkerson said. He glanced at the guards. "And the SLRs those two young thugs are holding certainly aren't from the 1940s." He forced a grin. "At least that's a sign we haven't sailed into a time warp."

Young Bjornson grinned back. "Like in the cinema, hey, Captain?"

"At least we know this isn't a film," Bokkerson said, trying to be cheerful. "None of us are good-looking enough to be movie stars."

"I did notice one thing, sir," Bjornson remarked. "The two fellows who brought that plastic-covered thing on board set it up on the containers just forward of the bridge. When they took off the covering, I could see it was an electronic instrument."

"What sort of electronic instrument?" Stensland asked.

"There were dishes on top," Bjornson said. "Sort of like one uses for television reception without cable. They seemed to be set up for reception or broadcast in all

directions at once. I think it might be for satellite communications or something."

"Interesting," Bokkerson said. "But why would they
want to communicate from our ship? I'm sure they have
the equipment they need aboard their own vessel."

"That is not a modern destroyer in any sense," Stensland observed. "Perhaps they are indeed from the past."

Bokkerson frowned. "Now listen—"

"*Katarumasen!*" One of the guards yelled out, placing
a finger over his lips to signal that no talking would be tolerated. He frowned fiercely to indicate he would not put up
with any disobedience.

Bokkerson took a drink of Coke, thinking of how he
would like to get his hands around the kid's neck.

CHAPTER TWO

Kakureta Island
The Pacific Ocean
February 1904

Like all islands in that part of the world, this one had been haltingly but violently formed during eons of volcanic activity through fissures in the ocean floor. The actual time the pyroclastic debris emerged slowly above the waves was never noted in the annals of man, since human eyes did not witness the event. The only visitors to the island were wind-driven birds that used its surface as a place to rest before going back to their regular habitats.

Countless centuries would roll by before any homo sapiens ever set foot upon the island. This landfall was far from the best fishing grounds and trade routes of the western Pacific Ocean, and was only vaguely noticed at rare times when vessels went off course due to bad weather or incompetent navigating. The mariners' sightings of this desolate isle judged it to be unremarkable, inhospitable, and useless in serious maritime enterprises.

But in the year of 1904, during the Russo-Japanese War, the strip of land was not only observed but visited. By then the volcanic explosions and rumblings had long ago died off, leaving a finished product that measured 41.8 kilometers long by 13.3 kilometers wide. This landmass rose an average of 10 meters above sea level.

A coaling ship of the Imperial Japanese Navy was en route back to Japan after delivering its cargo to the task force under the command of Admiral Heihachiro Togo. The grand admiral was busily and successfully engaged in actions against the Russian fleet at Port Arthur on the southwest Chinese coast of the Yellow Sea in that year of 1904.

The collier had not yet turned on course toward its Japanese home port when it ran into the northern extremities of a typhoon. The winds were strong enough to cause some structural damage to the vessel before passing on, and it seemed she would have to limp slowly back to Osaka. Unfortunately, this calm proved to be only temporary, as the other side of the storm whirled around and began approaching with disturbing speed. The sailors battened down for a rough tossing about since the damage sustained previously had reduced the control of the vessel to an absolute minimum. Luckily, an alert lookout standing watch in the maintop spotted the smudge of land on the sea and hailed the bridge.

The captain ordered a change of course—a laborious task due to the condition of the vessel—and they drew close enough for an observation of the potential landfall through binoculars. This was the first time in history that human eyes scanned the island with any curiosity or interest. The strip of land appeared to offer a harbor of sorts on the west side where the ocean moved in between a pair of stubby peninsulas. It would be a good place to wait out the coming tempest if it were deep enough. It might even prove to be a feasible place to make temporary repairs before continuing on to Japan.

A landing boat was launched without delay, and the strong arms of the crew rowed her across the space of open water into the sheltered area. When they eased between the peninsulas they found a perfectly formed harbor that was a near symmetrical hundred meters across. Sand, brought in by thousands of years of surf activity, had formed into gently sloping beaches. The officer-in-charge wasted no time in casting a lead line to determine the depth. The first effort indicated eight fathoms of water. It seemed too good to be true. More soundings were taken in various areas showing that eight fathoms was the minimum. A few spots were a bit more than ten fathoms. The officer turned to signal the ship to be brought in.

While the collier moved slowly toward the natural harbor, the boat crew rowed to the beach, dragging the craft up to where scrub brush began. These Japanese sailors knew this was a strong indication of subterranean sources of fresh water. Further searching discovered numerous springs and small creeks that sent water cascading from the higher to the lower levels of the terrain to eventually drain into the ocean. Landing parties could be brought ashore to replenish the ship's water supply.

The crew rejoiced in this cessation of their normal routine. These were not the best sailors in the emperor's navy. The work aboard coal-hauling vessels was filthy, backbreaking, and monotonous; just the place for the insubordinate, dull-witted and lazy. The arduous duty on a collier consisted of constantly loading and unloading the combustible cargo. Consequently, the men suffered from the constant inhalation of coal dust. This life-shortening condition even affected the officers and petty officers who supervised the labor.

When the collier returned to Osaka, the captain made an official report of the uncharted island to the Imperial Bureau of Charts and Navigation. This information was duly passed up through the various command and staff echelons until reaching the chief of staff, Rear Admiral Iwao Chinana. Chinana took special note of this uncharted island with its excellent harbor, fresh water, and its 556 square kilometers of land.

For the previous decade, the Imperial Japanese Admiralty had begun to grow wary of the Imperial Army's General Staff. The general officers had begun showing a disturbing tendency to intrude onto the political scene. Even the younger officers formed various fanatical right-wing militarist organizations and brazenly assassinated various individuals opposed to their aims. Imperial naval officers were a more conservative group and had their own agenda. Admiral Togo had expressed a desire for the navy to pull away from the military-political intrigues and establish a separate clandestine organization of its own. When this society was formed in 1905, they called themselves the *Kaigun Samurai*—"Naval Knights"—and only the most trusted and able officers were invited to enter its exclusive sea-warrior brotherhood.

The Kaigun Samurai quickly recognized a pressing need for a clandestine organizational headquarters. It seemed to Rear Admiral Chinana that this newly discovered uncharted island might just fill the bill.

June 1906

The Russo-Japanese War was over. A settlement between the two empires of Japan and Russia had been reached after a peace conference that was mediated by the American president Theodore Roosevelt. This occurred at Portsmouth, New Hampshire, during negotiations that went on from August 9 to September 5, 1905. In the ensuing settlement, Japan won the Chinese Liaodong Peninsula and half of Sakhalin Island, while the Russians were permitted to maintain their influence over northern Manchuria. All in all, it was a Japanese victory, though it had been an expensive struggle both in men and matériel.

Nine months passed before Admiral Togo was able to act on Rear Admiral Chinana's suggestion about the uncharted island recommended for the Kaigun Samurai. The great naval commander thought this important enough for his own personal attention rather than dispatching a subordinate to investigate the area. He set out for an inspection at the first opportunity.

When his flagship, the *Mikasa,* eased into the island's harbor, the admiral, his staff, and the ship's officers shared an initial optimistic reaction to what they saw. A trip ashore reinforced that approval, and orders were immediately issued to begin preparations for the construction of a secret naval base. This new facility would not only be fully operational, but known only to a select few. It did not take Togo long to come up with a name for the island. He chose *Kakureta,* the Japanese word for "Hidden." This was a typically Japanese gesture: a simple word with a strong significance. But—no matter the name—Kakureta Island was to never be shown on any maritime charts.

When the *Mikasa* returned to Japan, preparations began for the occupation of the island. Admiral Chinana used his many administrative talents to make sure all paperwork involving the supply, transport, and personnel actions was either ambiguous or completely false. In less than a year, the matériel for buildings, dockings, roadways, and other necessary structures and conveniences were brought ashore to be stacked in readiness. Machines and tooling for construction arrived soon after.

Non-Japanese-speaking Korean laborers were recruited to do the building under the supervision of Imperial Navy officers and warrant officers. These workers arrived after a long ocean voyage belowdecks, and would return the same way. They had no opportunity to view the sun or stars to ascertain in which direction they sailed. Within two years, the construction work was complete, and the laborers were sent back to their homeland.

The clandestine assignment of personnel—the most trusted officers, warrant officers, petty officers, and ratings—were carried on orders under code names that were familiar only to those within the highest echelons of the Imperial Navy. Everyone of all ranks fully recognized that Kakureta Island would serve their cause more effectively than a fleet of battleships.

1941–1946

Vice Admiral Noburu Chiteito of the Scientific and Technical Staff had been against the attack on Pearl Harbor from the outset. This outspoken senior officer was not one to keep his opinions to himself. Consequently, several death plots against him quickly developed and would have been carried out if it had not been for his best friend Admiral Isoroku Yamamoto. Yamamoto ordered Chiteito to keep his opinions to himself, then had him shipped off to Kakureta Island to avoid any potential assassination attempts.

Ironically, it was Yamamoto who planned and led the assault on the American fleet in Hawaii to start the war with the United States. On the evening before the treacherous sneak attack, he bragged that within a year he would dictate the peace face-to-face with President Franklin Delano Roosevelt and his cabinet in Washington, D.C. But a few months later he lost the battles of Midway and the Solomons, and those failures made his boasting no more than empty words. Then, as if things weren't going bad enough for him, the admiral lost his life when his transport plane was shot down by Americans who learned his whereabouts through broken Japanese codes.

During all that time Admiral Chiteito stayed on Kakureta Island, but he did not simply languish in isolation. As a member of the Scientific and Technical Staff, he knew of certain highly classified projects. He made arrangements for a supersecret technical team to be brought to the island from the Imperial Naval Laboratory of Scientific Research in Tokyo. Chiteito knew that foreign troops, i.e., American, would occupy Japan within a few years. He wanted nothing to interfere with the work of these specialists.

A twenty-year-old genius by the name of Gomme Zunsuno was in charge of a team of scientists working on a concept far ahead of the times. These men were striving to develop a force field that would generate an electronic waveform of protection around ships and planes that would stop radar or any other intrusive science from penetrating, observing, or recording the protected vehicle. Zunsuno had been a child prodigy and graduated from the Massachusetts Institute of Technology the previous year. It was there he developed the complicated mathematical conception of this invention. When he returned to Japan, he knew exactly where to take his idea: the Imperial Navy.

Admiral Chiteito personally approved the project and quickly organized the funding and facilities to set the development program into motion. This machine was named *Kamisaku*—"Sacred Barrier"—and any nation that was the first to use this device would be virtually undefeatable. But the project was going to take decades to be brought to a successful conclusion. Chiteito assured Zunsuno and his scientists that they would have those long years to work undisturbed. It was in order to fulfill this promise that he had them brought to Kakureta Island.

Due to his pessimism about the outcome of the war with America, the admiral kept the rest of the island just as it had always been in its clandestine state. He realistically felt that the Imperial Navy would need a safe haven before the last shot was fired. The admiral used his trusted staff to arrange for picked individuals to report to his island command as soon as it was evident the war was lost. They were authorized to bring their wives and children with them. The atomic bombings of Nagasaki and Hiroshima prompted those orders to be issued.

The Japanese surrender was signed aboard the battleship *USS Missouri* on September 2, 1945. By mid-January of 1946, all the picked Imperial Navy officers and their immediate families were settled on Kakureta Island. At the first staff meeting of his enlarged command, Admiral Chiteito announced that the Imperial Japanese Navy was *not* defeated; in fact, it was going to continue the war against the Western democracies. And this time victory was assured. All that was needed was for the Kamisaku program to be completed.

1947–1989

Chiteito and his senior staff were not foolish dreamers. They knew they would need outside help if their plans were to be fulfilled. Special agents—voluntary or not—would have to be recruited and organized in Japan. These would be ex-naval and army officers, industrialists, educators, financiers, and others, who, with their superior education and contacts, would be in the highest levels of the new Japan. The Kaigun Samurai organized an intelligence service to send picked men to make contact with people who would be the most useful to the cause. It was expected that the majority would be more than happy to cooperate for the renewed glory of Imperial Japan. But for those who were hesitant, certain incentives could be put forward to encourage cooperation, such as the safety and well-being of their families. If any raised even the slightest suspicion of betrayal, they would have to be killed without hesitation. Those who cooperated would be known as *hokannin*—"the trusted ones"—and would be rewarded as their deeds deserved.

As time passed, the Kaigun Samurai eventually developed into two castes. This class system began when the officers fully realized that along with an educated and intellectual leadership, they would have need for individuals with more manual skills. These could be obtained in the ranks of the Imperial Navy's *jun-i,* the warrant officers who filled the technical ranks aboard ship and ashore. This included machinists, carpenters, armorers, mechanics, and other trades and skills. These men were all long-service veterans, fully trustworthy and faithful to the cause of the Imperial Navy.

The children of both officers and *jun-i* shared a basic education. This was the indoctrination of *Yamato Damashii*—"the Japanese spirit"—and *Bushido*—"the Code of the Warrior." The one change from the old beliefs was the divinity of the emperor. Recent history had rendered that doctrine as totally false. Philosophical emphsasis was directed to create a fear of shame rather than the love of pride as the driving force behind every individual's decisions and conduct. These lessons created a doctrine that the individual was subordinate to the group. Even one's life must be sacrificed without hesitation if it would benefit the Kaigun Samurai. Only the strictest of obedience and conformity would be tolerated. The front of the school building on Kakureta Island displayed a banner with the bold red *Kana* characters that thundered the words:

DEATH IS LIGHT AS A FEATHER WHILE DUTY IS
HEAVIER THAN A MOUNTAIN!

The schoolboys' natural inclination to compete and roughhouse was encouraged with a sports program designed along traditional Japanese lines. The youngsters trained and played hard in *kendo* sword fighting, various hand-to-hand martial arts including karate and jujitsu, and Japanese-style archery. Sumo wrestling was formalized to include tournaments and championships with the best boys advancing up the ranks as was done in the professional *bashos* in Japan. These latter events became the favorite spectator sport on the island.

Girls, on the other hand, were taught to be gentle, obedient, and submissive. They learned that their place in that sphere of society was to please the men, respect all male authority, and produce children for their lords and masters. As good Japanese daughters they accepted their place in the order of things humbly and passively.

After a few more years, the leadership of the Kaigun Samurai had another fact of life to face up to. They were growing steadily older and knew that they would probably never see the glorious realization of their goals. The Kamisaku machine simply was not going to be ready in their lifetimes. They would have to depend on their sons, grandsons, and even great-grandsons to renew the battle against the enemy.

Through the benefits provided by the *hokannin,* the sons of officers were sent off to the best schools and universities on the Japanese mainland. At the same time, boys from the *jun-i* families were dispatched to apprenticeships and trade schools. Elaborate cover stories and backgrounds were arranged for them.

The *hokannin* saw to it that when these young men completed their education and training, they had no trouble finding choice careers as they moved deeply into the new Japanese industrial establishment. Those with university degrees worked their way into managerial and executive positions. Even the banks were infiltrated as elaborate embezzlement schemes were carried out with the protection of *hokannin* accountants who not only reported no irregularities but helped cook the books.

Kaigun Samurai who worked in the logistical areas of all industries adjusted and manipulated inventories and dispatched thousands of units of items to Kakureta Island. This included tooling machinery, electronic parts, and other industrial and technical material. State-of-the-art instrumentation for the Kamisaku program was supplied as new scientists took over the project from the older ones who passed on to their heavenly rewards. However, the program's originator, Gomme Zunsuno, was only twenty-five years old at the war's end. He still had plenty of productive years left in him.

Other island supplies were handled by a small flotilla of *suiraitei* patrol boats. These sixty-foot vessels, formerly used by the Imperial Navy of World War II, were rerigged to appear as interisland trawlers. The *jun-i* manned these old boats, making calls on various ports to purchase food, clothing, and other items for life's necessities.

Kakureta Island thrived, and thrived well.

The 1990s

Keizo Hara came home in 1995.

Of all the boys sent out to be educated and prepared for service in the Kaigun Samurai, Hara was the best. He was born in 1948 to Rear Admiral Hirobumi Hara and his wife Mariko, both descended from prominent samurai families. Keizo displayed a quick mind and agile body at an early age, and got the attention of Admiral Chiteito the first time the great officer laid eyes on him. Something about the boy bespoke an inherent superiority, even though he was just a toddler. From the age of four he was given special instruction and tutoring by picked individuals. His schooling consisted of not only academia but technical subjects taught him by special members of the *jun-i* class. When Keijo reached the age of six, he was sent off to Japan for years of education, training, and polishing.

His progress through the demanding curricula of Japanese education was nothing short of magnificent. In addition to being a superb scholar, he excelled in *kendo* and *sumo*. The latter sport of wrestling had no weight classes, and he beat boys much heavier and older than he. The Kaigun Samurai staff feared that his natural superiority would attract too much attention. But Keizo was well prepared for dealing with the outside world. He avoided betraying too much information about himself, dispensing just enough true and false data to avoid raising suspicions. It helped when he turned down a chance to attend Tokyo University in lieu of the Japanese Defense Force Academy. The intelligentsia, who had sought him for much higher education, lost all interest in the student in spite of his superior mind. They did not consider a naval or military career as especially prestigious. In truth, they were very disappointed in Keizo Hara.

By the time he began his career as a *kaigun-shoi kohesi*—"midshipman"—Keizo Hara was a handsome, strapping young man. He stood five feet ten inches tall and weighted a trim, muscular 170 pounds. He excelled even more under the strict military discipline of the academy, graduating in four years at the head of his class. He was commissioned an ensign in 1970.

Thus began a naval career noted for Keizo Hara's superlative efficiency, leadership, and administrative skills. The outstanding officer never married in spite of attracting several beautiful women of good families. This bachelorhood was looked on as a result of his total devotion to duty.

Hara served twenty years of active service, retiring in 1990 with the rank of vice admiral. He quietly withdrew to a small seaside village. He let five quiet years slip by as the attention normally paid him by the Japanese Self Defense Forces slowly evaporated. When he was certain he was out

of the limelight, he made an unobtrusive move from his retirement abode back to his real home on Kakureta Island.

He married the beautiful seventeen-year-old granddaughter of now-deceased Admiral Chiteito. Hano was totally unlike the women he had met in modern Japan. She
readily accepted the arranged marriage to a much older
man with humility and complete obedience. Hara was
happy with his new bride, and within a year she gave birth
to the first of three sons.

Meanwhile, Hara joined the staff of the Kaigun Samurai Admiralty, and when the present fleet admiral died, he
was chosen to take the man's place.

On the same day that Hara was elevated to the position
of supreme leader, Gomme Zunsuno, now in his seventies,
appeared before the new fleet admiral to announce the successful completion of the Kamisaku machine. It had been
tested and retested to the old scientist's satisfaction. The
advent of transistors and integrated circuits for use in au-
dio, digital circuits, logic gates, and other components had
not only brought about an earlier completion than expected, but resulted in a much smaller machine than the
original design. An unexpected benefit not originally taken
into consideration was that the machine made Kakureta Island invisible to the intrusive electronic observations of
spy satellites orbiting the earth. The Kamisaku Force Field
was truly ready for active operations in the modern world.

Everyone, officers and *jun-i* alike, looked upon this as a
good omen, since it coincided with Hara's ascendancy to
supreme leadership. This officer, trained and practiced in
contemporary naval warfare, was just the man to change
the brotherhood back to the Imperial Navy and continue
World War II to a glorious Japanese victory. The staff
dusted off old operation plans, and Hara began studying
the concepts, making changes and appointing the right
men to the right jobs.

Unfortunately, this was the exact time that things began
to unravel for the Kaigun Samurai.

The first misfortune involved one of the officers' sons.
He had worked himself up to a high position within the

Toyota organization in Kyoto. After years of education and career-building in modern Japan, he found the concepts of *Yamato Damashii* and *Bushido* barbaric and outdated. He dropped from the program, removing himself forever from the Kaigun Samurai.

His father committed ritual *seppuku,* the traditional suicide of disemboweling one self before being beheaded by a chosen second. The act was performed on the highest point of land on the island. A platform, covered with a white sheet, had been set up for the gruesome occasion. Everyone, including the man ready to kill himself, was dressed in his most expensive, formal kimono.

After reading a poem of apology he had written, the disgraced officer sat down. He opened his kimono to bare his belly as his second, holding his sword at the ready, stepped up to one side. The self-condemned man took the short *wakizashi* sword and held it to his belly. This was the weapon traditionally used in the ritual suicide ceremony. He looked upward, then plunged the blade deep into his abdomen, cutting across to spill out his intestines. At that exact moment, the second sliced down with his *katana* sword, decapitating the man to end his dying agony.

In spite of that dramatic event, a couple of weeks later, a half-dozen sons of the *jun-i* who had joined labor unions in various factories also disavowed any association with the old traditions. Their fathers were also shamed and made many tearful public apologies for their sons' collective treachery. They would have killed themselves, too, but Keizo Hara forbade any further *seppuku* ceremonies.

Within six weeks, other young men withdrew from the Kaigun Samurai, and the *hokannin* who had been cowed for decades now sent word they would no longer assist in obtaining funds or matériel. Almost immediately all the bank accounts that had been growing regularly since 1947 began to run dry. There was nothing that could be done about the situation. Sending assassins to set a couple of examples would only lead to unwanted publicity cascading down on the Kaigun Samurai. The former *hokannin* would begin turning to the authorities for help and protection. By

Japanese custom, if these defecting auxiliaries or families were not harmed, they would not betray the secret naval organization. They had been paid for their past cooperation, and it would shame them to reveal their treachery to their own legitimate employers and stockholders.

Everyone now turned to Keizo Hara for his leadership and counsel. He accepted the responsibility gracefully and confidently, promising them that he would see that the Kaigun Samurai not only recovered from the setback, but came back stronger than ever.

And that was the time he declared himself *shogun*.

This was not an egocentric act; it was a decision based on established traditions and rituals that only the Japanese could understand. Hara knew that by taking this ancient title that meant "the Lord of Lords," he made a statement that he was powerful enough to attain any goal he set for himself. The other officers joyfully accepted his pronouncement, and the people in the *jun-i* village wept with happiness that now a truly great leader had come forward to lead them to their triumphant destiny.

Much of Hara's self-confidence came about because the Kamisaku was now working perfectly. Several new models had been produced and tested. Now the only problem was to figure out the best way to employ these powerful instruments before all the money was drained away from the dwindling accounts. Then Hara remembered something he had learned at the Naval War College in America some years back, before he was promoted to captain.

The class was about eighteenth- and nineteenth-century naval warfare. The lessons that fascinated Hara were those involving privateers. These were ships' captains who received letters of marque from governments to attack and capture enemy ships. These documents legitimized the privateers as legal combatants, meaning they could not be hanged as pirates if they lost a sea battle. When they captured a ship, they would bring it back to a friendly port where they received prize money for the worth of the vessel. If the captured ship happened to be a merchantman, then the monies earned would include the cargo's value as well. Hara was surprised by how many of those privateer captains retired from the sea with great wealth and property.

He reasoned that if an organization, such as the Kaigun Samurai, acted as their own privateers by issuing themselves letters of marque, they could earn millions for any ships and cargo they captured. It was a matter of ransom. He sent out an invitation to an old friend from his Japanese Self Defense Forces days to join him for an evening of conversation and *sake* at the officers' *geisha* house. This was retired Captain Heideki Tanaka. They had served together on many naval operations, and Tanaka was one of the best ship's captains that Hara had met during his service days.

That evening the two old comrades sat in front of the low *cha* table, sipping rice wine and talking tactics as two beautiful *geishas* tended to the refreshments. The pair of old comrades paid little attention to their lovely companions as the plan for privateer cruises came together. The main problem would be obtaining ships capable of waging war, but Tanaka had an excellent suggestion: purchase the vessels from Russia. Since the fall of the Soviet Union they had plenty of ships sitting idle at naval docks. They would be happy to make some sales for hard cash.

"*Mochiron*—of course!" Hara exclaimed happily. "We have a special fund set aside for contingencies."

Tanaka laughed with delight. "In that case, I know of a cruiser and two destroyers just waiting for us at Vladivostok!"

CHAPTER THREE

***Destroyer* Isamashii**
East China Sea
28 May
0645 Hours

The MWB eased up to the accommodation ladder of the warship, and Lieutenant Gentaro Oyama nimbly leaped to the steps and ascended them to the stern deck. He walked briskly through the deck division working parties as he made his way to the bridge. Less than a year before, Oyama had been an officer in the Japanese Maritime Self Defense Forces. The Kaigun Samurai put an end to that career by ordering him to resign his commission and report back to Kakureta Island to begin his service in the Imperial Navy. He was fully aware of what was behind this unexpected call home and had spent his final night in Japan lying sleepless and restless in his rack, wakeful in his anticipation of the adventure ahead. The great day was now close at hand; the humiliation suffered by Japan in World War II would soon be avenged.

This transfer did not mean a promotion for him, but his Defense Forces title of lieutenant—*itto kaii*—was changed to the old Imperial terminology of *tai-i*. Additionally, his uniform sported the insignia of former days. He only wished the destroyer on which he served was also Japanese, but it was a recently purchased Soviet vessel. But that was only a temporary situation. He fully expected that within a year the Imperial Navy would steam to the Japanese mainland to take over the Maritime Self Defense Forces and renew World War II.

As Oyama made his way past sailors on the deck, they immediately ceased their tasks and stiffened to strict positions of attention before bowing to him with reverent respect. This attitude of obedience and dedication further encouraged the young officer. This was imperial discipline, not the emasculated style of modern Japan. He went up to the bridge, entering the command and control domain of the ship where Captain Heideki Tanaka sat in his chair overlooking the activities.

Oyama saluted sharply. "Sir! I beg to report that the Norwegian ship and crew are secured."

"Ah! *Sugureta!*" Tanaka exclaimed with approval. "Did you have any problems?"

"None, sir. We were able to approach the target ship completely undetected."

Tanaka smiled. "So! The Kamisaku has performed on operations as well as it did in training, eh?"

"Even better, sir," Oyama replied.

"Very well, Oyama-*Tai-i*," Tanaka said. "See that a signal is sent to Kakureta Island. You recall the code words to use, do you not?"

Oyama smiled. "Of course, sir! *Tora! Tora! Tora!* The same as used at Pearl Harbor in 1941."

Washington, D.C.
31 May
0920 Hours

The cab pulled up in front of the gated brick building located at 2720 34th Street Northwest, and the turbaned driver brought it to a quick halt. He glanced in his rearview mirror at his passenger with great interest. It wasn't often a man could be seen wearing a fedora in even a cosmopolitan city like Washington. In fact, the only time the driver ever saw one was in old movies on TV.

The customer was a small, dapper, middle-aged Japanese gentleman wearing a conservative business suit that matched the style of his outdated headgear. He paid the fare, adding a small tip, then got out of the vehicle. He stood gazing at the building in front of him for a moment as the taxi drove off. Then he walked up to the plaque on the gate and studied it.

AMBASADE
KONGEDØMME AV NORGE

Now that he was satisfied he was at the Norwegian embassy, the Japanese walked over to the guard post at the gate. The soldier on duty, a severe young man in a trim, blue uniform, greeted him in English, noting the visitor had no briefcase with him.

"Good morning, sir. May I help you?"

"Oh, yes. Thank you. I wish to speak to someone in the embassy."

"Do you have an appointment with anyone in particular, sir?"

"No. I am sorry. I have not procured an appointment."

The guard opened the small section of the gate used to admit pedestrians and turned to point at a door down the walk a few feet away. "You will find a receptionist beyond that door. She will be able to help you."

"Oh, yes. Thank you very much."

The Japanese strode cheerfully toward the door, opened it, and stepped inside to find a young blond woman sitting at a desk. He liked such women, especially if they were taller than he. His smile was a combination of politeness and admiration.

She was as courteous as the guard outside when she inquired about his business. She also took note of the lack of a briefcase.

"Yes," he said, taking off his hat. "My name is Mr. Kawaguchi. I wish to speak to your ambassador, please."

"I'm afraid our ambassador is not available, sir," the receptionist said. "Perhaps if you told me the nature of your business, I could direct you to someone else who might be able to help you."

"Ah, yes," Kawaguchi said, thinking what a delicious bedmate she would make. "Please. I wish to speak to someone about the Norwegian ship the *Edvard Grieg*."

"And what might be your concern about that particular ship, sir?"

"Ah, sorry. I am certain that if you made contact within your organization of a person concerned with merchant marine activities, he would be interested to see me."

The receptionist, already forming a solicitous brush-off in her mind, picked up her phone and pushed a button. She spoke a few words in Norwegian, then her eyes opened wide with surprise. She hung up. "Uh, yes! A gentleman will be here directly to fetch you." She indicated some chairs across the room.

Kawaguchi affected a slight bow. "Yes. Thank you so much."

He walked over to the chairs, chose one, and had just turned to sit down when a man with thinning light-brown hair appeared from a door behind the receptionist's desk. He approached Kawaguchi with a slight frown on his face.

"I am Mr. Olenstadt," he said. "Am I to understand you know something of the ship the *Edvard Grieg*?"

"Yes. Please. I would like very much to discuss the vessel with someone," Kawaguchi responded politely.

"This way, sir," the Norwegian said.

Kawaguchi was ushered through the door out of the reception area and taken down a hall to an elevator. From there they went up two floors and stepped out into another hall. The walk continued down to an office at the far end. When his escort opened the door, Kawaguchi stepped inside to find a second Norwegian sitting behind a desk. He had a mane of thick black hair and a well-trimmed beard.

The first man joined them, speaking to Kawaguchi. "This is Mr. Halverson."

"I am Mr. Kawaguchi."

"How do you do, Mr. Kawaguchi," Halverson said. "Please sit down."

"Thank you," Kawaguchi said. "Excuse me, please. May I inquire as to what is your position at the embassy?"

"I am the maritime shipping attaché," Halverson said. "Now what interest do you have in our container ship?"

"I can arrange to have the ship and crew returned to you within a short time," Kawaguchi said calmly.

Halverson asked, "Really? What makes you think the ship needs returning?"

Kawaguchi smiled widely. "We both know the *Edvard Grieg* is not where it is supposed to be."

The tone of Halverson's voice was flat. "What is your nationality, Mr.—ah—Kawaguchi?"

"I am Japanese," Kawaguchi replied.

"Very well," Halverson said. "State your business."

"I am an agent for the privateers that have taken it," Kawaguchi replied.

Halverson leaned forward in his puzzlement. "Privateers? There have not been privateers on the seas for over a hundred and fifty years!"

"Excuse me," Kawaguchi said. "I do not wish to appear disagreeable, but privateers have taken the *Edvard Grieg* and her sailors and her cargo."

"I do not think you mean privateers," Halverson said. "I believe you are referring to what we Norwegians call *sjøroveren*— pirates—are you not?"

"No," Kawaguchi replied pleasantly. "Privateers, if you please, with letters of marque."

"Letters of marque!" Halverson thundered. "From what country? Japan?"

"Ah, no. Not Japan."

"Then who in this day and age issued letters of marque to someone to act as a privateer?"

"The Japanese Empire."

Halverson sputtered. "There is no such empire."

"I do not wish to argue the point," Kawaguchi said.

Halverson took a few moments to calm down. He leaned back in his chair and studied the Japanese who sat on the other side of the desk. The fellow was obviously well-educated, polite, rational, and very sure of himself. He looked over at Olenstadt, who stared in wide-eyed surprise at their visitor.

"Please continue, Mr. Kawaguchi," Halverson invited.

"I am to inform you that the *Edvard Grieg,* her cargo, and her crew will be returned to you upon the deposit of twenty-five million dollars into a specific account in the *Banque Martime et Mercantile du Djibouti* in the city of Tadjoura, Djibouti." Then Kawaguchi added, "That is in eastern Africa."

"Thank you," Halverson said, knowing Djibouti had a port used only by the French and local Arabian dhows. He sullenly studied the small man who so pleasantly demanded ransom for a ship, humans, and cargo. "Well, Mr. Kawaguchi, what makes you think we will pay what you demand?"

"Then you will not see the vessel or people again," Kawaguchi said. "Sorry."

"I must pass this information up to my superiors," Halverson said. "They will hesitate at paying out such an exorbitant sum. I am certain the matter will have to be discussed further."

"Oh, sorry! I did not make it clear," Kawaguchi said. "The privateer will not negotiate."

Olenstadt lost his temper. "Just what makes you think you're going to come in here with a criminal demand like that and be allowed to walk away?"

"If I am not allowed to freely leave this building, you will never get your ship back," Kawaguchi said. "I do not know where it is. So I would be a most useless prisoner. And even if I was arrested, I would be quickly replaced." Then his countenance and his demeanor changed to threatening. "You have forty-eight hours." He stood up. "I will return for the final arrangements." Now he became smiling and polite again as he bowed to Olenstadt. "Please. Show me out."

Halverson asked, "Where can we contact you, Mr. Kawaguchi?"

"Please. Show me out."

Merritt Island, Florida
5 June
0715 Hours

Commander Gerald Fagin, USN, sat at his breakfast table, idly drumming his coffee cup with his fingers. He was a muscular Irish American in his early forties with graying red hair, a square jaw, and bright blue eyes. His wife Toni sat across from him, her low-calorie breakfast drink not yet touched as she read the day's edition of *Florida Today*. She glanced over the newspaper at her husband. She could see his mind had drifted away. This had become a constant habit with him as of late.

Toni, a thirty-six-year-old beauty, was one of those sexy, svelte women with large breasts. She attributed this part of her physique as well as her brunette good looks to a long line of lusty female ancestors from Italy. During her college days at Columbia University, she had been given several serious opportunities to begin a modeling career, but she turned them all down. Toni Maglione was a serious student majoring in economics, not prone to waste her time at what she considered useless activities.

Now she studied her husband as she took a sip of her liquid breakfast. "Scheming another getaway try?"

Fagin came back to earth and grinned. "Yeah." He looked at his untouched bacon and eggs. "I should never have gone for that master's at MIT."

"That's debatable," Toni said. "You were first in your class at Annapolis, darling. The navy saw the brainy side of you and didn't want to waste your intellect aboard some ship."

"I should have gone to the Coast Guard Academy," Fagin said. "They have too much to do to send gung ho officers off for scientific study when there're people to be rescued, illegal aliens to intercept, and dope smugglers to be caught out on the open ocean."

"You didn't have to go to MIT, as I recall," Toni said. "When they asked you, you volunteered. Right?"

"God!" he said. "I wouldn't have gone if I'd known how it was going to affect my career goals. I was my own worst enemy."

"I think things will turn out better in the end," Toni said. "You must be patient, darling."

"Everything was wrong from the start," Fagin said. "I hurt my knee at football tryout during my first year and never got the glory of playing against Army. That damn injury also meant no chance to become a SEAL. I should have—" He stopped in midsentence, knowing he was about to utter remarks he had already made hundreds of times. "I did not go to the academy to sit behind a desk as an electronic warfare intelligence officer." He grimaced. "Especially when I ended up billeted with a bunch of fucking air force types."

"Tsk! Tsk! Watch your language, darling," Toni said.

"Sorry," Fagin said. "I didn't mean to say *air force*."

Toni laughed. "God, Gerry! You really do hate it, don't you?" She folded her paper and stood up. "Why don't you get out of the navy and get a captain's ticket from the merchant marine? You could sail on a cargo ship or an oil tanker or something."

"There're not very many jobs in that line of work, dearest mine," he said. "Particularly when it comes to being master or an engineering officer."

Toni walked around the table and kissed him. "I have to get to work, and I don't want to be late. Unlike you, I like my job!"

"Maybe I should go into financial banking with you."

"No, thanks!" Toni exclaimed. "I wouldn't want you being angry all the time down at our office. You would scare the hell out of our accountants." She headed for the door. "See you later."

After she left, he poked around at his breakfast some more, then gave it up. Nothing left to do but go out for a

day's work. He scraped the leftovers into the garbage disposal and turned it on, leaving it to run while he put the
plate in the dishwasher. He turned off the disposal, glancing out at his screened-in patio with the swimming pool.

He really liked the house, and Brevard County was a
nice place to live. But he was more disappointed about his
duty assignment than he let Toni know. Commander Gerald Fagin's attitude was steadily sinking toward dangerous
depths, and he knew the other officers on the staff were beginning to grow weary of him. Especially the unit's boss. A
flash of Irish temper coursed through him, and he slammed
the dishwasher door closed. He headed for the garage, still
angry.

They wore civilian clothing in the office where he
worked, even though it was a military unit posted on the
Cape Canaveral Air Force Station. He continually groused
that if they didn't have to wear uniforms, they should at
least be allowed tank tops, shorts, and sandals. Hell, this
was Florida after all.

It only took him ten minutes to drive off Merritt Island
and down the 528 Beach Line to George King Boulevard
and get on State Route 401, which would take him up to
Gate 1. He glanced over at the cruise ships at dock in Port
Canaveral, thinking that being a steward serving drinks to
tourists would be preferable to what he now did. When he
reached the gate he held up his ID card so the guard could
easily see it as he eased by. Then he got up to speed and
headed for his office out at Area Seven.

Fagin's workplace was in a low-ceilinged cement block
structure with a noisy air conditioner. The entire inside was
open but filled with cubicles. The one exception was a
small walled-in area where the boss of the operation, an air
force colonel by the name of Don Wendt, occupied a small,
cluttered office. Fagin went around the outside of the cubicles to his own workstation. He started to sit down when he
noticed a yellow sticky informing him that "DW" wanted
to see him the moment he came in. A surge of hope bright-
ened Fagin's mood. Perhaps one of the myriad transfer requests he had submitted had finally borne fruit. He could

barely suppress a grin as he hurried over to Wendt's office. He knocked and stepped inside.

Wendt checked his watch. "You've come in late again."

"Fire me."

Wendt, a heavyset man who could do with some exercise, grinned without humor. "You'd like that, wouldn't you?"

"Right."

"Well," Wendt said, "not half as much as me. And let me tell you something. Blame the United States Navy that you're assigned here. It's not the air force's fault. And it sure as hell isn't mine, either. If you keep pissing me off, I'm going to write you up so bad that you'll end up supervising FOD walk-throughs at NAS Pea Patch in the middle of Kansas. Understand?"

"Yes, sir."

"Anyhow," Wendt continued, "you and I are going to be in better moods for awhile. You'll be getting out of here on a TDy assignment. There's something for you to look into just north of San Diego in a place called Del Mar."

"What's going on?"

"I don't have a hell of a lot on it, Fagin," Wendt said. "But it has to do with some missing merchant ships. This includes their cargos and crews."

Fagin was confused, and he grabbed a chair by the wall, quickly taking a seat. This was entirely different from the usual missions assigned the group. Mostly they dealt with analyses of software, hardware, and documentation. "This seems like something for the antiterrorist gang. Maybe the CIA."

"Normally it would be," Wendt commented. "But there is evidently some electronic slant on it. It could be complicated. You might be required to do quite a bit of traveling around to organize an intel packet for the navy. From what I gather, it will be putting together a puzzle of sorts. A piece here. A piece there." He reached in a drawer and pulled out a packet. "Here're your orders. You'll fly out of Patrick on a direct flight to NAS North Island. There's a C-130 waiting for you now."

"And what happens when I arrive on the West Coast?"

"A party will meet you and take you to wherever it is you'll be staying in Del Mar," Wendt said.

"Did you choose me for this assignment?" Fagin asked suspiciously.

Wendt shook his head. "You were handpicked for the detail. It seems the U.S. Navy has discovered some use for their wandering boy—thank God—so they more or less called you home." He took a breath and added, "And feel free to stay there."

Fagin stood up, feeling better. "Sure. Maybe I'll get some sea duty."

"I wouldn't know anything about that," Wendt said. "But you better leave a note for your wife. Tell her you're probably going to be gone for awhile."

Fagin nodded and left the office. They kept prepacked luggage in a supply annex for the unannounced travel that was required of them from time to time. He picked his out, then returned to his desk to arrange transportation down to Patrick Air Force Base.

CHAPTER FOUR

Del Mar, California
7 June
0945 Hours

Commander Gerald Fagin didn't give much thought to his coming stay in the Del Mar safe house during the long flight from Florida to California. Most of his stays in those clandestine domiciles were best forgotten. He had endured leaky roofs, bad plumbing, and insect infestations in some of the places he had temporarily resided while on classified missions. However, if he'd known what was waiting for him in this upcoming operation, he would have been in a much better mood.

The place was a luxury condo overlooking the beach a mile or so north of the Del Mar Racetrack. It was high enough on the concrete-and-steel-rod-reinforced hill where it was situated that the traffic noise of old Highway 101 was hardly noticeable. The only downside was that the area's seasonal "June Gloom" was going full force, making for very gray, cloudy days. The view out to sea was a blur where the Pacific Ocean and sky blended together on the far horizon. This was a source of irritation for unknowing tourists who had booked their vacations for that time of year.

When Fagin arrived at NAS North Island the day before, he was met by Lieutenant Pete Bledsoe. Bledsoe wore longish hair, and his faded knit shirt, cutoff denim shorts, and sandals made him appear as a typical Southern California beach bum. He had the tanned look of an older surfer still living his carefree youth at the seashore. Fagin wondered how the guy managed to get aboard the base with such a nonmilitary appearance. Even after wearing civvies for more than a year at CCAFS, the guy looked positively seedy to him. The young sailors in the terminal building hardly gave them a second look when they shook hands and greeted each other. Evidently a lot of people on special duty wearing all sorts of modes of dress passed through North Island.

During the drive up Interstate 5 to the safe house, Bledsoe didn't say much. But Fagin learned this rather uncommon officer was from the OTSI office in the city of Coronado near the SEAL installation at the Silver Strand. Just as Fagin and his air force cohorts in Florida, this California bunch was also interservice, and did not work in uniform.

If Bledsoe's appearance surprised Fagin, the safe house rocked him back on his heels. The community was gated, and the residences had every amenity one would expect when buying or leasing such posh property. This included a Jacuzzi room, small gym, and sauna in each unit. Fagin knew that meant most of the visitors to the hideout were VIPs who could demand the best in luxury living, even if they might be scumbag traitors, informers, or criminals in their own countries. Once someone becomes a valued asset to an intelligence program, his or her sins are overlooked if not completely forgiven. Fagin felt positively flattered.

Bledsoe gave him just enough time to dump his bag in his assigned bedroom before giving him a briefing on why he had been sent for. Through a terse recitation by the lieutenant, Fagin learned that since 27 May several international merchant marine vessels had been hijacked by an organization claiming to be privateers. The first, the Norwegian container ship *Edvard Grieg,* had been ransomed two days before. As of that moment, there was a freighter of Panamanian registry and a tanker of Liberian registry being held in parts unknown by persons unknown. Negotiations were in progress between the affected shipping companies and a Japanese gentleman known only as Mr. Kawaguchi, who represented the corsairs.

Fagin was puzzled. "What in the hell as this got to do with the Office of Technological and Scientific Intelligence?"

"It seems the raider was completely undetectable on radar," Bledsoe said, brushing back his long locks. "Even when she had drawn alongside the victims, she returned no signals from their sets."

Fagin frowned. "Now that's weird! Did the vessel seem to be constructed of, or covered by some radar-absorbing material?"

Bledsoe shook his head. "In the instance of the Norwegian incident, the interceptor has been described as a conventional-appearing destroyer, sir. After we were called into the case, we sent around the latest copy of *Jane's Warships of the World* for the Norwegian crew to study. They made a close examination of the photos and descriptions, and all agreed the bad guy matched an old Soviet Union *Krupny*-class destroyer shown in the book."

"Oh, God!" Fagin moaned. "Do you suppose that a bunch of crazy old renegades from the USSR are out extorting money on the high seas?"

"The officers and crew of the raider have been identified as Japanese," Bledsoe said. "Which makes sense when you consider that the mysterious Mr. Kawaguchi is also Japanese."

"Okay," Fagin said. "Now what?"

"One of the ship's officers off the *Edvard Grieg* has been assigned to us," Bledsoe said. "I'll be picking him up tomorrow at San Diego International and bringing him out here. I'll turn everything over to you once we have him on board." He stood up. "In the meantime, sir, make yourself comfortable. There's plenty of chow, coffee, beer, and some exotic liquor. We've had a rather international guest list here with myriad tastes." He went to a desk in the corner of the room, retrieving a thick packet of papers. "And there's this. All the documentation and reports on the takeovers is in here. You'll find it interesting reading."

"I'll have to admit my scientific curiosity has been whetted," Fagin said.

"Yes, sir. You're about to begin a cruise with a spinning compass."

Now, sipping the coffee on the balcony of the safe house, Fagin glanced down at the entrance to the gated community and could see Lieutenant Bledsoe's gray Ford van turn off Highway 101 and approach the facility. A moment later the gate swung open to admit the vehicle, and it was driven toward the residential parking area. Fagin turned and walked back inside, going to the kitchen to dump the remnants of the cold coffee into the sink. Then he went into the living room to wait for Bledsoe and the guest he had gone to fetch.

A couple of minutes later, the speaker next to the front door buzzed, and Fagin went over to it. "Yeah?"

"Bledsoe."

"Right," Fagin replied, disappointed that there were no passwords or countersigns. This seemed to be developing into an exciting secret-agent-style caper rather than the mundane searching through papers, blueprints, and other documentation the OTSI usually did. He hit the buzzer that would open the downstairs entrance to the building.

A few moments later, the doorbell rang. Fagin opened it to admit Bledsoe and a stranger. The man was dressed in a business suit and carried a well-worn suitcase. Bledsoe introduced them.

"Commander Gerald Fagin. Lieutenant Lars Stensland, Norwegian Navy."

"How do you do," Stensland said with hardly a trace of a Scandinavian accent. "Actually, I am in the Naval Reserve as are all merchant marine officers of my country. I have been ordered to active duty for this special operation."

"Glad to know you," Fagin said. "I take it you have all

the information about what went on aboard the Norwegian ship when it was captured."

"Yes," Stensland said. "In truth, I was part of the crew serving as bridge officer at the time. A cadet doing his sea duty from our national academy was with me."

"And you picked up no indications of the raider on your radar as he approached you?"

"No, sir," Stensland said. "And there is one more thing that has come up. It has to do with my digital camera when I took photos of the raider. I had almost forgotten the incident." He put his suitcase on the dining room table and opened it. He produced several computer printouts of the photographs. "Take a look at these."

Fagin took the pictures and studied them. The ocean, horizon, and parts of the *Edvard Grieg* were sharp and focused. But one large section showed a ship that appeared to have been cut apart and put back together in a hodgepodge pattern without regard to its original design. The bow was in the lower center of the pattern; while the forward gun turret was split in two sections, one above and forward of the other; and other sections of hull, superstructure, and weaponry appeared to be split up and scattered helter-skelter though the scene.

Bledsoe looked at the images. "Christ! The pixel signals have been bent and sent off in myriad directions. The analog-to-digital converter must have been hit with an electronic epileptic fit."

"Right," Fagin said. "But only in the area of the bad guys' ship. Look at the horizon, the ocean, and parts of the Norwegian vessel. They're clear as a bell."

"That destroyer must have some sort of a device aboard that tears up intrusive electronics," Bledsoe said.

Fagin studied the photos for a few more moments, then turned his gaze to Bledsoe. "What is the initial OPLAN for this—this caper—or whatever the hell it is?"

"Pretty preliminary, since we don't know much," Bledsoe replied. "Obviously they're going to eventually send out some decoy merchant ships and set up an ambush. That's why Lieutenant Stensland has been sent here. He's been detailed to take a target freighter out to draw in the bad guys."

Fagin grinned sardonically. "We're not near ready to take overt action yet."

"You're right," Bledsoe said. "And the launching of active operations depends entirely on you." He nodded to Stensland. "You'll be staying here awhile, Lieutenant."

Stensland glanced around at the plush surroundings, smiling widely. "I shall think of it as a great sacrifice for my country."

"Poor guy," Fagin said with a wink.

Bledsoe said, "This is your baby, Commander. Tell me what you want me to do for you."

"Is Dr. Levinson still out on Point Loma in San Diego?" Fagin asked.

"Yes, sir."

"And he's still doing experiments on underwater stealth?"

"As far as I know," Bledsoe said. "It's a highly secure area."

"Well, tell them to unsecure it enough to let me in," Fagin said, indicating Stensland's photos and the documents. "I need to go over this stuff with him."

Point Loma Submarine Base
8 June
1035 Hours

Point Loma is a peninsula that juts southward into the Pacific Ocean to the west of North Island. The Fort Rosecrans Military Reservation takes up a large portion of the area. Old gun emplacements and tunnels there can be traced back to when it was a U.S. Army Coast Artillery garrison for decades. Later the Army Reserves— including the crack 12th Special Forces Group—used the reservation for its activities. After that it became a submarine base.

This was the place where Dr. Harry Levinson established his laboratory for underwater stealth experiments in
one of the former headquarters buildings. His facility was
a spacious, climate-controlled environment dominated by a
large 22,000-cubic-foot tank of saline water along the entire
west wall of the structure. The other side of the building
was filled with a hodgepodge of electronic instrumentation
needed for simulation, recording, measuring, and conduct-
ing his many experiments. None of this equipment was
stock. It had either been jury-rigged or built by the scientist
himself. His specialties were radar, sonar, and stealth
methods under the sea.

When Commander Gerald Fagin walked into the lab, he
found the doctor standing by a printer that was spewing out
the data on his latest test run. The water in the tank still
sloshed a bit from the movements of the submarine mock-
up used in whatever data the doctor was monitoring. The
old man, a short, dumpy genius with a bushy white beard,
was completely lost in his work. Fagin cleared his throat to
get his attention. Dr. Levinson turned around, stared at the
unexpected visitor, then lowered his glasses from his forehead to his nose for a better look. His craggy face broke
into a grin.

"Fagin!"

"Hello, Doctor," Fagin said, holding out his hand. They
had met when Dr. Levinson was a visiting professor at
MIT. Fagin had taken several of his classes.

Dr. Levinson said, "I gather from your serious countenance as well as the briefcase you hold that this is not a social visit."

"I'm afraid not," Fagin said. "I hate to bother you, but
I've come to see you on a rather important matter."

The printer stopped whirring, and the doctor ripped off
the printed stack of sheets. "All right, my boy. Let's go
over to my office."

The office that the doctor referred to was no more than a
cluttered desk, a battered file cabinet, a couple of chairs,
and piles of paper on the floor next to the wall. As they

walked up, Dr. Levinson tossed the recently printed document over on one stack.

Fagin laughed. "I see you're still using the same filing system."

"It works for me," Dr. Levinson said. "Sit down."

After they settled into the chairs, Fagin gave him a quick but reasonably complete briefing on the situation involving the privateer and the merchant vessels. Then he handed the documentation over. The doctor took it and opened to page one. As he read, Fagin went over to the coffeemaker and poured out the remnants of what had to have been in the pot for at least a week, then began to brew some fresh.

Levinson was a caffeine addict, but many times he would become so engrossed in his work that he would forget to drink what he prepared. He also missed meals for the same reason, and would sometimes come back to the real world not realizing how long he had been lost in his work, and completely surprised by how hungry he was.

By the time the coffee was ready and Fagin had poured them a couple of cups, the doctor was a third of the way through the report. He took a cup from Fagin and sipped at it, so engrossed in the reading that he didn't realize what he was doing. Fagin settled down and waited. Another fifteen minutes went by before Dr. Levinson closed the report and slammed it down on his desk.

"There is more than stealth involved here," he announced. "This is some sort of very sophisticated ECM that can defeat radar. Do you have those photos mentioned here?"

"Sure do," Fagin said. He reached in his jacket pocket and handed them over.

The doctor's eyes opened wide. "Good God!"

"Yeah," Fagin agreed. "Everything is in focus except for the bad guys' ship. It looks like it came through a matter transformer that had gone awry."

The doctor returned the photos. "This has to be a force field of some sort."

"Like in *Star Trek*?"

"I don't know," Dr. Levinson said. "I hate science fiction. Never watch it. Never read it." He swung around to
his computer. "This is a stand-alone, but they ship in the
data I need to load on, when I request it. Plus I put in a few
things myself." He typed in: "Force Field." He tapped the
Search button and waited. A couple of file names popped
up, and he went into them. When he finished, he leaned
back in his chair. "There's nothing here that provides anything about the sort of science you're facing out there on
the bounding waves."

"Maybe there's another term for it," Fagin suggested.

"Let me turn to my historical search engine," the doctor
said. "There's myriad subjects in there. Some of this stuff
goes back centuries to specific theories that some far-
sighted individual dreamed up."

He called up his historical data and typed in the subject.
Once again about a half-dozen files popped up. One caught
his attention, and he turned to Fagin. "So the pirates or privateers or whatever are Japanese?"

"Right."

"Well, here's something from World War Two," Dr.
Levinson said.

"About the Japanese Navy?" Fagin asked. "The *Imperial* Japanese Navy, that is."

"Actually, it's about a force field mentioned from the
U.S. Navy's World War Two decoding program. They
were headquartered in Washington, as I recall. The Japanese code had been broken early on, and they were happily
monitoring and deciphering the emperor's sailor boys all
through the war." He studied the data. "There're only a few
insignificant sentences, however, and—oh! Here's something interesting. The code clerk involved with this was a
woman by the name of Anne Madigan. She worked in the
code office for her entire career. During World War Two
she was assigned to the Japanese section."

"Anne Madigan?" Fagin asked. He reached for the
phone and punched in a number. He got his party on the
first ring, and spoke rapidly. "Lieutenant Bledsoe, this is
Commander Fagin. I want you to look up somebody for

me. A woman by the name of Anne Madigan. A clerk in
the Navy's code operation in Washington during World
War Two. Get on this now. I'm with Dr. Levinson out at
Point Loma. I'll wait."

Now Dr. Levinson noticed the hot coffee. "I'm glad I
remembered to brew up a pot this morning."

Fagin grinned. "Yeah. Me, too."

CHAPTER FIVE

Georgetown, Virginia
9 June
1515 Hours

Anne Madigan was a ninety-year-old retired civil servant with a thirty-year career that had begun in 1930. The lady's service consisted of using her talents in various areas of United States Naval Intelligence, where she skillfully and effectively enciphered, deciphered, and designed codes.

Anne was far ahead of her time when she earned a Ph.D. in mathematical theory from Princeton University. She was an outspoken, headstrong twenty-year-old who damned convention and tradition. Not only was her gender a problem, but the fact that she was petite, pretty, and profane prevented her from being taken seriously. Timing was also against Anne, since this was back in the days when women were not encouraged to seek scientific educations. Consequently, she had been forced to compete on a decidedly uneven playing field.

When she completed her studies and sallied forth to begin her professional life, Anne found it impossible to find employment at any of the leading universities. But her old professor and mentor, an eccentric by the name of Lazlo Berczets, Ph.D. told her of the United States Navy's

little-known code center in Washington. They had requirements for people with special abilities in arrangement,
classification, and grouping of mathematical syntax. He
wrote out a letter of recommendation for her.

Armed with Dr. Berczets's letter, she caught a train for
the trip down from her alma mater to Washington to apply
for a job in the center. She was grudgingly and hesitantly
granted an audience with a crusty captain who greeted her
entrance into his office with an open scowl. He glanced
without interest at Dr. Berczets's letter, then quickly
launched into the interview to get it over with as quickly as
possible. Within only a couple of minutes he knew that a
very special young woman sat across his desk from him.
He quickly concluded she would prove invaluable in the
supersecret Japanese code section because of her unique
fascination and talents with word and number puzzles.
Anne was busy explaining her methodology in computa-
tive serializing when he interrupted her to say she was
hired.

Unfortunately, her first workday was met with more
than a little disdain by the section's staff, who were smug,
self-assured geniuses with egos that matched their exalted
mental capacities. Rather than being shaken by their churl-
ishness, it brought out a cool, calculated anger in young
Anne Madigan. She challenged them to a contest in solv-
ing a series of a half-dozen puzzles she had designed and
published in *the Journal of Analytical Mathematical Praxis.*
This quarterly magazine, in print from 1897 until 1939 by
a consortium of mathematical theorists, was one of those
money-losing projects that died out with the death of its
last editor, who also happened to pay all the bills out of an
inheritance.

Anne's challenge and her puzzles bested the learned
gentlemen in spite of their determination to solve them.
She had encoded mathematical symbols using consistent
Egyptian hieroglyphics for each one. What the mathemati-
cians had not realized was that the enigmas could not be
solved one at a time. They had to be worked as a whole, referring each puzzle to the other five to figure out the

matches. When they finally capitulated after more than a week of laboring at unraveling her vermiculate reasoning, Anne was called in to explain the solutions.

This lovely young woman, whose sexuality and beauty was lost on the nerds in the room, explained her self-designed enigmas on a blackboard in a back office used for group brain sessions. After carefully writing the puzzles out in a single line, she changed each hieroglyphic to a particular symbol. It still did not make sense to her audience until she took the last part of the first and put it with the first part of the third; then the last of the second to the first of the fourth and on through the process until the last of the sixth was written with the first of the second. This set up a string of logic, but it seemed like something designed by a dyslexic inmate of an insane asylum. After letting them frown over that for a few minutes Anne went back to the board and reversed the parts of the second, fourth, and sixth sets. *Voilà!* There was a ten-year cycle of orbits of Earth in conjunction with those of Mars projected mathematically across the blackboard.

One of the geniuses was so incensed he shouted, "A child's puzzle!"

"Really?" Anne said in her characteristic boldness. "Then why didn't you solve it, if it was so easy?"

Another protested, "Trickery! Plain and simple."

"Not plain and simple enough for you, evidently," Anne said. "And, yes! You got the trickery part right." She gazed at the frustrated men. "It's a code. Understand? It's a god-damn code! Isn't that what this department is all about?"

The naval officer in charge of the Japanese section was no mathematical genius, but he was a trained leader out of the United States Naval Academy, and he could recognize quality when he saw it. Anne was quickly thrown in the deep end of the code-deciphering program, where she served faithfully and effectively while being paid 25 percent less than her male coworkers. Her responsibilities and workload increased dramatically with the attack on Pearl Harbor.

During her rare free evenings, Anne enjoyed the wartime nightlife of Washington. There wasn't a nightclub, upscale bar, or restaurant that she didn't know. She attracted more than her share of men and enjoyed several torrid love affairs—more than a few simultaneously—but she never found the man who she would be happy with. Her eccentricities were not compatible with beings of lesser intellectual strength. Anne continued the cycle of working hard at that office during the day and partying vigorously when able at night. She kept this up until the end of the war.

After VJ Day she was transferred to other departments that served the Free World's cause in the Cold War. Anne's greatest accomplishment during this period was breaking a highly complicated technical code being used by various missile design facilities within the Warsaw Pact countries and the Soviet Union. She would have worked forever, but regulations and budget concerns forced her to take a mandatory retirement in 1960.

Now, even though in her ripe old age, Anne lived healthfully and happily in a modest townhouse in Georgetown. She was still a feisty lady with a sharp mind, and was a member of a local chess club where she beat the younger players on a regular basis. When not doing that, she swam laps in a senior citizen center's pool, played complicated word and number games, and submitted tough crossword puzzles to the *Georgetown Senior Citizen Review.*

When Commander Gerald Fagin called her from Andrews AFB to ask for a meeting, he had expected the trembling sounds of the ancient vocal chords of a very old lady. He was not only surprised by the firmness in her voice over the telephone, but also by the eagerness she showed in having him drop by for a visit. She evidently liked to have company.

An hour later, after a cab trip out from the base, he rang her doorbell. Anne answered the summons and gave the caller a flirtatious leer. "Hey, handsome," she said. "You know how long it's been since a sailor boy has called on me?"

Fagin smiled and shrugged. "I don't know. A day or two maybe?"

"Actually it was three decades back, but who's counting?" she said with a laugh. "Come in, please, Commander Fagin."

They walked through the small foyer into her living room. Fagin had been expecting tea and cookies if any refreshments were offered. Instead, a fully stocked wet bar with pretzels, peanuts, crackers, and various cheeses was laid out. Anne walked behind the bar and pulled out a tall can of Guinness stout for herself. As she carefully poured it into a proper pub glass, she said, "Name your poison."

His eyes scanned the bottles. "A Jameson on the rocks would do me fine, thank you, ma'am."

"Jameson Irish whiskey," Anne said. "That's what I'd expect from a man named Fagin." She fixed the drink and came around the bar, handing it to him. "And if you call me ma'am one more time, you'll be wearing the next libation for a hat."

"Aye, aye, Anne!" Fagin answered with a wide grin.

They settled down on the sofa, placing their drinks on the coffee table. "Now what can I do for you, Fagin?"

"I'm interested in a small segment of your code work," Fagin began. "It has to do with the Japanese naval codes of World War Two. One in particular about a force field."

"Force field? Force field?" Anne took a deep swallow of the stout and thought for a moment. "Of course. Kamisaku! The Sacred Barrier."

"Ah!" Fagin exclaimed. "So the devil's machine existed, did it?"

"I believe it was in the basic phases of design when I came in contact with it," Anne said.

"I would like to know what you remember of it," Fagin said.

"There wasn't a hell of a lot," Anne answered. "It was mentioned in several messages I decoded. One of them had a brief but rather detailed description and the machine's concept. It evidently caused an electronic invisibility of sorts. It was completely out of my field of expertise. But my boss thought it was important enough to be looked into.

He tasked me with taking the decrypted messages up to my alma mater—Princeton University—and turning them over to a qualified man for study and examination. There were several brilliant scientists and theorists such as Albert Einstein on campus in those days. I went to my old professor, Dr. Lazlo Berczets. I ended up having to spend two months up there while he worked out a theorem of how such a machine might function." She took another swallow of stout. "God! It was fascinating!"

"I presume he produced a paper or a report or something."

"He most certainly did," Anne said. "It was so complicated that I had to run checks on most of the mathematical formulas he formatted. We wanted to make sure all the i's were dotted and the t's crossed. Actually, I should say that we wanted to make sure two plus two equaled four throughout the paper."

"But this was only his idea of what the Japanese were talking about, correct?" Fagin asked.

"True," Anne replied. "But you must understand that Dr. Berczets was a brilliant man. Also, he had his work reviewed by Dr. Einstein, and they both agreed that he had reached the only logical conclusion possible about the damn thing and how it worked."

"I know Albert Einstein has gone to that great laboratory in the sky, but what about Dr. Berczets?"

"He died in 1947," Anne said. "And his son passed on in 1993. But the grandson, Lazlo Berczets III, is now working in the same old office and laboratory."

"What happened to the report you and Dr. Berczets worked on?" Fagin asked. "Is it somewhere in naval archives?"

"Oh, no," Anne said. "It's still up there in Princeton. The navy wanted hardcore intelligence, not conjecture. The papers would be in young Lazlo's office somewhere."

"It would seem I must see this latest Dr. Berczets," Fagin remarked.

"He doesn't have a doctorate," Anne said. "In fact he never completed high school. Lazlo III was even more brilliant than his grandfather and father. In fact, his giant intellect led him deep into insanity, but treatment, medication, and self-discipline brought him out of it. The powers that be determined that it was asking too much of him to follow a curricula to earn degrees. His father took him under his wing, and he evolved into an eccentric but sapient scientist."

"I'll go visit the guy then," Fagin said. "Will you be available if I need further explanation or enlightenment on this Sacred Barrier?"

Anne winked at him. "Sailor boy, I'm available for whatever you want." She leaned forward. "What do you want?"

"Well," Fagin said, "I could certainly use another Jameson."

Princeton, New Jersey
11 June
1635 Hours

Commander Gerald Fagin's inquiries revealed that Lazlo Berczets III was no longer at Princeton University. He worked in his house on Witherspoon Street just north of the cemetery. Evidently there was some problem with a high school dropout having laboratory and office space that was wanted and needed by others with doctorates in various sciences and disciplines. However, government grants funded Lazlo's studies and experiments, and he was able to purchase a large rambling brick home in which to live and work.

Fagin was greeted at the door of the residence by a Hispanic housekeeper who had answered his telephone inquiry as to how to find the house. The lady was a short, dumpy Puerto Rican wearing a gray maid's uniform with a large white collar. She ushered Fagin into the house, then led him through a neatly arranged and maintained living area toward the rear. When they stepped into Lazlo's work area, the environment quickly changed to one of clutter and disorganization. Bookshelves were lined up as if part of a library run by Curly, Larry, and Moe in conjunction with Laurel and Hardy. The shelving was close together, forming narrow aisles, and was crammed with volumes at all sorts of angles: some stacked, some on their sides, and other laid helter-skelter on top.

The housekeeper called out, "Mr. Lazlo! Your visitor is here."

A nasal voice came from out of sight somewhere in the clutter. "What? What was that? Are you calling me, Mrs. Gonzales?"

"Your visitor is here," she repeated. Then she turned and left the place as if she were fleeing the scene of a bloody train wreck.

Fagin stood there for a moment before the stooped, thin figure of sixty-year-old Lazlo Berczets III appeared from among the stacks. "Yes?"

"How do you do?" Fagin said. "I'm Commander Fagin. I called you yesterday about one of your grandfather's work projects."

Berczets walked up, showing gray unkempt hair, an overbite, and granny glasses pushed down to the edge of his nose. "Yes. Yes, you did."

A few awkward moments passed, then Fagin realized it was his turn to continue the conversation. "It involved some data discovered in a Japanese coded message, which proved to be a sort of force field."

"That is most interesting, is it not?" Berczets said. "A force field."

"Yes it is," Fagin agreed. "Do you think you might be able to locate the documents?"

"I already have," Berczets said. "Right after we talked and hung up our respective telephones, I went to Grandpa's file reference book and located the cabinet and drawer into which he had placed the documents of which we are speaking."

"May I see the file?" Fagin asked.

"Yes. Of course. You may see the file," Berczets replied. He turned and began shuffling back into the administrative wilderness that dominated the room. "Follow me, please."

Fagin had to turn sideways to make his way through a long, narrow space that was bordered by shelves. When they emerged from the book storage area, they stepped into a neat, open area with a desk, a long table, a drafting table, and several chairs. The contrast between the disaster area they had just traversed and this office space was like the difference between a junkyard and a hospital operating room. Everything was clean and orderly in the spacious study area. A thick cardboard file folder lay on top of the drafting table. Berczets took one of the stools and motioned Fagin to take the other.

"Everything is in here," he said, opening the folder. "After I perused it superficially to determine it was what you required, I became fascinated by the contents. I sat up all night going through my grandpa's papers. Perhaps now, you should go over these documents. I shall wait patiently while you do so."

"Thank you," Fagin said.

Berczets pulled the papers out. There were diagrams and many neatly typed pages of data. "The top page is the original copy of the decoded Japanese message," Berczets explained. "The date is indicative of the *Showa* era that ran from 1926 to 1989. *Showa* means 'enlightened peace,' and marks the reign of Emperor Hirohito. *Showa* 18 is our year of 1943. The date on the message is the third of November of that year."

"Thank you," Fagin said as he began reading the message that had been typed so many years before by Anne Madigan.

Date: 3/11/Showa 18
To: Admiral Chiteito
From: Commander Nakamigawa
Preparations are being made for Dr. Zunsuno and the Sacred Barrier Machine Team to be transported from Tokyo to Kakureta Island at the earliest date possible. All tests of the Sacred Barrier machine have indicated a great potential, but

there are various difficulties to overcome. I have the honor
of attaching a brief description of the results expected by
Dr. Zunsuno when the project is brought to fulfillment.

After this came the attachment that was made up of
three pages of single-typed descriptive data. Fagin read it
and came to the conclusion that if what was said was true,
the Sacred Barrier machine would somehow be impervious
to any electronic intrusions or impulses aimed at it. Fagin
glanced at Berczets. "What is this Kakureta Island?" he
asked.

"I haven't the slightest idea," Berczets answered. "None
of my reference material makes mention of it."

"Mmm," Fagin mused, "it's probably a code name. At
any rate I am most interested in what conclusions your
grandfather drew from this data."

Berczets handed him the thick document that was contained in a three-ring notebook, and Fagin settled down to
read. An hour drifted by, and he barely paid attention to
Mrs. Gonzales's voice when she announced she had
brought sandwiches and coffee. Berczets went to fetch the
refreshments and brought the tray back to the drafting
table. Fagin was barely aware of eating a sandwich and
sipping coffee as he continued to read. When he finished,
he had been studying the paper for three hours.

"You see?" Berczets said. "My grandpa has proven
mathematically that a machine can be made that would be
completely impervious to radar, laser, or any other electronic impulses or beams or influence."

"Yeah," Fagin agreed. "My education and abilities in
mathematics don't come close to your grandfather's skills.
Or yours either, I'm sure. Do you have any specific opinions yourself?"

"Yes indeed," Berczets said. "Such a machine would not
be passive. By that I mean it broadcasts or transmits this
force field."

"Would it be long range?" Fagin asked.

Berczets shook his head. "No. It wouldn't have to be,
you see. All it must do is provide protective covering in the

immediate area. It does not block electronic intrusions, it disintegrates them. Thus, it has only to be effective within a limited circumference. The source distance of the intrusions directed toward it is immaterial. Irrelevant. Meaningless, actually."

"You use the term *intrusions*," Fagin said. "Are you of the opinion that it is able to defeat any form of electronic warfare aimed at it?"

"Oh, yes," Berczets said. "If it were possible to build such a barrier—as the Japanese called it—whatever it was on or in would be invulnerable to modern weaponry. That is to say, the detection process and aiming capability of that ordnance. However, this is only theory, and no such technology exists. I myself cannot think of how it could be manufactured."

If you only knew, Fagin thought. That was how the Japanese destroyer was able to approach its victims without being detected on radar screens. The largest vessels on the ocean had all the latest electronics, making the crews complacent and self-assured as to their security.

"I had another thought," Berczets said. He spoke in a tone as if to see if Fagin would be interested in what he had to say.

"What were you thinking, Mr. Berczets?" Fagin asked, taking the hint.

"I was thinking that if such a barrier machine was aboard a ship or an airplane, the only way to destroy it would be the old-fashioned way."

"You mean a line-of-sight attack?" Fagin asked. "Such as aiming at it with the bare eyeball using gunsights, torpedo sights, or bomb sights?"

"Yes," Berczets said. "That's what I was thinking."

Fagin stood up. "I will have to take your grandfather's papers with me."

"Oh, dear! Must you?"

"I'm afraid it's very important. Very, very important."

"Somehow I think so, too, Mr. Fagin. Please feel free."

CHAPTER SIX

NAS North Island, California
12 June–25 June

When Gerald Fagin landed at North Island, he hurried from the aircraft to the terminal as rapidly as possible. He was once again met by Lieutenant Pete Bledsoe, but this time the laid-back lieutenant was not alone. He was accompanied by one of those sleepy-eyed gents whose unemotional countenance betrayed both the alertness and ferocity of a hunting tiger that dwelt within his psyche. A quick introduction was made by Bledsoe before they went out to the parking lot. The guy was beefy but moved almost gracefully as he led the way to their transportation. Fagin noticed his eyes continually scanned the area as they approached the car.

This ominous stranger had been assigned to escort them because someone in the local OTSI office had decided that the document Fagin brought from Dr. Berczets was important enough to be given some hard-core protection. This arrangement was one of those cover-your-ass details instigated by some anal-retentive individual whose mind-set was driven by imaginary worst-case scenarios. In other words, if someone were destined to steal the material, it wouldn't happen on his watch or area of responsibility.

After the trio settled into Bledsoe's Ford van, the lieutenant drove down the air station's McCain Boulevard to the main gate and out onto Fourth Street in the city of Coronado. He made a right onto Orange Avenue, then headed down the Silver Strand to where the OTSI office was located. After the stranger and documentation had both been deposited in the building, Bledsoe drove out toward Interstate 5 to take Fagin to Del Mar. The commander would be dropped off at the safe house to begin a period of waiting.

Safe House
Del Mar, California

During their enforced stay in the safe house together, Gerald Fagin and Lars Stensland formed an impromptu but sincere friendship. The two men had plenty of time on their hands as they waited for some decisive action to be taken by their shadowy command structure. They were completely in the dark about what was going on or what to expect. It was impossible to tell if sneak-and-peek operations would continue, or some sort of overt action was going to be taken. Meanwhile, Fagin had received direct orders not to discuss the details of his trip with Stensland, and the Norwegian knew better than to pry into the situation.

As they became more acquainted, the two naval officers were surprised that they had one big thing in common: both knew Florida's Space Coast intimately. Fagin and his wife Toni lived on Merritt Island only a ten-minute drive from Port Canaveral. That was the home port of Stensland's former tour ship the *Happy Vagabond*. He hadn't lived on Merritt Island, but he had had a small apartment in a high-rise a short distance down State Route A1A in Cocoa Beach. Both had enjoyed many of the same local restaurants and watering holes that were located away from the crowded tourist hangouts. They had also done a lot of boating on the Indian and Banana Rivers and gone biking through the Old Florida backcountry. Additionally, the pair was able to watch shuttle launches as well as the commercial launches of Lockheed Martin's fantastic Atlas Centaur rockets from their respective homes.

Fagin and Stensland were avid beer drinkers and liked to spend the cool evenings on the balcony of the condo consuming brew and watching the beach babes stroll along the street. Stensland enjoyed talking about the women he had known in various ports during his twelve years as a sailor. But he didn't mention the romance with Kristina Olson. The emotional wounds were still raw about the failed engagement. Another thing he held back was his days in the fishing fleet. His concern with his apparent cowardice made that too difficult for him to discuss openly with another officer. The Norwegian still carried a heavy emotional load about that last storm he had endured on the North Sea. He privately wondered if dealing with the experience was going to be a lifelong struggle.

Fagin also kept quiet about a few things. He was severely limited about what he could relate concerning his recent past as an operative in the OTSI. On the other hand, he was able to converse freely about his youth in Pennsylvania as well as his days as a midshipman at Annapolis.

During the afternoons, they went over to the beach to surf, which was another pastime both had enjoyed in Florida. They had to buy a couple of boards at a shop in Carlsbad, and the first time they walked out on the beach they quickly discovered that Southern California surfers were a territorial bunch. Hand-lettered signs had been erected at strategic points in the area. All read pretty much the same:

LOCAL SURFERS ONLY

Fagin and Stensland ignored the warnings as they strode out onto the sand with surfboards under their arms. Within moments they were approached by a couple of the local wave riders. Fagin cautioned Stensland that there was a possibility of trouble as they watched the two young guys walk up to them. The first surfer nodded a greeting and remarked, "It's pretty obvious you guys ain't from around here."

Fagin warily replied, "That's right. We can see by your signs that you don't welcome visitors."

"Oh, man! That don't apply to old dudes like you," the second surfer said. "Just them assholes from Orange and L.A. County. We wanted to tell you that the water here is cold. You ain't gonna like it without wet suits."

"Yeah," the first said. "Take a look around, man. Ever'body here is wearing one."

Fagin and Stensland now noted that the locals, indeed, were attired for cold water. Stensland, remembering his ordeal in the storm, said, "Thank you very much for your advice. But we shall manage."

"Sure," the second said. "Just thought we'd let you know."

The two kids walked away, and Fagin and Stensland headed for the waves. After a couple of runs they stood shivering and turning blue as the wind off the ocean added to the chill that gripped them hard.

"Damn!" Fagin exclaimed. "That water isn't much over fifty degrees!"

"I thought we were in the tropics, like Florida," Stensland said, vigorously rubbing his legs.

"I think we better go back to that Carlsbad shop again," Fagin suggested.

The next day they were back at the beach, this time wearing neoprene shorty wet suits. None of the kids gave them a second look, indicating it was true that "old dudes" weren't considered much of a threat by this young crowd.

As the wind-and-surf activities went on, the two officers found the California wave activity a lot more challenging and exciting than the long, lazy rolls that swept languidly up on the sands of the Space Coast. Their individual skills at the sport increased with every wave they rode. It was nice to look forward to a quiet evening of sipping beer on the balcony after becoming tired but exhilarated from the day's activities.

But even seemingly endless beer drinking and surfing can become boring, especially when the potentiality of real adventure loomed in the near future. Commander Gerald Fagin and *Løyntant* Lars Stensland were not disappointed at the arrival of the four people who would run the enigmatic project they had been assigned to. The quartet had come loaded down with all documentation needed to launch a combination overt and covert military operation.

The commander was forty-five-year-old Rear Admiral John Paulsen, who was from an unnamed supersecret desk in the Pentagon. He had spent the majority of his service in the SEALs, and this had led to several interservice operations on detached duty. Paulsen was one of those rare individuals with the highly inquisitive and questioning mind of the scientist combined with the physique of strength, agility, and endurance that would be expected of someone with his service background. His arrival to middle age had not dimmed these attributes one iota. This officer with black, short-cropped hair stood five feet ten inches tall, weighed in at 210 solid pounds, sported cauliflower ears from his collegiate wrestling days at Oklahoma State University, and had seen on-the-ground, nose-to-nose action in Bosnia, Somalia, and Afghanistan. His age and intellect had resulted in his being transferred to a supervisory and staff planning assignment in SPECOPS.

The air intelligence and operations officer was USN Lieutenant Commander Gray Hollinger. This man, who had been an aviation enthusiast since boyhood, had earned his spurs on various special air ops around the world. The slim, quiet officer looked positively scholarly with his thinning red hair, almost delicate features, and slender hands. His military flight credentials were impeccable. He had put in several successful stints as a test pilot between tours with the fleet and had been checked out in jets, props, and choppers. As if that wasn't enough, he was an avid airplane model builder, and his home in Norfolk was filled with beautiful examples of his hobby projects.

Commander Craig Davis, only recently assigned to the nuclear carrier *USS Jefferson,* had never had the chance to settle in on his new ship. He was immediately tagged for the job of sea intelligence and operations officer on the coming mission. He was a mustang who had come up through the ranks after studying technical manuals and orders in his rack when off watch or when his buddies were in some port raising hell. He pushed himself until at the beginning of his second four-year hitch, he qualified for the Enlisted Commissioning Program. The navy enrolled him as a full-time student in NROTC at San Diego State University to complete the business administration degree he had begun in his prenavy days at Gustavus Adolphus College in his native Minnesota. From the NROTC program, he went to OCS at Newport and earned a commission as ensign. Now this nononsense officer with a dozen years of service had established himself as a skillful and cool-headed sea officer who had solidly proven his worth to the United States Navy.

The scientist assigned to the operation was Fagin's old pal Dr. Harry Levinson. He had been transferred from his Point Loma laboratory to the OTSI facility in Coronado to turn his scientific expertise loose on the papers written by Dr. Lazlo Berczets so many decades before. Normally he would be perturbed about being pulled from his beloved experiments, but this latest assignment, complete with a mysterious force field, intrigued him with its unknown technology.

Gerald Fagin learned he was to be the technological intelligence and operations officer, and that Lars Stensland would be his assistant. They would be used actively on the operation, but at that point no one seemed to know quite what to do with them.

The first briefing was held in the spacious living room of the condo as the six men began the tentative steps into the unknown challenges they faced. Everyone settled down on the plush furniture of the residence, their books and notes arranged on the apartment's large coffee table. Rear Admiral Paulsen waited until everyone was comfortable, then he opened up the session.

"Before we get started," he began, "I'll give you the latest SITREP. A total of fourteen merchant ships of various nations have been taken by these privateers." He looked at Davis. "Would that be the proper term, Commander?"

Davis nodded his head. "That is exactly what they are as far as we know. Their spokesman is claiming they have letters of marque from the Imperial Japanese Navy. While the laws pertaining to privateering have all been eliminated, the concept of the activity is still recognized historically. Therefore, they are privateers."

"Whatever they're called, the bastards are pulling in some big bucks," Paulsen said. "The ships they've ransomed have earned them a total of two hundred and eighty million dollars. The others are being held until some eighty million is paid for them. These include oilers, tankers, freighters, and container ships. All were hauling valuable cargo that was badly needed by several international industries."

Dr. Levinson raised his hand. "Do you suppose the privateers have knowledge of what those vessels have on board?"

"It wouldn't matter," Davis interjected. "The merchant marines of the world don't take cheap loads. Any ship afloat that is stopped will have a costly cargo."

"Right," Paulsen agreed. He turned to Craig Davis. "Have you been able to identify and locate this mysterious Kakureta Island?"

"No, sir," Davis replied. "Every bit of research I've done has drawn a blank."

"Shit!" Paulsen said. "Then all we know for certain is that their method of operations is to approach their targets with a stealth machine of sorts. However, Dr. Levinson has been given a paper written by some genius at Princeton. Evidently the guy had a chance to read a Japanese description of the thingamajig. I think we should hear Dr. Levinson's report before we proceed. Doctor, the floor is yours."

"I began acquainting myself with this situation with an intense study of the report submitted by Lieutenant Stensland about his own capture by the privateers," Dr. Levinson said. "Next I turned my attention to the World War Two documents and that thesis written by Dr. Lazlo Berczets of

Princeton University. Fascinating! He correctly assumed that a machine—called the Sacred Barrier by the Japanese—created a force field of sorts to resist electronic intrusion such as radar. I am convinced that the capabilities of this defensive system counteract intrusion by bouncing it off into other directions."

Hollinger, the air intelligence and operations officer, leaned forward. "What about heat-seeking missiles, Doctor?"

"Heat-seeking weaponry is also electronic," Dr. Levinson said. "This damn thing is aggressive. It would be able to counter anything aimed at it. And that would include torpedoes or other underwater ordnance."

"How the hell do we attack it then?" Gray Hollinger asked.

"There's the rub," Dr. Levinson said. "You can't damage it with what's carried in the modern navy's weapon inventory."

"What are we supposed to do?" Hollinger asked. "Strip our fighter-attack aircraft of all that billion-dollar gadgetry we've put in them, then send them out looking for these guys?"

"First things first," Rear Admiral Paulsen said. "Any nineteen-year-old rifleman will tell you that the primary thing you got to do to destroy an enemy is to know where the son of a bitch is. We got to figure out a way to find 'em."

"We can't search them out," Commander Davis argued. "We'll have to draw them to us. We need a decoy."

"Decoys won't do us any good if we can't blow the bastards out of the water!" Paulsen pointed out.

"What the hell are we supposed to do?" Commander Hollinger said. "Fly over the sons of bitches, hang out the windows and drop bombs down on them, like they did in World War One?"

"World War Two," Fagin said impulsively. "That's the answer!"

Paulsen turned toward the speaker, irritated by the intrusion of what he considered a desk jockey. "Do you have a point to make—" He had to think a moment to remember Fagin's rank. "Commander?"

"Yes, sir!" Fagin replied. "Something I saw in an air show in Titusville, Florida, just came to mind. The Grumman Avenger."

"What the hell is a Grumman Avenger?" Paulsen asked. "It sounds like either a serial killer or a superhero in the movies."

Commander Hollinger interjected, "The Grumman Avenger was a torpedo bomber used in World War Two. It was quite effective in its day."

"It didn't carry laser- or radar-guided weaponry," Fagin said. "The pilot and his crew physically aimed at their targets and cut loose torpedoes, bombs, or fifty-caliber machine gun fire."

"Very interesting," Paulsen said impatiently. "But I hardly think there are any of those aircraft available in our carrier battle groups, Commander Fagin."

"You're absolutely correct about that, sir," Fagin said. "But I know where four real-live flying Avenger aircraft are located." He pulled out his wallet and went through it for a few moments before coming up with a dog-eared business card. "Here we go," he said, reading it. "An old guy by the name of Scotty Ross owns them. He takes at least one to various air shows all around the country during the summer. That's where I met him. At the annual event held in Titusville at the Space Center Executive Airport."

Commander Hollinger stood up and walked to the window. The others regarded him in silence as he gazed unseeing out at the beach. Then he turned. "TBF-1 Avengers were flown in the Battle of Midway in World War Two. They were instrumental in destroying enough Japanese ships to turn the tide of the war in our favor." He walked across the room as if speaking to himself more than the others. "The crew consisted of a pilot, bombardier–radio operator, and rear gunner. Two fifty-caliber machine guns were mounted one in each wing. Another fifty-caliber was rear-pointing in an aft turret, and a thirty-caliber in a ventral position also aimed rearward. The aircraft could also carry one hell of a torpedo, bomb, and rocket load. The pilots flew by the seat of their pants, going down close to the water to deliver their attacks. Nothing was aimed by laser or radar. Just the eyesight and judgment of the crew."

Commander Davis frowned. "How do you know so much about those old aircraft, Hollinger?"

"Are you kidding?" Hollinger said. "I grew up loving airplanes. I know the best ones of World War One as well." He looked over at Rear Admiral Paulsen. "Those Avengers wouldn't give a damn about a force field. Hell! They could take on a thousand force fields if they had to." He paused, then added, "But they still have to find the targets before they can shoot at them."

Jensen thought a moment before turning to Fagin. "Do you know where to get ahold of the geezer that owns these—these Avengers?"

Fagin waved the business card. "Yes, sir! I sure as hell do."

CHAPTER SEVEN

NAS Fallon, Nevada
26 June
1400 Hours

The trio of aged F-5 jet fighters, with their outdated Warsaw Pact camouflage paint schemes, swung off the base leg onto the final approach to the runway for landing. The three pilots driving the machines through the sky were bone tired after a long session of simulated dogfighting over the Nevada desert. They were among the handpicked pilots based at Fallon who were the U.S. Navy's bad guys, i.e., the "play" enemy. The number one requirement for a jet jockey to be assigned there was to be among the best of his profession. The second and third were to have a mean streak and enjoy humiliating people. The fourth was to be unpredictable and tricky.

These individualistic aviators were tasked with being skilled opponents in staged albeit dangerous dogfights against carrier air wings going through workups prior to heading out to the fleet for operations. The aircraft the bad guys flew were painted and marked as foreign adversaries that were likely to oppose the visiting squadrons when they went out into the wicked world of reality.

This particular trio of aviators were inseparable

mavericks who were among the best of that nonpareil group. Their off-the-wall personalities bonded them in a strong collective friendship with traits not unlike those of triplet siblings. Unfortunately, that uniqueness did not always work to their—or their commanding officers'—advantage.

They were all lieutenants, and the spokesman for the group was Westmoreland "Westy" Fields. Westy was an intellectual hell-raiser who read the classics and could speak French, German, Italian, and Spanish fluently. This tall, lanky man with patrician features was the youngest son of a wealthy, established New England family who traced their ancestry back to the Pilgrims of Plymouth Rock. Westy had received an excellent education through a series of tutors provided by his father. He was given this type of schooling not because his family could afford it but because he was continually being expelled from the finest, most expensive prep schools in New York, Massachusetts, Rhode Island, and Connecticut. The young hellion's behavior was so bad it overwhelmed his excellent academic accomplishments. Westy's rebellious attitude continued until he met a neighbor's son who was a naval aviator serving aboard the carrier *USS John F. Kennedy.* This exposure to the adventurous life of flying in a carrier battle group awoke ambition in the young man. The aviator was home on leave when Westy met him. The two spent a few afternoons together as the officer entertained the boy with tales of his flying experiences in the fleet. Westy could not imagine anything more exciting than being a dashing jet fighter pilot in the U.S. Navy, and he decided to make a try at earning the gold wings of naval aviation.

However, a school record filled with demerits and expulsions would hinder such ambitions. From that moment on, Westy showed a grudging respect for his bevy of private instructors. This influenced his pater enough to send the boy back to complete his education in the elite atmosphere of an exclusive prep school.

After Westy's eventual acceptance to the United States Naval Academy, the strict discipline and curriculum jarred him into becoming an even more responsible young man. However, after being commissioned and going to Pensacola, many of his old habits began regaining the upper hand in his personal conduct as he evolved into the quintessential fighter pilot.

Ariel Goldberg was born and raised in Brooklyn, New York. His family was strictly Orthodox Jewish, and he was brought up in the highest religious traditions of his people. His father was in the diamond business and wanted his three sons to join him in the enterprise that had been founded by Ariel's great-grandfather in the early 1890s. The two other boys were enthusiastic about learning the business and eventually running it. Ariel was the exception. He was the youngest child, and difficult from the start, being disrespectful of his father's attitudes as well as a reprobate in Hebrew school. Ariel chafed under family pressure, and his innate stubbornness brought him nothing but grief in the form of whippings and an almost permanent confinement to his upstairs bedroom. His natural sense of rebellion led him to run away from home when he was eighteen. He knew he could enlist in the service without his parents' permission, but he wanted to avoid the resultant confrontation such intentions would bring about. One night, while everyone slept, he quietly left his room and went down to his father's study. After sneaking his birth certificate from the family desk, he went back upstairs.

The next morning Ariel presented himself at the navy recruiter and enlisted for a four-year hitch. It didn't take Seaman Goldberg long to recognize that the United States Navy was something he had been searching for all his life. He applied himself in boot camp and "A" school, going to the fleet as a striker for aviation machinist mate. His experiences around aircraft kicked up further ambitions in the young man. After a year of repairing airplanes, he decided he wanted to fly them. He took the examination for acceptance in the officer candidate program and earned a reserve commission. After that came the opportunity for college and a bachelor's degree in economics from Florida

State University. This accomplishment in education pleased his parents enough to forgive him for spurning family tradition. They saw a great future for the former errant son as an investor or banker. But this initial approval of his stern sire faded with Ariel's decision to remain in the navy. Unperturbed, the young officer went to flight school, graduating as a fighter pilot to begin his career on aircraft carriers.

The third member of this intrepid team was a stout redhead with a pleasant, round face. Junior Stump was a native Alabaman whose family had been engaged in the distilling of illegal moonshine whiskey for untold generations. Junior had all the impetuosity and disregard of conventions displayed by any self-respecting moonshiner. Among the traits he inherited from his outlaw ancestors was quickness of mind and an innate alertness. These traits, while useful in evading federal revenue agents, also helped him with his studies in school. Junior had learned early in life to enjoy reading, and that natural mental sharpness combined with a heavy dash of intellectual exercise worked in his favor. Everything he read in books stuck solidly in his mind, never to be forgotten. He maxed all the tests in school and was even skipped over the second and fifth grades, a situation that was usually reversed in the wild Stump family. Most of them were flunked and held back until quitting the eighth grade when sixteen or seventeen years of age.

But in spite of his quick mind, Junior was still a Stump at heart. While other boys made extra money after school with paper routes or flipping burgers, Junior earned as much as $500 a night running souped-up tanker cars filled with illegal whiskey while making deliveries for his dad. Even at the age of fourteen, Junior's skill behind the wheel earned him the respect and admiration of drivers as far away as North Carolina. He would have probably kept at the business until he switched over to NASCAR racing as many tanker drivers did, but his excellent work in school earned him a scholarship to the prestigious Camellia Academy in Montgomery, Alabama. His dad hated to lose a good driver, but he considered this opportunity best for his daring son, and he encouraged him to do well in the conventional world.

This prep school for boys provided him with an excellent education and a chance to join the campus NROTC. His family background and history was not much admired by the majority of his fellow students, who were from wealthy, well-to-do backgrounds. They snubbed him as an inferior being who had forgotten his place in society. Junior didn't particularly mind their collective haughty attitude because he didn't like them either. It was this total disregard of their standards and mores that infuriated the rich boys more than Junior's humble origins. They decided to take some action to teach him a lesson. During a midnight raid on his room, he fought back a physical attack, beating the hell out of a half-dozen frat rats. This violent resistance on his part resulted in him becoming the leader of other disenfranchised boys who were also on scholarships or were social misfits.

Junior's bravado combined with that high IQ got him the attention of the NROTC program's commanding officer, who recognized the boy had the right attitude and daring to become a fighter pilot. This man arranged for Junior to take the competitive entrance examination for Annapolis. He, like his two best friends, ended up in flight school and flying jet fighters off carriers. The only detriment in Junior's life was the fact that in spite of all his education and the good writing habits he acquired during those years of schooling, his vocal skills remained relatively undeveloped. He still spoke in the moonshine idiom of his people.

One other problem he faced during his first year of active duty involved some marked difficulty in obtaining a security clearance. This temporary setback came about because so many of Junior's male relatives had served time in federal detention facilities on charges pertaining to the illegal manufacture and sale of moonshine whiskey. But this glitch was eventually put right.

On this particular day following the dogfight training, Westy, Ariel, and Junior had just stepped from the cockpits when a yeomen from squadron headquarters approached them. The guy showed an insolent grin as he informed them the CO wanted to see them without delay. The three were wary.

Westy Fields asked, "What sort of temper is our esteemed commander exhibiting?"

The yeoman grinned wider. "You want to know what sort of temper, sir? I can describe it in one word. Fucking bad."

"That's two words," Ariel Goldberg countered.

"'Scuse me, Ariel," Junior Stump interjected. "The word *fucking* don't count."

"It doesn't in Brooklyn," Ariel remarked. "But I thought it did everywhere else."

"Not in the armed forces of the United States," Westy pointed out. "It is an adjective that always becomes part of the word it modifies."

"Jesus!" the yeoman exclaimed. "You guys better knock off the bullshit and get over there."

"That does seem the appropriate thing to do," Westy agreed. He turned to his two best friends. "Let us hasten to our commander with confidence and optimism."

"But he's pissed off," Ariel reminded him.

"Then our display of cheerfulness will soothe his anger," Westy insisted.

"Like hell it will," Junior said glumly.

They hurried from the flight line to squadron headquarters to answer the summons. Westy marched into the CO's office with Ariel and Junior right behind him. When they were in a proper rank, the three came to a halt, made a left-face, and rendered faultless hand salutes.

"Sir! Lieutenant Fields reporting to the commanding officer as ordered."

"Sir! Lieutenant Goldberg reporting to the commanding officer as ordered."

"Sir! Lieutenant Stump reporting to the commanding officer as ordered."

The CO glowered at them over his desk. "Fields, Goldberg, and Stump. It sounds like a crooked law firm, doesn't it?"

"Sir," Westy said, "you haven't returned our salutes."

"I have no intention of returning your salutes, mister!" the CO snapped.

"I beg the commander's pardon," Westy said in a hurt tone. "But the highest-ranking admiral in the United States Navy is obligated by both tradition and regulations to return the salute of the lowest-ranking seaman."

"Shit!" the CO snarled. He returned the salutes, warning, "But you remain in the position of attention. I want you braced like your days at Annapolis. Understand?"

Ariel said, "I didn't go to Annapolis, sir."

"Then stay braced as if you did!" the CO yelled. He breathed rapidly and shallowly for a few moments before settling down. "Now! Let's get to the reason I summoned you." He glared at them. "When you three applied for astronaut training, I was very pleased. I thought that finally— *finally*—you had decided to get serious about being aviators and were anxious to spread your horizons in serving our country."

"Yes, sir!" Westy, Ariel, and Junior said simultaneously.

"I did not read your applications," the CO said. "I simply trusted your enthusiasm and signed the documents with my personal approval. Then I sent them up through channels."

"Thank you, sir!" Westy, Ariel, and Junior said simultaneously.

"Then the applications were quickly returned to me disapproved," the CO said. "That puzzled me. Accompanying them was a letter of reprimand made out personally to me. I was confused because the letter of reprimand said that the United States Navy did not make light of the astronaut training program. That confused me more. Then I carefully examined your applications and saw the reasons you gave for wanting to join the space program. Do you remember what you said?"

"Yes, sir!" Westy, Ariel, and Junior said simultaneously.

The CO ignored their answer. "You wrote down that you wanted to be astronauts so you could become millionaires and play golf with celebrities. That's what you wrote, wasn't it? That's what you wiseasses put on an official United States Navy form requesting transfer to the National Aeronautical and Space Agency for astronaut training, wasn't it?"

"Yes, sir!" Westy, Ariel and, Junior said simultaneously.

"Did you really think that the United States Navy would approve your application for the reason you gave?"

"Actually, sir," Westy said, "we were trying to make a point about people in the space program. Many become wealthy and hobnob with movie stars and the like."

"So that's what brought about that statement to play golf with celebrities, hey?" the CO asked sarcastically.

"Well, sir," Junior Stump said, "I was worried about that."

"Ah! You had a flash of good sense, hey?" the CO said. "And what concerned you about that reason, Mr. Stump?"

"I don't play golf, sir," Junior said. "I would really prefer just to hang out with celebrities and play tennis with 'em."

Westy looked at his friend. "It's really not that much of a falsehood, Junior."

"Shut up!" the CO roared.

"Yes, sir!" all three said simultaneously.

The CO clasped his hands in anger, fighting the urge to get physical. When he managed to speak, his voice was only a whisper. "You three just don't get it, do you?"

"We do have problems relating to other people, sir," Westy admitted.

"I give up!" the CO exclaimed. "You're dismissed. And forget about any more godamn salutes."

The three quickly made about-faces and hurried from the office. When they were outside the building, Ariel and Junior looked to their leader. Ariel remarked, "That was surprising, wasn't it?"

Westy nodded. "I must confess I did not expect such a fractious retort."

Junior frowned with worry. "D'y'all think he'll stay mad about this?"

"He's already making us fly the oldest aircraft in the squadron because of little things we did before," Ariel pointed out.

"I feel he's far from finished with venting his vengeful wrath in our direction," Westy said. "We can expect some rather unpleasant consequences from this in future."

Ariel moaned, *"Oy gevalt!"*

Kakureta Island
27 June
0400 Hours

Shogun Keizo Hara strode purposefully across the field located in the limited open countryside of the island. He wore a flat, wide-brimmed peasant hat of braided rice straw; his kimono was a plain blue color without decoration. He had slung a quiver of arrows over his shoulder, and he carried a four-man bow in his hand. The instrument was so named because it took four strong men to string it. As he approached his destination, the shogun slowed his pace and began breathing deeply to bring his spirit and body into the proper harmony.

The Japanese word for archery is *kyujutsu*. But that is the literal translation. In reality it would be like describing the ocean as a pond. The art—for it is more than a sport—must be performed in a deeply spiritual way in which the bowman transfers his spirituality into the arrows he shoots. Only when the bowman's inner harmony is in sync with *kyujutsu* is he able to perform the art with unfailing accuracy.

When the shogun reached the proper place, he came to an abrupt halt, then sank into a *zazen* sitting position and closed his eyes. After several long moments of meditation, he opened them, feeling refreshed and alert. As the shogun stood up, he reached for the bow that was eight feet, ten inches long. The grip was a little over two feet from the bottom, putting the strain of the draw on the lower third of the instrument. He had twenty-four arrows in the quiver, and one stood out from the others. It was the longest and was further distinguished by white falcon feathers at the end of the shaft. Tradition demanded that this would be the first he would shoot, since evil spirits and demons feared the color white. When they were frightened away, the conditions would be perfect for practicing *kyujutsu* that day.

Ashibumi!

The shogun withdrew the white-feathered arrow as he faced the target he had chosen for the preliminary and most meaningful shot. It was a leaf fluttering in the wind at the end of a tree branch fifty meters away.

Dozukuri!

He balanced himself as he began to control his breathing.

Yugamae!

He notched the arrow into the string.

Uchiokoshi!

He raised the bow to arm's length, still maintaining a tight control of his breathing.

Hikiwake!

Holding the string steady, he pushed the bow a third of the way down the arrow's length.

Kai!

Now the bow was fully drawn, and the shogun's powerful shoulder muscles kept the weapon steady.

Hanare!

He released the string, sending the arrow flying over into the leaf. It went through it, striking the tree trunk with a loud whacking sound.

The shogun reached for another arrow, beginning a steady, slow exercise in the spiritual practice of this demanding art. Other leaves, also dancing in the wind, were struck true as the vibrating missiles streaked through the open space, singing a whirring song that crossed over countless generations of *Bushido* and *Yamato Damashii*.

When the exercise was finished, the shogun left the arrows to be retrieved by others. He shouldered the bow and empty quiver and walked slowly back toward his villa, feeling a renewed surge of confidence and strength. The

archery practice had come as the result of a dream he had
the night before. In it an old man with a long, wispy beard
and wearing ancient robes had approached him out of a
dense, clinging fog. The elder spoke clearly, stating that
the shogun was to go out and shoot two dozen arrows.
When this task was finished, he would experience a great
revelation that was his *Karma*—his individual destiny—
and it would be a sacred order from the spirits of departed
samurai that he must obey implicitly.

Now, with the twenty-four wooden, steel-tipped missiles spent, that revelation flashed into Keizo Hara's consciousness like a sudden blaze. It was as if the rising sun
had burst forth from the dawn clouds: He was to be the emperor of Japan.

Aislado, Arizona
28 June
0930 Hours

The dusty desert town was small, with only twenty inhab-
itants and a scattering of buildings. One of the two edifices
that dominated that area was a square adobe structure that
was a combination office and home for the community's
leading citizen. This was eighty-one-year-old Scotty Ross,
who lived with his granddaughter Jennifer, aka Sparky;
and cantankerous Phil Paderewski, Chief Petty Officer Retired, United States Navy. This latter gentleman, who was
even older than Scotty, was known as Paddy, which made
strangers assume he was Irish. The geezer quickly and angrily corrected the misconception, always stating that the
Irish enjoyed an undeserved reputation as drinkers, and
that any self-respecting Polack could drink any Mick under any table any time. Paddy kept a more-than-ample
supply of Polish vodka in his freezer and was always
ready to display his prodigious capacity for hard, fast
drinking. Once, during a physical examination, the doctor
noted that blood tests showed problems with the patient's
liver. The physician asked the retired chief if he had a

problem with alcohol. Paddy had roared, "Hell no! I got plenty!"

The largest building in Aislado was a solidly constructed, air-conditioned, spacious airplane hangar that housed a quartet of airworthy Avenger torpedo bombers circa 1943. Numerous other scavenged examples of that aircraft sat on the floor in front of shelves holding miscellaneous parts. These had been collected during the many trips Scotty and Paddy made across the country. A well-appointed machine shop stood in one corner, and this was the domain of Chief Paddy Paderewski. Years of naval service as an aircraft machinist had made him a master of the trade.

During the previous couple of days, Scotty Ross had received several calls from the postmaster in the nearby larger town of Gonzales. This representative of the United States Postal Service told him that a registered letter from the U.S. Navy had arrived for him. Scotty happily ignored the news, knowing that by not fetching it himself, it would have to be brought over to him. The postmaster, whose name was Buck Derrick, had been a political rival of Scotty's on several local issues in the past. These involved tourism and development. Scotty wanted that part of the desert left alone, while Buck wanted to cash in on the holdings of his wide ranges of worthless desert land. They hated each other's guts and never missed a chance to make life miserable for the other guy. Although this had not come to fisticuffs, both men were the same age and both looked twenty years younger. Thus, when Buck came driving up to the hangar, Scotty grinned wickedly as the postmaster got out, bringing the mail with him.

"About time," Scotty said. "The godamn mail delivery in this part of the country isn't worth the powder it'd take to blow it to hell."

"Here's your letter, you lazy son of a bitch!" Buck snapped. "And it's got to be signed for. Is there anybody around here who can write?"

"Give me the form!" Scotty snapped back. He grabbed it and scribbled his name on it. "Only folks I know of who can't write their names are illiterate, useless postmasters."

"The three most overrated things in the world is home cooking, home fucking, and airplane drivers," Buck retorted as he stalked back to his car.

Scotty began opening the envelope as the postmaster drove away. Sparky and Paddy, who had been installing some new control cable in one of the aircraft, joined him. Sparky, though in overalls and with her hands covered with grease, showed a natural feminine attractiveness. She was petite with thick black hair cut short, and her eyes were bright and lively. Bald and grizzle-jowled Paddy looked in his element in his oily garments.

The retired chief asked, "Is it really from the navy, Lieutenant?" He and Scotty continued the habit of addressing each other by their respective ranks, even after the passage of more than a half century.

"Right, Chief," Scotty said. "It's from San Diego." He scanned the lines. "Now this is interesting. It seems that a couple of officers are coming to visit us. And one is flag rank."

Sparky shrugged. "They probably want to talk to us about being in one of the air shows at Miramar." The three went out a dozen or so times a year around the country, and Scotty would make flights of one of the Avengers to show the crowd a superlative example of U.S. Navy air power of World War Two.

"Honey," Scotty said, "they don't send admirals out on piddling stuff like that."

"Admirals is bad news," Paddy announced. "They don't come out and talk to nobody 'cept to send 'em in harm's way."

Sparky laughed. "After we finish with the control cable maybe we better load some machine guns into the number three bird."

Scotty smiled. "I don't think these birds will be going to war, honey."

Paddy frowned. "Just remember what I said about harm's way."

CHAPTER EIGHT

Kakureta Island
1 July
1200 Hours

The crowd stood along the quay as the cruiser eased into the island's harbor. The ship's crew, wearing their service-dress white uniforms, lined the main deck. These sailors stood at a rigid position of parade rest, facing outward as the spectators' uplifted voices cut through the bright afternoon atmosphere. The crowd was dressed in their finest traditional Japanese garments according to their standings in the Kaigun Samurai. The wearing of this ceremonial attire was in honor of the auspicious occasion they celebrated that day.

"*Banzai! Banzai! Banzai!*"

The cries of triumph and celebration came in choruses orchestrated by the senior *jun-i,* who stood to the front of the throng, raising his arms above his head to signal for each separate cry. Three more times he led the crowd to express its collective joy.

"*Banzai! Banzai! Banzai!*"

In the center of the gathering stood a large, shaded review stand that held the shogun, his wife, and a dozen people of the great man's personal staff and retinue. The

leader was resplendent in his formal *haori* suit made up of
a coat and skirtlike pleated pants decorated with a cherry
blossom design. His wife Hano was demurely beautiful in
her kimono and traditional hairstyle that accented her attractiveness.

Other officers and their families, similarly dressed,
were to the immediate right and left. Japanese rising sun
banners flew from tall poles behind the crowd, and everyone held small, individual flags, waving them in time with
the cries of *banzai*.

The ship that was the object of the exuberant accolades
was a *Sverdlov*-class cruiser that had been used by the Soviet Navy for a couple of decades. Agents of the Imperial
Navy had arranged the purchase of the vessel, and their negotiations were strengthened by the infusion of millions of
dollars into the shogun's coffers. A picked crew was sent to
take delivery of the warship at Vladivostok after a technical team had inspected and approved all alterations demanded by the sale agreement.

The mighty vessel displaced 17,000 tons and was capable
of speeds up to thirty-two knots. The original armament had
been refitted to meet the particular needs of the new Japanese Imperial Navy. A half dozen 150-millimeter guns were
mounted in a pair of triple turrets, capable of reducing any
merchant ship to a sinking wreck with only a few salvos. For
protection from any potential air attack, eight 37-millimeter
antiaircraft rapid-firing cannons were mounted on both starboard and port sides. Additionally, a pair of torpedo tubes
stood ready to accept any of the two-dozen Soviet *Strela* torpedoes that had been part of the purchase. These underwater
killers were 6 meters in length and 530 millimeters in diam-
eter. They could move through the water at speeds of thirty
knots to deliver 315 kilos of explosives to the target. All
these attack features were strongly augmented by one overwhelming defensive technology: the Kamisaku.

The commanding officer of this large newly acquired
sea killer was the shogun's best friend Heideki Tanaka,
who had taken command along with a promotion to the
rank of *shosho* (rear admiral). The proud skipper, along

with his officers and crew, answered the cheers of their compatriots with responding cries of *banzai!*

The engines were reversed and the anchor dropped as the ship was brought to a halt. At that time a colorfully decorated personnel boat moved up to the reviewing stands and docked. This small vessel was decked over with closed compartments fore and aft. However, for that day's events, the fore was open. Along with an imperial ensign on the bow, the sides were hung with *gohei,* the paper white lightning flashes that are seen at the entrances of Shinto shrines. The shogun, his wife, and immediate staff stepped aboard and settled down for the short trip out to the bow of the new cruiser.

When the coxswain brought the personnel boat to a skillful halt, his mate tied up to the cruiser's anchor chain. A moment after the shogun stood up, everyone aboard also got to their feet to begin the *meimei suru gishiki* ceremony in the tradition of the old Imperial Navy. This ritual had been adapted from foreign naval protocol just before the twentieth century after adding a few obvious Japanese touches.

The youngest officer on the boat, a twenty-year-old ensign brought along for the purpose, clapped his hands together as hard as he could three times to summon the attention of the gods. After that, he scooped up a handful of purifying salt and tossed it onto the bow of the cruiser. Then Hano-*san,* the shogun's wife, stepped forward with a bottle of *sake* rice wine. She swung it hard on the steel bow, breaking the bottle as she called out the name chosen for the vessel.

"Hayaken!"

The cruiser *Swift Sword* was now an official warship of the Imperial Japanese Navy.

Aislado, Arizona
8 July
1330 Hours

Scotty Ross, his granddaughter Sparky, and his plane captain Paddy Paderewski had gotten back from the July

Fourth air show at Modesto the day before. Scotty proved to be a great attraction as he put the aircraft dubbed *Avenger 1* through its paces for the festive holiday crowd. The aircraft looked like it was being skillfully whipped through the air by a pilot twenty years younger rather than the old salt who could still handle the stick and rudder pedals with such dexterity. The crowd appreciated the display, and they periodically broke into simultaneous applause while watching the demonstration.

After completing his routine and landing, Scotty stepped down on the runway, bowing to the accolades he could now appreciate. He was immediately approached as always by naval veterans of World War II from the spectators. He always looked forward to this opportunity for a bull session with the old guys. Although it was rare to meet somebody he had actually served with aboard the *Enterprise,* Scotty always met an ex-sailor who knew someone he had known.

Now, with *Avenger 1* back in the hangar with *Avenger 2, 3,* and *4,* Scotty, Paddy, and Sparky stood in front of the large building watching the expected approach of a Cessna 208 as it neared the airport. The thirteen-passenger aircraft was unmarked, but all the experience tallied up by Scotty and Paddy in the U.S. Navy told them this was a service aircraft, not a commercial model. It swung over and lined up for a landing, coming in on the only runway. After a smooth touchdown, it taxied over to the waiting people and came to a stop. A young man in civilian clothing pushed the door open and scurried down the steps to the ground with wheel chocks. He was immediately followed by Rear Admiral John Paulsen and Commander Craig Davis.

Paddy growled, "That's a hell of a lot of airplane for just two passengers."

"Their budget is bigger than ours, Chief. C'mon, you two." Scotty led Paddy and Sparky up to the visitors. "Welcome to Aislado," he said to the arrivals. "I'm Scotty Ross."

I'm John Paulsen," the admiral said. "This is Craig Davis."

"The young lady here is my granddaughter Jennifer Ross," Scotty said. "We call her Sparky."

Paddy gruffly introduced himself. "Phil Paderewski, Chief Petty Officer, United States Navy, Retired."

Scotty quickly noticed that Paulsen and Davis cringed a bit under the baking desert heat. "Let's get you gentlemen out of the midday sun."

"I'd appreciate that," Paulsen said. "Let's follow the poet's advice and leave it to mad dogs and Englishmen."

Scotty grinned and escorted them into the cool interior of the hangar. Sparky and Paddy gestured to the pilot by the Cessna, and he came over to join them. The three went back to the work area, while Scotty led the other visitors to his enclosed office in one corner of the building.

As they settled down with cans of Coca-Cola, Paulsen looked at Scotty, finding it hard to believe this robust man was eighty-one years old. "You weren't a career man in the Navy, correct, Mr. Ross?"

"No," Scotty replied. "I was in for the duration—as they used to say in those good ol' days—and came back home to Phoenix after the Japs surrendered."

Davis gazed admiringly out the large office window at the four Avenger TBFs. "You didn't seem to lose your interest in naval aircraft."

"No," Scotty replied. "The affection I felt for that particular airplane stuck with me over the decades. Kind of like an old girlfriend, I guess. Anyhow, when I returned to civilian life, I worked in real estate in Phoenix for about twenty-five or twenty-six years. Made me a kajillion dollars, so I sold out and came up here to Aislado to devote my time to restoring an Avenger. I traveled a lot around the country picking up parts here and parts there. Happily, I ended up with four flyable aircraft. That's how I ran into Paddy. He was my plane captain on the *USS Enterprise.* He was a mechanic for Northwest Airlines in Minneapolis. You can imagine our surprise at seeing each other after all those years."

Paulsen stood up and studied the interior of the hangar. "Is your granddaughter a qualified mechanic? She seems to know what she's doing to that engine."

"She knows her way around, all right," Scotty replied. "She was ten when her folks—my son and daughter-in-law—were killed in an auto accident, and she moved in with me. She really took to the airplanes. I wanted her to become a pilot, but she was more interested in working on the engines." He shrugged. "There's nothing wrong with that, so I let her have her way." He took a sip of Coke. "Now I'm real curious about why the hell you've come to see me. Can we get down to brass tacks?"

"Sure, Mr. Ross," Paulsen said. "But we'd like for you to indulge us first. My friend Davis has a few questions to ask you."

"Sure," Scotty said agreeably.

Davis began. "The first thing I'd like to know is whether those four aircraft out there are fully airworthy or not."

"They sure as hell are," Scotty assured him. "I don't want to wear 'em out, so I rotate using them at air shows. I flew number one in Modesto over the Fourth of July, so I'll be taking number two up to Portland in August."

"What about their bomb delivery capabilities?"

Scotty frowned in puzzlement. "You want to know if bombs can be dropped from them?"

"Yes, sir."

"Not the way they are right now," Scotty said. "We gutted the bomb bays since we don't do anything but a few aerobatics at the shows. But all the parts are stored over in Paddy's shelves. They could be installed. But I don't have any sights for the bombardier."

"What if there wasn't a bombardier?" Paulsen asked. "Could they be used as dive-bombers?"

"A bomb release would have to be installed in the cockpit for the pilot," Scotty said. "But I can tell you that it'd take one hell of an aviator to pull that off. Ripple bombing in level fight would be best for these babies." He chuckled. "My God! That's crude as hell in today's world with radar-guided, laser-guided, infrared, and all that stuff." He finished off his soda. "Now I'm *really* curious as to why you've come to see me."

Paulsen spoke carefully. "We need an aircraft capable of delivering bombs without any electronic aiming assistance of any kind."

Scotty gave him a quizzical look. "I take it we're discussing a training scenario here."

"Right," Paulsen stated flatly.

Scotty wasn't convinced. "I'd bet a million bucks this is a classified operation."

Davis ignored the remark. "What about those bombing capabilities?"

"All right," Scotty said. "The Avengers could be configured for basic bombing, but you might be better off delivering torpedoes to the target. A guy could come in low and cut loose, then—"

Davis interrupted. "A torpedo would be rendered useless in these exercises. Its motor would turn off and its gyros would go crazy. Then it would simply sink."

"What the fuck kind of target are you guys going after?" Scotty demanded to know.

"We can't get into that," Paulsen said. "But we'd like to send some pilots over to do a little experimenting with the Avengers."

"Where?" Scotty asked.

"Here's as good a place as any," Paulsen said. "It's isolated and doesn't seem to have many visitors."

"We don't have *any* visitors," Scotty said. "But I'm not sure I want anybody else flying my airplanes."

Paulsen spoke in an apologetic tone. "I'm afraid you don't have a choice, Mr. Ross."

"I'm going to insist on knowing your ranks," Scotty said testily.

"I'm a rear admiral," Paulsen replied. "And Craig is a commander."

"Please try to understand, sir," Davis said. "The reason we're here is of the utmost importance." He paused. "Excuse me, Mr. Ross, but as of this moment your aircraft and these facilities are being confiscated for use by the United States government."

Scotty groaned. "I feel like I'm back in the navy."

"You may not be," Paulsen said, "but your aircraft sure as hell are."

Del Mar, California
1400 Hours

Lars Stensland, lying supine on the workout bench, reached up and grasped the bar of the Olympic barbell just above his face. He took a deep breath, then pulled the weight off the rack, struggling as he held it up at arm's length.

"All right, Lars!" Gerald Fagin said. "This is going to be a personal record for you. Ninety kilos. Go for it!"

Stensland lowered the bar until it touched his chest, then pushed upward, driving the barbell up until it slowed just before he could lock out his elbows.

Fagin growled, "Get mad at it, Lars! Godamn it! Get mad at the damned thing, and teach it who's the boss."

Stensland grunted and put everything into the effort, making the bar slowly rise. Then he summoned the inner strength he needed and locked it out. Fagin quickly grabbed the weight from his hands and set it on the rack. "Good lift! No competent powerlifting ref would turn it down. Way to go, Lars!"

Stensland sat up, grinning and pale from the effort. "There is a word in the Norwegian language that best describes that damn barbell. *Tung!* That means 'heavy.'"

"Well, ol' buddy, now you can start thinking of going for ninety-five kilos," Fagin said.

Stensland stood up and rubbed his aching shoulders. "I cannot believe you are able to bench one hundred and fifteen kilos."

"I've been training with weights since I was in middle school," Fagin said. "After you've been pumping iron for three months or so, you'll be surprised at how strong you are. If you keep going for years, you'll look completely different than you do now."

The American and Norwegian had decided to use the empty hours of waiting to improve their physical conditioning. There was more than vanity behind the vigorous exercise program they had organized. If the mission got to the point where they would be decoys set up for capture, they wanted to be well prepared for one hell of an ordeal. They included aerobics in their workouts by jogging from Del Mar up to Carlsbad State Beach and back. The two officers ran barefoot just inside the surf line, letting the pressure of the water and the sand add to the physical demands of the exercise. Sore calves and thigh muscles plagued them for the first few days, but now they could make the ten-mile circuit without too much agony, but it still took maximum effort on their part.

"Se opp!" Stensland exclaimed, turning toward the rack where additional plates were stacked. "I am going to load on another five kilos and go for it!"

CHAPTER NINE

USS Jefferson
East China Sea
9 July
1400 Hours

Commander Gene "High Roller" Erickson felt like a pariah, even though he had been recently promoted to his present rank and given his first squadron command. He had also been transferred from the carrier *USS Lincoln* to take on special duties aboard the *USS Jefferson*. In spite of the career advancement, the F/A-18E aviator was as much an outsider as a hopeless drunkard at a WCTU convention. At the moment, he lived among the pilots of the *Jefferson*'s air wing, assigned as a sort of supernumerary.

Officially he was the commanding officer of a VFAX, an experimental naval aviation fighter-attack squadron, but he had no proper unit to command. He was in possession of only two aircraft: an F/A-18E one-seater and an F/A-18F two-seater. The one solitary human being under his direct command was Chief Petty Officer Earl Monger, who had also just been elevated in rank. Monger had been Erickson's plane captain on the *Lincoln,* and kept his boss' aircraft maintained and fueled during a brief air war with North Korea. This had occurred when their carrier battle group was attacked by the North Korean Air Force without provocation or warning. The outrage was instigated and commanded by a trio of rogue general officers and resulted in a lopsided victory for the Americans. The carrier pilots went up against ill-prepared and inadequately trained pilots who had an inflated opinion of their flying and fighting abilities. Dozens of aircraft belonging to the Democratic People's Republic of Korea had been shot out of the sky in a series of deadly dogfights that culminated in nothing less than a massacre.

Erickson's latest duty assignment came about because of a book he had written. It was entitled *A Naval Aviator's Book of Fighter Tactics,* in which he spelled out his theory of how to employ modern carrier aircraft in combat. His basic tenet was to join up one- and two-seater airplanes into teams with the RIO in the second acting for both aircraft. The pilots were to concentrate on the enemy while the backseat guy monitored their battle environment on his instrumentation, passing out information to help the lead aviator make timely decisions as the combat situation evolved. Erickson's theory interested the admiral in command of the *Lincoln*'s carrier battle group, who arranged to have him assigned to the *Jefferson*. The idea behind the transfer was to give Erickson a squadron to put his proposed system to the test through training exercises and mock aerial combat. The assignment had been made, but so far that promised unit had yet to materialize. In fact, the pilots who had served with him, and were supposed to transfer to the *Jefferson* as part of his command, had stayed aboard the *Lincoln* and were now with an air wing at NAS Lemoore in California.

Erickson did not participate in any flying activities with the four other squadrons—one F-14 Tomcat and three F/A-18s—on his present carrier. He went out on his own, putting in a few hours doing touch-and-goes on the flight deck to keep himself sharp. Monger did all the mechanical work on the aircraft, bullying avionics, electrical, and structural airmen from the other squadrons into helping him out at odd moments.

Now, well into the boring routine in which they seemed to be permanently stuck, Erickson and Monger sat in the F/A-18F as it came in for a smooth landing, the tail hook grabbing the third cable that snapped it to a halt. After the aircraft was disengaged, Erickson taxied over to the parking area and, following the directions given by a blue shirt, cut the engine. Erickson and Monger had just spent two hours buzzing the ocean at different altitudes. Monger had kept himself amused by finagling with the knobs and switches on the radars as Erickson whipped his aircraft through its paces. They were stiff from all that g-force battering as they disengaged from the harnesses and climbed from the cockpits to the deck.

Monger, a short, husky, morose man, took off his helmet as he followed Erickson off the flight deck. "You gonna need me for anything else today, sir?"

Erickson shook his head. "If things don't pick up for our neglected outfit, I won't need you for the rest of my life."

"What about today?" Monger asked. He didn't like vague or humorous answers to his questions. "That's what I'm asking. I don't give a rat's ass about the rest of your life, sir."

"No, Chief Monger, I won't need you for the rest of the day," Erickson assured him.

"Right."

Erickson watched Monger walk away in his usual slow, deliberate stride, then turned and headed for pilot country. His shoulders ached from the day's demanding flight, and he needed a hot shower to flush away the lactic acid built up by the muscle-straining activity. He took his time moving through the passageways and up a series of ladders until reaching his quarters. He could swear the crew members he passed were sneering secretly at him as a useless mouth to feed.

"Let's not start getting paranoid, Erickson," he mumbled to himself under his breath.

When he reached his quarters, he found an envelope had been taped to his door. He pulled it off before stepping inside. When he opened the message, he saw it was from Admiral John Miskoski's office. The battle group commander wanted to see him at the earliest possible moment on his bridge. A surge of excitement bucked up the aviator's morale. A summons from an admiral could only mean big happenings. Perhaps the projected arrival of personnel and aircraft to flesh out the VFAX was now in the foreseeable future.

Erickson headed topside to the admiral's bridge, where the flag officer could watch launch and recovery operations in privacy and comfort. When the aviator arrived, he saw a marine sentry on duty just outside the door. The young man snapped to attention and rendered a salute sharp enough to cut through Kevlar armor.

"May I help you, sir?"

"Yes. I'm Commander Erickson," he replied. "I received word the admiral wants to see me."

It took the marine only a few seconds to step inside, then reappear and hold the door open. "The admiral is waiting for you, sir."

Erickson stepped in to see Rear Admiral John Miskoski at ease in his swivel chair. The wide windows around the structure he occupied gave him an excellent view of flight deck activities. Miskoski's greeting was, "I saw your landing, Commander. Damn good. Caught the third wire, hey?"

"Yes, sir," Erickson said, already knowing the landing was near perfect, or Monger would have made a sarcastic remark at the earliest opportunity. "I hope you've called me up here with some welcome information about my squadron-to-be."

"Sorry," Admiral Miskoski said. He studied the pilot for a moment. "You look like you're bored and a little wrung out, Commander."

"Yes, sir," Erickson replied. "I don't have a hell of a lot to do under the circumstances."

"Well, I've received a message regarding you," Miskoski said. "Special orders."

"I hope *that* has something to do with my phantom squadron."

"I'm afraid not," Miskoski said. He reached over to the table by his elbow, picking up a sealed packet. "Here you go. Straight from the Pentagon."

"I'm flattered," Erickson said in a tone of disappointment.

"You're being given a temporary assignment, but you'll remain a permanent part of the *Jefferson*. I was supposed to give you these papers unopened. I suggest you peruse them here and now."

"Aye, aye, sir," Erickson replied. He opened the packet and found only a single piece of paper inside. He quickly read it, then glanced up. "Chief Monger and I evidently have to go on a trip. We're ordered to North Island to meet some OTSI brain by the name of Fagin. From there we're going over to a place in Arizona. Then coming back here to the *Jefferson* on an operation they're calling Yesteryear. That's weird."

"I'm aware of the mission," Miskoski said. "I think you'll find your stretch of the doldrums is about to be kicked into a bit of excitement."

"I don't have any problem with that," Erickson said.

"Fine," Miskoski said. "You'd better get the word to Monger. You two will be flying over to Osaka at 1900 in a Greyhound to meet your flight to San Diego. See you when you get back."

"Yes, sir," Erickson said. He saluted, then hurried away, wondering how long it was going to take him to find Monger on the massive carrier.

Kakureta Island
2015 Hours

Gomme Zunsuno, inventor of the Kamisaku, had been happily married to his wife Hikui for sixty years. She had never been a particularly attractive woman, but there was something about her that appealed to the scientist. He had met her during a visit to her father's house before the war. The gentleman was a professor of some renown at Tokyo

University, and it was considered an honor to be invited to visit him. Zunsuno's first sight of Hikui set his cold, scientific heart glowing. She had a long face, and her eyes were set much too close together, but her gaze was open and friendly.

Zunsuno became a regular visitor to the house, and his affection for Hikui continued unabated. After a year had passed, the young scientist had his parents make a formal proposal of marriage for him. The professor was so pleased to be able to marry off the unattractive oldest daughter that he readily and gratefully accepted the offer. They were married in the summer of 1941.

Hikui was not a submissive woman in any sense, though she observed most of the customs and traditions assigned to Japanese wives. Zunsuno recognized she had a lively intellect and many times considered what she might have accomplished with a proper scientific education. He could tell that her life was filled with frustrations that she dealt with by writing innumerable *haiku*. These were simple seventeen-syllable poems composed in three lines. He remembered one he had read that had been indicative of her most secret inner thoughts.

> *Tradition tells us*
> *how life must be lived*
> *as it binds us in silk rope.*

Zunsuno, in spite of his logical, scientific psyche, caught the full meaning of those words that Hikui had brushed on rice paper in her lovely calligraphy. He was touched deeply by her obvious pain and went out of his way to be caring and kind to her. He began to teach his wife English to give her some intellectual exercise for her brilliant mind. He was not surprised when she was completely fluent in the language after only a year.

Hikui sensed her husband's deep consideration and appreciated the affectionate respect he showed her, knowing he did it out of love. Her devotion to him was deep and lasting.

• • •

Zunsuno sat on his haunches in front of the *shokutaku* table that held the evening meal. Hikui knelt beside him, ready to serve her husband as he consumed the chicken *supu,* boiled *kani,* and rice.

This was a custom they had established many years before in the earliest days of their long marriage. No matter when Zunsuno came home from his laboratory, Hikui had his food ready, even if it were past midnight. She tended to the tired man as he ate, keeping his plates and bowls filled and the teacup brimming with steaming brew. It was during those quiet times that the scientist conversed with his attentive spouse, telling her of how the day's work went, subtly complaining when things were not quite right, and sharing his good feelings when the project moved along quickly and efficiently.

Since moving to Kakureta decades ago, they kept the family custom going. Their home was smaller on the island than the one in Japan because there was not much room for large, rambling residences. All the officers, including Hara-*sama,* lived in more confined quarters than they would have enjoyed on the mainland. The *jun-i* were housed along the coast in small apartments stacked up to three or four stories high.

Hikui put more rice in the *ine* bowl, taking note of Zunsuno's somber quietness that evening. Usually he had something to say, even though the hectic work on the Kamisaku had subsided to leisure experiments in bettering the devices. But he seemed preoccupied, almost sad, as he slowly ate.

Hikui asked, "Is something bothering you, *shujin*?"

He took a sip of tea, then slowly set the cup down. "Yes, *kanai.* Lately I have been troubled by thoughts that come to me from deep in my heart. Since I perfected the Kamisaku enough for practical employment, I have been able to relax my mind and contemplate what I have accomplished over all these decades."

Hikui knew he was about to settle into a period of elucidation about whatever it was that bothered him. She poured him more tea, silently waiting until he was ready to talk. Zunsuno took a sip from the cup before speaking.

"Many of the grandchildren of our people who have been sent to Japan for schooling and training do not wish to return to Kakureta Island," he stated. "They do not consider this old way of life worth pursuing."

"That is true," Hikui agreed. "It is good that Hara-*sama* has forbidden any more ritual *seppuku* by the fathers of wayward children."

"One of the janitors at the laboratory has spoken of a *jun-i* boy who ran away," Zunsuno said. "He tried to sneak aboard one of the *suiraitei* boats. But he was caught."

Hikui shuddered. "Was his punishment severe, *shujin*?"

"He was clubbed unconscious and locked away for weeks on a diet of food that barely kept him alive," Zunsuno said.

"Such is the way of the Imperial Navy."

"Life is not the same in Japan as when we left to come here during the war," Zunsuno said. He looked into Hikui's face. "The young women there are allowed many things that you could only dream of, *kanai*."

"As is the life for the young men, I am certain," Hikui commented. "I am sure they are no longer drafted into military life and taught that death in battle is the ultimate goal they can achieve on this earth."

"Mmm," Zunsuno acknowledged.

"Would you like more tea, *shujin*?"

"I believe I would prefer *sake*," Zunsuno said. *"Arigato."*

She rose to fetch a bottle of the rice wine.

NAS Fallon, Nevada
10 July
0500 Hours

Lieutenant Junior Stump placed the last khaki uniform in the garment bag, zipped it up, and grabbed the kit bag off his bunk. He left his room and walked down the hall of the bachelor officers' quarters to Westy Fields's room. When he stepped inside, he saw that Ariel Goldberg had already arrived. His luggage was on the floor by the door, and he had perched himself on Westy's desk.

"Hello, fellers," Junior said. "It looks like we're ready to pull a Hank Snow, huh?"

Ariel frowned in puzzlement. "What does pulling a Hank Snow mean?"

"It means we're 'movin' on' like the song he sung," Junior explained.

"I've never heard of the guy," Ariel said.

"He was a singer in the hillbilly genre of music," Westy explained as he zipped up his ditty bag after cramming his toilet articles in it. "It's a unique American style somewhat similar to folk music."

"I know what hillbilly music is," Ariel said.

"It ain't hillbilly, Ariel," Junior protested. "You're confusing country-western with bluegrass. It's differ'nt."

"I don't know hillbilly or country-western or bluegrass from *drek*," Ariel said.

"Is *drek* one of them Yiddish words you use now and then?" Junior asked.

"Yeah," Ariel said. "It means 'shit.' "

Westy finished his packing and turned around. "The thing I appreciate the most about the Yiddish idiom is the way the words sound like the things they describe."

"You bet," Ariel agreed. "Here's a good example. Our commanding officer is a goddamned *shtik drek*—a piece of shit."

"Ease up, old boy," Westy said. "You must remember that our esteemed commander has a pretty good reason to be disenchanted with our behavior. Those words of irony and sarcasm we put on our applications for astronaut training were not appreciated by higher headquarters."

"So write us up a lousy OER," Ariel said. "Why ship us out from a job we like?"

"Yeah!" Junior agreed. "Which is also a job we're the best at."

"I beg to differ with your OER suggestion," Westy said to Ariel. "A couple of bad ones, and you're passed over for promotion. Once that happens, you are quite literally dead in the water career-wise."

"Where is it we're being shipped to again?" Junior asked.

"We are going to North Island," Westy replied. "From there we're to fly to a place called Aislado, Arizona. I tried to find it on a map, but it only showed a small landing strip. I don't think it's a naval or military facility."

"Maybe we're getting kicked out of the service," Junior suggested.

"They wouldn't be that sneaky about it if we were," Ariel said.

"It's a shame we're not permitted to take our wheels," Junior commented sadly.

"There's something most extraordinary about this assignment," Westy said. He was thoughtful for a moment. "A classified mission in the hinterlands of the desert. Now that stokes the imagination, does it not?"

Junior grinned, saying, "It worries the *drek* out o' me." He turned to Ariel. "Did I say that right?"

"Perfectly," Ariel remarked, grinning back. "I'm arranging for your *bar mitzvah* already."

"I don't know what that is," Junior said, "but I like the sound of it. Particular the *bar* word."

Westy checked his watch. "We'd better head for the terminal. Our aircraft is due to leave at oh six hundred hours."

The three friends picked up their gear and walked out into the hall. After Westy locked his door, they headed downstairs to begin whatever adventure was offered by the mysterious TDy assignment.

Junior chuckled. "*Drek!* That's a good word all right."

"Let us hope it doesn't prove to be prophetic in our case," Westy cautioned him.

CHAPTER TEN

Over Arizona
11 July
0840 Hours

Commander Gene Erickson sat alone in the front row of the Cessna 208's passenger compartment. Behind him, scattered throughout the aircraft's seats, were eight other naval personnel. Everyone, Erickson included, were dressed in casual civilian attire. They had taken off from Gillespie Field in El Cajon, California, a little more than an hour previously, looking for all intents and purposes like a group of people heading for some sort of outdoor sporting vacation.

Erickson turned from staring down at the sparse desert terrain some six thousand feet below to pull the mission roster from his shirt pocket. He wanted to peruse the list yet one more time to further familiarize himself with the team that had been given him.

Erickson, Gene, Commander
Fields, Westmoreland, Lieutenant
Goldberg, Ariel, Lieutenant
Stump, Junior, Lieutenant
Monger, Earl, Chief Aviation Machinist's Mate

Warrenton, James, Aviation Ordnanceman 1st Class
Martinez, Emiliano, Aviation Machinist's Mate 2nd Class
Torino, Gianna, Aviation Machinist's Mate 2nd Class
Harrigan, Michael, Aviation Ordnanceman 3rd Class

This was all Erickson had in the way of dossiers; a simple list of names, ranks, and rates. He knew Monger well, but there was no indication of education, special skills, or aptitude of the others. The three pilots—Fields, Goldberg, and Stump— were unknown to him, but he knew they had to be top-notch from what he'd learned of their permanent assignments. The aviators chosen to fly adversarial roles at Fallon were among the best in the fleet. The trio had the look and demeanor of being nonconformists with little regard for naval regulations. He appreciated individualism and a certain amount of disrespect for rules and regulations, but he hoped they were not the troublemaking type. Maverick behavior only went so far, then it became disruptive.

He had to assume the enlisted personnel were also fully qualified in their fields if they had been chosen to participate in a highly classified mission. Two machinists and two ordnancemen meant that he would have to assign one of each skill to two aircraft. That would leave Monger as the maintenance and repair supervisor.

They were a cosmopolitan group; Goldberg was Jewish, Warrenton an African American, Martinez a Latino, Harrigan was Irish, and Torino was not only Italian but female. Erickson guessed her age to be in her late twenties, and she seemed to fit in well with the others. At least that was indicative she'd been around and earned her spurs. Her self-confidence and ease in the company of men was reassuring. Most women in the service went that extra mile to prove their worth in what was almost a totally male society.

Erickson turned and glanced back at this unexpected command for another look. Most were dozing as would be expected of veterans of the armed forces. A wise soldier or sailor always grabbed a few z's whenever the chance was available. The woman, Torino, was reading, while a couple of the others gazed out the window with the stoic acceptance of a new, unknown assignment. This was a professional attitude developed from years of being transferred around the world.

Erickson turned back around to face the front as he folded the roster, sticking it back in his pocket. He decided it was a perfect time for him to take a nap, too.

Aislado, Arizona
0920 Hours

Scotty Ross sat at his desk in the air-conditioned office built in the southeast corner of the hangar. He had an appointment book organized for the next year's exhibition flying, and he worked at writing various air show dates in the calendar pages. It was always a good idea to plan ahead when it came to those public events, even if the godamned navy had commandeered all his airplanes. Since he had no idea when the aircraft would be returned, he couldn't afford not to be optimistic. He had to have his schedule organized ahead of time to avoid losing out on all those potential public appearances. There was actually more planning spent on the ground activities than the actual flying at the air shows. Granddaughter Sparky drove the van with Paddy Paderewski, bringing all the spare parts and tools needed for the shows. This meant picking out the best routes and times for traveling.

Scotty was interrupted when Paddy opened the door. "Aircraft approaching."

"All right," Scotty said. He stuck the schedule in the desk drawer and followed the retired CPO out into the bay. Sparky was standing in the big door, gazing skyward. The two men joined her, watching the speck in the sky gradually form into a plane as it drew closer.

"Mmm," Sparky mused. "It looks like the same one that brought in those other two guys."

"One of those *guys* was a rear admiral," Scotty reminded her.

"That doesn't mean much to me," she remarked.

Another quarter of an hour passed before the Cessna landed on the threshold of the runway. It rolled along the concrete as it taxied up to the waiting trio. After it came to a stop with the engine still running, the door was opened. The copilot hopped out with a set of portable steps, secured them, then stood back to allow the passengers to disembark. As soon as they were out with baggage in hand, he reversed the process and leaped back inside. The Cessna began heading back to the runway.

"Hey!" Sparky cried out. "One's a girl!"

Paddy scratched his armpit. "She prob'ly does the cooking."

"I bet she doesn't," Sparky said. "I bet she's a pilot."

"Maybe so," Paddy allowed. "They say gals can fly planes nowadays. But it takes a special one who can fix 'em."

Sparky laughed. "By golly, Paddy! You just paid me a compliment."

"You're a good mechanic," he stated in a matter-of-fact tone.

The group walked up to them with Erickson in the lead. "Hello. I'm looking for Mr. Scott Ross."

"I'm Scotty," he replied, offering his hand.

"I'm Gene Erickson." He turned around and gestured to the others. "What we have in this intrepid group are three pilots, a chief petty officer, two ordnancemen and two machinist's mates."

"We got four aircraft," Paddy said, looking at the three men identified as pilots.

"I'm the fourth pilot," Erickson said. "Or I should say the lead pilot. I'm in command."

Sparky nodded to Gianna. "Hi there. I'll bet you're one of the pilots too, huh?"

"Not me, honey," Gianna said. "I'm an aircraft machinist's mate second class, halfway into my third four-year hitch." She glanced inside the hangar at the quartet of old aircraft. "Oh, my God! What do we have here?"

"The best airplane in the world," Scotty said proudly. "The TBM and TBF Avenger. Or maybe I should say facsimiles and combinations thereof. None of them are purely stock, but they fly as beautifully as the originals."

"World War Two stuff, huh?" Gianna observed. "Where's the aircraft we're going to work on?"

Erickson interrupted. "I'll have a full briefing for you on this mission you've been volunteered for. I was told to hold off until we arrived here."

"The navy ain't changed much," Paddy commented dryly. "Still sticking folks into situations without giving 'em any idea of what's going on."

"Roger that," Erickson agreed.

Scotty noticed the pressing morning heat of the desert was beginning to affect his guests. "Let's go inside the hangar and get out of the sun. We've got some cold drinks. Beer. Soda. Bottled water. It's in the fridge inside."

"We appreciate that!" Emiliano Martinez said. "I feel like I'm baking, man."

"The U.S. Navy sent the drinks in," Paddy said. "We didn't pay for 'em. Same goes for your chow."

Erickson and Scotty led the crowd into the interior of the hangar. "I have to brief my people," Erickson said. "They're not aware of the wheres, whens, and whys of this assignment. This is classified, so I'm afraid we'll have to get off by ourselves."

"I understand perfectly," Scotty said. "Use my office over there. It's air-conditioned."

"Thanks," Erickson said. He turned to his people. "Grab something to drink and follow me. I'll give you the skinny on what your loving navy has sent you into."

They all snatched cans of soda, leaving the beer alone. The old veteran Paddy Paderewski couldn't believe his eyes. "This is a new class of sailor," he muttered to himself. "In my day, we'd've grabbed at least three of them cans of suds apiece."

"I've heard happy hour in the clubs isn't what it used to be in the old days," Scotty commented.

Erickson took his charges into Scotty's office. They crammed into the limited space, lining up against the walls as their leader took up a position behind the desk. "This is going to be short and sweet," Erickson said. He pointed through the glass at the four Avengers out in the hangar. "Take a good look at those aircraft, people. You're going to be flying, arming, and fixing them up for a real-life combat mission."

Westy Fields chuckled. "I knew the navy's budget was somewhat sparse, but this is ridiculous."

"It seems that way, doesn't it?" Erickson remarked with a wry grin. "But evidently these old-fashioned airplanes are the only ones around that are capable of dealing with the mission we've been assigned."

"So what are we going to do?" Ariel Goldberg asked. "Drop retardant on a forest fire somewhere maybe?"

"Here's the SITREP," Erickson said. "Merchant ships, tankers, and such have been disappearing off the high seas, then held for ransom. Actually, to be more specific, I should say they've been disappearing off the East China Sea."

Junior Stump frowned. "I haven't seen nothing about that in the paper or on TV."

"It's being kept under wraps," Erickson explained. "These bad guys evidently have a force field of some sort that neutralizes radar, infrared, laser, and other weapon guidance systems. They use this stealth technology—or whatever it is—to sneak up on their victims. The only way we're going to sink the bastards is find them physically, then fly the Avengers out and do some ordnance delivery on the targets by the seats of our collective pants."

"Dang!" Junior Stump exclaimed. "You mean we're gonna have to *aim* at 'em?"

"That's right," Erickson said. "I'm not sure of the physical sighting system we'll employ, but it'll be what our grandpappys used in World War Two. Hence those Avengers are the airplanes of choice."

Westy was confused. "Why not use some Viking S-3Bs? It seems they would be perfect for the job."

"The S-3B is designed to use instrumentation and ordnance that would be useless against the bad guys," Erickson explained.

"Just who is this enemy, sir?" James Warrenton asked.

Erickson shrugged. "I don't know. In fact, I don't know any more than I've just told you. Even the echelon directing this show isn't sure who the bad guys are. And I want to emphasize one thing very strongly. This is a highly classified mission. You are not to discuss the situation with anyone outside this group. And that includes Scotty Ross, the chief out there, and the girl."

"Where's our base of operations gonna be?" Junior Stump asked.

"We're going to be flying off the *Jefferson*," Erickson replied.

Mike Harrigan, the junior ordnanceman, stood up and looked out at the Avengers. "Sir, them aircraft ain't armed. I hope somebody's noticed that."

"That problem is being addressed even as we speak," Erickson said. "But we pilots are going to have to learn to fly the damned things, and the machinists are going to have to learn how to maintain and repair them before we give much thought to shooting and bombing anybody." He studied their faces, noting the skeptical expressions shared by everyone. "Well! I'll be the first to admit that this is a crazy situation. But we're going to have to make some sense out of it. Therefore, let's start our training program right now by going out in the hangar and getting an orientation on the airplanes from Mr. Ross."

Scotty turned from watching Paddy and Sparky working on the engine of number two when he heard the scuffling of approaching feet on the concrete floor. He walked over to the crowd who were gazing intently at the Avengers. "You look like some people in search of information," he remarked.

"We are," Erickson said. "An introduction to the birds seems to be in order."

"You bet," Scotty agreed. He gestured to the line of aircraft. "These, unfortunately, are not exactly like the originals. A shortage of certain materials and parts has brought about some very nonregulation configurations. But, basically, what you have here are four TBM-slash-F aircraft that have been determined to meet the requirements of your mission. I flew TBMs in the Pacific Campaign of World War Two. They proved to be reliable, tough aircraft."

"These were mainly torpedo bombers, right?" Westy asked.

"Unfortunately, American torpedoes were unreliable in those days, so we used them mostly as glide bombers," Scotty replied. "The navy folks I've talked to want these four to also be used in that manner. I'm not sure why, but they're afraid that even modern torpedoes might not be feasible for what you folks are going to do."

"Can you give us a brief history of the Avengers' beginnings?" Erickson asked. "I like to know all about an airplane I'm going to fly. Especially an exceedingly old one with an interesting historical background. It might be helpful to us in understanding the original missions they were designed for."

"I don't know all the particulars of their past," Scotty said. "The maiden flight was in August of 1941. About ten thousand Avengers were built during the war years. They made their combat debut at Midway in June of 1942. Of the six aircraft committed to battle, only one survived. And it crash-landed with a wounded pilot and radioman. The gunner was dead."

"Not too auspicious a beginning," Westy remarked.

"Our people at Midway were heavily outnumbered," Scotty explained. "And this was early in the war. As a matter of fact, the airplane was given the name Avenger after the Japs' sneak attack on Pearl Harbor. It turned out to be an appropriate sobriquet, since they were instrumental in American naval victories in the years that followed."

"You told us these four models aren't stock," Erickson said, "but do you have any reliable specifications?"

"I fly these a lot," Scotty said. "So far I've determined the nineteen hundred–horsepower Wright engine—which is air-cooled and radial—can push it up to around two hundred sixty miles an hour. I estimate the range could stretch out to fifteen hundred miles, but I've never checked that out seriously. Back in my day they could install a two hundred and seventy-five-gallon fuel tank that added over two thousand miles to our range. We'd burn up the gas in those auxiliary containers first, then jettison them."

"That might come in handy for us," Erickson said.

"Sorry," Scotty said. "We don't have any of those tanks. Since I don't have use for one in my air show display flying, I've never looked for any in my trips to find parts. However, we did have some tail hooks we picked up over the years. Paddy has already installed them after we learned the planes would be used from a carrier. The control switch is on the left side of the pilot's seat."

"How soon can we take them up for some familiarity flying?" Erickson asked.

"They'll be ready to go later this afternoon," Scotty said. "Meanwhile, we'll get you folks settled in. You're going to be here awhile."

1500 Hours

Sparky Ross and Gianna Torino took turns with the propeller blades of *Avenger1,* as they pulled them through four rotations to pump oil up into the aircraft's cylinders. When they finished, Chief Earl Monger worked the starter engine hand crank to get it up to half speed before the power plant was started. This saved battery energy that the big airplane used greedily and continually in flight operations.

Gene Erickson was buckled into the cockpit, ready to fly. He had been given a thorough briefing in piloting the airplane by Scotty Ross. Now he moved the battery switch to the **On** position, then placed the fuel selector valve to the center main tank and switched on the electric fuel pump. After pushing the throttle one-third open, he engaged the starter. The engine kicked to life in a sputtering roar, caught on, and settled into a smooth cadence. At that point Erickson shut off the fuel pump, turning to the takeoff checklist mounted on a rotating, two-sided panel beside him.

TAKEOFF

CHECK FUEL
MIX. RICH
LOW BLOWER
SET PROP
WINGS LOCKED
COWL FLAPS
CHECK TABS
TAIL WHEEL

After the check, he released the brakes and began a slow, short taxi to the takeoff point in front of the hangar. When he reached a position leaving him looking down the runway, he braked again, locked the tail wheel, and revved the engine to 2,600 rpm. Then he released the brake and began rolling down the runway, quickly gaining speed.

The Avenger aircraft takes off from a three-point liftoff with all the wheels down touching the ground. As soon as he was airborne, Erickson throttled back to 2,400 rpm for the climb, keeping in mind that at sixty-five to seventy-five knots, the airplane would stall. He brought up the landing gear, continuing to climb to 3,000 feet before leveling off.

After thousands of hours in jets, the aviator felt like he was lumbering almost motionless through the air. But when he performed a few basic maneuvers, he realized this was one beautiful aircraft. It responded quickly and smoothly, going in and out of the demands he placed on it with nary a complaint.

He continued the flight for another half hour of familiarization, before making the turn to line up with the runway threshold. He reached over and turned the takeoff checklist panel around to reveal the landing criteria.

LANDING

TAIL WHEEL
LOW BLOWER
CHECK FUEL

MIX. RICH
WHEELS DOWN
SET PROP
FLAP DOWN

Erickson ran through the procedure, slowed to eighty-five knots, and began descending for the touchdown. Scotty had advised him that three-point landings, like take-offs, were the preferred method. He pointed out that making contact with the ground on the tail wheel was much preferable to having the front gear hit first. Erickson instinctively went nose up and pulled the throttle to idle at the correct altitude.

The landing was flawless, and Erickson used the brakes to slow down as he taxied back toward the hangar. He turned into the parking area under Monger's direction, then stopped and cut the engine. Westy, Junior, and Ariel walked up to the wing and waited as he climbed from the cockpit and hopped down to the ground.

"How was it, sir?" Westy asked.

"I was surprised," Erickson said. "This airplane really loves to fly. I can see why Scotty never lost his affection for it."

Junior Stump wasn't that impressed. "He never flew an F-14."

"True," Erickson conceded, "but when this baby was state-of-the-art, it was the best aircraft in the Pacific Campaign."

Ariel studied the big fuselage with the ball turret in the rear of the cockpit. "It's gonna have to be the best again out there."

Scotty walked up with a big grin. He could tell that Erickson was impressed. "So! Will it do the job, Commander?"

Erickson nodded. "If all our briefings and intelligence are correct, it might just be the thing. But—" He let the sentence hang.

"But what?" Westy asked.

"We still have to work up a weapon delivery system for

it," Erickson said. "If that can't be done, this whole operation is going to be a washout."

"Your ordnancemen have been working on that with Paddy," Scotty said. "We've picked up some dummy five hundred–pound bombs during our wanderings over the years. At one time I was going to use them in my air show act, but the idea made the airport managers nervous."

"How many of those play bombs do you have?" Erickson asked.

"A couple of dozen," Scotty said. "They're rusty and dented, but they'll do the job for training you guys."

"We're lucky there're still a few of the real ones in the navy's weapons inventory," Erickson remarked.

"Yeah," Scotty agreed. "But unfortunately, bombsights designed for the Avenger are nonexistent. It looks like you pilots are going to be bombing by the seats of your pants."

"We knew about that," Erickson remarked.

Junior Stump was impatient. "Meanwhile, how about the rest of us going up? The other aircraft are ready to go." He gave Erickson an imploring glance.

"Okay," Erickson said. "I'm officially approving the Avenger for Operation Yesteryear. The sooner you start flying the aircraft, the better."

Westy, Junior, and Ariel whooped simultaneously and turned toward *Avenger 2* through *4,* sitting in front of the hangars. "Hey!" Scotty yelled after them. "Don't forget to make three-point takeoffs and landings!"

14 July
1000 Hours

It took the professional expertise of Chief Aviation Machinist's Mate Earl Monger and Aviation Ordnanceman first Class James Warrenton in coordination with Paddy Paderewski to work out the best system for bomb delivery in the renovated aircraft. It was tougher on Warrenton, who was caught between the two verbose and opinionated chief petty officers who were not averse to expressing themselves at the tops of their lungs. These expletive-filled verbal bombasts occurred mostly during disagreements between the two opinionated veteran sailors.

The trio spent two loud evenings and nights banging heads, making diagrams, and pilfering bits and pieces of equipment from Paddy's workbench as they worked out the best method possible under the circumstances.

It would not only take all the pilot's flying skills to deliver the ordnance accurately, but he would have to coordinate the bomb release with the bombardier in the bay. Under normal conditions the bomb droppers would have been somebody like the SENSOs who flew on fleet ASW operations in Viking 3B aircraft. But both time constraints and security considerations precluded bringing in four more personnel for the operation. Thus, it would be the ordnancemen and machinists already on the team who would do the bomb release work. Monger wanted to be assigned to one of the planes, but Erickson preferred to have his chief petty officer kept out of harm's way to guarantee an experienced hand to take care of any mechanical problems that might arise.

The younger crewmen were overjoyed to find out they would be flying on the missions, and Gianna Torino was particularly pleased with the arrangements. She would be the first female to fly combat missions in an Avenger in the history of the United States Navy.

After Monger and Warrenton's ideas were put into work, *Avenger 1* was rigged for a trial bomb run. Erickson would be the pilot, while Warrenton acted as his bombardier. Scotty's old surplus Mark 7 bomb hoist was used to load a quartet of dummy 500-pounders into the bay of the aircraft. Desert sand had been shoveled into the tanks of the pseudo-ordnance to bring them up to the correct weight. Paddy had to supervise this operation, since he was the only one who had actually participated in loading Avengers for combat missions. He directed and taught the procedure at the same time as the four crewmen struggled with the device that hauled the bombs up into position, one at a time.

When *Avenger 1* was pronounced ready, Erickson

climbed into the cockpit, while Warrenton squeezed himself through the door on the starboard side of the aircraft. When he was inside the bombardier's station, he buckled himself onto the narrow seat at the rear of the bay. A quick check of the intercom system was made before the start-up procedure was begun. At the same time the others loaded into Scotty's van and headed out for the target area.

The bombing target was an easily discerned stand of barrel cactus on a slight rise some five miles from the airport. Scotty and Paddy recommended that the bomb release lever be set to make a ripple dispersal of the ordnance to spread them out. Without the advantage of being able to dive-bomb or use a proper sight, this offered a better chance for at least one of the bombs to strike the target.

Erickson took the airplane some ten miles out before turning toward the target area. He flew at an altitude of twenty-five hundred feet, maintaining a straight line toward the unoffending cacti that were about to be sacrificed for the cause. He eased the throttle back to a speed of a hundred knots.

"Pilot to bombardier," he said over the intercom, feeling like he was in a World War Two movie.

"This is the bombardier," Warrenton said, getting into the spirit of moment.

"Bomb bay open," Erickson said.

"Bomb bay open."

"Safety pins out."

"Roger. Safety pins out. Bombs armed," Warrenton replied even though the dummies weren't actually armed. SOP demanded that all procedures be conducted as if this was not a dry run.

Erickson was now headed straight for the cacti. "Steady," he said more to himself than his bombardier. "Steady . . . steady . . ." He waited until the front of the target was just a bit in front of the aircraft nose. "Drop 'em!"

Warrenton pulled on the lever. The Avenger shuddered and rose a bit as each bomb left the bay and hurtled downward at one-second intervals. "Bombs away!"

"All right!" Erickson said, gunning the engine up to normal flying speed.

Down on the ground the others watched as the four bombs moved on a forward, downward trajectory. The first and second hit in front of the cacti, the third plowed through the patch, and the fourth hit just outside.

"By God!" Scotty exclaimed. "If that'd been a ship it would've been sunk."

"He let loose too soon," Monger said. "It'd be better to get two bombs in the cactus. That way when a real ship is hit, it could be the first, second, and third bombs making hits or the second, third, and fourth."

When Erickson returned to the airport and taxied up to the hangar, he found the others waiting. Monger wasted no time in reporting the results. Erickson had experienced a deep Scandinavian pessimism during the flight back to the airport and was pleasantly surprised with the good report on the bomb strikes.

"Okay. I know what to do then," he said, turning to the other three aviators. "Here's the skinny, guys. We'll go in at a hundred knots in file. Altitude twenty-five hundred feet. Fly straight and level. Try to maintain a quarter mile between each aircraft. Just as your nose starts to cross the near edge of the cactus patch, make your release. Any questions?"

"Let's do it," Ariel said.

"Warrenton will stay with me," Erickson said. "Fields and Martinez go in number two; Goldberg and Torino in three; and number four will be Stump and Harrigan."

The bombs had already been loaded onto two through four, but the mission had to be delayed while the bombardiers reloaded number one. When that task was satisfactorily completed, the aircraft taxied for takeoff. Monger, Scotty, Sparky, and Paddy once more headed for the target area.

The Avengers were specks in the distant sky as the quartet of observers stood around the van. Scotty and Monger had binoculars, while Sparky and Paddy squinted against the brilliance of the Arizona summer sky.

The roar of the aircraft could be discerned as they drew closer. Monger, looking through his field glasses, nodded approvingly. "They're lined up straight as arrows. And I'd say they were pretty close to that quarter-mile interval that the commander wanted."

Scotty glanced over at Paddy. "Those kids are damn good."

"They'd have helped out a bit against the Japs," Paddy allowed.

Erickson's lead aircraft released first, and the four falling projectiles arced downward. His first bomb hit at the edge of the patch, the second and third creamed the center, sending bits of cacti and rocks zinging through the air. His fourth grazed the outer edge. As the others came in, the procedure continued. The end result was that the plant life was obliterated, leaving the top of the knoll scarred, pitted, and barren of cacti.

"A few more runs, and they'll be pretty fair," Monger announced.

"Yeah," Paddy said. "Fair."

"Fair?" Sparky exclaimed. "They're as good as can be now."

Scotty smiled at his granddaughter. "These two are chief petty officers, my darling. When they say 'fair,' they mean 'superlative.'"

"Well!" Sparky said. "I'd hate to be around them if somebody did a lousy job."

Monger ignored her remark. "We'd better get back to the hangar. I got to bring them folks back here to pick up these bombs for tomorrow's practice."

They got into Scotty's van for the short ride back to the airport.

CHAPTER ELEVEN

East China Sea
SS Dileas
15 July
1415 Hours

Captain Angus Crookshanks, skipper of the Liberian-registered cargo liner *Dileas,* took a deep swallow from the bottle of scotch. The fifty-year-old merchant marine officer sat at the desk in his cabin, morose and drunk, feeling like the entire world had turned against him. This was not the life he had envisioned for himself during his youth when he first opted for a career at sea.

The *Dileas,* once a proud ship that sailed between the United Kingdom and North America in her heyday of the 1920s and 1930s, was now a rust-streaked bucket. She was propelled by a gasping turbine engine that could barely move the vessel at ten to twelve knots on a smooth sea. And even this pitiful speed needed a stiff wind off her stern. If the sea was even the slightest bit rough, she slowed to a crawl, wallowing like a harpooned whale as she struggled toward her destination. It took all the skill and cursing of an expert engineering officer to get eight knots out of the old girl under normal conditions.

Nowadays her routes were in the Far East where she

carried such dismal cargo as hides for soccer balls and assortments of cloth to be made into clothing lines bearing celebrities' names. This cargo was destined for sweatshops in Bangladesh and Pakistan, where child labor and starvation wages were the norm.

All this was bad enough for Crookshanks's self-esteem, but what really drove him to heavy drinking was the makeup of his crew. He had Singaporean officers with varied ethnic backgrounds of Chinese, Malayan, and Indian, and his seamen consisted of a combination of Filipinos and Pakistanis. Crookshanks was the only European aboard, and he longed for the old days of what he considered a racially pure ship's company, i.e., all whites, though a few Greeks or Italians were okay as long as there weren't a lot of them. And of course it was also acceptable for the Filipinos or Chinese to be stewards. Crookshanks was an equal-opportunity racist; he hated all non-Europeans with the same intensity.

The captain took a few more deep swallows from the bottle, emptying it. He tossed it aside and got to his feet to lurch across the cabin and grab another from his sea bag. He pulled a fresh liter out and opened it up. After a long belch and a longer fart, he put the container to his lips and gulped generous helpings of the liquor. He wiped his mouth and took a deep breath. Suddenly his temper rolled up from his psyche and into his alcohol-soaked brain like the burst of an emotional volcano.

"Enough is bluddy enough!" he growled.

The captain slammed out of his cabin and staggered forward to the bridge. The Singaporean Chief Officer Syed Lujamalail was startled by the skipper's unexpected appearance. "Yes, Captain?"

"Shut yer face!" Crookshanks roared. "Ye blowzy Wog bastard!"

Lujamalail glanced over at Third Mate Mohandas Kalpayee from India, who was the duty watch officer. Kalpayee shrugged to show he didn't give a damn if the captain was roaring drunk again or not. They had endured so many insults from the skipper that the words he spat out meant nothing other than the ramblings of a hopeless, racist drunkard.

The helmsman also ignored the hullabaloo, keeping his full attention on his task. The *Dileas* had no automatic steering system and had to be manually pointed in the direction she was to go and kept there by a constant monitoring of the compass.

The captain stumbled across the bridge, stopping between the two officers. "So what've ye been up to then, hey? Planning a mutiny, are ye? Ye bluddy black bastards! I ought to shoot the lot o' ye and send ye to hell where all heathens go."

"Yes, Captain," Lujamalail said patiently, wondering how long this latest jag was going to last. Generally, after Crookshanks had vented his hatred enough, he would go directly back to his cabin to sleep it off.

Now the captain noticed the helmsman. "What's the course, ye bastard turd what was shit out by a Pakistani whore?"

"Two-eight-three," the man reported.

"Two-eight-three *what*?" Crookshanks roared.

"Two-eight-three, *sir,*" the helmsman calmly replied.

"Tha's better, goddamn yer slanty fucking eyes to hell!"

The ancient radio speaker suddenly crackled, catching everyone's attention. A voice said, "Attention, the Liberian ship. Heave to and prepare to be boarded."

"What the hell is that about?" Crookshanks bellowed. He turned to the watch officer. "Where away is that bastard?"

Kalpayee checked the radar screen. "There's no reading, Captain."

"How could the son of a whore be boarding us if he's out o' radar range?" Crookshanks said. He went over to the port windows and saw nothing. He turned and staggered across the bridge, pushing the two officers out of his way. It took him a moment to focus his eyes on the sea view to starboard. "There she is, ye dumb blind bastard! It's a bluddy fucking cruiser!"

"There is nothing on the radar, Captain," Kalpayee insisted.

Now Lujamalail was angry. The long months of putting up with the captain's binges came to a head at that moment. He quickly checked the radar, noting that there was no indication of any nearby vessel. He turned to the captain. "There is *no* reading on the radar!"

"Is that right?" Crookshanks shouted. "Well, take a look out there then, and tell me what ye see."

Lujamalail reluctantly walked over to where the captain stood. He glanced out, and his eyes widened. A fully armed cruiser had drawn up some one hundred meters off their starboard beam. "I don't understand."

"Ye stupid slope!" Crookshanks snarled.

Once again the speaker crackled. "Attention, Liberian ship. Heave to and prepare to be boarded."

The captain grabbed the microphone. "I'll no have nobody telling me to heave to without a goddamn good reason. So who the hell are ye, then?"

The question was ignored, and another terse warning to heave to for boarding was issued. This time a threat accompanied the order. "We will fire on you if you do not obey immediately."

"Go to hell, ye cheeky son of a bitch!" Crookshanks said. He glared at Kalpayee. "Flank speed, damn it."

"Sir!" Lujamalail protested. "That is an armed warship that has threatened to fire at us. Our flank speed at best in these waters is eight or nine knots."

"I'm ordering flank speed, and I want it now!"

"Aye, sir," Lujamalail said. He nodded to Kalpayee. "Flank speed."

Kalpayee reached for the engine telegraph and cranked out the order.

Imperial Japanese Cruiser **Hayaken**

Captain Heideki Tanaka studied the *Dileas* through his binoculars from his position on the bridge. "*Hakuchi*—idiot!" he said under his breath.

This was no prize ship, but it would fit well in intrais-land travel normally used by the *suiraitei* boats. Orders had been issued to capture such a vessel if and when one be-came available. A lot more cargo could be carried aboard a freighter than on the ancient patrol boats now used by the people of Kakureta Island.

Newly promoted Lieutenant Commander Gentaro Oyama frowned in puzzlement. "Is she trying to run away?"

"Have one of the one hundred and fifty-two–millimeter forward guns fire over her bow," Tanaka ordered.

"*Hei, Taisa-san!*" Oyama responded. He grabbed a fire direction control microphone and issued the order. Imme-diately the sound of the shot echoed across the sea, and a splash erupted on the far side of the old cargo liner.

"Warn her again," Tanaka said.

"Attention, Liberian vessel," Oyama said. "Heave to and prepare to be boarded. Do you understand?"

Once more an answer came back in the form of a slurred voice with a Scots burr. "Ye kin go straight to hell, ye bastards. This is Cap'n Angus Crookshanks, and I don't heave to fer no bluddy mon!"

Tanaka ordered another trio of warning shots, but the *Dileas* continued its pitifully slow run for freedom. Oyama looked inquiringly over at his commanding officer. When Tanaka issued his next order, his voice was low and calm.

"Sink her."

SS Dileas

The first explosion erupted on the bow, sending shards of iron spewing in all directions. Lujamalail grabbed Crook-shanks's arm. "They're firing on us, Captain. For the love of Allah! Heave to!"

"I'll do no such thing!" Crookshanks yelled drunkenly. He spoke again into the transmitter. "Go on, ye bastards! I'll no heave to for nobody!"

Another explosion hit the starboard bow just above the

waterline. Third Officer Kalpayee pressed the general alarm button on the control console. Immediately the *whoop-whoop* signal blasted throughout the old vessel.

"Who told ye to sound abandon ship, ye Hindu son of a bitch?" Crookshanks asked furiously.

Both officers on the bridge ignored him as they ordered the helmsman to leave his post. The next order of business was to lower lifeboats. As they rushed off the bridge, Crookshanks sneered openly at them. They were cowardly dogs as far as he was concerned, and if he had to defend his ship single-handed, he would do it.

Two more hits rocked the ship, and Crookshanks went to his cabin to retrieve the old Webley revolver he kept in the safe. His drunken clumsiness made it difficult to spin out the correct combination on the dial. He finally managed it on the third try and reached in to grab the pistol.

"Repel boarders!" he roared as he rushed back to the bridge and out onto the signal deck. He could see that the cruiser was only fifty meters away, and he could make out the features of the crewmen on deck. "Hey! Ye Jappo sons o' bitches. Take this!"

He pointed the revolver at them and began to fire. The crewmen on the cruiser reacted swiftly to this armed defiance. The first strikes of the 7.62 machine gun rounds splattered around Crookshanks; then the gunner found the target. A half-dozen bullets stitched across the drunken captain's chest and abdomen, knocking him to the metal deck.

The cannon hits on the old ship increased to a rapid staccato of roaring explosions. Within short moments the old *Dileas* began to break up under the pounding.

Imperial Japanese Cruiser **Hayaken**

Captain Tanaka and Lieutenant Commander Oyama watched as the *Dileas* shuddered and slowly sank deeper into the water. Suddenly the bow broke off and floated outward for a few moments before tipping forward to slip under the waves. Then the stern moved backward while rolling onto her port side. In less than a minute it also was swallowed by the sea and sent to the bottom. Now there was no sign of the cargo liner on the surface of the water. Only floating debris and the two lifeboats the crew had managed to launch gave evidence that a vessel had been there only a short time before.

Tanaka gazed impassively at the lifeboats where the occupants sat in shocked silence. Hara-*sama* had pronounced a decree against sinking any merchant ships unless absolutely necessary. The only situation where such action was permitted was exactly as this one with the *Dileas*. She had refused to obey orders to heave to. Thus Tanaka had obeyed the shogun correctly and precisely. Hara-*sama* had also issued instructions as to what must be done with any crew who survived a sinking. Tanaka had no choice in the matter. The oath he had sworn upon his commission in the Imperial Navy left him no alternative. He was required to follow Hara-*sama*'s dictates to the letter. Tanaka turned to Oyama.

"*Shosa-san*," he said softly.

Oyama turned and saluted. "*Hei,Taisa-san!*"

"You are to have the port side machine guns fire at the men in the lifeboats."

Oyama was confused. "Do you mean over their heads as a warning?"

Tanaka shook his head. "They are to be killed. I want no survivors. *Hitotsu*—none!"

"*Hei!*" Oyama responded.

He left the bridge and went down the ladder leading to the port side where two of the ship's 7.62-millimeter machine gun stations were located. The gunners and their assistants turned toward the officer as he stepped out onto the deck.

"Lock and load," Oyama said. "Then fire into the lifeboats out there until all the men in them are dead and the boats are broken up."

The young sailors, disciplined in the tradition of the old Imperial Navy, turned to the task. The gunners cranked back on the loading handles, then aimed directly at the lifeboats bobbing on the waves. Oyama watched, noting the *chunka-chunk* sound of the firing along with the metallic *pings* of the expended shells bouncing on the metal deck.

At first the *Dileas*'s crewmen were confused as the first fusillades splattered around them. But when the reality of the horror sank in, they turned to the oars in a futile attempt to get away. As more of them buckled under the impact of the steel-jacketed bullets, the others leapt overboard and tried to swim away. Several dived deep, hoping the slaughter would have ceased by the time they surfaced. But the Japanese sailors waited for them to reappear, then began hosing them with fiery sweeps of bullets again. The *Dileas*'s crewmen died gasping for air as the rounds splashed around and into them. Within a very short time the boats were sunk and bodies floated amid the debris of the mass murder.

On the deck above, Hyojun Someikona stared in horror at the sight he had just witnessed. His ears had been battered by the rapid detonations of the machine guns, and his eyes shocked by the violent death suffered by the foreign crewmen. Now he cringed in shock as he noted that sea's normal green gray color was crimson around the area where the corpses floated. Someikona was a technician of the Kamisaku and worked directly for Dr. Zunsuno. He had spent his entire youth and manhood under the scientist's direct supervision, and had not been indoctrinated in the finer elements of Imperial Navy practice and standards.

Below where the emotionally stunned technician stood, Lieutenant Commander Oyama ordered the machine gun crews to secure from battle stations and return their weapons to the ship's armory.

CHAPTER TWELVE

Kakureta Island
16 July
2100 Hours

Dr. Gomme Zunsuno stood on his house's back veranda, looking out toward the harbor. He could see the superstructures of the destroyers *Isamashii* and *Chujitsuna* twinkling with lights above the horizon. A bit farther out, the recently returned cruiser *Hayaken*'s illumination was not as clearly visible.

The elderly scientist was dressed in a simple, functional kimono as he waited patiently for a visitor. The young man had sent him an apologetic request to see him only a scant hour before. Dr. Zunsuno sensed there was an urgency involved in the missive, and he had immediately sent back an acquiescence.

The wood-and-paper door of the house slid open, and Zunsuno's wife Hikui stepped outside. "Someikona-*san* has arrived," she announced grumpily.

"Bring him to me, *dozo*."

"It is very late, Gomme," Hikui said, obviously thinking the caller most rude.

"Then the reason for his visit is more imperative than impolite, *kanai*."

She nodded, then turned and went inside, shutting the door. A few moments later, the flimsy entrance was opened again. Hyojun Someikona hesitantly appeared and bowed deeply. "*Gomen kudasaii*—excuse me please for this late visit, Zunsuno-*san*. It is unforgivable of me to disturb you in this manner."

Zunsuno studied the younger man's face, noting the distress he displayed. "Do not bother yourself with such thoughts. We will have some tea."

As if on cue, the maid appeared with a tray holding a teapot and cups. She set the refreshments on a nearby table and served the two men, pouring them each a cupful. At a nod from her venerable master, she made a quick exit. Hyojun stared numbly down at the tabletop.

"Please have some tea," Zunsuno invited. "It will make you feel better."

"*Arigato,*" Hyojun said. He took a polite sip, then suddenly exclaimed. "Something terrible has happened, Zunsuno-*san!*"

Now Zunsuno recalled that Hyojun had gone out on a voyage aboard the *Hayaken* a couple of weeks earlier to serve as a technician on the Kamisaku. He must have just returned. "What is troubling you?"

Hyojun set his cup down. "An attempt was made to stop a ship," he said. "The foreign captain refused to obey the order and tried to flee. The guns of the *Hayaken* fired and sank his vessel."

"One must expect such action under those circumstances," Zunsuno said, "even though it is most distressing to witness it."

"The crew of the foreign ship was in the water in their lifeboats," Hyojun said. "For some reason the officer Oyama went to the machine guns and ordered them to shoot at the helpless sailors. I was on the deck above and saw everything."

Now it was Zunsuno who showed a troubled expression. "Did the sailors on the machine guns obey?"

Hyojun nodded his head. "*Hei!* They began to fire without hesitation. All those poor foreigners were killed. It was *gyakusatsu*—a massacre!"

Zunsuno took a deep breath, letting it out slowly. "It is unbelievable."

"Is a crime such as this a part of our science?" Hyojun asked. "I feel as if I am at fault for those innocent men's deaths."

"It is understandable," Zunsuno said, feeling his own sense of guilt.

"I thought of the Kamisuku as a defensive device."

"Warriors now own it," Zunsuno said glumly.

Hyojun looked as if he might break out weeping. "I want to serve Imperial Japan, but I do not want to be a participant in cruel murder."

"Nor do I, my young friend," Zunsuno said softly.

"Please, Zunsuno-*san!* Do not make me go on another voyage on a warship!"

"This situation requires much contemplation and thought," Zunsuno said. "I will assign you tasks that will keep you in the laboratory. Another technician can take your place aboard the *Hayaken.*"

"*Arigato*—thank you!" Hyojun cried.

"But do not speak to anyone of this incident or how you feel about it," Zunsuno warned him. "The *Bushido* code of the Imperial Navy would demand you be given harsh treatment. Perhaps you would suffer even death."

Hyojun finished his tea. "Excuse me, Zunsuno-*san,* but I do not feel well. I humbly request your permission to withdraw from your honorable presence."

"Of course. I understand."

Hyojun bowed, then went to the door leading to the interior of the house. After he left, Zunsuno poured himself more tea, sipping slowly from the cup. Hikui came onto the veranda and joined her husband. She said, "The young man seems to be disturbed about something."

"Yes," Zunsuno said. "He was on the cruiser as a technician, and they tried to stop an uncooperative foreign ship. It was sunk and the crew killed by machine guns as they sat helpless in their lifeboats."

Hikui's eyes opened wide in shock. *"Osoroshii!"*

"I shall request an audience with Hara-*sama* first thing

in the morning," Zunsuno said. "He will see that the captain who ordered this outrage is punished."

"He will not!" Hikui exclaimed. "Are you forgetting that it is the shogun's best friend Heideki Tanaka who commands the cruiser? If you raise a fuss, it will be you who is punished, *shujin!*"

"Ah!" he said in despair. "You are right."

"Forgive me," Hikui said, "but you no longer hold such an honorable position on Kakureta since the Kamisaku is finished."

Zunsumo frowned. "We must get away from this cursed island and everything it stands for!"

"I have been waiting for years to hear you say that."

"There has to be some way we can escape to the Japanese mainland," Zunsuno said.

Hikui knew her husband well. She returned to the house to fetch the *sake* tray. The rice wine would calm him and allow a clearer contemplation of what must be done.

Aislado, Arizona
17 July
0400 Hours

The lights inside the hangar attracted the desert's flitting night insects from the outside. The pesky creatures fluttered around the illumination in a frenzy of dysfunctional stimulation that ended when they collided with the hot bulbs and exploded with little pops. The human beings laboring around the four Avenger aircraft down below paid no attention to the insectile drama going on above them. Strafing runs were scheduled for later that morning, and the planes had to be ready on time.

It had taken almost three days before the multiple problems of mounting and firing machine guns were solved. With no manuals available, the two ordnancemen went by instinct and logic as they figured out how to install the pairs of .50-caliber machine guns allotted to each airplane. The weaponry had been flown in from MCAS Miramar along with the ammo belts and boxes. The holes for the barrels to protrude were just inboard of the breaks in the wings that allowed them to be folded up for parking in a carrier hangar bay. Starting at that point and working back, Warrenton and Harrigan got the weaponry positioned properly. In very short order they had figured out the proper layout of box and belt that provided each gun a total of 335 rounds of ammunition. Finally the more difficult problem of configuring and activating the firing mechanism to work from the stick was solved. When that task was finished, the two intrepid airmen hopped down to the hangar floor. Chief Earl Monger joined them to see how things were going.

"They're all set," Warrenton informed him.

"Oh, yeah?" Monger remarked. "How the hell are they gonna aim the damn things?"

Warrenton shrugged. "I guess with the sights."

"There ain't any sights," Monger pointed out.

A frantic search of Scotty's and Paddy's parts boxes and shelves produced no sights in the whole of their inventory. Nor were there any of the reflective sights that could be mounted above the instrument panel and reflected off the front cockpit windshield.

"They ain't gonna use them guns for air-to-air anyhow," Warrenton said.

"Right," Harrigan agreed. "They can follow the strikes on the ground or in the water when they close in on a ship."

"Ain't good enough," Monger said. "Not even with tracers." He thought a moment. "Okay! Here's what we do. First thing is we'll paint a ring-and-bead sight on the windshield in the pilot's point of view. We can cut a stencil and have the pilot sit in the aircraft and let us know when it's in front of his eyes. At that point dab her with paint."

"Great idea!" Warrenton said. "Hell, that's plenty good for ground strafing, provided we zero 'em in at a specific range."

"One thousand yards," Monger said. "That'll do the trick."

The trio went to work on the idea. It was amazing to see Monger's thick fingers daintily draw the pattern of a gunsight on a piece of thick vinyl, then cut it out smoothly and accurately with an X-Acto knife. When the job was finished, the pilots were called out one by one to climb into their cockpits and adjust the seats to their most advantageous elevation. The first was Junior Stump. After settling himself into the proper position, he waited for further instructions.

Monger straddled the engine cowling, ready to stencil the gunsight onto the windshield. "Okay, Mr. Stump. Are you right-eyed or left-eyed?"

"What're you talking about, Chief? I'm right-handed, if that helps any."

"No, sir, that don't mean shit," Monger said testily. "Put your palms together with your arms stretched out in front of your face. Now point 'em at something in the distance with both eyes open."

Junior stood up and followed the directions by pointing to a window in the hangar some twenty yards away. "All right, Chief."

"Now close your left eye and look with your right."

"All right, Chief."

"Are you still pointing dead on at the window?"

"No, Chief."

"Now close your right eye and look with your left. Are you pointing dead on at the window?"

"Yeah, Chief!"

"You're left-eyed then," Monger announced. "Now sit down and close your right eye and tell me when this here center of the stencil is dead on in front of you so you could sight on a target through it."

Junior gave instructions for a few minor adjustments until he announced. "That's it!"

Monger slapped some masking tape around the stencil, then leaned down and took the brush and can of paint that Harrigan handed up to him. He daubed the black flat color through the gunsight stencil onto the windshield glass. "All right, Mr. Stump. You're done."

The procedure was followed with Erickson, Westy, and Ariel until they, too, had the sights painted in the correct position. Erickson had always been amazed at the knowledge the chief petty officer had stored in his pragmatic, humorless mind.

"Chief, I didn't know people could be right- or left-eyed," he said when his aircraft was taken care of.

"Hell, yes," Monger said. "Did you know that the best baseball hitters are either right-eyed and left-handed or left-eyed and right-handed?"

"No. I didn't know that," Erickson said.

"Well, it's true," Monger said. "Mr. Stump is right-handed and left-eyed. He's one of o' them lucky guys that's got a perfect angle on the ball because his sighting eye is on the side it's coming at him. Understand?"

"Sure," Erickson said, considering the theory. "Makes sense."

Monger hopped down from the plane. "All right! Now let's get these airplanes out to the edge of the runway. We'll set up a target a thousand yards out and start the work of zeroing in them machine guns."

The sun was already coming up as Monger drove Paddy Paderewski's pickup truck out a thousand yards from the edge of the runway. Four targets to be used for zeroing in the machine guns had been put in the back of the vehicle. These devices were simple but practical under the circumstances. A stack of six-by-six-foot pallets left by a construction crew had been bleaching in the sun behind the hangar. Monger and his crew loaded them up for the morning's main activity.

The tail of *Avenger 1* had been set up on a jury-rigged work platform at the exact height for the fuselage to be level. Erickson, sitting in the cockpit, looked through the painted sight on his canopy, making hand signals until the wooden target was directly in front of it. Then he fired a burst of six .50-caliber rounds from both guns that came together, splattering violently into the pallet.

Monger trotted up to the target with his tape measure. After checking the bullet strikes, the chief petty officer used Sparky's cell phone to call Warrenton, who had borrowed Scotty's. "Twelve right, up fourteen," Monger reported.

Warrenton and Harrigan each went to one of the guns, adjusting the elevation and deflection with the weapon's aim-adjustment knobs. Each turn moved the strike of the bullets one inch at the thousand-yard range. "All right," Warrenton hollered when they finished. "Try it again, sir."

Erickson leaned forward for another sighting, then made a quick pull on the trigger. The Avenger shook momentarily as the rounds streaked out. Monger went back to make another measurement. "Four right! Up six!" he said to Warrenton.

Once more the ordnancemen reached inside the gun compartment doors to make the proper adjustments. When they finished, Erickson squeezed off another short burst.

"Close enough for government work," Monger said. "Okay. Let's do *Avenger 2* now."

Erickson's aircraft was taken down and pushed out of the way. Westy Fields's plane was made ready for its zeroing task. The routine made for hard but short work as each Avenger was muscled into position. By 1000 hours the task was completed, and the bullets from each set of machine guns came together at the thousand-yard range.

Ariel Goldberg was anxious to try some real strafing, and turned to Erickson. "Let's give 'em a go, sir. It's going to take us a little while to get used to those painted sights."

Erickson felt the beginning of the day's big heat as the sun's intensity slowly but perceptibly increased. The desert would be a baking hell within an hour. He shook his head. "We'll do it tomorrow morning just after dawn. By the time we get fully loaded today, there won't be a lot of lift in the atmosphere. Between the thin air and thermals, we'd have a hell of a time making steady runs."

Monger, driving the pickup in from the target area, rolled onto the concrete of the runway, coming to a loud, squeaky halt. "All right, people! Let's get the aircraft out o' the hot sun and into the hangar."

Harrigan looked hopefully at the chief petty officer. "What're the chances of a siesta after noon chow, Chief?"

"If you want a goddamn siesta, then join the Mexican Navy," Monger snapped. "Now let's get moving on these planes! There's scheduled maintenance to take care of."

The four enlisted personnel turned to the task. As they started moving *Avenger 1* toward the hangar, Westy, Junior, and Ariel joined them to help with the effort. Their willingness to lend a hand at the difficult menial tasks was something Commander Gene Erickson liked best about the three pilots. Their collective attitude of not considering themselves above anything because of rank was also much appreciated by the aviation machinists and ordnancemen.

Erickson joined Gianna and Martinez on the left wing.

Washington, D.C.
Noon

Captain Lyle Nelson was an egotistical, self-centered man. The merchant marine officer was quick to be offended by a slight or insult and would seethe for months over the incident, no matter how trivial. When any chance for payback presented itself, Nelson moved in on his prey relentlessly and viciously. On the other hand, he responded to favors and consideration from others with the same amount of passion and dedication. When shown a kindness or done a favor, he was willing to reciprocate an almost unlimited amount.

Some twenty years before, he had stood accused of gross misconduct when the tanker he captained for the Petroleo Atlantico Oil Company ran aground off the coast of Venezuela. He had quite properly turned over the bridge to his chief officer after clearing the port of Puerto Cumarebo, bound for Buenos Aires with 5,000 cubic meters of crude oil for Argentine refineries. Two hours later, the vessel ran aground on the shoals of the Piedras Escondidos, spilling the thick, gooey cargo into the Atlantic Ocean. The spillage spread quickly, threatening to drift southward to destroy the beaches of Caracas. Only the quick action of the Venezuelan Navy, helped by advice and guidance from United States Coast Guard personnel, contained the damage to the local vicinity.

The chief officer, backed by the helmsman, claimed he was following the exact course laid out by Captain Nelson. They were able to produce a chart showing the skipper's instructions. Although it bore nothing of Nelson's signature or handwriting, it was the only chart found on the bridge. Venezuela's *Directiva de Actividades Marítimos* wasted no time in charging the unfortunate gringo captain with felony crimes of misconduct and negligence. A conviction would result in Nelson's license being permanently revoked. If that happened, he would be lucky if he could find a third mate's berth aboard a Hoboken garbage scow. His career was on that proverbial thin line.

Oil spillages were the hot news items in those days, and a young American journalist by the name of Pamela Drake had been assigned to cover the trial by her employer, *Global News Magazine*. She was not pleased with the assignment since it seemed a simple open-and-shut case against the American. Pamela was looking for stories of political intrigue filled with mind-boggling revelations. This oil spillage seemed dull and routine, with a predictable outcome. But after she had attended the first three days of the hearing, she was convinced of Nelson's innocence.

Something about the man bespoke of the quiet confidence and steady professionalism of a seasoned saltwater ship's officer. The chief officer, Nigel Throckmorton, on the other hand, was a much older Englishman who seemed unsure of himself. This trait titillated her journalistic instincts. Where others saw an overweight, run-of-the-mill ship's officer with average but steady abilities, Pamela Drake perceived a failed, angry little fellow who had never commanded a ship in his more than twenty-five years at sea. At first she thought of arranging an interview with Throckmorton through the maritime board, but the budding journalist knew it would be useless. After listening to him testify, she realized the fellow had a sort of crude guile in which he would happily lie to cover his miserable ass.

The key to more enlightening information lay with the helmsman, a young, pliable, Irish lad who had been on duty at the time of the accident. Therefore, she made arrangements for a one-on-one meeting with Sean O'Reilly of Ballycotton, a small seaside town in County Cork.

The meeting between the journalist and the sailor took place in an unused office of the Maritime Directorate's building. The two sat down across from each other at the only table in the room. Pamela began by delving into the youngster's background, asking questions about his hometown and short career. She quickly noted Sean was an open sort of fellow who liked to talk about himself, especially if he thought it would impress an attractive woman. She let him go on making long, complicated answers to her preliminary innocuous questions. When he was relaxed and enjoying himself, she slowly turned the interrogation to the more serious matter of the accident.

"Tell me, Sean," Pamela said, "did you hear Captain Nelson give the course to Mr. Throckmorton?"

"Ah—ah! Indeed. Yes, indeed, I did, miss," Sean replied.

"And he handed him the chart with the proper course drawn on it, did he?"

"Yes, miss. That he did."

"Oh!" Pamela said. "I just remembered that Mr. Throckmorton said that *he* drew the course on the chart following Captain Nelson's instructions."

"Indeed."

"Then the captain didn't draw the course on the map, did he?"

Sean frowned in puzzlement. "Well—well, now. Sure and I'm not certain o' that, miss."

Pamela kept on about the chart for a few more minutes before going back to the verbal orders issued by Nelson to Throckmorton. She noted that Sean was very self-assured when he said that Nelson had given Throckmorton the course to follow, but the Irishman would stutter and mumble when it came to discussing exactly what was said. As a helmsman, he would have to have been well informed on the subject to perform his job properly.

After hammering at the subject, Pamela stopped talking and looked straight into Sean's eyes for long moments. The young man began to squirm and diverted his gaze from hers. Finally, Pamela spoke plainly.

"Captain Nelson did not give the same course that Mr. Throckmorton drew on that chart, did he, Sean?"

"Well, now—I mean to say that—ye see—well, now, miss—no, he didn't."

Then the whole story came out. Throckmorton had convinced Sean that if they sailed into the Piedras Escondidos and ran aground, then blamed the captain for the accident, Nelson would be dismissed. In that case, Throckmorton would become the captain, and he promised Sean a third mate's ticket if he backed him up about the instructions and the map. Sean had nothing against Nelson, but this was a quick chance for a promotion that would have taken years of going to sea under normal circumstances.

Sean explained, "I thought o' how proud my parents would be when I came home wearing an officer's uniform."

When the hearing resumed the next day, Sean refuted his earlier testimony. Nelson was cleared with all charges against him dismissed. Throckmorton lost his ticket, and it was his career that was dead-ended abruptly, not Nelson's. Sean lost his job with the shipping company as would be expected, but he was able to sign on another ship as an able seaman. Nelson gave Pamela a brief, gruff expression of gratitude, then went back to take command of another tanker for Petroleo Atlantico.

Pamela returned to the States with a feature story on the crude frame-up attempt. The article changed her from an unknown to a popular writer with guaranteed bylines on everything she turned in for publication. It was her first big step up a long journalistic ladder where she would end up reigning supreme. Captain Lyle Nelson faded back into the dim corners of her memory.

The El Senador Restaurant in Washington was one of the best eating establishments the public never heard about. The owner was a former liberal politician from Chile who

KEITH DOUGLASS

had been forced to flee a right-wing military junta that took over the country after a short but violent *coup d'état*. When he opened the business, he decided to operate an establishment that would provide the powerful and wealthy a secluded place to meet and dine.

Lyle Nelson sat alone at a back table, sipping a glass of rum. His back was to the wall, and he had a good view of the dining area. When the person he was waiting for appeared among the tables, he stood up and beckoned to her.

Pamela Drake walked up to him, smiling as she offered her hand. "I had trouble remembering who you are, Captain Nelson."

"Well, I've never forgotten you, Miss Drake," he said. "Please sit down." He walked over and held the chair for her.

"I see you're still a perfect gentleman, Captain," she said, noting that he seemed to have prospered since his troubles of twenty years past.

He retook his seat. "Actually, I'm not a captain anymore, Miss Drake. I head up accident investigations for a large maritime insurance corporation in Baltimore."

Pamela thought a moment. "Would that be East Coast Surety?"

"The same," Nelson said. "Actually, they're not insurers *per se*. The company puts up front money for various maritime activities. Ships and cargo mostly. And I look into more than accidents. I also investigate sabotage, thievery, and other crimes." He smiled. "As you remember, I've had a bit of experience when it comes to certain problems."

"I do recall," Pamela said. "An oil spill and a frame-up conspiracy."

The waiter appeared to take their drink orders and to leave menus. Pamela had been in El Senador many times and already knew what she wanted. She recommended the creamed salmon, and Nelson took her advice when the waiter returned.

The former captain took a sip of his fresh rum. "I know you must be bursting with curiosity, Miss Drake."

"You've made a sudden unexpected appearance after a

couple of decades," she said. "So, yes! I am frankly wondering why you called me."

"I owe you, Miss Drake," Nelson said. "You saved me big time down there in Venezuela. If you hadn't broken down that Irish kid, I'd have ended up on the beach someplace. Disgraced and broke."

"All right," Pamela conceded, surprised that he would feel indebted after all those years.

"I have some information that might interest you," he said. "I've noted you're no longer on TV. I wondered what happened to you until I ran across your column in the *Washington Herald-Telegraph*."

"I had a disagreement about broadcasting some information I'd dug up on government antimilitia activities," she explained. "Anyhow, the show-biz glitz of TV news was holding me back." Her journalistic instincts were flashing on full speed. "What sort of story do you have?"

They were interrupted by the waiter bringing the salads. Pamela fought down a desire to yell at the man to hurry up as he slowly twisted the pepper mill over their dishes. Nelson waited until the server left before speaking again.

"Ships, crews, and cargos have been disappearing off the East China Sea for the past several months," Nelson said in a low voice. "East Coast Surety assigned me to look into things after a couple of cargos they had financed went off to parts unknown."

"What did you find out?" Pamela asked.

"There is a maritime criminal organization that is capturing ships and holding crews, vessels, and cargos for ransom," Nelson said. "It's being kept out of the news, and those of us who've become involved have been told to keep our mouths shut. The lid is on tight."

"You could get in a lot of trouble talking to me about this," Pamela warned him.

"Like I said," Nelson remarked casually, "I owe you." He paused. "I've delivered a couple of ransoms myself. One was at the Panamanian embassy here in Washington, and the other was in New York City at the Liberian consulate."

A busboy showed up to remove their salad plates just before the waiter returned with the main course. When they were alone again, Nelson spoke slowly and softly as they ate. Pamela Drake only played with her food, listening intently to the startling revelation of twenty-first-century piracy.

Aislado, Arizona
18 July
0630 Hours

The target area used for the bombing runs had been reduced to a battered, cratered patch of ground. All the cacti had been blown away, leaving a miniature wasteland in the middle of the desert. The night before, chief petty officers Earl Monger and Paddy Paderewski had used the latter's pickup truck to drag a dozen hulks of abandoned autos into the area to add some realism for the aviators' strafing runs. The old junkers came from an abandoned junkyard on the other side of the road from Scotty's compound. Monger had a bit of a problem dealing with the half-dozen rattlesnakes and one Gila monster they encountered during the task. Paddy chuckled each time his companion jumped back from an unexpected encounter with a poisonous reptile.

Now, with the sun just off the horizon, the four Avengers flew in trail with Gene Erickson in the lead. James Warrenton sat behind the pilot on the aft cockpit seat. A small door allowing access to the bombardier's station below was situated just to the right of the position. But Warrenton, like his enlisted companions in the other aircraft, had only come along for the ride rather than to perform bombing duties. It was a sort of reward for all their hard work.

Westy Fields flew on Erickson's "six" in *Avenger 2* with Emiliano Martinez; Ariel Goldberg was paired with Gianna Torino in *Avenger 3,* while Junior Stump and Mike Harrigan brought up the rear in *Avenger 4.*

Erickson pushed forward on the stick as he eased into a thirty-degree dive toward the target. By the time he was at 2,500 feet AGL, he was some 3,000 yards out, and he continued on, sighting through the stenciled gunsight, until within range. He squeezed off short fire bursts, keeping track of the clouds of dust kicked up by the heavy .50-caliber slugs. When the strikes of the bullets passed the impact area, he pulled up and rolled to the left.

The other Avengers followed, each making a strafing run in turn. The flight circled around and came back three more times, plowing the earth and blasting holes in the old car hulks, rattling and shaking them.

When the aircraft turned into their landing pattern, Monger and Paddy drove out to see how they'd done. It was obvious that an overwhelming majority of rounds had come in with accurate devastation. Paddy walked over to the riddled remnants of a 1951 Chevrolet pickup. He grabbed the bullet-battered door and easily pulled it off the remnants of the cab. He glanced over at Monger. "Looks like they were right on target."

"Time to go to the fleet," Monger said.

The two walked back to Paddy's truck for the short return drive to the airport.

CHAPTER THIRTEEN

USS Jefferson
East China Sea
20 July
1315 Hours

The wind streamed down the flight deck fore to aft as the carrier moved into position to receive the addition of four aircraft to the wing already on board. Lieutenant Commander Todd Irving, an F-14 pilot acting as LSO, glanced toward the deck. It was now condition green, i.e., cleared for the landing operations that were due to start almost any minute. The pickle in his hand was ready to flash the lights that would inform the incoming aviators if their approaches were correct, slightly out of kilter, or potential disasters. His assistant, an ensign working the detail for the first time, tapped him on the shoulder.

"ATCC just called to say the incoming flight was fifteen minutes out," he reported. "Four aircraft. And—well—are you ready for this, sir?"

"Ready for what?" Irving asked.

"They're prop jobs," the ensign said, suppressing a grin.

"No shit?" Irving said, unconcerned. "What've we got? Greyhounds bringing in some VIPs or something? There must be a lot of 'em. This is supposed to be something special from Osaka."

"No, sir, they're not Greyhounds," the ensign said. "And not Ospreys or E2s, either. Are you ready for this, sir?"

"Don't ask me that again, mister!" Irving snapped.

"They're Avengers," the ensign informed him. "World War Two jobs. Johnson up at PriFly said they were about sixty years old." He chuckled. "I hope he wasn't talking about the pilots, too. That'd be a hell of a situation, wouldn't it?"

Irving glanced sternward, his eyes raised to the sky. "Whatever or whoever they are, here they come."

The four Avengers and assigned crews had flown from Aislado to NAS North Island on the first stage of travel to the operational area. There was one other important matter to tend to upon their arrival at the California air station, and technicians were standing by to tend to the task. The small, short-range radios used in air shows by Scotty Ross and Paddy Paderewski would hardly do a proper job of communicating while out with the fleet, and the proper operational transmitter/receivers had to be installed in each airplane.

When the ancient aircraft landed at North Island, they were directed over to a hangar where technicians waited with the radios. Even the most casual of observers were curious about the arrival of the vintage airplanes, but when they attempted to get closer for a better look, they were kept away by marine guards.

Later that day the communications systems were given a brief but conclusive test. This was done by making spot transmission checks while flying out to sea and inland over the mountains of the Cleveland National Forest and into the desert. When that last detail was taken care of, the aircraft were ready to go. The four returned to North Island to prepare for sea transport to the naval base at Osaka, Japan.

The wings were folded back and locked, tape put across the canopy glass with great care to see that the stenciled gunsights were not marred, and landing gear brakes locked to avoid any unnecessary rolling. After those indignities, the Avengers were loaded on the back of flatbed trucks to be driven down to the dock, where cranes worked by civilian contractors waited for them.

Chief Earl Monger irritated the workmen by personally checking each twelve-inch nylon strapping that was wrapped around the airplanes. He insisted on tentative liftings of no less than a dozen feet to check balance and stability. Only then were the crane operators allowed to hoist the modified airplanes off the trucks and onto the bow of the combat supply ship *Wichita*.

All munitions, spare parts, and other supplies were already in the holds of the vessel that would go to Osaka to drop off the Avengers, then continue out to deliver the rest of the goods to the *USS Jefferson*.

After the arrival and unloading at Osaka, the aircraft were given a thorough preflight inspection by the aviation machinists before everyone's gear was stowed in the various bomb bays. A proper warm-up followed before the crews climbed aboard, and the Avenger flight took off. Commander Gene Erickson flew his command directly toward the location of the waiting carrier battle group.

Erickson, with James Warrenton buckled in the backseat, received the LSO's request for him to "call the ball" to acknowledge he had the light signal in sight. "Roger ball," he responded, wishing the old airplane had some sort of ILS in it.

Erickson, used to coming in for carrier landings in his F/A-18E Super Hornet, felt like he was creeping as he lowered his wheels, flaps, and hook. The plane crawled downward but flew steadily without a waver as she continued on the correct flight path. The wheels hit the deck, and the hook grabbed the second wire—not good form in a jet—but the Avenger stopped solid.

Warrenton let out a long sigh of relief. "Whew! That was scary as hell!" he pronounced through the intercom.

Erickson grinned. "Someday I'll bring you along in an F/A-18 and show you the real thrill of a carrier landing in a jet."

They taxied under the direction of a blue shirt plane handler who took them to the correct side of the deck to stop. By then, *Avenger 2*, with Westy Fields, Earl Monger, and Emiliano Martinez, was detached from the arresting wire. In less than five minutes, *Avenger 3* and *Avenger 4* had joined them in the parking area. After everyone and their personal gear were unloaded, the wings were once again folded and locked back. The enlisted personnel helped a team of blue shirts push the Avengers onto the elevator for the trip down to the hangar bay. This time the officers did not lend a hand. They properly stayed out of the way so that people assigned to such tasks could complete the work quickly and efficiently.

A young marine appeared from some unknown location and requested to see the flight commander. Erickson took his salute and was crisply informed that he was to follow the messenger up to flag country. Rear Admiral John Miskoski, the battle group commander, was waiting for him with Rear Admiral John Paulsen.

Erickson followed the marine's brisk pace as the pair went up ladders and down passageways until reaching that portion of the carrier where the admiral and his staff maintained their working spaces. Erickson felt a twinge of nervousness as they walked across the blue tile deck that marked the bailiwick of the top brass. People of high rank always made Erickson nervous, even when he wasn't in trouble. The marine stopped in front of the admiral's cabin and knocked.

"Come!"

Erickson waited as the marine stepped in and announced him. The aviator entered the hallowed domain and saluted the two flag officers. "Commander Erickson reporting as ordered, sir."

Miskoski returned the salute. "Welcome back, Commander. This is Admiral Paulsen, who is heading up Operation Yesteryear."

Paulsen shook hands with the visitor. "Glad to meet you, Erickson. They tell me you really kicked ass during that Korean fiasco."

"Yes, sir," Erickson replied. "I was in the air wing on the *Lincoln*."

"How do things look for this operation?"

"We're ready, sir," Erickson informed him. "We've worked out all the bugs in converting the old aircraft to the specifics and requirements of the mission."

Paulsen nodded. "Great. I imagine there were quite a few expediencies to be taken care of."

Erickson grinned. "Yes, sir. Like stenciling gunsights on our canopies to simulate the old reflective models. My chief petty officer thought that one up."

Paulsen smiled back. "That's what the chiefs do best, isn't it? Are you satisfied with your personnel? I'm referring to both pilots and technicians."

"A hundred percent," Erickson said. "The procedures we've worked out include having the ordnancemen and machinists act as bombardiers when we conduct the actual missions."

Miskoski frowned. "Those people aren't flying personnel, are they?"

"No, sir," Erickson said. "But they've got their assignments down perfect. It would take a great deal of time and effort to train someone to take their place."

Miskoski looked at Paulsen. "Why weren't qualified aircrews provided for this operation?"

"We didn't know they would be needed," Paulsen explained. "As a matter of fact, none of us were familiar with Avenger aircraft."

Miskoski shrugged. "Well! Nothing to be done about it now. It looks like some enlisted folks are going to earn aircrew badges, huh?"

"One of them is a woman, sir," Erickson said. "She's an aviation machinist's mate second class with lots of experience."

"Then she's more than qualified," Miskoski said.

"What about ordnance delivery?" Paulsen asked. "I've

received reports about the five hundred–pound bombs and point five-zero-caliber machine guns. How have they worked out?"

"We've developed a more than adequate accuracy in hitting stationary targets, sir," Erickson said. "We used a patch of desert terrain and old junker cars. The problem was that we got no practice on moving targets. But my pilots are top-notch. None of us should have any trouble adapting to whatever operational situations pop up."

"Good!" Paulsen said. "Your munitions and other supplies should be aboard by midmorning tomorrow. We'll give you a full briefing in the morning and let you in on the big picture. Any questions?"

"No, sir."

"All right. Dismissed, Commander. See you tomorrow."

Erickson saluted and made his exit, feeling damn good about being back on a carrier with a real job to perform.

Oriental and Occidental Commodities, Ltd.
Executive Building
Bethesda, Maryland
2010 Hours

Pamela Drake had been surprised by the payback of an old favor given her by the former merchant marine Captain Lyle Nelson. The information he passed on to her led the journalist to call in an additional favor from yet another source. Pamela's superb ability to balance collecting debts with discretion was the crux of her personal journalistic program. In some corners this might be considered a sophisticated form of blackmail, but Pamela Drake had no problem with this. She followed the old adage that the end justified the means.

She had once done Chinese American businessman John Tshek a particularly great service by suppressing a story involving dealings some of his employees had with a Thailand drug cartel. Although Tshek had known nothing of the affair, the fact that his company was involved could have done irreparable harm to his reputation in the Asian and U.S. business communities. It was his good fortune that it had been Pamela Drake who discovered the situation.

Now she sat across the desk from the entrepreneur in his austere office located on the top floor of his commercial empire's headquarters. Pamela was always set back a bit by the contrast between the expensively dressed businessman and his stark working environment.

Tshek seemed very pleased to see her. "How have you been, Pamela, dear?"

"Quite well, thank you," Pamela answered. "The switch from TV news to the print media has had its difficulties, but I'm well settled in now."

"I read your weekly column faithfully," Tshek said in his accented English. "Am I to conclude that this most pleasant surprise of your visit has to do with your professional interests?"

"Yes," Pamela said. "I have been given certain information regarding incidents on the high seas. On the East China Sea, to be exact. Since that is within your sphere of commercial operations, I thought you might be able to enlighten me on the situation."

Tshek knew she was referring to the hijacked ships. But he said nothing, having learned early in his career that subtlety and patience were more advantageous than an eager revelation of prior knowledge. "How may I help you?"

"My source has informed me that modern-day pirates are prowling that area of the world," Pamela said. "They seem to operate with impunity as they capture ships and cargo, then hold them for ransom. Is this true?"

"Unfortunately, what this person has told you is filled with truth," Tshek said. "I, too, have suffered the humiliation of buying back cargo that was stolen from me."

"But how can this be, John?" Pamela asked. "This is the twenty-first century, with spy satellites and other technology. I can see how Moslem terrorists can hide in mountain caves, but operating on the high seas puts the bad guys right out there in the open."

"I, too, have pondered this enigma," Tshek commented. "But I've not managed to learn much about it. However, I will be happy to relate to you my latest knowledge of this sorry state of affairs."

"Please do," Pamela said, retrieving pad and pen from her purse. "I promise to be most discreet."

"I trust you, dear Pamela."

"Then may I have what information you can give me?"

"This time a ship has disappeared, and no ransom was demanded," Tshek said. "The vessel, a Nigerian-registered freighter named the *Dileas,* was last heard from on July fifteenth. A couple of days later, some debris was spotted by a South Korean naval vessel. It appeared to be remnants of lifeboats. They also recovered the bullet-riddled body of a ship's officer." He reached into his desk drawer and took out his personal activities journal. After flipping through the pages, he continued. "He was a Singapore man by the same of Syed Lujamalail. This unfortunate is listed as the chief officer of the missing freighter."

"Isn't anybody doing anything about these outrages?" Pamela asked.

Tshek instinctively lowered his voice. "I can tell you this. The United States Navy is taking some sort of action. They are working out of the big base at Osaka, Japan." He now spoke in a normal tone. "Pamela, my dear, that is all I can tell you. Not because I wish to conceal anything, but because I know nothing else."

"You've been a great deal of help, John," Pamela said. "Thank you."

"You are most welcome," Tshek said.

Pamela replaced her pen and pad in her purse as she stood up. "You've told me enough to go farther up the trail. Thank you so much. I hope to see you again soon."

"It was my pleasure, Pamela," Tshek said. "Please do not hesitate to call on me if I can be of any further assistance to you."

"Again, thank you."

As Pamela rode the elevator down to the lobby, she thought of how John Tshek had actually been very helpful.

He had unwittingly saved her much time and effort by mentioning the naval base at Osaka. One of her best naval contacts, Lieutenant Junior Grade Wilma Dietrich, was the assistant public relations officer at the facility.

USS Jefferson
Operation Yesteryear Ready Room
21 July
0830 Hours

Rear Admiral John Paulsen, Lieutenant Commander Gray Hollinger, and Commander Craig Davis sat at the table in front of the room facing the audience. Commander Gerald Fagin and Lieutenant Lars Stensland occupied two seats in the front row. The four pilots—Commander Gene Erickson, Lieutenants Westy Fields, Junior Stump, and Ariel Goldberg—sat in the second row. Behind them, spread out between the third and fourth rows, were the machinists and ordnancemen of Operation Yesteryear. Chief Earl Monger sat in the back row by himself.

Paulsen stood up. "I believe everyone has been introduced now. So, without further ado, I'll begin the briefing of Operation Yesteryear. Commander Fagin and Lieutenant Stensland have had the full story for a couple months now. In fact, our Norwegian friend was an officer serving on the first ship captured by the raiders. The information he provided after his release was the basis for the planning of this mission."

Admiral Paulsen brought the others up to date on the ransomed ships, crews, and cargos that were captured on the high seas by people who were Japanese or of Japanese ancestry. He emphasized that they insisted they were part of the Imperial Japanese Navy. He further informed his audience of the stealth aspect of the raider vessels that was so sophisticated that Stensland was unable to get a clear picture of the culprits with his digital camera. Now Erickson and his group understood why the Avengers had been chosen for the mission. Their simple delivery systems of unsophisticated ordnance would not be adversely affected by stealth technology.

"The latest word on this situation is very ominous," Paulsen said. "A ship has completely disappeared. This would be a freighter called the *Dileas*. The South Korean Navy discovered debris of lifeboats and a corpse floating in the water in the area of latitude thirty-six degrees east and longitude one hundred and thirty-one degrees north. The dead man was identified as the chief officer of that vessel. He had been killed by gunshots obviously from an automatic weapon. Unfortunately, no other clues were discovered, and it is impossible to tell how far the body and boat remnants had drifted from the scene of the crime."

Erickson raised his hand. "Sir, what is this stealth aspect of the raiders? Is their ship constructed of some super new material?"

"We believe they have a special machine aboard their ship—or ships—that is capable of blocking intrusive signals such as radar, lasers, and the like," Paulsen explained. "Commander Fagin can give you what details we have."

Fagin stood up and faced the flight crews. "We believe that this machine is called the *Kamisaku* in Japanese. This translates as the 'Sacred Barrier,' and work was begun on it during World War Two but not completed. Somehow and somewhere the device was perfected and is now in use. Everything else about it is unknown." He shrugged. "Sorry. But that's what we're working on, and most of that is speculative. There's no telling what we'll find when we manage to make contact."

"Thank you, Commander," Paulsen said. "The one positive aspect of the situation is the fact that the raiders do not seem to have employed spies or informers to learn about ship movements. They are going out on the shipping lanes and attacking targets of opportunity. The advantage to that is that we don't have to worry about anyone knowing our operational procedures. And speaking of those methods, I'll let Commander Davis explain the seagoing part of our caper."

Craig Davis took the floor. "Okay, folks, here's the skinny on how we plan to make that contact. Commander

Fagin and Mr. Stensland are going aboard a freighter picked for this mission. It is the *SS Buenaventura* of Panamanian registration." As he spoke he passed out aerial photos of the ship that had been taken from different angles. "This will familiarize you with the vessel's appearance. She will be carrying some innocuous nonperishable cargo with a phony manifest to give the appearance of being a real working ship. The crew will be made up of selected individuals of various Oriental ancestries. These guys are from a number of U.S. intelligence agencies. Their seamen IDs will match their cover nationalities. All speak their ancestral languages fluently. The officers will be European, like Fagin and Stensland. They'll sail out there on the East China Sea until the raiders make contact with them. Since that damned machine makes the bad guys invisible, the *Buenaventura* won't know they're being captured until the last moment. At that time, a commo buoy will be launched from the stern of the ship. The device will stay underwater while traveling approximately a hundred meters. At that point it will surface and begin broadcasting. Its signal will be picked up here on the *Jefferson*."

"Excuse me, sir," Erickson said. "If that holy machine or whatever it is can break up signals, won't that neutralize the buoy?"

"It might for awhile," Davis admitted. "But we hope that hundred-meter distance will get it far enough away to be effective. The moment it's picked up here, the Avenger flight will be dispatched to deliver that simple unguided weaponry you folks are going to have to use." He gestured to Commander Gray Hollinger. "Gray, will you give the details on the flight operations?

Hollinger didn't bother to stand up. "It's short and simple, people. The direction-finding instrumentation you'll use to home in on the *Buenaventura* is being installed in your aircraft even as we speak. No big deal. It's no more than a box that picks up the signal like the devices put in cars to track down thieves. Unfortunately, the avionics people say whoever is monitoring it won't be able to use those radios you were given at North Island, so I recommend that only one of you use it at a time."

Erickson turned to Westy Fields. "You'll be our direction-finder aircraft." He looked back at Hollinger. "So we fly to the buoy, search around for a visual sighting of the bad guys, and attack."

"It's not *that* simple," Hollinger cautioned him. "We don't want you to sink the son of a bitch. We need prisoners to sweat information out of them. Also, you want to avoid hitting the *Buenaventura,* which will be close by."

Fagin winked at Erickson. "Just remember it's the bad guy you bomb the shit out of. Not the *Buenaventura.*"

"Not to worry," Erickson said, waving the photos at him.

Fagin continued, "Those of us on the decoy ship will board the raider after you've pounded him to a standstill in the water. We'll have all the weapons necessary to pull that off."

"The battle group will have closed in pretty much by then," Admiral Paulsen said. "And that sacred barrier should be switched off. The minute that devil's contraption is out of action, ship and airborne radar will locate the scene very quickly. Anything else?"

"Yes, sir," Hollinger said, nodding to Erickson. "There'll be flight quarters for the Avengers tomorrow. You're going to have to practice launching and landing to sharpen those new skills your old aircraft will demand."

"Great, sir," Erickson said. "It's a hell of a lot different landing them than a controlled crash in jet fighters."

"All right, people," Paulsen said. "Consider Operation Yesteryear launched. You're going to be mighty busy even while waiting for things to heat up. That is all."

Everyone stood to attention as the admiral and his staff left the ready room. Erickson turned to Monger. "Are we ready to fly?"

"Yes, sir," Monger replied. "As soon as we finish fueling."

CHAPTER FOURTEEN

Kakureta Island
22 July
0915 Hours

The *suiraitei* boat, with its engine chugging, sat at the dock waiting for the passengers scheduled for a twenty-four-hour voyage to Japan. A few minutes passed before the small Mitsubishi van that served as the island's only ambulance pulled up and parked at the head of the wharf. The driver quickly jumped out and rushed around to the passenger side, opening the door. Hikui Zunsuno stepped out and turned to watch as the back was opened, and two men emerged. Her husband Gomme, sitting in a wheelchair, was taken from the interior and gently lowered to the ground. The driver gestured toward the boat, indicating that was where everyone was to go. One of the medical orderlies carefully pushed the patient onto the wharf as Hikui walked at their side. The other orderly followed, carrying two suitcases.

The feeble old man was picked up and carried aboard the vessel by two waiting crewmen. Hikui was helped off the dock and onto the deck. She waited until Gomme was carried into the cabin, then she followed, carefully watching her step in the unfamiliar environs of the boat. Almost immediately, the master barked his orders, and the stern and bow lines were cast off. The vessel moved out into the harbor and turned toward the open sea.

Medical care on Kakureta Island was outdated at best and rudimentary at worst. The last physician with a valid M.D. degree from an accredited medical school died in 1992. Not a single young man sent to Japan for an education in medicine ever returned to establish a practice on the island. The amount of money to be made on the mainland proved too much of an enticement to remain. After three such defections, no more potential doctors were sent abroad.

At that point, ten-year medical apprenticeships were established in which the remaining M.D.'s on Kakureta gave on-the-job training to their surgery assistants. When these older physicians eventually passed way, the new healthcare givers took over all medical care and training. They taught others in basic classes on diagnosis, pharmacology, and simple surgery such as setting broken bones, appendectomies, and other procedures that could be done with the simplest of instruments. The best that could be done for acutely ill patients was to administer narcotics to make their last days as comfortable as possible. Only those of great importance and trust were transferred to Japan for proper treatment.

Dr. Gomme Zunsuno and his wife Hikui had decided to take advantage of this situation. Even though he was in his early eighties and only worked part-time in the laboratory, Zunsuno was still considered a respected member of the Kaigun Samurai community. The old couple reasoned that if he could convince one of the journeymen medics that he was seriously ill, the authorities would not hesitate to send him to the homeland for whatever modern medical treatment would save his life. They also knew that Hikui would be permitted to accompany him.

Once they were in Japan, they would have to look for the first opportunity to defect to freedom and expose the criminal acts being conducted with the Kamisaku. This dangerous task they had set for themselves would be almost impossible because of their age, and if things went wrong, would result in a forced return to Kakureta. Neither had any doubts about what fate awaited them if that happened. However, Gomme pointed out to Hikui that their execution would be most merciful because of his past service. They would no doubt be given lethal injections of drugs that would ease them into unconsciousness and then death. Hikui was not comforted by the grim revelation.

At least they would have no financial problems when they arrived in Japan. Although no need for money existed on Kakureta Island, bank accounts had been set up for the island elite in the National Nipponese Bank in Japan. Each of these families had records of deposits made in their name, and the Zunsunos had some fifteen million yen in their account. This was equal to over $125,000 American.

The first step in their escape plot began in the middle of the night when Hikui sent their maid to fetch one of the medical people. When the young man arrived at the house, he found old Gomme writhing with supposedly horrible abdominal pains as his distraught wife sought to comfort him. Hikui tearfully pleaded, "Please help my husband, *Isha-san!*"

"Do not worry, Hikui-*san*," the young man said as calming and professionally as he could. "We will soon have him put right."

He retrieved his diagnostic book from his bag, turning to the chapter on acute stomach discomfort. To his chagrin, he found the symptoms could be the result of numerous maladies, some trivial and others decidedly fatal if not properly treated. "I will take Zunsuno-*san* to the hospital for a more complete examination."

He gave the old man some painkillers to calm him, then arranged to have him transported to the island's hospital. The van arrived quickly, and Gomme was hurried away for an examination via an ancient fluoroscope that had been a feature at the medical center for over five decades. Although Gomme was under the influence of sedatives, he grinned secretly to himself at the medic and his colleagues as they attempted to decipher the blurred image on the screen of the machine. They whispered in worried tones with each other, and he kept hearing the word *gan*—cancer. The chief of the hospital was summoned, and upon his arrival, he began the examination all over again. When finished, he huddled in one corner of the room with his subordinates, and they spoke in low voices and hoarse whispers. Then the chief went out into the hall where Hikui waited.

"*Gomen kudasai,* Hikui-*san,*" he said. "We fear that Zunsuno-*san* is seriously ill. I do not want you to worry. I will see that arrangements are made to have him taken to Japan for appropriate treatment. I am sure they will have him back to good health in no time at all."

Hikui bowed respectfully. "Your kindness and consideration is well appreciated, *Isha-san.*"

"In the meantime he can go back home where he will be comfortable," the chief told her. The hospital did not offer the amenities available in the Zunsuno home. "I will have one of our doctors visit daily."

Hikui was provided with more painkilling medicine along with instructions on how to administer it. They were returned to their house where Gomme was tenderly placed back in his bed. After the medics left, Hikui settled on a chair next to him. Gomme sat up and smiled at her. "Do you think we are spry enough to carry through our plan?"

"As of this moment," she replied, "I am thankful that you are truly not ill." She shuddered. "I hate to think of the fate of sick *jun-i.*"

The boat rocked forward in the swells of the sea as it labored toward Japan. The old couple sat down in the cabin, bracing themselves with each roll as the sound of the noisy engine throbbed through the small vessel. Hikui opened her suitcase and showed her husband all the strong sedatives the hospital had been delivering to them on a regular basis. She asked, "Should I throw these away, *shujin*? You really didn't need the medication."

"Keep it handy, *kanai,*" he advised her. "If our ploy fails, we can use the drugs to end our lives by our own hands rather than have the shogun's men do it."

USS Jefferson
1020 Hours

Avenger 1, with Commander Gene Erickson at the controls, sat in position with the engine at idle in this first carrier launch of the old airplanes. The morning's flights were particularly important to work out any bugs in that phase of adapting the ancient aircraft to a modern nuclear carrier. No one knew what problems might arise as carrier and aircraft reached across the decades to each other.

In the case of launching a jet aircraft, the nose wheel is positioned just behind the catapult shuttle prior to the gear strut being lowered into the device. But the Avenger's launch system consisted of a cable bridle hooked to both the port and starboard landing gear doors. This was attached to the shuttle for the trip down the catapult track, and it dropped off into the sea after the aircraft was airborne.

No other activity was taking place on the flight deck, and everyone's attention was on this operation. Loud laughter burst out among the catapult crew when the jet-blast deflector was raised behind the prop job. Erickson grinned out at the green shirts who were enjoying this little joke being played on him and his old-fashioned airplane. Another green shirt raised the board that displayed the aircraft's takeoff weight of 18,200 pounds. This was quite a bit less than a fully loaded F-14's 70,000-plus. Erickson hoped the steam pressure could be set low enough to accommodate his aircraft. Mental pictures of the Avenger being violently hurled off the bow into pieces flitted through his mind.

Erickson had the flaps fully extended as he pushed the throttle all the way open at the signal from the catapult officer. The aircraft moved forward to the limits of the cable bridle and shook violently under the pressure. Another signal was given to the catapult launch control pod, and the shooter inside hit the button that sent the Avenger down the track and off the carrier. The force of the takeoff was minuscule compared to what Erickson endured in his

F/A-18E, but there was a good bit of discomfort neverthe-less. He held the stick back and raised the flaps after reach-ing an altitude of 500 feet ASL. The airplane quickly gained speed and began a strong, steady climb powered by the engine.

That last night at Scotty Ross's airport in Aislado, Arizona, was dominated by a barbecue and a couple of kegs of beer. The four airplanes were already fully prepped and fueled for the flight to North Island, and everyone had packed for the trip. The festivities had not quite started when Paddy Padarewski wheeled out a crate balanced on a dolly. He pushed his load to the front of the flight line and stopped.

"Something's been buzzing in the back of my mind ever since you people got here," he said. "I didn't know what it was until about fifteen minutes ago when it came on me like a bomb blast."

Earl Monger looked up from his task of cracking the first keg. "What the hell are you talking about, Paddy?"

"Well, I got to thinking about you fellers launching off a carrier in a sort o' sad, nostalgic way," Paddy explained. "It made me think o' them long-ago days in the Pacific War and how it was. I closed my eyes and remembered them Avengers heading off the flight deck and going out to at-tack the Japanese fleet."

Monger showed a rare grin. "An old salt and his memo-ries."

"Yep!" Paddy agreed. "Then I had what we call a *ujawniene* in Polish—a revelation." Now the pilots were interested in what the old chief had to say. They delayed filling their paper cups with beer and walked up closer to listen. He continued, "It dawned on me that these Avengers prob'ly ain't configured for launching off a modern nu-clear aircraft carrier. Then I remembered something." He reached in the crate and pulled out a length of cable with snaps on the end.

"I'll be damned!" Scotty exclaimed. "Launching cable bridles that are hooked on catapult shuttles. I forgot we had them."

"They was in that airport there outside of Duluth," Paddy said. "The guy there didn't know what to do with 'em, so we just took 'em along as historic objects. Hell, there must be a couple o' hunnerd in this crate."

Erickson walked up and took the bridle, examining it. "What were these doodads doing in Minnesota?"

"The navy had a couple o' carriers on Lake Michigan to use for qualifications during World War Two," Scotty explained. "They were the *Wolverine* and *Sable* that had been converted from a couple of Great Lakes cruise ships. These were left over from the program."

Now the other aviators gathered around to check out the devices. Ariel Goldberg looked into the crate. "*Gants goot!* It's a good thing you remembered these things, Chief."

"Yeah," Junior Stump said. "We'd've looked real stupid out there if there was no way to launch us."

"You could still take off," Scotty told him. "You would have to start out at the stern, lock your brakes, and rev the engines, then release and go like hell down the flight deck. With the vessel turned into the wind, those Avengers with flaps down would be flying before you were halfway down the length of these modern carriers."

"It'd be quicker using the catapult," Westy Fields pointed out.

"Yeah," Monger said, "not to mention you'd be in ever'-body's way during takeoff operations."

"Points well taken," Scotty said. "So I suggest you transport these with you. We have no use for them in our air shows."

Monger had gone back to the keg. "C'mon, people! Are we gonna have a party or what?"

Everyone impatiently lined up as the CPO finished installing the keg taps. It was a hot night, and the beer was cold.

Erickson made a wide turn to port, heading into the race-track area off the carrier's beam. After going three-quarters of a mile past the stern, he turned in for a landing approach. The LSO's lights invited him to come in, and he came down smoothly on the flight deck, snagging the second arresting wire. By then Westy was in the air, and Ariel's Avenger was hooked to the catapult shuttle, ready to be hurled skyward.

Pusan, South Korea
23 July
2000 Hours

A heavy fog had settled in the harbor area of the city as the taxi eased down the street toward Gate 3 of the cargo docks. The headlights reflected off the heavy floating droplets of moisture, making it difficult for the driver to see. His destination suddenly loomed up, and he had to brake to a stop. The passengers in the back—Gerald Fagin and Lars Stensland—almost slid off the seat.

The driver was apologetic. "*Choesong hamnida!* I am sorry."

"Perfectly all right," Fagin assured him, taking out his wallet. To show his pardon was sincere, he gave the man a good tip.

"Oh, thank you very much," the cabbie said. "I wish for you a happy voyage."

The passengers got out, taking their roll-along luggage with them. The taxi slowly turned around for the return trip downtown as they walked up to the gate that offered entrance to the dock area. A pair of grim-faced guards of the *Hangu* Police dully watched their approach. The law enforcement unit was responsible for area security, and Fagin knew these were tough guys well-trained in not only firearms but who also had earned black belts in the Korean forms of karate.

The policemen held out their hands to indicate they wanted to look at ID papers. Fagin and Stensland produced their passports, shipping papers, and merchant marine officer tickets showing the Norwegian was a captain and the American a deck officer. All had the proper photographs and seals. After the documents were given a thorough scrutiny, they were directed toward the door of a nearby building. The two, deep in their cover as merchant marine officers, went to the indicated place where their luggage was given a complete inspection. Since they were the only visitors, the police had plenty of time to leisurely poke through their belongings, emphasising their suspicions with occasional frowns at the two round-eyes. When that was done, the Occidentals were once more pointed in the direction they were to go. This time they stepped out of the building and straight into the wharf area itself.

"I almost forgot where the *Buenaventura* was docked," Fagin said, a bit irritated after the minute inspection of his bag.

"Number twenty-three," Stensland said. The number was etched in the stone of his orderly Scandinavian mind.

They didn't have far to go, since Gate 3 was just in front of Dock Ten. They walked the hundred meters down the line of other moored vessels until coming to the slip where the ship was tied up. Stensland paused and gave the *Buenaventura* a close look. This made Fagin feel an absolute amateur. He had never served at sea, and here he was paired up with a professional merchant marine officer who was silently making a study of what was to be their home for the next several weeks. All Fagin saw was a generally sloppy-looking civilian freighter with some streaks of rust.

"She is a good ship," Stensland announced.

"Then let's go aboard," Fagin suggested.

A man standing on deck at the gangplank leaned against the railing. He was a muscular Oriental with a friendly, open expression on his face. "Where you gentlemen bound to?" he asked.

Fagin completed the challenge and password process by answering, "Yesteryear."

The man laughed and offered his hand. "I'm beginning to feel that this is more of a time machine than a ship. My name is Steve Wang."

"Gerald Fagin here. This is our captain, Lars Stensland."

"As I understand it," Wang said to Fagin, "you're in

overall command while Stensland runs the ship, and I'm in charge of the combat teams."

"Correct," Fagin said.

Stensland asked, "Are we ready to get under way?"

Wang shrugged. "The navy guys that were here said everything was ready. But don't ask me. I'm army."

"Army?" Fagin asked, surprised.

"Let's get you guys settled in, and I'll explain this setup to you," Wang said. In actuality, he was one of an interservice group assigned to Admiral Paulsen's SPECOPS organization. He looked at Stensland. "I understand you're a real ship's officer."

"I am," Stensland said, feeling as unsettled about a soldier being in on the operation as Fagin.

They went from the deck up the ladder to the bridge. Wang led them down the passageway to the officers' cabins. Fagin wanted to get the scoop on the ship's setup before making himself comfortable. "Let's settle in my cabin for a talk. I'm a commander, U.S. Navy."

"Lieutenant colonel, Special Forces," Wang said.

"Tell us about the crew," Fagin said, wanting to get directly to the point.

"They're all Americans," Wang said. "Multiracial in the right mix to appear as a typical merchant ship crew. The guys are Filipinos, Arabic, and a mixture of Chinese and Japanese. We're all fluent in the languages of our ancestries. I speak Cantonese."

"Are they all Green Berets, too?" Fagin asked.

"Some are, but just about every American branch of service and intel agency is represented," Wang explained.

Fagin frowned. "Aren't there any Force Recon or SEALs on the ship? They'd come in handy when we have to board a raider vessel."

"Force Recon and SEALs are like Army Rangers," Wang said. "They are primarily raiders. Hit, kick ass, and exfiltrate. Paulsen chose us on an individual basis because of our abilities to stay in an area and blend in with the native population for long periods of time. Obviously, this is breaking every known rule of the Geneva Convention. The admiral decided Operation Yesteryear needed a crew that could pass as not being American."

Stensland appreciated the logic behind the organization. "That will come in handy if things go wrong and we are taken prisoner. We will all be interrogated. The Japanese who captured my ship were very thorough."

"I understand you were caught by the bad guys," Wang said.

"Yes. I can teach the men what to expect if the raiders take over the ship."

"Let's hope that doesn't happen," Wang said. "And I don't expect it to. My people are experienced in combat. Some of the Arabic guys are Moslems who served in Afghanistan. We have a strong dislike about becoming prisoners. If the bad guys figure out who we really are, then a very unpleasant situation quickly develops."

"Understood," Fagin said. "It appears we have to work out an SOP on how to handle ourselves when trouble starts."

"It's already worked out," Wang said. "That's my job as the combat leader. I'll bring you guys up to date. Meantime, we're going to have to get ready to get under way. There're enough seamen among the spooks to handle the job with the right officer in charge." He winked at Stensland. "That'd be you, Captain."

"I am told we sail at 0400," Stensland said.

"That's in about seven and a half hours," Wang said. "This would be a good time for you to meet the crew."

"Then let's get to it," Fagin said, stinging a bit about not being considered a ship's officer.

"Aye, aye, sir," Wang said. He laughed. "Isn't that what you're supposed to say?"

Fagin didn't appreciate the humor.

CHAPTER FIFTEEN

Yoiummei, Japan
23 July
0800 Hours

The *suiraitei* boat rounded the outcrop of rocks extending from the shore, then turned in toward the small harbor that served the fishing village. The vessel's arrival was expected, and the community's headman along with four husky young fishermen stood at the dock, eagerly waiting. Kiyoe Yamata, a member of the Kaigun Samurai *jun-i* class, was a bit past middle age. He had dressed in his best suit to greet the venerable guests who had been passed into his care by his superiors on Kakureta Island.

The boat's motor slowed to a dull throbbing and was reversed as it drew alongside the dock. Two crewmen, one in the bow and the other in the stern, tossed lines to the fishermen, who deftly caught them. They secured the small vessel with quick wraps of the lines around the pilings. At the exact moment the engine was cut, Yamata jumped aboard. The captain greeted him with a bow, then led him down into the crew quarters.

Gomme and Hikui Zunsuno looked up as the headman entered the small cabin. He bowed politely to them.

"Ohayo gozaimasu," he greeted. "I welcome my honored guests to our humble village."

"Arigato," Hikui said. "Please forgive my husband if he does not speak. He is very weak from his illness and the voyage from Kakureta."

"I understand," Yamata said. "I have brought four strong men with me. Shall I have them lift him to the dock?"

"Yes," Hikui said. "It will be good for him to get off the boat."

Yamata turned and barked some orders. Immediately the four fishermen appeared through the door. They easily lifted Gomme and his wheelchair and took him out on the deck before gently placing him up on the dock. Two of them went back to get the luggage, while the remainder aided Hikui to disembark.

With that taken care of, the procession headed off the dock and into the village. The entire population was turned out, lining the path, and they bowed politely as the old couple passed by. The short walk continued to a large house where Gomme was picked up yet again. This time he was carried inside, while Hikui followed with Yamata just behind her.

The interior of the dwelling, although sparsely furnished, was airy and clean. A Western-style bed sat in one corner. Within moments, Gomme was lifted from the wheelchair and gently placed on it. He lay back gratefully. Although his illness was feigned, the discomfort from the rough trip on the small boat was not. His old body was sore and tired from the buffeting, and he had been miserable with seasickness. Hikui, not any better off, was glad to be able to settle down on a wooden chair beside him. The piece of furniture did not offer a soft seat, but at least it wasn't rocking back and forth.

Two young women with trays appeared from another room. Tea and *ine* cakes were placed on a nearby table. Hikui gratefully took an offered cup of tea, but Gomme's stomach was still upset from the voyage he had endured for almost twenty-four hours.

Yamata treated the Zunsunos to another bow. "You will

stay here until the day after tomorrow. Arrangements have been made for Zunsuno-*san* to go to the hospital in Osaka. We trust his recovery will be comfortable and quick under the expert care of skilled physicians and surgeons."

"Thank you," Hikui said.

"We have seen that an apartment will be ready for you, Hikui-*san*," he said. "It is near the hospital. Also a driver has been arranged to take you there when you wish to visit your honorable husband."

"*Arigato,*" Hikui said. "You are most kind."

"I can see that you are both very tired," Yamata said. "If you require anything else, please do not hesitate to ask us. We are honored to serve you."

"My husband and I only desire to rest at this time," Hikui said.

"Of course," Yamata said. "We shall withdraw and leave you alone."

After Yamata had taken himself and others from the room, Hikui leaned over and spoke softly to Gomme. "How are you feeling, *shujin*?"

He grinned weakly. "I have not been seasick since the journey from Japan to Kakureta. And that was sixty years ago."

"Let us hope there will be no return trip."

He sighed. "I do not know what we will do in the hospital, *kanai*. Eventually the doctors will discover I am not really ill."

"Do not forget our money," Hikui reminded him. "We will need much if we are to travel around."

"That will be difficult even with money," Gomme said. "We do not know this new Japan or how one buys train tickets."

"Whatever happens is in the hands of the God of Fortune."

"We are old, so we have had a long life," Gomme pointed out.

"But I want to find death in Japan, not on that awful island," Hikui said sadly.

"Let us hope our Karma will be kind to us."

Hyatt Regency Hotel
Osaka, Japan
1800 Hours

Pamela Drake's outstanding career had netted her an exalted status in the world of journalism. Her accomplishments made her a celebrity, and as such she went first-class wherever she traveled. The bills she ran up at hotels, restaurants, and airlines were readily accepted by her employers, who knew better than to expect a detailed accounting from the prima donna reporter.

Her room in the hotel was a Hyatt Regency Club accommodation made up of a luxurious suite of rooms along with the preferential service she always expected when on the road. Now, relaxing in the living room with a bottle of mineral water after a sauna and massage, she waited for the arrival of her caller, who had just telephoned from the lobby.

Lieutenant Junior Grade Wilma Dietrich had been a student at the Naval Academy when she first met Pamela. Wilma had been detached from duty during one summer to serve as a journalist intern at the television network where the older woman worked. Wilma was disciplined, not pretty but intelligent, did not talk back, and took suggestions as if they were gospel. This made her the perfect piece of clay for Pamela to mold into her own image. She designed an ad hoc program for Wilma that included exposure to proper writing, presentation, makeup, and fashion.

Wilma was assigned as an aide on various in-house projects that Pamela had already written and filmed. These were specials to be included in the hour-long evening news show broadcast Monday through Friday on the network. Pamela always did her own tape editing because she didn't trust the staff to get her stories across in the right way. When she introduced Wilma to this very difficult art, the young woman showed an innate talent in piecing segments together for the best presentation. Her expertise increased to the point that Pamela trusted her to edit a presentation on runaway children in New York City. It wasn't absolutely perfect in Pamela's eyes, but it was good enough to be considered as a nomination for a local news Emmy. Unfortunately, it didn't win, but Wilma's potential was definitely out there for everyone to see.

Pamela tried to talk her into leaving Annapolis and come to work for her in TV news. But Wilma's heart was set on a naval career, and she returned to Annapolis to finish the grind for a commission in the rank of ensign.

The knock on the hotel room door broke into Pamela's reverie. She set the mineral water down and went to answer the summons. Wilma Dietrich stood there in the hallway with a wide smile. The two women embraced, and Pamela led her into the room.

"Wow!" Wilma exclaimed. "This is ritzy!"

"I tried to talk you out of the navy, remember?" Pamela remarked, noting that Wilma had put on a bit of weight since she last saw her. It was also obvious she had forgotten everything she'd been taught about makeup and fashion. Wilma had returned to being a dowdy young lady. Pamela thought it might be the uniform. In the fashion-sensitive reporter's opinion, there was nothing more unflattering to a woman than military attire. "You should have listened to me. I told you I'd have you hired straightaway into the big time."

"Yes," Wilma said. "And I was really flattered, but I think the career choice I made was the right one for me. And I'm also flattered at being invited to dine with you this evening."

"I hope you don't mind if we order in room service," Pamela said. "I'm here in a semi-incognito mode. Also, I have some rather pertinent questions to ask you."

"You're working on a story, right?"

"I can't deny that," Pamela said.

"I'll be happy to help you out if I can," Wilma said. "I've used everything you taught me to great advantage in the navy. I did a stint as host of a half-hour TV armed forces program that was broadcast on Sunday mornings in San Diego. Of course it aired at five a.m."

Pamela almost shuddered at the thought of that gig compared with what Wilma could have had in the way of a career in broadcast journalism. She sighed, asking, "Shall we peruse the room service menu? And don't deny yourself anything. This is all on my boss's dime."

Pamela settled for a baked Pacific salmon dinner while Wilma chose the steak and shrimp. They decided to split a chocolate mousse dessert as well as share a carafe of Sauvignon Blanc wine. After the order was phoned in, they had cocktails from the suite's courtesy bar while Wilma brought Pamela up to date on her career. It was painful for the journalist to listen to what she considered a tale of wasted potential. When the young officer brought up the subject of her boss, Pamela interrupted with a flash of temper.

"Why in the hell is that guy in the navy?" she asked.

Wilma, surprised, stammered, "Well—uh—I guess it's what he wanted."

"The guy is in public relations, for God's sake!" Pamela said. "If he wants to wear a uniform, he ought to do something like go to sea, fly an airplane, be a SEAL or a marine. He's doing a civilian job! Doesn't he feel stupid with epaulets on his shoulders that don't mean shit?"

Wilma shrugged. "You might say the same thing about me."

Pamela calmed down. "He's a man, honey. He could reasonably hope to be an admiral someday." She forced a laugh, afraid she might have offended this potential source of news. "Oh, don't mind me. I just get crazy thoughts in my head now and then."

"I know it's hard for you to understand," Wilma said. "But I'm doing the job I've always wanted. And serving my country at the same time."

"I know, honey," Pamela said, still thinking the younger woman had made a poor choice.

When the meals arrived and were laid out in the dining area, the two settled down to a pleasant repast. Pamela purposely kept the conversation light, asking questions about Wilma's job as if she really gave a damn, knowing the young woman liked to talk about her varied duties and the problems she faced with the media. When the final bite of the mousse was shared, they finished off the wine and went back to the living room. Pamela mixed a couple of more cocktails, and they sat down.

Wilma took a sip of her vodka tonic. "Pam, you said there was something I might be able to help you with."

"Yes," Pamela replied. "There most definitely is. And, don't worry; it has nothing to do with classified information."

"If it did, I would be totally useless to you," Wilma said. "The Public Relations Department is the last place the navy confides its deepest, darkest secrets."

"What I'm after is actually a merchant marine matter," Pamela said. "Civilian stuff, y'know? I've been told by a most reliable source that cargo vessels are being stopped on the high seas, then held for ransom. Actually, this has been happening in the East China Sea, very close to here. Have you heard anything?"

"No," Wilma said. "But I have a friend in intelligence who might be able to help out as long as it doesn't concern national security. His office keeps tabs on current events in its assigned area. That would include the East China Sea. He might have read some reports or something."

"I would appreciate it if you would look into it for me," Pamela said. "Frankly, you're my only hope. Nobody in Washington is talking, and all I have are bits of information that are not general knowledge."

Wilma frowned in puzzlement. "You mean ships have been captured at sea and held for ransom without making the news?"

"I mean exactly that."

"Pam, dear, you have one hell of a problem, don't you?"

Pamela smiled wryly. "Thanks for reminding me." She stood up. "Care for another drink?"

"Why not? The evening is young."

Kakureta Island
The Shogun's Residence
2300 Hours

Hara-*sama* and his best friend Heideki Tanaka, now a rear admiral, sat in the *shagamu* position at the low table that held the sake cups and bottles. Both were dressed in the *mijikai* jackets and *fukuro* trousers of ancient Japan. Additionally, the shogun had the top of his head shaved and the remaining hair drawn up into a topknot in the feudal style of samurai noblemen from centuries past. Tanaka, because of his duties, had his hair cut as per regulations of the Imperial Navy.

Hara-*sama,* slightly intoxicated from several cups of the rice wine, spoke approvingly, saying, "I commend your decision to eliminate the crew of the troublesome freighter."

"I am pleased that you do," Tanaka said. "I felt I was following your orders on how to deal with a stubborn captain who would not obey commands to bring his vessel to a stop."

"One must admire the fellow," the shogun said. "He resisted capture unto death."

"The reason his ship sank was that he continued under power until it had sustained so many hits of our cannon that it could no longer stay afloat," Tanaka said. "I myself witnessed him on the signal bridge, actually firing a pistol at the *Hayaken* until he was riddled by machine gun bullets."

"A noble death," the shogun commented. "How unfortunate for him that he was not Japanese. The gods of *senso* would have honored his soul."

"Ah! But his crew did not share his courage," Tanaka said. "They had already taken to the lifeboats. Naturally we did not wish to ransom them without a ship and cargo. Hardly a fitting transaction for the Imperial Navy. Thus, they had to die."

"As I have said both privately and publicly," the shogun said, "your decision was the correct one."

"Our agents in Japan report that no news of the freighter's loss has been on television or in print," Tanaka said. "Thus, everything worked out well, as it always will when orders are obeyed without hesitation or question."

"*Hei!*" the shogun agreed. "What is our tactical situation now?"

"The *Hayaken* is in port for resupply," Tanaka reported. "The crew will be given liberty." He laughed. "The comfort girls will be busy all through this night."

The shogun smiled. "Our lads must be able to relax properly." He took another deep sip of sake. "What ship will go out on operations?"

"The destroyer *Chujitsuna* sails at dawn tomorrow," Tanaka said. "The captain is Ichino Montonishi."

"A magnificent officer!" the shogun exclaimed in approval. "I feel sorry for any ship that dares to defy him. The fury of his personal courage and fighting spirit is unlimited."

"He is a *shishi*—a lion!"

The shogun raised his cup. "A toast to Montonishi-*san!*" They downed the sake and poured refills. "And another toast to our honored old scientist Gomme Zunsuno, who now suffers from the effects of old age and ill health!"

"May he recover and live long!" Tanaka added.

The shogun poured the last of the sake from the bottle. A maid, discreetly sitting in the corner of the room, rose to her feet and padded across the mats to replace it with a full one.

Hyatt Regency Hotel
Osaka, Japan
24 July
1800 Hours

Pamela Drake and Wilma Dietrich stood on the hotel's veranda that looked out over the nearby business complex. The early evening was warm, and both wore comfortable sleeveless blouses. Pamela had donned shorts and sandals,

while Wilma, having to come by taxi across town, sported
slacks and open-toed shoes that did not go with the rest of
the ensemble. She had arrived a quarter of an hour earlier
and called from the lobby for Pamela to join her downstairs. They had gone to the veranda for privacy as soon as
the older woman stepped off the elevator.

Wilma glanced around. "I don't like to discuss things
such as this on the telephone. We've been warned that
Japan is swarming with all sorts of intelligence agents who
are unfriendly toward the U.S."

"No surprise about that," Pamela commented. "I assume you found out something."

"Yes and no," Wilma said. "I met with my friend from
intelligence, and he tells me that he has absolutely no information regarding lost ships and cargo out on the East
China Sea."

Pamela was disappointed. "Then you found out nothing."

"There was a little something," Wilma said. "Some very
unusual activity has been going on in this area. A combat
support ship arrived from North Island in California on
nineteen July. It off-loaded some vintage World War Two
aircraft that were trucked to the airfield. And some strangers
who had been quartered at the BOQ went out to the ship.
The vessel sailed out to the west at the same time those old
airplanes flew off in the same direction."

"Your intelligence friend took notice of all that?"

"Yes," Wilma said. "They have journals in which
everything—and I mean *every*thing—that happens is jotted
down with times and dates. Nothing is trivial enough not to
be listed."

"Mmm," Pamela mused. "And all that activity moved
out westward." She thought a moment. "That's the direction of the East China Sea where all this pirate stuff is supposed to be going down."

"Right," Wilma said.

"And who's out there on the East China Sea?"

"The only outfit I know about is the Fourteenth Carrier
Battle Group," Wilma answered.

"Oh, my God! That's the *USS Jefferson!*" Pamela said.

"There was a big air battle out there, too," Wilma reminded her. "But it was to the north on the Sea of Japan. That was the one where some rogue North Korean officers ordered an attack on the *USS Lincoln.*"

"I'll bet this has something to do with that," Pamela said. "It could be that the North Koreans are up to more mischief. They're crazy enough to try a bit of piracy." She turned toward the entrance to the hotel. "Excuse me, Wilma. I have to make a phone call right now."

"Are you going to get in touch with your newspaper?"

"Hell, no!" Pamela exclaimed. "I'm canceling my flight back to the States. There is a story here, and I'm going to dig it out, even if it's buried under tons of official bureaucratic navy bullshit!"

CHAPTER SIXTEEN

SS Buenaventura
East China Sea
25 July
0300 Hours

Lars Stensland had taken over the bridge for the midwatch and now had an hour to go before Commander Gerald Fagin relieved him for the morning watch. Normally Stensland would not be pulling such duties as the ship's captain, but a shortage of qualified officers aboard made it imperative that he share the watch bill with them. Only one other seagoing naval officer was assigned to the vessel. This was Lieutenant Frank Larcos, a Filipino American who spoke fluent Tagalog. His normal duty assignment was aboard the missile destroyer *USS Terral* of the Fourteenth Carrier Battle Group.

Fagin had moved easily into the sea routine of the ship in spite of his many years ashore in technical and scientific intelligence. His education at Annapolis had prepared him for shipboard life, and he understood all that was expected of him. The hours the middies spent learning the proper techniques of handling sailboats ingrained seagoing skills in them that would never fade. However, it also proved very beneficial that the small cadre of professional sailors

aboard took care of the actual running of the ship, and if
Fagin was a bit slow or made a questionable decision, they
would offer advice. These corrections were made most respectfully since the man held the rank of commander,
USN. The most important thing for Fagin was to be ready
to make a quick reaction in the case of being overhauled by
that mysterious raider. He was tasked with supervising
launching the directional buoy that would broadcast its
location to the *USS Jefferson*.

The *Buenaventura*'s work routines evolved quickly and efficiently in spite of the crew being diverse and for the most
part not acquainted with each other. The sailors' duties
were not that much different from normal shipboard activities, except that they had no set destination or course to
follow. Their voyaging consisted of moving back and forth
across the East China Sea, doing their best to go into
harm's way. Other than that, the ship and her equipment
still had to be operated and maintained normally to stay
under way.

Lieutenant Colonel Steve Wang and his attack detachment had little to do other than remain alert and fully prepared to engage the enemy. But this action would not start
until the raider vessel had been pounded to a standstill by
the Avenger aircraft. Wang was not authorized to execute
his assault until cleared by Commander Fagin or Lieutenant Larcos. The Special Forces officer had been more
than a little disenchanted by that order, arguing that he was
capable of determining when the raider was a listing hulk.
It had been Lieutenant Larcos who pointed out to the army
officer that if he erred in the timing of boarding, and began
it prematurely before the raider was adequately disabled,
the bad guys would be warned of the true situation they
faced. If that happened, they would simply draw off and
blast the unarmed *Buenaventura* into bits of scrap metal.
The merchant vessel carried no ordnance and could not defend herself, and the weaponry of Wang's men was no
match for the warship's big guns. Any shelling by the enemy would send the merchant vessel and all her crew to

the bottom within a matter of only minutes. After being presented with those tactical facts, Wang agreed it would be a good idea to leave the timing of his boarding attack to qualified naval officers.

The success of taking over the raider ship also depended heavily on Commander Gene Erickson and his people. If the pilots attacking in the old World War II torpedo bombers failed to disable the enemy, then the *Buenaventura* would be compromised. In that case, the weaponry and equipment of Wang and his men would remain hidden in the cargo containers while everyone aboard went into captivity. They would not only be under the control of this unknown Japanese raider navy but also hidden from sight by the unknown stealth force field used by the bad guys. Wang estimated that they could maintain their safe covers for no more than a month before the plot would start to unravel. Once the raiders discovered they had captured a boatload of intelligence and special warfare people, they would turn particularly nasty. The lieutenant colonel summed up what their reaction would be in two words: "Mass execution."

Stensland yawned and stretched, then glanced over at the two men who shared his dark, lonely watch that night. One was a radar operator and the other a modern version of a helmsman, which meant he monitored the autopilot and checked the ship's actual position from time to time via the navigational instrumentation. Their faces showed in the dim lights of the bridge instruments that gave their features an eerie appearance. Stensland grinned as he recalled this was the way Oriental villains were pictured in old movies on late-night TV.

Harry Chin, the electronics warfare technician first class who stood the radar watch, suddenly called out, "I've got a blip, sir. Whoops! It's gone."

"How far out was she?" Stensland asked.

"Twenty nautical miles," Chin replied.

Stensland joined him to gaze down at the green cathode-ray tube mounted in the control console. It was blank, but an instant later the blip reappeared for a moment, showing it had moved a bit closer to the *Buenaventura*.

"Now that's some weird shit," Chin remarked. "He's going in and out of view."

"He's working out an interception course," Stensland said. "His own radar gets jumbled up by that technology, and he has to turn off the force field to get a reading on us. As soon as he's worked out a course and is sure he can catch us, he'll disappear completely."

"I'd say he's sure now," Chin said. "He's clicked off."

"Keep monitoring your scope," Stensland said. He looked over at the navigator. "Set a course of two-seven-zero and maintain a speed of twelve knots. Do not alter a thing. We want to make it very easy for him to catch us."

"Aye, aye, sir."

Stensland checked his watch, deciding to wait awhile longer before signaling general quarters.

Destroyer Chujitsuna

Captain Ichino Montonishi came onto the bridge, his puffy eyes giving evidence of having just been awakened. The watch officer saluted briskly. "Sir! We have made contact with a vessel traveling a course of two-seven-zero. Speed twelve knots."

"*Sugureta!*" Montonishi said with approval. "How much time until we catch him?"

"Approximately three and a half hours," the watch officer reported. "It depends on how he maintains his course and speed."

"Very well," Montonishi said. "Turn off the Kamisaku every half hour to check our progress."

"*Hei!*" the watch officer said to acknowledge the order. "Shall I sound general quarters, *Taisa-san*?"

"*Iie,*" Montonishi said, shaking his head. "Let's let our lads have another hour of sleep. They're going to be quite busy this morning."

Hyatt Regency Hotel
Osaka, Japan

Pamela Drake stared up at the ceiling above her bed. She had been lying there over three hours in a sleepless, agitated state. The one situation that made her angrier than anything else was being frustrated. And at that very wakeful moment in the darkness of the hotel room, Pamela was very frustrated. This emotional agitation was compounded by a feeling of having been foiled and stymied. This wasn't the first time she had hit a blank wall, but she had always been able to regain complete control of the situation or people involved. In this instance, however, it appeared as if this was one barrier that she wouldn't be able to knock down.

Things started out smoothly enough when Lyle Nelson informed her of the people she now referred to in her notes as the Raiders of the East China Sea. After John Tshek not only substantiated the story but added a couple of more tidbits, it appeared she was on her way to another Pulitzer prize in journalism. Here was a staggering situation made to order when it came to earning professional kudos. Things looked even better after she reconnected with Lieutenant Wilma Dietrich. Pamela was convinced she was heading for what could very well be the apogee of not only her entire career, but a triumph of the Fourth Estate that would not be eclipsed in the entirety of the twenty-first century.

But now the glow of glory had faded to the blackness of defeat. Wilma was no longer returning her calls. That meant the navy brass had gotten wind of Pamela's prying and had shut down her access to their activities. There was also the matter of the price Pamela was adding to her expense account. The suite was running twenty-five hundred dollars a day, room service meals cost another two hundred, and with the addition of saunas, massages, the beauty parlor, and the bar bill, Pamela was costing her boss over three thousand dollars every twenty-four hours. So far, counting this new day, her hotel bill added up to a staggering nine thousand dollars. If her humongous salary were included, the entire cost of the previous seventy-two hours was thirteen thousand two hundred seventy-three dollars. And, of course, her first-class round-trip airline ticket wasn't a small change item, either.

The bean counters in the financial department of the *Washington Herald-Telegraph* would be having kittens if she stuck to her guns and didn't return to America within a very short time. If that happened, the big story of the year would be how prima donna Pamela Drake was fired for wasting thousands of dollars on a useless gamble. It wouldn't matter that her presence on the newspaper had boosted circulation by 150 percent.

It was more than innate stubbornness and pride that kept Pamela Drake from going home. She knew there was a tremendous, consequential story within all that murkiness of secrecy. If she didn't bring it to light, the news would eventually come out at some future press conference conducted by a U.S. Navy public information officer. He or she would be the one who informed the world press of the extraordinary events that had occurred on the East China Sea. The story would be broadcast and published simultaneously on every TV station and newspaper over the entire world. No glory in that situation for Pamela Drake. But the lady now had to be realistic. She could only allow herself another forty-eight hours, then she had to return Stateside.

She groaned, knowing she couldn't sleep, and reached for the telephone to call down for room service.

SS Buenaventura
0610 Hours

The lookout on the signal deck swept his binoculars along the northern horizon as he had been doing for the previous hour and a half. His eyes burned from the intensity of the task, and the sailor cursed whatever strange machine it was that had made the radar ineffective.

He was using the same lookout methods that the ancient sailing navies had employed: scanning the surrounding sea by studying the physical features of the environment by eye.

A few more moments passed before he lowered the binoculars for just enough time to blink rapidly to generate some soothing tears. The instant he went back to his surveillance, he stiffened.

"Ship approaching! Bearing one-three-five!" he hollered loudly.

Lars Stensland displayed a half grin. "No surprise there. They have made a perfect intercept of our course."

"Are you sure it's them?" Gerald Fagin asked. When he showed up for the morning watch to relieve Stensland, the Norwegian had remained on the bridge because of the tactical situation.

Stensland turned the radio speaker up to full volume. "We shall see, my friend." He walked over and checked the radar, noting the screen was blank. There was no indication of an approaching vessel within visual range. "Ah, yes! It would seem that Operation Yesteryear is now entering its serious stage."

A few moments passed before an accented voice spoke in English over the communications system. "Attention the Panama ship! Attention the Panama ship! Heave to and prepare to be boarded."

Fagin nudged Stensland, saying, "I'm going to have the directional buoy cast off as quickly as possible."

As the American turned to the task, the Norwegian picked up the microphone. "This is the SS Buenaventura. Say again your last transmission, please."

"You must heave to immediately. Be prepared to receive boarders."

"I see no reason to comply with that order," Stensland said. "Identify yourself."

"This is a warning," came the reply. "You will obey, or we will fire on you."

"This is an outrage," Stensland said in his role as a merchant captain. "I insist you identify yourself. We are in international waters."

A few moments passed, and an explosion erupted from the water a hundred meters off the port bow. This was followed by the sound of the gun that fired the shell.

"We are not a warship," Stensland said, biding for time. "Why do you attack us?"

"Heave to, or the next shot will hit you," came the terse reply.

Fagin reappeared on the bridge. "The directional buoy is off and moving, submerged on a bearing of two-two-five."

"Very well," Stensland said. He turned to the helmsman. "Take a course of three-one-five."

The *Buenaventura* responded to her rudder, going forty-five degrees to starboard to put more distance between the buoy and the two ships. Belowdecks, Lieutenant Colonel Steve Wang and his two-dozen professional gunmen were on their feet, ready for the job ahead. Their faces were grim and set with the knowledge that combat was less than an hour away. All wore protective vests over their dungaree sailor garments. Kevlar helmets and ammunition pouches made up the rest of their outfits. Each carried an M-16A3 rifle with thirty-round banana clips. They were organized into two rifle teams of ten men each, while Wang and four others formed a command-and-support element.

"Team leaders report!" Wang called out.

"Alpha Team ready!"

"Bravo Team ready!"

"Move into position and hang tight," Wang ordered.

The Alphas went to the forward ladder of the compartment, mounting it until the first man was under the hatch. The Bravos took the same action at the aft ladder. Wang led his quartet of riflemen to the hatch located amidships. At his command, the entire group would burst up on the deck in one simultaneous maneuver.

No one had the slightest idea of what would happen after that.

USS Jefferson
Operation Yesteryear Ready Room
0645 Hours

"Scramble!"

The one word shouted through the door by Lieutenant Commander Gray Hollinger, the air operations officer of Operation Yesteryear, brought the Avenger crews to their feet. Commander Gene Erickson led his people through the door and down the passageways toward the ladders leading to the flight deck. The eight people, rigged out for air ops, kept the formation tight in spite of having to move as fast as possible past other crew members going about their normal duties. One small yeoman was sent sprawling when she bumped into Erickson, and the documents she had been carrying flew upward to float downward in a small paper storm.

"Well!" she exclaimed as she scrambled to her feet. "That was certainly rude and uncalled for!"

Short moments later, the Avenger Flight crews burst out from the island onto the deck and sprinted across to where their aircraft were warming up. Erickson and James Warrenton used their respective ingresses to get inside *Avenger 1* while the others did the same at their own aircraft. Erickson strapped himself in, then began taxiing down to the catapults for launch. Warrenton, now buckled in his seat in the bombardier's station, reached up and patted the nearest five hundred–pound bomb.

"Showtime, baby!" he yelled in a voice that was drowned out by the big Wright engine's roar. "Now you'll be able to strut your stuff big time!"

The catapult crews worked quickly in the tumult of the launch activity. In less than five minutes all four Avengers were off the deck and in the air. Erickson raised Westy Fields on the radio. "Where the hell are we going, Westy?"

Westy had already checked his directional instrumentation. "Make that a course of one-seven-two. We got two-zero-zero miles to go."

Erickson, his command behind him in trail, coordinated stick and rudder to get on the correct azimuth.

CHAPTER SEVENTEEN

Avenger Flight
East China Sea
25 July
0715 Hours

"Target in sight!"

Commander Gene Erickson could not hide the excitement in his voice as he communicated the news to the other Avengers flying in trail to his rear. This was the payoff for all that hard work and risk in preparing themselves and the aircraft for the coming moments of truth.

Erickson's adrenaline kicked in hard when he sighted both the *Buenaventura* and a destroyer side by side in the water a mile ahead. He reached down to his kit bag beside him to pull out the aerial photos supplied in the briefing. A quick check of the pictures made identifying the decoy ship easy. The warship lay some fifty meters off the *Buenaventura*'s starboard beam.

"Lay those eggs with care, guys," Erickson cautioned his pilots. "Those two ships are close enough that a stray bomb could damage them both." As soon as the other aircraft acknowledged his announcement, he spoke into the intercom to alert Ordnanceman James Warrenton. "This is it. How're you feeling?"

Warrenton's voice came back tinged with excitement. "Ready to kick ass, sir!"

Destroyer Chujitsuna

Commander Genjiro Tani, the executive officer, monitored the action of the merchant ship that was slowing dramatically in the water, its bow dipping slightly as it dug into the waves. A sound-power telephone man stood beside him, ready to relay any orders or messages he received. Tani was about to call for the lowering of boats for the boarding party when the telephone man suddenly shouted, "The watch reports aircraft approaching directly off the stern!"

Tani turned toward the rear of the ship and could see four shadowy shapes of aircraft bearing down on the *Chujitsuna*. He knew the stern antiaircraft guns were not manned at that time. There had been no reason to take precautions against any unexpected aerial attacks. The AA crews had been detailed to board the merchant ship, since the Kamisaku would protect their vessel from marauding aircraft. Tani rushed off the deck onto the bridge, where Captain Ichino Montonishi sat in his chair as his crew prepared to take over this latest victim.

"Taisa-san!" Tani said, saluting. "Four unknown aircraft are approaching us on the stern."

Montonishi's eyes opened wide in surprise. "An unexpected event, *Chusa-san.*" Then he abruptly laughed. "We are obviously not indicated on the aircraft's weapon or surveillance instruments. The pilots are no doubt going mad trying to figure out why what they see with their eyes is invisible to their avionics systems." He shrugged. "Nevertheless, order the boarding party to stand fast until we see how things are going to unfold in this situation."

Tani saluted again. *"Hei, Taisa-san!"*

Avenger Flight

Warrenton pulled the bomb bay handle, and the twin panels snapped open to offer a view of the ocean streaking past a couple of thousand feet below. "Bomb bay open!" he reported to Erickson as he reached over to the release lever that would ripple the ordnance out in a straight-line trajectory. "Ready for drop!"

Erickson went down to fifteen hundred feet, leveling off and lining up his flight path on the raider vessel on a stern-to-bow angle. He cut the throttle back to drop the speed to a hundred knots an hour. When the stern of the warship was just in front of his engine cowling, he spoke again to Warrenton. "Execute! Execute! Execute!"

The ordnanceman pushed the release lever and watched the bombs drop through the bay a second apart. Just as the fourth one went through the open space, Erickson banked the Avenger. The first bomb hit the water behind the stern of the raider ship, the second struck the stern waterline, and the third slammed into the vessel amidships. The fourth and final bomb hit the bow, blowing the foredeck open.

Destroyer **Chujitsuna**

Captain Montonishi was thrown from his chair to the deck as the *Chujitsuna* rocked from four rapid explosions. He got to his feet, noting that the others on the bridge had also been slammed around by the violent shocks and concussions of the detonations. He was about to issue orders when Tani reappeared from the signal deck, hatless and with a bleeding wound across his forehead. "They have bombed us, sir!"

"That is quite obvious, *Chusa-san*," the captain said impatiently. He turned to the helmsman. "Hard to starboard!"

The sailor turned the wheel, but it spun loosely around with all tension gone. "We do not have steerage, *Taisa-san!*"

Suddenly more explosions pounded the ship from stern to bow, sending her into a series of shuddering rocking motions. Eight more followed as the *Chujitsuna* began to list to port.

Avenger Flight

Erickson was now flying in the opposite direction of the attack. He glanced to his left to note that *Avenger 4,* with Lieutenant Junior Stump, had turned away after delivering his bomb load. The raider ship was now motionless in the water, her gun turrets ripped open and flames coming from several hatches. All that practice in Arizona had paid off handsomely.

Erickson made a sweeping turn to line up on the enemy's stern once more. He noticed the vessel seemed to be going in a slow, uncontrolled turn to starboard. He went down to a little under a thousand feet, leaning forward to sight through the gunsight stenciled on the front windshield of his cockpit. Even though the target vessel continued to turn slowly, this strafing run was as easy and satisfactory as the ones made on the junk cars in the cactus patch back at Scotty Ross's airport.

Lieutenant Westy Fields, in *Avenger 2,* could see the mass of sparks flying off the metal deck of the raider ship as Erickson made his run with both .50-caliber guns spitting the heavy cartridges at the target. Now Westy came in, flying low and slow as he squeezed the trigger on the joystick to send fire bursts across the length of the crippled target.

When Lieutenant Ariel Goldberg made his strafing run in *Avenger 3,* he noted the white figures of corpses in sailor uniforms strung out along the raider's decks on both the port and starboard sides. Down in the bombardier's station, Aviation Machinist Gianna Torino had gone aft to the unused rear gunner's position for a rearward glance at the battle. She could see the black columns of smoke beginning to boil out of the doomed ship as the old aircraft flew directly over the target. A brief sight of Junior Stump

coming in for his attack came into Gianna's view just as
Ariel turned to keep his place in the formation.

A new voice sounded in Erickson's earphones. "*Avenger
One,* this is Decoy. Over."

"This is *Avenger One,*" Erickson replied, knowing it
was the bridge of the *Buenaventura* raising him. "Over."

"Cease your attacks. We are going to begin our boarding operations. Over."

"Wilco, out," Erickson said. He flipped over to the flight
channel. "Avenger Flight, we're going into orbit. The guys
down there are going to jump on the bad guys' asses. Maintain the formation until further orders."

Jihi Hospital
Osaka, Japan
0800 Hours

Hikui Zunsuno gingerly opened the room door and took a
careful look out in the hall. The aged lady eased the door to
a half-closed position and walked across the room to the
bathroom. "*Hayakumasu*—hurry!" she urged her husband
who was inside, changing from his hospital gown into his
street clothing. She wore a traditional going-out kimono
that bore an attractive pink cherry blossom pattern across
the dark blue garment.

"I am ready, *kanai,*" Gomme Zunsuno said, stepping
out to join her. He was attired in the same rumpled suit and
hat he'd worn when he checked into the medical center the
day before. "Let us leave this place."

Hikui once more surveyed the hallway, then nodded a
signal of all clear as she stepped out of the room. "The elevator is to our left."

"I remember," he said with a nod.

They walked as nonchalantly as possible under the circumstances. Every nerve in their ancient bodies trembled
with anxiety as they approached the elevator landing where a
half-dozen other people waited. The elders used the special
license provided by their age to get to the front of the small

crowd. The other people, all polite Japanese, stepped back to allow them to stand directly in front of the door. The Zunsunos were not pulling age rank simply for convenience; they wanted the concealment provided by the other people.

Hikui turned and nodded politely to the young medical orderly at her side. He smiled and bowed. She looked back the other way, then grabbed Gomme by the arm. "Nurse-*san* is approaching."

Gomme looked out of the side of his eyes and caught sight of his personal nurse coming down the hall toward them. If she stopped to get on the elevator, their escape would end then and there. Both husband and wife instinctively lowered their gazes to the floor as if by turning their faces they would be hidden. A few seconds passed, and Hikui took a quick look to the left and saw the nurse's back as she turned down another hall. Luckily she wasn't on her way to Gomme's room. Since she wasn't due in to check on him until ten o'clock, they had a little less than two hours to disappear into this modern Japan they had already found confusing and noisy.

When the elevator arrived, the Zunsunos went to the back. The other people crowded in, giving the couple feelings of claustrophobia. They were not used to the close proximity of crowds after decades on Kakureta Island.

The conveyance continued down, making two more stops in which additional passengers crammed themselves into the small space. By the time they reached the lobby, Gomme and Hikui felt as if they were suffocating. They stepped out, grasping each other's hands as they took deep, calming breaths.

"We must get a taxi," Hikui said, glancing around. "Where is the door?"

"It is difficult to tell," Gomme said. "There are windows all around this place. Everything seems open, but I see no way out."

They walked toward the outer perimeter of the lobby, now desperate for an exit. Neither would feel safe until they had gotten out of the building and down the street. The flow of walking people seemed to move in one direction, and they discreetly followed after the crowd until reaching a door. They gave each other reassuring looks as they stepped outside. After continuing down a shallow flight of concrete steps, they were on the sidewalk, by the curb.

Gomme pointed to the right. "A line of automobiles, *kanai*. Perhaps there is a taxi among them."

"Hei!" she said hopefully.

They walked through the throng of people traveling to and fro in the area until reaching the first car in a line of four vehicles. A neatly dressed man wearing what appeared to be a chauffeur's cap noticed them. He bowed respectfully. "Do you have need of a taxi?"

"Hei," Gomme replied affirmatively.

The driver opened the door for them. They got into the back and settled on the seat. The interior of the cab was immaculate. "Ah!" Hikui exclaimed. *"Seiketsuna!* So clean!"

The driver got in. "Where do you wish to go?"

"A moment, *dozo,*" Gomme said. He reached into his inner jacket pocket and pulled out an account booklet to read the words on the front. "We would be pleased for you to take us to the Kogyo Branch of the National Nipponese Bank. Do you know where it is?"

"Hei!" the driver replied.

The cab ride took them from the center of Osaka out toward an industrial area on the south side of the city. The old people, remembering the Japan they knew in the pre–World War II years, were amazed at the changes in their native land. The younger people, many of whom were dressed outlandishly with garish hair arrangements, attracted most of their attention. Gomme smiled wryly and leaned close to his wife. "Could you imagine any of those young fellows in the Imperial Army or Navy?"

Hikui grimaced, whispering back, "I cannot imagine them anywhere except in a *hakkyo shita byoin*—an insane asylum!"

It took twenty minutes before the driver eased out of the heavy flow of traffic and pulled up at the curb. He motioned to the building to their direct left. "Here is the bank you wish."

Gomme paid the meter from the bundle of yen notes that had been provided them in the fishing village of Yoiummei. The driver opened the door and bowed deeply as they got out of his taxi. The couple walked up to the glass doors of the building, surprised by the guard inside who opened the portals for them. Once more they were treated to a bow, and the uniformed man asked, "May I direct you somewhere?"

"Yes, *dozo*," Gomme said. "We are here to make a withdrawal."

The guard pointed to a row of teller cages across the room. They walked over, entering a roped area where a line of some eight people had formed up to wait for their turns to see the tellers. As the oldsters joined the queue, the man to their direct front bowed and gestured for them to go ahead of him. The next customer, a lady, did the same. Within moments, they were at the head of the line. The couple didn't have long to wait before a teller was available. Gomme, grasping the account book, walked to the cage with Hikui following.

The teller was a pleasant-looking young lady dressed in a tasteful pants suit. Hikui thought she looked too masculine in her attire. She would have been more attractive with a traditional hairdo and kimono. The young woman smiled. "May I help you?"

"Yes, please," Gomme said. "We wish to make a withdrawal from our account."

"Of course," the teller said, taking a withdrawal slip from the forms on her desk. "How much do you wish?"

"One million yen, please," Gomme said.

"Yes. What is your account number?"

Gomme gave her the deposit book. "I think it must be in here someplace."

She looked at the document. "Oh, yes! Please excuse me. Our manager will want to personally handle a transaction of this amount."

Both Gomme and Hikui felt a flash of fear. Once more they grasped hands, wondering if they should have asked for much less.

The teller left her station and walked toward the rear of

the room where a secretary sat next to an office door. She handed the deposit book to the woman. "This is a transaction that must be handled by Kagawa-*san*. The deposit book bears the special chrysanthemum symbol."

The secretary took the book and went to the door, rapping lightly. She stepped inside, bowing to the middle-aged man behind a desk. "Excuse me, Kagawa-*san*," she said. "It is a special transaction brought by one of the tellers."

Michuro Kagawa looked up from the monthly reports he had been working on. When he glanced at the deposit book, his eyes opened wide for just an instant. He went to the door and opened it, motioning to the teller. "Who is the party wishing to make this withdrawal?"

The teller pointed to the pair of old people at her station. "There they are, Kagawa-*san*," she said.

"All right. Wait here."

Kagawa returned to the office and dismissed his secretary back to her desk. He sat down and studied the deposit book of Gomme and Hikui Zunsuno. The bank manager was a *hokannin,* one of the trusted outside agents of the Kaigun Samurai. He was among the few who had chosen to continue to serve the secret naval society after the majority of the agents had opted out of the arrangement.

The account belonging to the old people was one set up in their names by the officers of Kakureta Island. The only withdrawals from these accounts had been done by very special people who had been cleared ahead of time. He had received no word about anybody by the name of Zunsuno coming to Osaka to get money. He pressed the buzzer for his secretary. When she appeared, he spoke tersely. "Have the teller bring the old people into my office, please."

His first instinct was to refuse to hand over any funds. But that could lead to unpleasantness for him. The couple might kick up a fuss that would attract the police. In that case, the Kaigun Samurai officers would become angry with him for not honoring the request. On the other hand, they might even be angrier if he did. Of course there was fifteen million yen in the account, and they were withdrawing but one million of the total. He made up his mind to give them the money. His thoughts were interrupted by a knock on the door.

"Come in."

The secretary ushered in Gomme and Hikui Zunsuno, introducing them to Kagawa. He smiled and bade them sit down. "I do not believe you have been to our bank before."

"No, Kagawa-*san*," Gomme said.

"Are you visiting Osaka?" Kagawa asked.

"Yes. This is our first time."

Kagawa displayed a wide smile. "I am so pleased to welcome you to our city. Tell me, please. Where are you staying?"

Kikui replied, "We have not obtained rooms as of yet."

"Oh? May I recommend a hotel? It is very reasonable and in a good location," Kagawa said.

Gomme looked to Hikui, who nodded her assent. The old man said, "That would be most kind of you."

"The Anraku Hotel is near here," Kagawa said. "The bank would be most happy to provide transportation for you. We can send for your luggage as well."

Hikui thought fast, saying, "We have already made arrangements to have it delivered when we are settled."

"In that case, I can still have one of our drivers take you to the hotel," Kagawa said.

"That is most kind," Gomme said. "*Arigato*—thank you."

"Now!" Kagawa said. "Let's see about getting your money for you." He punched out some numbers on his phone, making a mental note to contact Kakureta Island as quickly as possible after the transaction.

Destroyer **Chujitsuna**
1000 Hours

The destroyer continued to drift slowly, making a languid circle away from the *Buenaventura*. The warship was a smoking hulk with corpses scattered across the decks. It had taken repeated poundings from the four Avenger aircraft in the form of sixteen bombs and some 2,600 rounds of .50-caliber machine gun fire during the aerial attack.

The boarding of the stricken vessel took place immediately after the aerial attack was called off. This had been a classical exercise under the command of Lieutenant Colonel Steve Wang. His command-and-control element provided covering fire while Alpha and Bravo Fire Teams went across the open space between the ships in motorized whaleboats. The return fire from the Japanese had been sporadic and mainly ineffective as spots of resistance were raked with volleys of 5.56-millimeter rounds from the M16A2 rifles used by the attackers. The range was short enough that they could leave their selectors set on fire bursts of three rounds. As soon as the Alphas and Bravos had climbed aboard the *Chujitsuna,* using grappling hooks thrown over the deck railings, Wang brought his support element over in the remaining whaleboat.

The boarders launched a two-prong attack, sweeping both outside decks before moving to the interior of the ship. The devastation they found shocked even the battle-hardened veteran warriors. The old Soviet destroyer had been deeply penetrated by the bombs, blowing holes and gashes into the bulkheads and decks while at the same time shredding and pulverizing her crew into charred, slashed hunks of meat barely resembling human beings. Pieces of corpses were in piles where waves of concussions had violently rolled them into the corners of compartments.

The last man to board the destroyer was Commander Gerald Fagin. He was glad of the hours he and Lars Stensland had spent pumping iron when he had to pull himself from the boat and up to the deck by rope. Fagin's task that day was to find the force field generator or whatever it was that the bad guys used to make themselves electronically invisible. When he arrived on deck, he could still hear the burps of three-round fire bursts. He contacted Steve Wang with the handheld radio and was advised to hold up until the entire ship had been cleared.

Commander Genjiro Tani, although badly wounded with his original head injury, now suffered from a ripped and dislocated left shoulder and a badly gashed upper thigh. The determined man managed to keep moving as he penetrated deeper into the bowels of the *Chujitsuna*. When he reached the third deck, he forced himself along in spite of the pain and extreme fatigue that was so intense it made him dizzy with near unconsciousness. When he reached his destination in the Kamisaku compartment, he stepped into the interior, almost falling down. The Kamisaku sat humming, while the technician, a thin, bespectacled youth from Dr. Zunsuno's department, sat curled up in one corner. Tani glared at him. "Get up! You must help me!"

The technician looked at the officer with a dazed expression on his face, not hearing the words yelled at him. The concussion from the explosions in the over decks had pounded his eardrums into bleeding, battered organs that were beyond medical help.

"I said get up!" Tani screamed so loud that it aggravated his wounds. "The enemy will be here soon!" When the technician continued to stare at him without comprehension, Tani pulled his Nambu pistol. He would have had to kill the man anyway, since the ship was lost, but he needed help in bringing about the vessel's full destruction. Unfortunately, the technician was beyond being useful. Tani aimed and shot the man three times in the head, blowing out one side of his skull.

Now Tani turned to the destruct button for the Kamisaku, unlocking it with a key he had brought with him. When the yellow light came on, he pushed the large black button underneath it. The red light next to it began blinking, indicating one minute before the explosives placed around and under the machine would detonate.

The officer went out into the passageway, going to a series of emergency lights that ran the length of the ship. Other triggers for explosive devices were located at each one. He began systematically unlocking and setting them as he staggered and stumbled from one to the other. He didn't get to all the destruct stations and abandoned any attempt to do so. Instead, he turned to a ladder that led below to the last deck. More antiarmor steel-cutting charges were located in that area. These would blast and burn through the bottom of the ship while blowing off the sea cocks.

Finally, the determined officer ran out of strength and consciousness. He sprawled to the deck, oblivious of his surroundings. A couple of seconds later, the explosives on the Kamisaku went off. This was followed by another series of detonations that blew holes and bulges in the ship's hull as blown sea cocks allowed thousands of gallons of sea water to gush into the interior of the vessel in simultaneous floods.

"Abandon ship!"

Gerald Fagin bellowed the order as well as speaking it continuously and rapidly into the radio. Wang's men had been knocked off their feet by the series of explosions from below that rolled and heaved the destroyer from side to side. It wasn't necessary to be a sailor to realize the vessel was in its death throes and would soon be slipping beneath the waves.

The men came up on deck and made an orderly descent down the ropes to the boats that were maneuvered into position by the coxswains. Fagin and Wang were the last ones down. The coxswains fired up the motors and turned toward the waiting *Buenaventura*.

Fagin turned around to watch the raider ship as it went down on an even keel. The infernal force field generator was going into the deep with it. For a moment he thought about getting an exact position from Lars Stensland to get a diving vessel out for a retrieval attempt. But he realized those explosives that destroyed the ship would also have been designed to blow the machine into unidentifiable pieces.

Fagin turned around and sat down beside Wang, muttering, "We're right back where we started."

Wang, who knew nothing of the force field, shrugged. "What the hell, Gerry! We sank the son of a bitch, didn't we? I think that means we won."

"It's what would be called a hollow victory."

CHAPTER EIGHTEEN

Anraku Hotel
Osaka, Japan
26 July
0700 Hours

Gomme and Hikui Zunsuno had awakened two hours earlier and now sat fully dressed in their small room. The oldsters had slept fitfully the night before, having been disturbed a bit past midnight by loud, drunken voices coming from the lobby downstairs. The noisy ruckus alarmed them, but it subsided after ten minutes.

Now they sat stiffly in two straight-backed wooden chairs placed next to the narrow window that looked out on a side street. The buildings within view were occupied by small stores that sold a variety of groceries consisting mostly of fish and vegetables. Early shoppers out for the freshest edibles went from place to place, carrying baskets to hold their purchases of poultry, fish, vegetables, and other items.

Hikui smiled wistfully. "The scene there reminds me a little of when I was a girl."

"I suppose there are still places where the simple life can be lived in Japan, *kanai*," Gomme said. "Even in a big city like Osaka."

"Are you hungry, *shujin*?" she asked.

"Not especially," he replied. "I suppose my stomach is too nervous for food." He chuckled lightly. "It should be. The rest of my body is very close to trembling with stark fear."

"The hospital people have undoubtedly discovered that we are gone."

Gomme nodded. "I wonder if they will inform Yamata-*san* in that little fishing village. If they do, he will send the news to Kakureta."

"If we are not careful, we will be quickly caught."

"And punished," Gomme added.

"If we are sent back to the island, we should act like we are old fools," Hikui suggested. "We can make them believe we have *korei*—senility, eh? Perhaps they will think our old age has made us confused and bewildered, *iie*?"

"That would be a logical defense," Gomme agreed. "But first, let us do our best not to be found. We must make contact with somebody who can help us."

"How can we go to the authorities?" she asked. "If we see the police and tell them we are from an unknown island, they will think we are *hakkyoshita*—crazy. Especially after we reveal the existence of the Kaigun Samurai."

"I know the exact location of Kakureta Island and can tell them," Gomme said. "I memorized it from some papers I saw many years before. It is the longitude and latitude."

"You mean those lines on maps you showed me once?"

"The very same," Gomme answered. "With that information they can go to the exact spot in the sea and find the island." He sighed. "But will the authorities take the trouble to search out a location given them by a silly chattering old man?"

"We also must run the risk of inadvertently making contact with a *hokannin*," Hikui said.

"I have been trying not to think of such an awful thing like that happening to us."

Hikui lowered her eyes. "I am ashamed, *shujin*. I must tell you that I am very afraid! It all seems so hopeless."

He leaned over and put his arm around this old woman he had loved for so many decades. "Do not fear, *kanai*. If our Karma is kind, we will be free to live out our final years in peace. If not—" He didn't finish the sentence.

Hikui was silent for a few moments before speaking again. "I think we should go out and get something to eat. I remember seeing a restaurant nearby."

"And there is a little park," Gomme said. "It was just down the street. We will feel better if we take a walk in the fresh air and look at flowers."

"It will clear our heads, and we will be able to form more lucid thoughts."

"Yes!" Gomme said. "At this moment I am so nervous I cannot think logically."

They stood up slowly, and Gomme got his hat.

USS Jefferson
Operation Yesteryear Ready Room
0745 Hours

The six men—Rear Admiral John Paulsen, commanding officer of Yesteryear; Lieutenant Commander Gray Hollinger, air operations; Commander Craig Davis, sea operations; Commander Gerald Fagin; Lieutenant Lars Stensland of the Norwegian Navy; and Commander Gene Erickson—sat sipping fresh, hot coffee. The mood in the room was somber.

Paulsen reached in his briefcase and pulled out several photographs. "Here are the photos of the raider ship taken from the bridge of the *Buenaventura*."

"I suppose these weren't taken with a digital camera," Fagin remarked.

"Just an old-fashioned model that uses film," Paulsen said. He handed the batch to Craig Davis. "Take a look at these before you pass them around. Tell us what we're looking at."

"Aye, aye, sir," Davis said. He studied each of the dozen photos. "This is a Russian—I should say *Soviet*—destroyer.

Krupny class. Outdated and old-fashioned in weaponry."

"I wonder how a bunch of godamned pirates got their hands on it," Paulsen wondered.

"They probably purchased the damned thing out of mothballs from the Russians," Davis opined. "But we won't be able to get that confirmed. The Russkies are really sensitive about the decline from their former glory. They're not going to want to discuss sales made by their poverty-stricken military."

"I doubt if the Russian government knows about it," Fagin said. "Most of those transactions are done by officers of the armed forces who are hard up for money. I'll bet it was some admiral making fifty bucks a month who sold that destroyer. He probably ended up with enough dough to buy a luxury dacha out in the country somewhere."

"The mystery behind this situation seems to have deepened," Paulsen complained. "I wish to hell we could have taken a couple of prisoners."

"When I debriefed Colonel Wang," Fagin said, "he told me the crew fought to the death. On several occasions he and his command witnessed suicides when the pirates fired their last bullets into their own brains."

"Just like the Arab suicide bombers, huh?" Erickson remarked.

"More like World War Two *kamikaze* fanatics," Fagin said.

Paulsen turned his attention to Erickson. "Give your people a well done, Commander. They knocked that ship down in nothing flat."

"All done by eyeball, sir," Erickson said proudly.

"We got to find their home port," the admiral said. He looked at Stensland. "Do you remember where they took you during your captivity, Lieutenant?"

"We spent all our time belowdecks, sir," Stensland said. "I am sure we were nowhere near land. I recall they put a machine on our deck in front of the bridge as quickly as they could after they captured the *Edvard Grieg*."

"I'm willing to bet dollars to donuts it was an extra force field generator used to mask their victims," Fagin suggested. "That way, both their ship and their captives' were invisible to curious radars."

"Well!" Paulsen said, standing up to stretch. "Our orders are to continue as before. The *Buenaventura* will go out again on decoy duty. Maybe if we have enough run-ins with the sons of bitches, we'll eventually end up with that infernal machine of theirs."

Fagin interjected, "Or at least enough of one to figure out how the damn things work."

"When do we go, sir?" Stensland asked.

"Your ship is being refueled, restocked, and re-everythinged even as we speak, Lieutenant Stensland. You'll be back out there by late this afternoon." He glanced around the small crowd. "Any questions? All right then. Dismissed."

Fagin and Stensland headed up to the flight deck for a helicopter ride over to the *Buenaventura*. The merchant ship was nearby, hooked by line and hose to the combat support ship *Wichita*.

Kimben Park
Osaka, Japan
1115 Hours

Pamela Drake strolled slowly along the walk that passed through an area of carefully cultivated hedges. She was dressed in a sleeveless white blouse, a wide cotton skirt decorated with a dull green and orange leaf pattern, and sandals. Her hand-tooled leather handbag was slung loosely across her shoulder by a wide strap. If she'd been back in Washington, she would have clutched the purse close to her, but here in Japan there was no reason to anticipate a purse snatcher.

Pamela had no reason to remain in her hotel suite. No calls were expected from informers or whistle-blowers; though she was surprised she hadn't heard from her boss at the *Herald-Telegraph* lately. But that was one man she did not want to talk with on the telephone. She would save her explanations of this money-wasting trip for a face-to-face confrontation. It was better to handle such sensitive subjects in person, when her flashing eyes were there to match the angry defiance in her voice.

She had decided to return to the States the next day. It had become obvious that the story she had pursued so diligently was buried deep under a military security blanket that even she could not penetrate. She had failed, been beaten actually, and it galled her more than she could stand.

Pamela came out of the hedges, continuing down to where a wide, clipped lawn was maintained. Benches were set at intervals along the pathway, and she noticed an old couple sitting on one as she approached. They were looking at her, and she decided to greet them, even if she didn't know any meaningful Japanese. Foreign languages were not Pamela Drake's forte.

"Good morning," she said with a half smile.

Gomme Zunsuno stood up and bowed. "Good morning. Are you American?"

Pamela reluctantly stopped to be polite. "Yes. I am an American."

"I attended schoor in your country."

"Schoor?" Pamela asked, confused.

"Actuarry, it was MIT," Gomme said.

Pamela realized he, like many Japanese, couldn't pronounce the letter *L*. "Where did you say you went to school?"

"MIT," Gomme repeated.

Pamela's eyes opened wide. "The Massachusetts Institute of Technology?"

"Yes," Gomme said. "This is my wife. Her name is Mrs. Zunsuno."

Hikui stood up. "I am preased to meet you."

"Oh!" Pamela said. "You speak English, too?"

"My considerate husband has taught me the rangridge over many years," Hikui explained.

"How nice," Pamela said, thinking the lady's problem with *L*s more than likely came from her husband's instruction.

"Ah!" Gomme said, not quite sure why he had spoken to the woman. "Are you here in Japan on horiday?"

"No," Pamela said, grinning as they continued to struggle with *L*s. "I am here on business."

"Oh!" Gomme said. "May I ask what is your business?"

Pamela felt like telling the little old guy that *her* business was none of *his* business, but she sort of liked the little couple. They were cute and charming. "I am a journalist."

"A journarist!" Gomme exclaimed.

Hikui was amazed. Here was a woman who did a man's job. A journalist! *Odoroku beki*—unbelievable!

Gomme turned to his wife, speaking rapidly in Japanese. Hikui kept nodding her head affirmatively. Gomme looked back at the American woman. "Can you assist us? We have knowredge that is of importance, but we do not know to whom we can speak."

Pamela knew a panhandler when she saw one, and decided she'd give them a couple of hundred yen to be rid of them. She was reaching for her handbag when she asked, "What sort of knowledge do you have?"

"It is about ships," Gomme said. "Ships that stop other ships. I speak of pirates."

Pamela's mouth opened wide, and she stared at them in such surprise that it frightened them. She quickly recovered. "May I invite you to my hotel suite for lunch?"

Gomme smiled and bowed. "Very nice. We are happy to accept your kind invitation."

Kakureta Island
27 July
0800 Hours

The castle of Hara-*sama,* shogun of the Kaigun Samurai, was more of a rambling frame house than a fortification. Hara-*sama* had it remodeled in the style of the old samurai palaces of ancient Japan, thus its purpose was more symbolic than pragmatic. In fact, the walls of this palace wouldn't stop a rifle bullet, much less heavy artillery. Another problem confronted in the construction was the up-turned cornices on the roof as was traditional in old Japan. The *jun-i* carpenters were not capable of constructing the features, and the problem was solved by creating a two-dimensional false front on the house, with the simulated cornices drawn, then cut out with coping saws.

The castle was not the only traditional item the shogun activated on Kakureta Island. Hara-*sama* set an example when he cut his hair in the ancient fashion, then continued the program by insisting on wearing traditional Japanese clothing. He issued an edict that all officers were to follow his example when ashore, and that included the wearing of two swords—the long *katana* and the shorter *wakizashi*—to show they were of the island's upper class, the true *samurai*. These new regulations did not affect the females of the population, since the island's original laws and traditions had dictated they dress in the old ways from the beginning.

Now Hara-*sama* sat in his throne room on the curved, backless chair from which he conducted his most important business. Rear Admiral Heideki Tanaka and Commander Gentaro Oyama, who had just been appointed the Kaigun Samurai intelligence officer, sat on the floor to the shogun's direct front. A sailor guard, armed with an Arisaka rifle circa World War II, sat by the door. He quickly looked up at the shogun's signal.

"Bring in Yamata-*san!*" Hara-*sama* ordered.

The sailor stood up, bowed, then opened the sliding door and stepped outside before closing it. Moments later it opened again, and the sailor led in Kiyoe Yamata, the headman of the Yoiummei fishing village on the mainland. He was dressed in a simple kimono and bore no swords. He walked up to a position in front of the shogun and knelt down in a deep bow with his head touching the floor.

"*Ohayo gozaimasu, Hara-sama!*" he greeted.

"*Konnichiwa,*" the shogun replied.

Yamata sat back up, his face twitching with nervousness. He had not been invited to the shogun's throne room for a social event. He lowered his gaze to the floor and waited to see what would happen.

"We have received your report that Gomme Zunsuno and his wife have gone missing," the shogun said. "What are the circumstances of their disappearance?"

"I arranged for a driver to take them to the medical center in Osaka," Yamata explained. "I accompanied them on the journey. When we arrived at our destination, I sent the driver inside to bring a nurse to aid them into the building."

"I see," the shogun said. "What was the old couple's physical appearance?"

"They seemed to be very weak," Yamata answered. "When they first arrived in Yoiummei, Dr. Zunsuno was pale and ill. I was alarmed enough that I delayed their journey to Osaka for twenty-four hours to give him a chance to rest from the sea voyage."

"Very commendable," the shogun said.

"*Arigato*—thank you, Hara-*sama!*"

"How was the doctor's wife?" the Shogun asked.

"She seemed old and frail but not ill, Hara-*sama*."

"What did you do after you accompanied them inside the hospital building?"

"I checked Dr. Zunsuno in as per arrangements I had made," Yamata said. "A small apartment in the medical center's visitor complex was made available for Mrs. Zunsuno. After a brief conversation with the attending physician, I returned to the car for the trip back to Yoiummei."

"When did you hear about their disappearance?"

"I received a phone call from the hospital administrator on July twenty-six," Yamata said. "I radioed a coded message here to Kakureta for instructions. The next day I received word to report here."

"What is your opinion of why the old people walked away?"

Yamata shrugged. "I am not an expert, Hara-*sama*, but they appeared confused. I think maybe they went out for a walk and became lost. I did not call the police because of security reasons."

"I agree with your reasoning," the shogun said. "You are

in no way at fault here, Yamata-*san*. I can find nothing wrong in the way you conducted yourself. You may return to Yoiummei at the first opportunity. You are dismissed."

The relief on Yamata's face was apparent as he bowed again, touching his forehead to the floor. He stood up, turned swiftly, and walked rapidly from the throne room, wanting to put distance between himself and what had been a very real potential of serious punishment.

The shogun waited until the man had left before speaking to the intelligence officer, Gentaro Oyama. "And now you know the old couple's exact location?"

"Yes, Hara-*sama*," Oyama answered. "Our communications net has forwarded me a message from one of the *hokannin*, who is the manager of the bank where they made a withdrawal from their account. He has had them taken to a small hotel called the Anraku in Osaka. They have a room on the second floor."

"What is your interpretation of this situation?"

"I believe the old people had a plan to run away," Oyama said. "Why else would they go to the bank and withdraw funds? That is a logical act done by clear-thinking people." He shrugged. "But they have never shown any indication of desiring to leave our society."

Admiral Tanaka spoke up. "Dr. Zunsuno is a scientific intellectual. His sort are unreliable. They invent systems of war, then have regrets later on. I do not think the doctor can be trusted."

"I agree, Hara-*sama*," Oyama interjected. "Even if they simply wish to return to life in Japan, they are a security risk. Old ones babble at times, and it would be foolish of us not to react to what would be a worst-case scenario."

"Mmm," the shogun said thoughtfully. "In truth, old Zunsuno's usefulness has faded away since the Kamisaku is fully operational." He gave the matter some more consideration, then stated, "Make arrangements to have them put to death. *Suguni*—immediately!"

Oyama stood up and bowed. "*Hei, Hara-sama!* The system to accomplish this is well in place." He left the room to attend to this most recent order.

Now the shogun looked at his old friend Heideki
Tanaka. "And there is the other problem, *iie*?"

"We have not had contact with the *Chujitsuna* for forty-
eight hours, Hara-*sama*," the admiral replied. "Something
is wrong."

"Has there been any mention of anything amiss in the
outside world press?"

Tanaka shook his head. "No, Hara-*sama*. And that has
brought to mind another thing that worries me. Commander Oyama says his intelligence organization has finally
noted that none of our captures have ever been mentioned
in the outside news media. It makes me think that a serious
clandestine campaign is being mounted against us."

"What about the ship *Dileas*?" the shogun asked. "Have
there been any discoveries of her dead crew?"

"Under the present circumstances I cannot answer that,
Hara-*sama*," Tanaka replied.

"Then I shall order a full state of war be declared in the
Kaigun Samurai," the Shogun said. "Every officer, sailor,
and ship will be called to duty to make sure all our resources are prepared for any eventual attack."

"*Hei, Hara-sama!*"

Osaka Naval Base
0930 Hours

Lieutenant Joel Weatherby pulled the van up to the curb in
front of the Public Relations building. He was a thin,
severe-looking man in his late twenties who considered his
desk job in naval intelligence as a divine calling to protect
his country. It was also a hell of a lot safer than serving in
the SEALs, Force Recon, or some other active combat
unit. Weatherby quickly exited the vehicle and hurried to
the door, stopping immediately at a desk occupied by a
journalist second class. Weatherby practically sneered at
the young man. He had nothing but contempt for those
fools who purposely broadcast information about the U.S.
Navy to the clodhopping public.

"Can I help you, sir?" the kid asked.

"I'm here to see Lieutenant Dietrich," he said impatiently.

"Go down the hall to the fourth door on the left," the kid said. "Her name is on it."

Weatherby hurried to the indicated place and found the door open. He stepped inside to see Wilma Dietrich behind her desk. A commander occupied a chair set at the far side of the wall.

"Hello, Joel," Wilma said. "This is my boss, Commander Lipton."

"How do you do, sir?" Weatherby said. "I'm here in regards to the phone call Lieutenant Dietrich made to me a few minutes ago." He dated Wilma from time to time, but not out of any romantic interest. He took her out to make subtle inquiries about her job to find out just what sort of information her office was giving out to the news media. It would be a real coup to catch public relations issuing classified or sensitive material. A report like that would look great in his OER.

"I'll let Wilma explain the situation to you," Lipton said. "I'm here in my capacity as the CO of this office."

Wilma pulled her phone closer to her. "Joel, are you familiar with Pamela Drake?"

"The journalist? Sure," he replied. "I recall that awhile back you said she was interested in navy operations on the East China Sea."

"Actually, she was interested in a particular aspect," Wilma said. "Anyhow, when I came in this morning, I found this message she left me on my answering machine."

She pressed the button, and the tape whirred a moment before Pamela's voice came on: "Wilma, this is one call you better return. I have discovered the full story on those raiders on the East China Sea. My contact knows who, where, and what is involved. I am ready to pass this on to the navy, but only under the following conditions. I wish to be the only journalist embedded with any forces taking action against the raiders. I also want to be allowed to publish the complete story in the *Washington*

Herald-Telegraph a full twenty-four hours before any official announcements are made. I'll be waiting for you to get back to me."

Weatherby's face reddened with anger. "Who the hell does she think she is? That bitch isn't going to dictate to the United States Navy! We'll have her arrested and force her to give us the information!"

Commander Lipton remained seated, glaring at Weatherby. He had disliked the young officer the moment he walked into the room. Lipton folded his arms across his chest and looked up at the intelligence officer. "Oh, yeah! That's a good idea. The taxpaying public can find out that a reporter dug out the full details on a classified operation. Pamela Drake will also tell them we had been unable to discover a single goddamn thing about a situation in which acts of piracy were being committed right under our noses. I would think that would cause a congressional hearing or two, don't you?"

Weatherby snarled, "She's breaking the law, goddamn it! And I intend to do something about it."

"Do me a favor, mister," the commander said. "See if you can get this hullabaloo moved to some other naval base. I don't want to have to try to put a damper on this public relations disaster you're about to create."

Weatherby started to sound off, but simmered down. After a moment, he said, "I have to report this to my commanding officer."

CHAPTER NINETEEN

Kimben Park
Osaka, Japan
0900 Hours

Pamela Drake sat on the park bench, looking down the sidewalk at the woman approaching her. The stranger was a Caucasian dressed in a stylish pants suit and carrying a briefcase. The closer the woman came, the more Pamela disliked her. When the stranger reached the bench, she came to an abrupt halt.

"Good morning, Ms. Drake."

"Good morning," Pamela replied, now spotting a couple of husky young men she had not noticed before. They had stopped at a bench ten yards away, sitting down in a manner that allowed them to keep both women in view.

"I am Captain Fontenac," the woman said. "I run the intelligence activities aboard the base here."

Pamela noted that Fontenac was a short, hard-bodied female with a few streaks of gray beginning to run through her short-cropped hair. Obviously the woman was not the type to be concerned with hair coloring for a more youthful appearance. Pamela guessed her companion to be a tad over forty. That made them about the same age, and she felt smug that she was more youthful in appearance.

Fontenac set her briefcase down. "Lieutenant Dietrich of Public Relations has given us the taped message you left on her phone."

"That was what I was told when they called me about meeting you here," Pamela said.

"We appreciate your cooperation."

"It seems there's some rather remarkable activity going on out there on the East China Sea," Pamela remarked.

"Naturally we're very curious about your source of information."

"I'm not surprised."

"Would you be kind enough to reveal the name or names to me now?" Fontenac asked.

"You evidently forgot I mentioned distinct conditions for such information," Pamela said. "I think we should discuss them right now."

"I'm afraid not."

"This is too lovely a morning to waste," Pamela said, getting to her feet. "Have a nice day, Captain Fontenac."

"Please sit down, Ms. Drake."

Pamela looked her straight in the eyes. "I'm in no mood for bullshit."

"Nor am I," Fontenac replied. "Sit down, Ms. Drake. Please."

Pamela complied. "The ball is in your court."

"You have become involved in a highly classified situation," Fontenac said. "National security is at stake here."

"I know what's at stake here," Pamela said. "Mysterious attacks on merchant shipping have occurred on the East China Sea. Crews and cargos have been held for ransom that has been paid. No mention of these crimes has been released to the media. That makes me think that the U.S. Navy's attempts to put a stop to the outrages have come to naught. Am I right so far?"

"I'll not answer that," Fontenac said, not really knowing the full story herself.

"I have come across information that will enable the navy to wrap up that little problem in a pretty package and tie it with a big red bow," Pamela said. "But—and I repeat myself—I have absolutely no intention of revealing that information until the terms I'm demanding are met. Understood?"

"You are breaking federal law, Ms. Drake," Fontenac said in a firm voice. "In fact, your reluctance to cooperate could bring about your prosecution under several of the new antiterrorist statutes that came on the books after nine/eleven."

"You listen to me, Fontenac. I am a well-known journalist with celebrity status. You lean on me, and I'll be on every goddamned television talk show that exists. I'll write articles that will be put on the front page of the *Washington Herald-Telegraph*. I presume you've heard of that little publication."

Fontenac, knowing full well the power of the *Herald-Telegraph*, controlled her desire to tell the journalist to roll up the latest edition of the newspaper and shove it where the sun doesn't shine.

Pamela continued, "And I'll write a book that will be on the best seller lists even before the damn thing rolls off the press. So don't get tough with me, lady. I can ruin your career."

"My career is in the hands of the United States Navy," Fontenac said. "If you can ruin me in my profession, then I was on my way down the tubes long before you came on the scene."

Pamela smiled in a most unfriendly manner. "I know you'd love to make admiral someday, right? You'd think that wonderful, wouldn't you? Just think of bossing around all those macho men and making them toe the line for Admiral Fontenac. Even tough marines would snap to attention when you swaggered by feeling like you just cut their balls off. Well, Fontenac, I am Pamela Drake. You fuck with me, and you'll be lucky to last until your retirement." She stood up again. "Now, here's what you do. You get your ass back to your superiors and tell them in no uncertain terms that if I don't get my way, they can all go shit in their hats."

She turned abruptly and walked away after waving to the two agents on the other bench.

Anraku Hotel
29 July
0200 Hours

The young Japanese gangster standing in the shadows across the street from the hotel was a professional killer. If he'd removed the conservative business suit he was wearing, the massive tattooing of his upper torso would have been revealed. These images on his skin told the ancient legend of the Forty-Seven *Ronin*. These samurai warriors' master had been forced to kill himself in a *seppuku* ceremony after committing the unpardonable *faux pas* of drawing his sword in the presence of the shogun. This breach of good manners happened after he was goaded into the act by a jealous rival. After the master killed himself, all his land was confiscated and his family banished from their ancestral home. This left his forty-seven retainers masterless and poverty-stricken. The warriors came up with an elaborate plan of revenge against the man who had caused their master's disgrace. For more than two years they acted the part of hopeless drunks who had been morally destroyed by their bad luck. They patronized women in the lowest brothels, borrowed money they could never repay, and followed a life of debauchery for all to see. They were soon forgotten in the samurai world as useless scum.

However, on the second anniversary of their master's death, all forty-seven men gathered together to attack the man who had brought about their disgrace. They broke into his castle and captured the villain. After beheading him, their carefully planned mission was complete. At that time all forty-seven committed *seppuku* in an elaborate ceremony, dying proud and happy they had avenged their dead leader. In Japanese tradition, they became martyrs and true followers of *Bushido*.

The gangster was a member of the brutal and merciless *yakuza*, the Japanese equivalent of the Mafia. They operated their criminal gangs in a ritualized system of honor based on that same *Bushido* code. The name *yakuza* came

from an ancient card game in which the worst hand was
made up of the three cards: *ya* (eight), *ku* (nine), and *za*
(three).

On this night, that particular *yakuza* mobster had been
assigned to kill two old people on the second floor of the
hotel across the street. He was particularly anxious to accomplish the deadly mission. The stub of his right pinky
finger still tingled with pain. He had severed it and sent the
digit to his gang leader as an apology for bungling a loan
collection assignment. If he succeeded in the murder of the
elderly couple, he would be solidly back in good standing
with the chief.

The sound of drunken revelry attracted the gangster's
attention. This was what he had been waiting for. A group
of a half-dozen intoxicated businessmen came staggering
down the street. The gangster undid the knot of his tie and
unbuttoned his suit coat. As soon as the boisterous men
passed his hiding place, he stepped out and joined them.
They swung across the street toward the hotel and lurched
into the lobby.

The hostelry had a special hall of berths built in three
tiers. These were designed for one-night rentals in which
the inebriated could sleep off the effects of the liquor they
had consumed during an evening of partying. The accommodations were quite comfortable, and the rentals included a kimono and slippers for each guest.

As soon as the noisy drunks congregated in front of the
desk and took all the clerk's attention, the gangster slipped
away. He quickly ascended the stairs to the second floor,
going down to the room taken by Gomme and Hikui Zunsuno. He deftly used his skeleton key to open the cheap
lock on the door. After a quick look in both directions, he
slipped inside the dark room. The neon light on the front of
the hotel blinked in a red glow. The illumination showed
that the room was completely empty.

Angry and frustrated, the gangster climbed through the
window to the fire escape and descended to the street below.

Hyatt Regency Hotel
0800 Hours

Pamela Drake had moved into a larger suite the evening before. The new accommodations included an extra bedroom now occupied by Gomme and Hikui Zunsuno. She had brought the couple up to her rooms without informing the Hyatt Regency management, so there would be no record of their location. It was this urgent need for secrecy that prompted her to insist on meeting Captain Myra Fontenac in the park rather than at the hotel.

When Pamela ordered that day's breakfast from room service, she offered no explanation to the clerk as to why the meal was for three people rather than one. The kitchen staff took no notice of the request, and when the bellboy delivered it, he didn't inquire about the situation either. The morning meal was a busy time for all servers, and Pamela knew they had more on their minds than to keep count of guests in each room. But just in case, she made sure that Gomme and Hikui stayed out of sight when the cart was wheeled in with the food.

Now, seated at the table in the dining area, the three occupants of the suite ate the ham and eggs Pamela had called for. She wasn't sure what Japanese people had for breakfast, but she did order a pot of tea for them in addition to one of coffee. However, Gomme started drinking the coffee, quickly consuming three cups before he took his first bite of food.

"I have not had coffee in decades," he said apologetically. "That was something I rooked forward to every morning when I was a student at MIT."

"I'm sure you'll be back in the States very soon," Pamela told him. "You'll be able to have all the coffee you want." She laughed. "In fact, you can begin having coffee regularly right now. Anytime you want some, I can call down to room service for a fresh pot."

"You are very kind," Gomme said. "Thank you."

Hikui enjoyed the meal, especially the rye toast. But she had to be shown how to open the little containers of jelly.

She was also intrigued by the hash brown potatoes and scrambled eggs. Like many old women, her appetite was small, but it was obvious everything tasted delicious to her.

Pamela had barely begun to eat when the phone rang. She excused herself and went into her bedroom to answer the call. The voice on the other end belonged to her very perplexed boss, Dick Harrison, the executive editor of the *Washington Herald-Telegraph.*

"What the hell is going on, Pamela?" he pleaded. "You've got to tell me."

"Everything is under control, Dick," she assured him, "so just relax. Okay?"

"I've got the finance department riding the hell out of me, Pamela!" he exclaimed. "It won't be long before the publisher hears about the thousands of dollars a day that are being paid out on your story without anything coming in."

"Damn it, Dick!" she said. "I can't blab about this over the phone. Especially in a foreign country, for God's sake! You remember the story I'm chasing down, right?"

"Yeah," he replied. "It's about those shipjackings or whatever they're called."

"Well, I've hit the ol' jackpot, buddy," Pamela said. "I've got the inside information to break it wide open. Right now I have the U.S. Navy eating out of my hand, trying to figure out how to accommodate my demands to be imbedded with their outfit at the scene of action while they try to solve their problem at the same time."

"Wow!" Harrison said, the relief obvious in his voice. "I should have known you had the situation under control, Pamela, my dear. Is there anything we can do from this end?"

"Yeah," Pamela said. "I need you to make arrangements for two Japanese aliens to be allowed legal permanent entry into the United States. These are going to be high-profile people with extra-special importance attached to them. One of them is a graduate of MIT."

"I shall see to it immediately," Harrison promised. "What are their names?"

"I can't give that to you at this time."

"Well, shit!" he complained. "I can't get visas and permits and all that without names. Even the *Herald-Telegraph* doesn't have that much juice."

"Can't you get things started?" she asked. "Maybe get the forms you'll need ahead of time? Give somebody in the Immigration and Naturalization Service a heads-up. We've got good contacts in that department."

"Okay," he conceded. "I know somebody who can at least get the ball rolling. Is there anything else you need?"

"Just be ready to tear out the front page and replace it when this thing breaks," Pamela said. "And don't worry about the publisher. The Murray family will be handing us big bonuses for this scoop."

"As businesspeople, the family that employs us is notoriously stingy."

Pamela laughed. "They won't be when all this is revealed."

"I feel a hell of a lot better, Pamela, my dear," Harrison said. "I'll be talking to you later."

"You bet, Dick. Bye."

Pamela went back to the dining room, where Gomme was slurping down yet another cup of coffee while Hikui played with her food. Pamela sat down and gave them a big smile. "Everything is going along fine. It won't be long before you'll be legal and permanent residents of the United States of America."

Gomme set his cup down. "Excuse me, prease, Miss Drake. I would be most honored if my wife and I are given permission to reside in Cambridge. That is rocation of MIT, and I spent four very productive years there. I would rike to return to that happy scene of my youth."

"I'm certain that can be arranged," Pamela said. She looked down at her breakfast. "My! I am absolutely famished!"

Gomme felt a little guilty. He was purposely not disclosing any information about the Kamisaku to his hostess. He fervently hoped all knowledge of the machine would be swept away in the tumultuous days to come. But he sadly recognized the very slim chance of that happening.

Osaka Naval Base
Intelligence Office
0900 Hours

Lieutenant Joel Weatherby sat off to the side of the conference room, looking over at the table where his boss, Captain Myra Fontenac, sat with Rear Admiral John Paulsen and Rear Admiral John Miskoski. Weatherby knew that Miskoski had a large command responsibility, since he was the head honcho of Carrier Battle Group Fourteen, but Paulsen was well-known in naval intelligence circles as one powerful individual, who had been involved in some of the deepest, blackest, and most dangerous missions in modern United States Naval history. Paulsen had a reputation that struck fear in Weatherby, who preferred to do his intelligence work from a desk. He hoped like hell he wasn't going to be tapped for some perilous clandestine work in this raider mess going on out there on the East China Sea.

Captain Fontenac was upset, too, but not over any potential of going into harm's way. The smug brush-off by Pamela Drake rankled her deeply. She didn't care if Drake was a famous journalist or not, she didn't care if Drake worked for the powerful and influential *Washington Herald-Telegraph*, and she damn well didn't care that the woman was maintaining her physical beauty up into her forties. Myra Fontenac was a captain in the United States Navy, and as such, she deserved more respect than some celebrity who made obscene amounts of money sticking her nose into places it didn't belong.

"Pamela Drake should have her ass thrown in a federal penitentiary," Fontenac blurted out when Paulsen mentioned her name.

"I agree," Paulsen said, a bit taken aback by the captain's anger. "But I don't think the Department of the Navy is going to see it that way. The woman can get into some pretty high places where she's well-known. Lots of ears tune in when Pamela Drake speaks."

"Big deal!" Fontenac snapped. "So she's fucked her way to the top."

"Pamela Drake has a Pulitzer prize," Miskoski said. "She should be taken seriously."

"I just hope I'm CNO someday when she tries one of her cute tricks," Fontenac said. She immediately regretted revealing one of her deepest, most secret fantasies. Fontenac made herself grin. "As if *that's* going to happen, huh?"

"You're one of the best intel officers I've ever known, Captain," Admiral Paulsen said. "You may well end up with those four stars on your epaulets."

Fontenac blushed, then blushed deeper as she realized her girlish reaction to the words just uttered. But her bad feelings about Pamela Drake were not forgotten with this compliment from one of the masters.

"We're not here to discuss whether her demands should be met or not," Miskoski said. "It's a moot point now that the Department of the Navy has sent down the word that she will be fully accommodated. She *will* be embedded on the *Jefferson;* information on the raider campaign *will* be withheld until twenty-four hours after it's appeared in the *Washington Herald-Telegraph.* Of course all this is contingent on the value of the information she passes on to us. But if she's this pushy about it, it must be good."

"Orders are orders," Fontenac said. "When do we entertain the famous Ms. Drake to get this fantastic information she has for us?"

"How long does it take to make a phone call?" Miskoski said, answering a question with a question.

CHAPTER TWENTY

Kakureta Island
30 July
0900

Commander Gentaro Oyama had come a long way since he resigned from the Japanese Maritime Self Defense Forces and returned to the Kaigun Samurai. The young officer had progressed upward from a deck officer in the rank of lieutenant to the position of chief intelligence officer in the rank of commander. He had not quite moved into the inner circle of power, but his job now involved him in conferences with the secret naval society's three top men: Hara-*sama* the shogun, Rear Admiral Heideki Tanaka, and Admiral Sonkei Hanagawa.

The latter gentleman was the senior adviser to the shogun. He had been a captain in his early thirties at the end of World War II. Although he had never taken a command position in the Kaigun Samurai, his sage advice had contributed greatly to the secret society's operations. The ninety-year-old was still physically active and mentally sharp. He actively participated in the Kaigun Samurai's *kendo* fencing program and could hold his own against opponents decades younger than he.

Hara-*sama* had called the elderly warrior to attend an

emergency meeting involving the disturbing situation of
the destroyer *Chujitsuna*. The old man's wisdom and guidance had never been needed more. That morning Hanagawa sat with Hara-*sama*, Tanaka, and the youthful Oyama
in the shogun's throne room.

Hara-*sama* had fallen into silence for several moments
after initial greetings were exchanged among the four. His
normally calm countenance was creased by a deep frown
of worry and concern. He looked up, turning his gaze to
old Hanagawa. "So it is your opinion that the *Chujitsuna*
has been lost at sea, eh?"

"Yes, Hara-*sama*," Hanagawa said. "She has not been
heard from in five days. There have been no storms or
other natural disasters that could have sunk her."

Tanaka said, "I can only conclude that she has been attacked and either destroyed or captured."

"Captured!" Hara-*sama* shouted in fury. "Captain Montonishi would never surrender his ship! He would fight to
the death, but only after ordering all the scuttling charges
detonated. And that includes the destruction of the
Kamisaku!"

"Of course, Hara-*sama*," Tanaka agreed, chagrined
about seeming to have insulted another Kaigun Samurai
officer. "That is an accepted truth."

The shogun turned to Oyama. "Has there been any mention of the ship's destruction in the news media of the outside world?"

"No, Hara-*sama*," Oyama replied. "Our agents have perused the press and television in Europe, America, and all
over the Far East. It is like always. Nothing is ever said
about us or the ransoming of ships and crews."

"Mmm!" Hanagawa muttered under his breath. "I feel
this secrecy maintained about our activities is a sure sign
there is a clandestine war being waged against us."

"Another warship could not have sunk her," Tanaka
pointed out. "The Kamisaku would have neutralized their
weaponry."

"But what if the machine had malfunctioned?" Hara-
sama asked.

"Then why would another warship attack her?" Oyama interjected. "She would not have shown any hostile intent toward a naval vessel if the Kamisaku was not functioning properly. The only ships she would approach would be merchant vessels that could be easily captured and ransomed."

"You are right," Hanagawa said. "I cannot think of any—" He suddenly stopped speaking. After pondering the problem for a couple of moments, he exclaimed. "A decoy! *Hei!* A decoy ship must have lured her close. That is a trick used in World War One by the English against German submarines. They called such vessels Q-ships. They were unarmed merchantmen from all outward appearances, but had concealed gun positions on their decks. These vessels sailed alone rather than in convoys to avoid torpedo attacks from U-boats."

Oyama was confused. "But how would that keep the Germans from using their torpedoes against the Q-ships?"

"If a ship was alone, they could save their torpedoes by surfacing and attacking with their deck gun," Hanagawa explained. "It would seem an easy victory for the submarine captain. In the instances when his boat drew near to fire, the Q-ship would uncover its guns and commence a surprise shelling. The submarine would be caught unawares and sunk before it could react. Even in emergencies it required long minutes for those old U-boats to submerge."

"Do you think that is what happened to the *Chujitsuna*?" Tanaka asked.

"Of course," Hanagawa replied.

"But wouldn't the Kamisaku protect the *Chujitsuna*?" Omaya asked.

"They would not use radar to aim their guns at such a short distance," Hara-*sama* explained. "And I think our victims have now figured out a force field has been used to thwart any attack by modern technology. Thus they have learned to use basic ordnance against us. They must now feel confident that they can easily sink our ships."

Tanaka's fists were clenched in angry frustration. "Have we lost this fight?"

Hara-*sama* suddenly smiled. "There is a solution to this problem. We will send out the *Hayaken* with orders to approach the next few merchant ships and open fire on them without warning. Sink them! Even the decoy ships will be destroyed if they are suddenly attacked. Our enemies will not know whether to continue with decoys or not. The shipping companies will become alarmed if they lose cargos and crews for what is apparently no good reason. They will strongly insist that the decoys not be used in the future."

"This appears to be only a temporary solution," Tanaka pointed out.

Hanagawa interjected, "But it will buy us some time. We must take some prisoners for interrogation to see if we can obtain intelligence about these decoys. Therefore not all lifeboats should be machine-gunned."

"Hara-*sama*," Tanaka said, turning to the shogun. "I humbly beg to be allowed to command the *Hayaken* on this mission."

Oyama's eyes were wide with excitement. "I, too, request to go to sea on the cruiser, Hara-*sama*. As intelligence officer I wish to question the prisoners. There are certain things I must investigate that the average officer would not think of pursuing."

"Both your requests are granted," Hara-*sama* said. "Further orders and procedures will be drawn up. Meanwhile, prepare the *Hayaken* for sea."

"It is ready to go now, Hara-*sama*," Tanaka replied. "I ordered it provisioned, and canceled all shore leave for the crew when our concerns for the *Chujitsuna* first became apparent. Everyone is aboard the *Hayaken* even now as we speak."

"*Sugureta*—excellent!" Hara-*sama* said. "I shall see that a proper send-off is organized for this most auspicious mission. You both are dismissed to the *Hayaken*. *Banzai!*"

Tanaka and Oyama quickly got to their feet. They bowed deeply, then hurried from the throne room to attend to their newly assigned duties. Hara-*sama* looked at the old adviser. "I will be calling on you much in the future, wise Hanagawa."

"I am honored to serve you."

Hyatt Regency Hotel
Osaka, Japan

Gomme and Hikui Zunsuno sat close together on the sofa in Pamela Drake's suite. Pamela stood to one side of the oldsters while, scattered among the other divans and chairs, sat Rear Admiral John Paulsen, Rear Admiral John Miskoski, Captain Myra Fontenac, and Dr. Harry Levinson. This latter gentleman had been flown to Japan from the Point Loma Submarine Base in San Diego, California.

Little Hikui, who had not seen Occidental people in her entire life, was extremely nervous. She kept her eyes diverted downward toward the floor, grasping Gomme's arm as she leaned against him. Her husband had at first felt quite comfortable, since some of the fondest memories of his youth centered around his days at MIT. But that sense of ease had begun to evaporate under the Americans' intense questioning. At that moment, he realized they were fully aware of the Kamisaku.

Dr. Levinson had an $8\frac{1}{2}"\times 11"$ notebook on his lap into which he had been scribbling notes almost continually during the short period they had been there. Admiral Miskoski had spoken most impatiently to Gomme about the location of the mysterious island the old man referred to as Kakureta. After the old Japanese gentleman gave him the latitude and longitude as he had memorized it, the admiral wanted to know the size of the place.

Gomme was apologetic. "I am so sorry, sir. I have not measured it, nor have I seen a map of Kakureta."

"Well then," Miskoski said, "are there maps of this island anywhere?"

"I am sure some must exist," Gomme said.

Dr. Levinson interrupted. "I would like to ask you some questions about that force field machine, Dr. Zunsuno."

Pamela was surprised. "What force field machine?"

"This is a matter you'll not be concerned with, Ms. Drake," Miskoski said. "Please do not make any inquires about it."

"I might make some very pointed inquiries, Admiral!" Pamela snapped.

"That would most definitely be to your disadvantage," Miskoski warned her. He turned back to Dr. Levinson. "Right now we must concentrate on obtaining information on which to base plans for an attack on the island."

"But this force field generator has all the potential of re-vising modern warfare into completely unheard-of applica-tions," Levinson said testily. "This will revolutionize international relations even more than nuclear weapons did."

"Shut up, Doctor!" Miskoski snarled. "Didn't you just hear me admonish Ms. Drake? You are discussing a highly classified matter in front of unauthorized personnel."

"Sorry, Admiral," Levinson said.

Pamela Drake had grown worried about Gomme and Hikui's obvious uneasiness. She walked to the middle of the room and wheeled to face the navy people. "Cool it! Goddamn it! Cool it! I'm not going to sit here while you upset these two old people. Do you understand? This situa-tion calls for patience and tact."

"Ms. Drake is absolutely correct," Paulsen said. He ac-tually had time in grade on Miskoski when it came to their ranks. "I suggest that we speak to Dr. Zunsuno one at a time on the subjects in which we are all interested. I'm sort of neutral here, since I'm a special warfare type. So we'll let Admiral Miskoski get what information he needs on Kakureta Island, then Dr. Levinson can have his turn."

"Meanwhile," Miskoski said, "I'll have to ask Ms. Drake to leave the room. I'll have Captain Fontenac ac-company her."

"Yes, sir," Fontenac said, thinking she'd rather be in the company of an enraged cobra than Pamela Drake. The two women glared at each other but obediently walked from the suite out into the hall.

Miskoski spoke to Gomme in a friendlier tone. "I am sorry if I upset you, Dr. Zunsuno."

"I am fine," Gomme replied. "Prease ask me any question you wish."

"What is your best estimation of the size of Kakureta Island?" Miskoski inquired.

"I should say thirty-five to forty kirometers rong and perhaps ten wide," Gomme answered. "I am sure those measurements are crose enough to be usefur to you."

"I see," Miskoski said. "And what about defense?"

"The only defenses are a series of Kamisaku machines," Gomme answered. "They are positioned about the irand in a way that their generated energy overraps each other."

"Overwraps?" Miskoski asked.

Gomme shook his head. "No. Overraps—raps!"

Paulsen, who had dealt with Japanese in the past, said, "The doctor means overlaps."

"Yes!" Gomme said. "Overraps."

"Thank you," Miskoski said, suppressing a smile. "Thus the entire island would be invisible to radar or other electronics because of those overlapping machines, correct?" He made a few notes in his own journal. "Now you say those are the only defenses. Are there no gun placements? No coast artillery? Nothing like that?"

"No," Gomme said. Hikui leaned over and whispered in his ear. Gomme nodded and looked at Miskoski. "My honorable wife has reminded me that the ships in the harbor have big guns."

"How many ships?"

"Three," Gomme answered, not knowing about the loss of the *Chujitsuna*.

"Are there any soldiers?"

"No sordiers. Sairors. But I do not know how many."

"Do you know the population of the island?" Miskoski asked. "By that, I mean the number of people who live on it."

"I think maybe five thousand," Gomme said. "There are men, women, and chirdren that rive along the coast in an arrangement of apartment comprexes that goes around from one side of the harbor to the other. These residents are what is known as *jun-i* in the navy. They are workers rike carpenters, erectricians, and that sort. The *samurai* who are the officers rive in the center of the irand in houses. We who are crassified as *kagakusha* have our residences on the perimeter around the *samurai*. We, too, rive in houses, but they are smar."

"What material are the buildings made of?"

"Everything is constructed of wood," Gomme answered. "No brick, no concrete, just wood."

"My God!" Paulsen exclaimed. "The place would burn like gasoline-soaked logs if it were bombed or shelled."

"Oh, yes," Gomme said. "If somebody sets something on fire even accidentry, the punishment is most severe."

"Now here is a very important question, Dr. Zunsuno," Miskoski said. "If outsiders come onto the island, would the population resist their arrival?"

"Oh, yes," Gomme said. "To the death. Everyone there is *Bushido*. To surrender is a disgrace. If they catch me, they would cut off my head with a sword."

"It sort of sounds like we're back in World War Two," Miskoski remarked. He leaned back in his chair. "That's all the questions I have for right now."

"Thank you, Dr. Zunsuno," Paulsen said. He nodded to Dr. Levinson. "Your turn."

"At last!" Levinson said impatiently. "Can you give me a brief description of how this Kamisaku machine works, Doctor?"

"So sorry."

"Perhaps if I gave you my notebook, you could sketch out the barest details and formulas," Levinson said. "At least enough for me to get the gist of the theorem."

"So sorry," Gomme repeated. "I do not wish to give away information of the Kamisaku. Thank you. So sorry."

Levinson's eyes opened wide. "Surely, Dr. Zunsuno, you would share your knowledge with the United States. We are the leaders of the Free World."

"If a strong nation gets the Kamisaku, it can command mankind and make everybody do what it says," Gomme said. "That is a bad thing."

Now it was Paulsen who was edgy. "You might as well tell us, Doctor. We'll capture one or two when we take the island anyway."

"Hara-*sama* will order them destroyed when he thinks the irand is rost," Gomme said.

"Who is Harasama?" Miskoski asked.

"He is the shogun," Gomme said. "The supreme reader of the Kaigun Samurai."

"What is it you wish from us, Doctor?"

"I wish to rive in United States at Cambridge in Massachusetts," Gomme replied. I wish to have a raboratory in which to do scientific experiments at MIT."

Dr. Levinson still held on to his notebook. "Then don't you think you owe the United States something, Dr. Zunsuno? I would think you would be happy to share the Kamisaku technology with us in exchange for being granted asylum and a place to work in our country."

"So sorry."

"Sorry?" Dr. Levinson said. "You will be a hell of a lot sorrier if some other nation gets their hands on you. They won't be so kind and understanding, Doctor."

"If I cannot go to the United States to rive under protection, then my dear wife and I will go to rive with our ancestors," Gomme said with soft determination.

"Relatives," Dr. Levinson said. "You mean you'll go to live with your relatives."

Admiral Paulsen's experience in dealing with indigenous people of other cultures made him understand exactly what Gomme meant. "I think we've gone far enough for today." He walked to the door and opened it, allowing Pamela and Fontenac to come back in the room.

Pamela was upset. "You've all been extremely rude to this nice old couple."

Paulsen stood up. "You're right. But we'll be leaving security people here for your protection until arrangements can be made for you to move aboard the base."

"Understood and appreciated," Pamela said. She waited until the guests departed, then turned back to Gomme and Hikui. "Don't you worry about a thing. I can absolutely guarantee you that the *Washington Herald-Telegraph* will see that you get everything you desire. So you can make serious plans about having a laboratory at MIT."

"Maybe they won't want me," Gomme said.

"Those institutions of higher learning are so dependent on the government that they'll do anything that is asked or demanded of them," Pamela said. "Everything is going to turn out just fine."

Gomme put his arm around Hikui.

Kakureta Island
1100 Hours

The ceremony had been quickly organized but was still impressive. All the officers, warrant officers, petty officers, and sailors who made up the cruiser *Hayaken*'s crew were drawn up in ranks on the wharf in front of the vessel. They wore their dress white uniforms, and the officers sported their *samurai* swords. The spectators had gathered in an area set aside for them next to a row of warehouses. Everyone in the crowd—men, women, and children—wore traditional kimonos and held small paper flags displaying the red disk symbol of the rising sun. They waved these tiny banners enthusiastically.

A small decorated platform stood in front of the crew. The crowd instantly ceased its chattering when Hara-*sama*, the shogun, suddenly appeared with an escort of a half-dozen men dressed in the costumes of ancient Japanese warriors. The shogun looked grand in his suit of ancient *senso* armor, complete with the traditional helmet. In his right hand he carried the *saihai* command baton decorated with a tassel of oiled paper. He was armed with both the *katana* and *wakizashi* swords stuck in the *obi* around his waist.

When he stepped up on the platform, a ship's officer marched to the front of the cruiser's crew and bowed deeply. Then he turned and gestured to the entire assemblage to signal for cheers.

"*Banzai! Banzai! Banzai!*"

At the conclusion of the shouting, Hara-*sama* stepped forward. "I greet the officers and crew of the *Hayaken*. You are about to set sail on the first war voyage of the Kaigun Samurai! Your mission is not to capture ships, but to destroy them. Our aggression will goad the outside world to humble themselves to our demands. It will be a war we shall win because of the Kamisaku. Within a year the Kaigun Samurai will rule all the oceans and seas. Thus, you are now truly warriors on your way to claim your place in imperial glory. Those Japanese fighters of generations past who died for our race look down on you with favor from *Okii Kusho* as you begin this step in the final act to bring back the former glory of our empire.

"This mission, on which you are about to leave, is one of vengeance. Samurai vengeance! You must avenge more than the humiliations of World War Two. You must also make the enemy account for the loss of our ship the *Chujitsuna* and her crew. Their fate is not fully known at this time, but we must accept the fact that they have disappeared from the sea, and we shall never see our dear compatriots again.

"I remind you this day that your most important duty is loyalty. Remember the sign on our school building that has taught you that duty is weightier than a mountain while death is lighter than a feather. To die for the Japanese Empire is a glory beyond mortal comprehension.

"You must also conduct yourselves with valor. You should not sneer at an inferior enemy nor fear a superior one. Remember you belong to the Imperial Japanese Navy. Be brave! Be faithful to your cause and your race.

"And as we move into this war you must adopt the austerity of your *samurai* forebears. Strive to make simplicity an important part of your life. If you do not, you will acquire a desire for luxury and extravagance. This is uncomplimentary to the Japanese warrior.

"Never surrender, but kill yourself if you are not able to fight to the death. You must never fall into enemy hands. Such a thing shames you, your family, your ancestors, and your race. It also shames me.

"Above all, obey all orders from your officers and petty officers as if I, the shogun, had personally issued them to you. For in truth, that is the case. Now go do your duty."

The shogun drew his *katana* and held it high. This time he personally led the cheering.

"Banzai! Banzai! Banzai!"

SS Buenaventura
Noon

Gerald Fagin and Lars Stensland sat in the latter's cabin engrossed in a game of cutthroat pinochle. Fagin had been forced to play a ten that Stensland trumped with a nine. "Shit!" Fagin exclaimed. Stensland led with a jack of trump that forced Fagin to give up another ten. Fagin glared at him. "All you've got left is trump, right?"

"Right," Stensland said with a leer. "Want to give up?"

Fagin turned over his remaining cards. "What chance do I have? How much do I owe you?"

"Ten million dollars," Stensland answered.

Fagin shrugged. "That's not too bad."

They had been playing a running series of games betting outlandish amounts of money that were never meant to be paid. At one point Stensland was down some twenty-five million dollars, but since then he had won thirty-five million.

Fagin leaned back in his chair. "I'm tired. Want to quit?"

"Fine with me," Stensland said.

They had now been to sea some four days and hadn't had any contact with raiders. Everyone was getting restless, and the scuttlebutt around the ship was that the bad guys had packed it in after losing their destroyer; or at least had temporarily ceased activities. Stensland insisted that the vessel that was scuttled by her crew was not the same one that captured the *Edvard Grieg*. That meant the pirates had at least one more around somewhere.

Everyone, especially the boarding group, was edgy because of the need to get prisoners. The idea was to call the

Avenger aircraft off before the enemy ship was so badly bombed and strafed that most of the pirates would be dead. Survivors were needed to guarantee captives. It also meant more people shooting back during the storming of the ship. This would make any suicidal last stands by the enemy particularly dangerous. Lieutenant Colonel Steve Wang had pulled in some M60 machine guns for his support element. Series of well-directed fire bursts would make the bad guys instinctively duck their heads, even if they were willing to fight to the death. All this meant the boarding operation would be hairy as hell.

Fagin yawned and looked at the deck of cards. "Maybe we should play another game anyhow. I got to win back that ten million."

Stensland grinned and began shuffling.

Geological Exploration Corporation
Head Office
Wichita, Kansas

Bainbridge Collins, seventy-six years old, grumpy, dyspeptic, and as mentally sharp now as when he was a quick-minded young lawyer, sat at his desk. He was the chief operating officer of the Geological Exploration Corporation, also known as Geo-X. The old man was never addressed by his job title. Instead, he was known by everybody as the Senator. And for good reason.

He had spent thirty years in that legislative body as a Republican, ending his political career as chairman of the Senate Intelligence Committee. He had steered the right bills onto the floor for votes, put the chiefs of American intelligence on the hot seat when he thought they'd screwed up, and had been privy to some of the deepest secrets of the Cold War with the Soviet Union and other unfriendly nations. Now he dozed contentedly at his desk, his hands folded across his ample belly. He had just taken a deep, snoring breath when the phone on his desk rang. He groaned and picked it up. "Yeah?"

"Martin Albright is here, Senator," his secretary Mona announced from her desk just outside the door.

"Tell him to go to hell."

"I'd be happy to," Mona said. "But you ordered him to be here today."

"Tell him to go to hell anyway."

"Yes, sir." There was a slight pause, then she spoke to the visitor, "The Senator says for you to go to hell."

"Okay," Albright replied in a barely audible voice. "But does he want to see me before I leave for Hades?"

"Send the rascal in," the Senator said.

A moment later Albright stepped into the office. He was a muscular, fit, middle-aged man with gray hair thinning noticeably on top. Although he was wearing a business suit, he looked as if he belonged in a set of camouflage fatigues. "Howdy, Senator."

"Hello, Martin. How's it going?"

"Pretty good, I guess."

The Senator reached for his humidor and withdrew a five-dollar cigar. He snipped off the end, then stuck it in his mouth. "There's some potential work for Geo-X."

"The first question I have is where?" Albright said.

"Somewhere in the East China Sea," the Senator said, lighting the stogie. "An uncharted island, as a matter of fact."

"If the damn thing isn't on maps, how the hell are we supposed to find it?"

"I gather from the information given me that they're working on that little problem right now."

"Okay. How many do I take with me?"

"Two assault teams and a fire support team," the Senator answered. "You'll go to the safe house out on East Kellogg for isolation. The others will be dribbling in here between now and in the morning." He took a drag off the cigar, then languidly exhaled the smoke. "But tell them to stay cool. They might not be needed."

"What's the story?"

"You and that ragtag bunch of paramilitary hooligans

you refer to as a commando may have to back up one of Paulsen's groups."

"We'll be ready if the admiral needs us," Albright said.

"Any questions?"

"About two hundred," Albright replied.

"Well I don't have any answers," the Senator said dourly. "Good-bye."

"Good-bye. Sir."

Albright got to his feet and walked out of the office. He felt pretty good. Normally he wasn't given that much information. The Senator had been unusually talkative.

CHAPTER TWENTY-ONE

SS Buenaventura
East China Sea
31 July
1115 Hours

The ripping sound of the shell flying through the air had
barely been perceived by the crew on the forenoon watch
before the explosion shattered the late morning. The deto-
nation, just off the port bow, was close enough that the resultant splash sent water splattering down on the deck like
a heavy, instantaneous squall.

Gerald Fagin, on the bridge with Lieutenant Frank
Larcos, was shaken from his reverie by the unexpected det-
onation. Almost immediately another incoming shell announced its violent arrival when the deck directly forward
was hit, sending white-hot shards of metal flying out in all
directions. The windshield directly in front of Larcos shattered inward, showering him with broken glass. Fagin ran
out on the signal deck and stopped in shock at the sight of
an old cruiser some two hundred meters off the starboard
beam. At that moment one of its deck guns fired again, giving Fagin only an instant to leap back inside the bridge before the shell struck and detonated into the side of the ship.

"These sons of bitches mean business!" he yelled at

Larcos. "I'm going to order the directional buoy cast adrift!"

Fagin bumped into Lars Stensland coming on the bridge as he rushed to the task. Stensland had been dozing in his cabin when the shelling started, and the shock of the attack brought the Norwegian to full wakefulness. Three more simultaneous hits rocked the *Buenaventura* as the barrage built up in intensity. Larcos's face was cut badly by glass, and he wiped at the blood blinding his left eye.

"It's a raider, Captain!" he gasped in pain.

"Did she challenge us to heave to?" Stensland asked.

"No. The first we knew of her being there was when a shell landed in the water just forward."

Now the cruiser was accurately zeroed in on the target, and the incoming rounds were raking the *Buenaventura* from bow to stern. The cabins at deck level where Lieutenant Colonel Steve Wang and his men were quartered had been reduced to smoking wreckage strewn with bodies, and the superstructure of the freighter was a twisted mass of steel, some of it molten from the heat of the explosions.

"Power is gone!" the helmsman reported.

"We're settling toward the stern," Larcos said. "They must've knocked out the engine room. The poor guys down there didn't have a fucking chance."

Gerald Fagin reappeared. "I managed to get the directional buoy loosed. But the whole ship's a burning wreck."

The smoke was now bellowing up around the bridge and coming in where the windshield glass was blown out. The deck suddenly slanted sternward, forcing the men on the bridge to brace themselves against the jarring movement.

"We've had it!" Larcos said. The front of his shirt was soaked in blood from the deep gashes in his face.

Stensland pressed the alarm to order abandon ship. But no sound came from the siren. All power was gone, and no damage control personnel were available to activate the emergency source.

A massive explosion suddenly took out the forward section of the bridge, sweeping Larcos and the helmsman away. Fagin and Stensland frantically donned flotation devices as they struggled off the bridge and down the ladder to the main deck. The *Buenaventura* listed heavily to starboard and shuddered heavily as the two leaped over the port side into the water.

"We must get away from the ship," Stensland said, spitting out a mouthful of oily salt water. "When she goes down, we'll be pulled with her."

They paddled as rapidly as they could to put some distance between themselves and the doomed vessel. The shelling had slowed by then, and after two more rounds hit the *Buenaventura,* the raiders ceased fire. The freighter was not a warship and had not been built to withstand heavy hits from big guns. But even if she had a series of watertight compartments belowdecks, there were no survivors to seal off the flooded sections. The ship was dead in the water, except for a movement sternward where she was sinking. When the *Buenaventura* finally died, she went quickly under, rearing up until the bow was pointed straight to the sky. Then she disappeared, slipping under the surface with the loud sounds of heavy steel plates twisting and breaking.

Fagin and Stensland looked around for more survivors, but the sea in the near vicinity was empty, except for some floating debris. They spotted a whaleboat being launched from the raider.

"Shit!" Fagin said. "That's our only chance for rescue unless the *Jefferson* is a lot closer than I think she is."

"A last position check showed her beyond two hundred and fifty miles away," Stensland said. He took a close look at the armed sailors in the boat, thinking of the massacre of the *Dileas*'s crew. *"Se opp!"* he warned Fagin, instinctively speaking Norwegian before switching to English. "Take care!"

"It looks like they spotted us," Fagin said.

The boat came toward them with a submachine gun–toting sailor in the forward sheets. He carried what appeared to be an AK-47 that was locked and loaded. He motioned in a threatening manner at them as the small craft drew closer. Both Fagin and Stensland braced to be murdered in cold blood, knowing it would be useless to dive under the water. But no staccato of automatic weapon fire swept over them. Instead, rough hands grabbed the two men and hauled them aboard.

Fagin looked out at the area where the *Buenaventura* had gone down. Neither crewmen nor their corpses could be seen in the water. He glanced at Stensland. "All hands went down with her."

One of the sailors viciously slapped his face. "*Katarumasen!* No talk!"

Stensland, who had swallowed some oil, leaned over the side and vomited into the ocean. When he finished, he took a deep breath and wiped his mouth. He looked at Fagin, who gave him a reassuring wink. In less than five minutes, the boat was at the side of the cruiser and had been secured to the end of the sea painter. Slings and steadying lines were attached to the boat cleats, and it was hauled upward to the deck.

A pair of armed sailors hopped off first, then signaled the two prisoners to follow. Fagin and Stensland did as instructed, waiting to see what else was going to happen when they were on the deck. A ship's officer, complete with samurai sword, walked up grandly and arrogantly as he surveyed the captives who shivered slightly from both emotion and the chill of the breeze that whipped across their sopping-wet clothing.

The Japanese officer gave Fagin a quick look, then turned toward Stensland. He studied the Norwegian's face impassively for several moments, then barked an order at the sailors. They roughly shoved the two survivors in the direction they were to go.

Stensland took a deep breath. He recognized the officer as the one who had come aboard the *Edvard Grieg* when it was captured back in May.

Avenger Flight
1250 Hours

Commander Gene Erickson looked down at the empty sea. "Westy," he radioed. "Are you sure that directional finder of yours is functioning properly?"

"All indications give me no reason to think otherwise," Westy Fields replied.

"I don't see shit down there," Junior Stump broke in.

"Let's make a low, slow orbit and see what gives," Erickson said. "I want all bombardiers to give a hand. The more eyes the better."

Ordnanceman James Warrenton, down in *Avenger 1*'s bombardier station, went forward to look out the viewing window as his pilot pushed the stick forward and pulled the throttle back. James had settled in, his sharp eyes peeled for the buoy, when he caught sight of some items in the water.

"Hey, sir!" he said over the intercom. "You just went over some floating crap down there."

"Roger," Erickson responded. He turned to the flight channel. "Warrenton's seen something. Let's tighten up a bit. Tell your people to stay alert."

He made a steep turn, losing some more altitude, and straightened up to run back over the area again. Almost immediately came back reports of more debris. Michael Harrigan in *Avenger 4* saw the directional buoy and quickly reported it. But it was Gianna Torino who spotted the most ominous feature.

"Dead ahead, maybe two or three miles, sir," she said to Ariel Goldberg. "An oil slick."

The word was passed to Erickson, who led them in the indicated direction. When they arrived on scene, they saw the numerous unidentifiable items floating in the muck that was visually spreading across the waves.

All eight members of the flight felt the sickening reality in the pits of their stomachs: the *Buenaventura* had been sunk, and Operation Yesteryear had hit the proverbial brick wall.

CHAPTER TWENTY-TWO

Kakureta Island
1 August
0730 Hours

The cruiser *Hayaken* approached the island harbor, but instead of entering the small port as was the usual practice, she dropped anchor just outside the facility. This return was unexpected by the general population, and those who sighted the ship stopped what they were doing to hurry to the seashore. The word of the unusual event quickly spread through the dock area, and others joined the gathering throng until some fifteen hundred people gazed out at the unforeseen arrival of the ship.

No special activity was visible on the vessel other than a few sailors tending to routine duties or standing anchor watch. After a half hour, a personnel boat with a coxswain and two armed sailors chugged out of the harbor toward the cruiser. It arrived at the accommodation ladder where an officer and four men waited. Two of them were Europeans wearing khaki-colored clothing. Immediately the officer and the white men boarded the boat. The spectators noted that the Caucasians needed guidance in stepping down into the small craft. A moment later it was apparent the two were prisoners; they were blindfolded with their hands tied behind their backs. As soon as the captives had been sat down, the coxswain swung the tiller and gunned the motor, quickly turning for a return trip to the wharf area.

Commander Gentaro Oyama glared down at Gerald Fagin and Lars Stensland, who sat in the forward sheets, facing aft. A small contingent of armed sailors waited on the dock for the boat. When it arrived, the guards formed a small perimeter to keep the curious spectators back. Oyama was the first to get on the wharf, and he turned to wait. At this point the blindfolds were removed from the prisoners, and they were manhandled out of the small craft to join the officer.

Fagin and Stensland looked around, bewildered by the sight of dozens of Japanese staring at them. The place seemed to be an ancient village like those seen in the *samurai* films that were popular back in the 1950s. All the women wore kimonos, but the vintage appearance was spoiled somewhat by the naval uniforms of the men, along with some small vans and automobiles that were parked around the area. Electric and telephone lines also intruded on the ambience of ancient Japan, as did the twentieth-century destroyer tied up nearby.

Oyama barked orders, and the prisoners were prodded by rifle butts into following him. The little procession moved through the crowd and across the dock to the gangplank of the destroyer. Oyama, guards, Fagin, and Stensland went aboard, and the prisoners were quickly hustled belowdecks down to the brig. After being untied, they were shoved into a cell. The door was banged shut, and the two officers were alone for the first time since they'd been plucked from the sea.

Stensland looked at Fagin. "This is much different than my last experience with the raiders."

Fagin's expression was serious. "Have you had any prisoner-of-war training, Lars?"

The Norwegian shrugged. "I do not even know what that is."

"That's where you learn how to conduct yourself when captured by the enemy," Fagin explained. "And, believe me! At this moment we are definitely in that situation."

"Then tell me what I must expect," Stensland said.

"They brought us here because they're suspicious," Fagin said. "You said you recognized that Japanese officer. Well, he probably recognized you, too. These people aren't stupid. They suspect a ruse of some sort, and they're going to talk to us about it."

Stensland shrugged. "So? We simply stick to our story of being officers on a merchant ship."

"They're going to try to pressure us to talk," Fagin said. "It may come in the form of beatings or other torture—"

"Torture?" Stensland exclaimed.

"I'm afraid so," Fagin said. "It depends on how upset they are. I imagine the loss of that destroyer has pretty well wound 'em up tight."

"What does one do under torture?"

"Everybody eventually breaks," Fagin said. "The thing is to try to last as long as you can. The longer it takes them to get information from us, the more advantageous it will be for Operation Yesteryear. The loss of our ship will have closed things down temporarily."

"Then we might be here for a long time," Stensland said.

"We're going to come under some very unpleasant pressure," Fagin reiterated. "Be ready for it."

"I will do my best."

"As will I," Fagin said. "But after so much time passes, you'll become disorientated enough to go through a personality change. You'll feel alone and isolated, like the whole world is made up of you and the guys who are tormenting you. You'll talk. You might lie to them at first and maybe get away with it for awhile. Then you'll find you've done yourself no favors. So you decide to tell them what they want. You might start spilling your guts to simply to make them stop hurting you, or you might have gone crazy enough to want to establish a friendly rapport with your interrogators."

Stensland was puzzled. "Why would I want to do that?"

"You'll feel it's a logical way to improve the hellish environment you've been thrust into," Fagin explained. "I know this is quick and abbreviated. When I went through POW training, I had two full weeks."

"Gud i himmel!" Stensland exclaimed. "I was not expecting a situation like this."

"Me neither," Fagin admitted.

The noise of a steel door opening was followed by the sound of footsteps scurrying down a ladder. The sounds grew louder as a group of people came up to the door. It was opened, and a tall Japanese gentleman wearing the old-style garments of a high-ranking samurai stepped inside. Oyama quickly followed, frowning furiously at the prisoners.

"Bow!" he commanded. "Bow before Hara-*sama*, the shogun of Kakureta and the Kaigun Samurai!"

Fagin and Stensland, who had been sitting on the deck, stood up slowly. They weren't quite sure what was wanted of them. Oyama furiously rushed around behind the prisoners and grabbed both men by the backs of their necks, pushing their heads down.

"Bow!" he screamed. "I command you to bow to the shogun!"

Hara-*sama* nodded to the prisoners in recognition of the forced subjugation. "Good morning," he said in almost unaccented English.

"Good morning," Fagin replied sullenly, staring down at the deck.

Stensland preferred his own language. *"God morgen."*

"Please stand straight," Hara-*sama* said in a pleasant tone. He had been waiting for the prisoners to arrive and wanted to see them for himself. He noted Fagin's American accent, but Stensland's ethnicity puzzled him. He looked at the Scandinavian quizzically for a moment. "Where are you from?"

"Norway," Stensland answered.

"What is this place?" Fagin asked.

The question earned him a sharp rap on the jaw from Oyama. "You will ask no questions of the shogun!" he yelled. "You will only speak if he asks you a question or orders you to speak!"

Fagin glared at the officer but wisely kept his Irish temper under control.

Hara-*sama* made several brief inquiries into their backgrounds. Both prisoners stuck to their cover stories of being merchant marine officers aboard the freighter *Buenaventura*. The shogun inquired about their ports of calls, cargo, course, and other information. After less than ten minutes he abruptly ended the interview.

"Bow!" Oyama yelled.

This time Fagin and Stensland immediately obeyed as the shogun left the compartment. Oyama followed, and the door was closed. Stensland examined Fagin's face.

"Are you all right?"

Fagin rubbed his sore jaw. "I'll be okay." He forced a grin. "Another thing you must remember as a POW is to avoid physical punishment if it is at all possible. That also means not to be insulting or disrespectful toward your captors. You want to stay healthy for escape attempts."

"Escape?" Stensland asked. He gestured at the steel bulkheads around them. "How does one sneak out of the bowels of a warship?"

Fagin emitted a humorless chuckle. "I think it calls for a rather large can opener."

Osaka Naval Base
Secured Area
0900 Hours

The accommodations provided Gomme and Hikui Zunsuno in the fenced, heavily guarded area were unadorned but comfortable. They had a living room, bedroom, a small kitchen area, and a bath. The double bed was comfortable, and the sofa, easy chair, and TV in the parlor were of a late modern design. A table and chairs for eating were situated in one corner of the room.

At that moment, the first of two expected visitors sat on the easy chair while the old couple occupied the sofa. This guest had been introduced to them as Hajiri Onwani from the Japanese Foreign Ministry. He was the perfect Japanese gentleman, having removed his shoes before entering their abode. He was very respectful and polite, smiling as he asked them questions.

"We have been told that you wish to go to live in America," Onwani said. "Is this true, Dr. Zunsuno?"

"Yes," Gomme answered. "I have been given assurance that I will be provided with a place to begin a new series of study."

"I see," Onwani said. He glanced at Hikui. "And this is your wish also, Mrs. Zunsuno?"

"If it is my husband's wish, then it is also my wish," Hikui said, surprised by the inquiry. In her day, a wife's opinion would not have been taken into consideration.

"The Japanese government desires for me to inform you that any type of facilities for living or work supplied for you in America can also be made available to you in Japan," Onwani said. "We have many electronic industries with projects that would interest you greatly, Dr. Zunsuno."

"Of course," Gomme said. "But I have a special desire to return to America in order that I might conduct my work at MIT. So sorry."

"I understand," Onwani said. "I have some questions about the place that you have identified as Kakureta Island. How did you come to go there?"

"I was a scientist for the Imperial Navy before and during the war with America," Gomme said. "I was working on a project the authorities in Tokyo considered important. For that reason my wife and I were taken to Kakureta to live. I was provided with a laboratory and equipment. Assistants were also placed at my disposal."

"Excuse my rudeness," Onwani said, "but may I inquire as to the nature of your work?"

"I am sorry," Gomme answered. "I prefer not to speak of it."

"Of course," Onwani said. "Did you continue to work for the Imperial Navy after the war?"

"Yes," Gomme said.

"Did you know that Japan lost the war?"

"We were told it was only a temporary setback that was going to be put right," Gomme answered.

"Do you know how your work was financed?"

"Not exactly," Gomme said. "Sorry. All I know was that funds came from Japan through the Kaigun Samurai. They had agents there. Of course we learned of capturing ships for ransom later."

"Yes," Onwani said. "I read the report on what you revealed about that secret society. Most interesting." He made some notes. "What do you know of the *hokannin*?"

"Again, my knowledge is severely limited," Gomme said. "I believe they were people in Japan who were not members of the Kaigun Samurai, but who served them."

"Do you know any of them?"

"No," Gomme answered. Hikui leaned close to him and whispered. "Ah!" Gomme said. "My wife has just reminded me of a man by the name of Kiyoe Yamata. He was the headman at the fishing village of Yoiummei, where we landed when we came to Japan from Kakureta."

"Yes!" Onwani said, obviously pleased by the revelation. "Can you recall others?"

"No. Sorry."

The visitor tried to get some sort of slant on the history of the founding of Kakureta, but Gomme knew next to nothing except that it was a secret base used by the Imperial Navy for many decades. He also had no information on the three ships, other than their names, and he was not sure of the origins of the shogun called Hara-*sama,* who was the leader of the Kaigun Samurai.

Onwani asked more questions, sometimes repeating the same one in several different ways, until he was sure he had exhausted all the knowledge Dr. Gomme Zunsuno had about the secret naval society and an uncharted island. He closed his notebook, stood up, and bowed deeply.

"Thank you very much for indulging my impolite meddling, Dr. Zunsuno," Onwani said. "I will now unburden you and your honorable wife from having to endure my rude presence."

"I must apologize for my miserable ignorance,

Onwani-*san*," Gomme said. "I have wasted your valuable time with my inane prattling."

With the proper good-byes made, Onwani left the apartment. Another gentleman appeared so quickly that Gomme hadn't had time to close the apartment door. This caller, an American, had obviously been waiting outside. The old couple was surprised to hear him speak in fluent Japanese.

"*Ohayo gozaimasu,*" he said. "I am Glen Fox from the United States Immigration and Naturalization Service. I have the honor of being assigned as your personal caseworker."

"Please come in, Fox-*san*," Gomme invited.

Fox removed his shoes and entered the apartment. After bowing to Hikui, he explained he had brought some forms for them to sign. He also had good news that the process of arranging their permanent residency in the United States was well under way. He pointed out that if they wished, they would be able to become American citizens. But there was one unpleasant aspect of their immigration he did bring up.

"I have been instructed to tell you that the revelation of your knowledge regarding a certain technology would be looked upon as a great favor by the government of the United States," he said. "I am not aware of the details, of course, but there are many highly placed officials who hope you will change your mind about not divulging the information to our scientists. Please give this matter some thought."

"Of course," Gomme promised.

Fox wasted no time in getting their signatures on the forms he had brought with him. With that task completed, he walked to the door, stopping to hand Gomme his card.

"If you require anything of me, please do not hesitate to call. I have an office at the American consulate in Osaka."

"Thank you," Gomme said. After Fox took his leave, he turned to Hikui. "I wish I had never conceived that awful machine."

"Then perhaps we should stay in Japan, *shujin*," she suggested.

"But the Japanese government wants it, too," he said mournfully. "Everybody in the world wants Kamisaku!"

Destroyer **Isamashii**
Kakureta Island
1400 Hours

Gerald Fagin and Lars Stensland, sitting in total darkness, could only guess how much time had passed as they sat on the deck of the unlit brig cell. Their watches had been taken away quickly after their capture at sea.

"I noticed something," Fagin remarked in a whisper. "They've not been locking the cell door." He chuckled. "Evidently the keys didn't come with the ship."

"It may make an escape attempt more feasible," Stensland suggested.

"Right," Fagin agreed. "We won't need that big can opener after all."

Stensland was in no mood to respond to the poor joke.

They were uncomfortable from the cold steel, but their body heat was slowly warming the area where they sat. Their conversation was at a minimum because of their shared feelings of uneasiness, and both now felt the pangs of empty stomachs as well as a growing thirst. Fagin suggested they try to nap and conserve what reservoir of energy they could because of not taking in nourishment. Both managed to doze off a couple of times, but after five or ten minutes of fitful sleep, they would come awake in their grim surroundings.

A sudden clanging of a door opening was followed by scuffling footsteps. The noise brought them out of their restless reveries. The cell was opened, letting in a weak light. Two truncheon-toting sailors stepped inside and pointed at Fagin.

"Kurumasu!" one growled in a gruff voice.

Fagin, not sure what they wanted, stood up. He was quickly grabbed and dragged outside to the passageway. The cell door was slammed shut, then the guards pushed the prisoner in the direction they wished him to go. They went up a ladder to another passageway that led to an office compartment. Fagin was taken inside, where Commander Gentaro Oyama sat behind a desk. The guards left them alone in the room.

Oyama leaned back in his chair. "What is your name?"

"Gerald Fagin."

"What is your ship?"

"My ship is—*was*—the *SS Buenaventura*."

"What port did you sail from?"

Fagin fell into the cover story already created for them. "We began our voyage in San Pedro, California. We had a miscellaneous cargo of raw material for Tokyo, Taiwan, and Bombay."

"What is your rank?" Oyama asked.

"I have a deck officer's license," Fagin replied.

"You misunderstand me. What is your navy rank?"

"I'm not in the navy."

"How many times have you experienced being halted on the high seas by the Japanese Imperial Navy?"

"None."

"You are mistaken," Oyama said. "I am an officer in the Japanese Imperial Navy."

"The only Japanese Navy I know about is the Maritime Self Defense Forces," Fagin said. He took a deep breath. "All this is illegal. I must respectfully protest."

"I advise you to keep such thoughts to yourself!" Oyama said in a loud voice. "And do not tell me lies about not being in the United States Navy. I know your companion well. His name is Lars Stensland, and he was aboard a Norwegian ship we captured months ago."

"I know nothing of that."

"How many decoy ships have been sent out to capture us?"

Fagin shrugged. "I don't know anything about any decoy ships."

"Was it your ship that sank the other destroyer?"

"I don't know about any destroyer being sunk," Fagin insisted. "The only sinking I'm aware of is the *SS Buenaventura*."

Oyama glared at him for a full minute, and Fagin did his best not to sneer in the Oriental's face. Oyama suddenly yelled, "*Mihari*—guards!"

The two guards stepped in, unceremoniously grabbed Fagin, and frog-marched him out into the passageway. He was pushed and pummeled down to the brig deck, but this time he was shoved into a different cell.

Once more, Fagin was in darkness. He sat down in a far corner of the compartment, fully aware that this preliminary interrogation was just the beginning of what would be carefully applied hell.

GEO-X Safe House
Wichita, Kansas
2 August
0430 Hours

Martin Albright came wide awake the instant his shoulder was touched. He sat up in an instinctively quick movement. "Yeah?"

"Your team is alerted," said the custodian who was a permanent resident of the house. His duties were to act as monitor and messenger when required. He was given the cushy assignment after losing a leg to a land mine in Bosnia.

"What condition of alert?" Albright asked.

"Red. You're going into action. The asset will be here in an hour."

"Right," Albright said, putting his feet on the floor. "I'll get the guys up. Is the coffee ready?"

"Naturally. And we've got some jelly rolls to kick you into a sugar high."

"We'll all need it," Albright said, reaching for his trousers.

Geological Exploration—aka Geo-X—was similar to the CIA's program they'd employed in Southeast Asia in the mid–twentieth century with Air America, except this

twenty-first-century version had a lot more kick. The overall parent organization was called Global Resources Corporation, located in Houston, Texas. This was the general
headquarters of the paramilitary conglomerate that mas-
queraded as a petroleum and mineral prospecting enterprise.

All communications, including interception and monitoring of unfriendlies, was carried out by yet another
branch business. This was the Global Industrial Communications and Electronics Company, with offices scattered
among certain strategic locations worldwide. To outsiders,
they appeared to be a small but effective electronics equipment manufacturing firm.

Satellite imagery operations were the responsibility of
Global Aerospace Television Services, Incorporated,
which put its own spacecraft into orbit through commercial
launches made at Cape Canaveral, Florida. Their cover
was to appear to be involved in broadcast TV activities for
various networks around the world.

All necessary air transport missions were the responsibility of Global International Air Services Corporation,
which operated out of a dozen or so airports located in
North and South America, Europe, Africa, and Asia.

All the way down the line of echelons and chains of
command in the Global Resources Corporation was the
Geological Exploration office. This unfriendly group was
run by Bainbridge "the Senator" Collins from a small commercial complex in Wichita, Kansas. It was here where
could be found certain talented individuals with socio-
pathic tendencies augmented by an innate evil cunning-
ness. The sophisticated thugs worked under the command
of Martin Albright. All had extensive military backgrounds
and had seen combat, intelligence, and bodyguard service
in Afghanistan, Kurdish areas of Iraq and Turkey, Bosnia,
East Africa, and other hot spots.

These were the people called in when a problem demanded violent, head-to-head action to be fixed quickly
and permanently.

• • •

The safe house in Wichita was a large, rambling residence located in a rural area just off old Highway 54. Its two stories of large rooms along with a basement provided ample room for people and equipment needed on the special missions the Senator organized.

The full basement, which covered the entire expanse under the safe house, was where briefings and debriefings were held. Now, slurping coffee and munching pastries, were a hundred men of Albright's commando crammed into the space. A map of an island was mounted on the wall to their direct front.

Martin Albright, carrying a sealed packet, came down the stairs to join his men. He went to the podium at the head of the room. He put the bundle of documents on a table next to him, breaking the seal. With that done, he looked up and surveyed the athletic-looking males who gazed back at him in open anticipation of an exciting event. He was always amazed at how clean-cut some of those professional killers could appear.

"Listen up!" he said. "You've already had a preliminary briefing on the potential mission that brought you here. Well, it ain't potential anymore. It's on. The latest situation isn't a good one. The decoy ship that took out a destroyer has been sunk with no known survivors. This included some pals of ours who work for Admiral Paulsen. John Wang is among the dead."

"Shit!" somebody said.

"Yeah," Albright agreed. "Shit. What this boils down to is an invasion of an island." He turned and pointed. "It's shown here on the map. I don't know how accurate this is, and our asset don't either. He tells me all this information was gotten from an old guy in his eighties. Anyhow, they don't want American or Japanese armed forces involved in this operation."

One of the men raised his hand. "What the hell do the Japanese have to do with it?"

"I haven't a clue," Albright answered. "Like always,

you're supposed to do what you're told without any displays of impolite curiosity. Any questions regarding this?" Nobody said anything, so he continued. "I've already got an OPLAN worked out, but I need a few more details before it becomes an OPORD. Okay? Meanwhile, let's hear what the asset has to tell us." He nodded to the custodian.

A moment later, Lieutenant Joel Weatherby from the Office of Naval Intelligence at the Osaka Naval Base stepped into the room. It was SOP that he was not identified to the crowd.

"Good morning," he said, feeling a little uneasy in this less-than-refined company. It took him a moment before his nervousness subsided enough to allow him to speak. He cleared his throat and aimed his laser pointer at the map. "What we have here is Kakureta Island. It is an uncharted feature located in the East China Sea."

The men of the commando leaned forward as Weatherby began his intelligence briefing.

USS Jefferson
East China Sea
1900 Hours

Pamela Drake's arrival on the carrier would have been unsettling for all officers and sailors except for one thing: Captain Myra Fontenac had been assigned as her escort. And this naval officer conducted her duties in a viciously efficient manner.

When the two ladies arrived on a C-2A Greyhound from Osaka, Fontenac, as would be expected, was properly dressed in summer khaki and brought along a kit bag and clothing bag for extra attire. If Pamela had been able to have her way, she would have arrived with close to a dozen pieces of luggage filled mostly with personal items for which she would have no use aboard ship. However, she conformed to regulations—though grudgingly—and brought only one suitcase and a clothing bag. The limited packing space forced the lady journalist to be most efficient and moderate in the selection of her onboard wardrobe.

Pamela brought comfortable running shoes, blouses, slacks, and two sets of safari clothing. This latter attire, which appeared military, consisted of lightweight tan jackets and pants that sported a multitude of pockets. She had a matching baseball-style cap to wear with the outfits. This was the costume she had used in her TV news days. It made her look more of an adventurous participant in the stories she filed from various war zones.

The *Washington Herald-Telegraph* sent a photographer to join her, and it took some extra persuasion on her part to allow him to accompany her out to the carrier. This young man was an eager participant in the story and was thrilled with the assignment. His name was Tommy Dawson, and his feelings for the beautiful Pamela Drake bordered on romantic adoration.

When they first stepped off the Greyhound, Pamela pointed to some aircraft parked on the stern of the flight deck. "Let's go get some pictures of the airplanes," she said to Tommy.

Myra Fontenac, just behind her, reached out and grabbed Pamela's sleeve. "Hold on, Drake," she said. "You don't go anywhere at any time without my okay. Got it? I've been assigned as your escort. In the navy that means I approve where you go. It does *not* mean that I follow you around."

Pamela jerked her arm free. "Let go of me, Fontenac. I have a solid agreement with the United States Navy in regards to this story assignment. So don't start getting bossy and abusive with me."

"The agreement was that you would be imbedded aboard the *USS Jefferson* during this operation," Fontenac said. "Now! You've been imbedded, and here you are. But you're not going to be allowed to have the run of the ship. And that goes for interviews, too. I want all your requests for interviews and photos, no matter how trivial, turned in to me personally. And in writing."

Pamela reacted with a furious glare, and she started to protest but wisely stopped herself. She stood white-faced, struggling with her emotions. Finally she said,

"Fine, Captain Fontenac. May I be escorted to my quarters? I would like to unpack and settle in as quickly as possible. Evidently I've got a shitload of requests to write out. By the way, do you want those in triplicate?"

"Don't trouble yourself," Fontenac said. "If I need any extras, I'll have a yeoman Xerox me some copies."

"Of course," Pamela said.

Tommy Dawson, smiling uncertainly, warily watched the two women as their conversation deteriorated into a staring contest. His heartbeats quickened when Fontenac turned her eyes to him.

"Give me that camera equipment!" the captain said.

"Uh—huh?" Tommy stammered.

"Hand it over! You'll get it back for those times when taking photographs is authorized."

"Yes, ma'am," Tommy said, complying.

"All right," Fontenac said. She turned back to Pamela. "Before you go to your quarters, I'm going to take you to meet Captain Tarkington. He's the skipper, and I believe he wishes to have a few words with you about protocol, conditions of your visit, and other odds and ends."

"Lead on!" Pamela snapped.

The pair walked across the flight deck with Tommy scurrying after them.

Destroyer **Isamashii**
Kakureta Island
3 August ·
0230 Hours

Lars Stensland lay on the deck of the brig cell in a semi-conscious state, naked and sweating heavily in the heat. His body and face were covered with bruises and welts that were the result of prolonged vicious beatings. A bright electric bulb lit the compartment in a stark glare. Between this illumination and constant waking by the guards, he had gotten only brief snatches of sleep during the previous twenty-four hours.

• • •

Stensland's first trip to Oyama's office had begun calmly
enough. The Japanese officer displayed a polite, almost
friendly attitude toward him. But this quickly evolved to
sarcasm when he began talking extensively of the *SS Edvard Grieg* and the time Stensland and the rest of the crew
had been held for ransom.

Then the serious questioning began. Oyama, as with
Gerald Fagin, brought in the decoy ship angle. "Your ship
was in the pay of the Americans, was it not?"

Stensland shrugged. "I am afraid I do not understand.
We were a merchant ship with a normal cargo. Why did
you not order us to heave to like you did the *Edvard Grieg*?
You fired on us without warning and sank us. All my crew,
save Mr. Fagin, died in the incident. That was a criminal
act."

Oyama stood up, walked around the desk, and gave him
a traditional hard Imperial Japanese Navy slap that almost
knocked the Scandinavian off his feet. "Do not complain
or make demands of me, *bakamono!* You are at my mercy.
Do you not understand that?"

Stensland, angry about the smack on the jaw, restrained
himself as he recalled Fagin's advice not to become arro-
gant and impolite. He forced himself to adopt a humble attitude. "I am sorry."

"Tell me about your friend Fagin," Oyama said. "What
is his rank in the American Navy?"

"He is a merchant marine officer," Stensland said.

"Liar!" Oyama screamed. "He has the look of a navy
officer. What is he then? CIA?"

"He is a deck officer," Stensland insisted.

"*Mihari*—guards!" Oyama yelled.

Immediately two burly sailors in shorts and T-shirts
came into the room. They worked efficiently, grabbing
Stensland by the wrists and dragging him to a spot between
two hammock rings in the bulkhead. They tied each of his
hands to one, then stepped back, leaving the Scandinavian
facing the wall with his arms stretched out between the re-
straints.

Oyama came up to Stensland's back. He thrust a wooden staff in front of the prisoner's face. "Do you see this?"

"Yes," Stensland replied warily.

"It is called a *bokken*," Oyama explained. "It is a wooden sword used to practice the art of *kendo*—sword fighting. It is most unpleasant to be hit by one, thus those who are fencing are encouraged to do their very best to avoid the pain of receiving a blow from the *bokken*."

Stensland closed his eyes and clenched his teeth. He knew what was coming. Oyama lifted the *bokken* into the high preparatory position for a horizontal stroke. When he swung, he did so with all his strength. The force of the blow knocked the wind from the prisoner.

"Who is your friend Fagin?"

Another stroke.

"How was the destroyer *Chujitsuna* sunk?"

The third heavy stroke followed.

"How many decoy ships are out looking for us?"

The serious phase of the interrogation quickly moved into a higher gear.

Now in the brightly lit cell, Stensland was in such great agony that he couldn't tell where the pain was exactly coming from. He gingerly struggled to a sitting position, gritting his teeth against the acute discomfort. He carefully felt his upper left arm and could tell it was broken; and some pushes with his tongue showed he had several loosened teeth. When he tried to look around, he found it almost impossible to see out of his swollen eyes.

The door of the cell suddenly opened, and two pairs of hands grabbed him and began dragging him across the deck. The heavy grip on his broken arm caused him to scream.

CHAPTER TWENTY-THREE

Japanese Foreign Ministry
Tokyo
3 August
0815 Hours

The two men in the small meeting room did not rank as cabinet ministers in their respective national governments. Nor did they hold elective offices, enjoy official authority, nor were they well-known by their fellow citizens. But they did have those two tangible qualities so important in international relations: influence and the right contacts.

Horace DeVoss had served several United States presidents as a sort of supernumerary in the State Department. This tall, thin, unimposing man with a Ph.D. in American history from Yale, was one of those career diplomats who had just about seen it all. The bulk of his twenty-five-year career had consisted of shuttle diplomacy in which he went into sensitive areas before any official negotiations began. DeVoss cleared the way by removing stumbling blocks that would hinder deals being made between the United States government and whoever else might be concerned. Many times this involved working with intelligence agencies and even criminal elements from both the United States and foreign countries.

DeVoss's counterpart, who sat across the table from him, was Hajiri Onwani, who was also employed in an apolitical career in which he had provided valuable diplomatic services for a variety of Japanese prime ministers. He was now on the Kaigun Samurai case while maintaining official contact with Gomme and Hikui Zunsuno.

Onwani and DeVoss had known each other for more than three decades and had smoothed the way for open talks on such things as American troops remaining on Okinawa, and U.S. Navy nuclear vessels visiting Japanese ports.

Now they had this new sensitive subject to deal with: Kakureta Island, the Kaigun Samurai, and the Kamisaku force field machine. DeVoss had shown up in Tokyo with full disclosure on those subjects. The U.S. government did not think it wise to conceal this technology. Eventually the Japanese would hear about it from the people on Kakureta in any case. Therefore, it was considered a diplomatic necessity to reveal its existence to a small sphere of the Japanese leadership.

DeVoss opened the meeting between himself and Onwani with the emphatic statement that the United States of America claimed the island, the force field machine, and the right to punish any criminals involved in international piracy and murder committed on the East China Sea.

Onwani's reaction to these demands was one of quintessential diplomatic nonemotion when he replied, "The Japanese government recognizes the expenses incurred by America in discovering the facts behind this unprecedented situation, Mr. DeVoss. We do not know the details, of course, but we assume there may have been certain physical risks taken by U.S. citizens."

"We are pleased that the Japanese government appreciates the extent of our efforts, Mr. Onwani," DeVoss assured him.

"However, the Kaigun Samurai is obviously made up of Japanese citizens," Onwani said. "And the island, though uncharted, is Japanese sovereign territory. It goes without saying that this technology known as the Kamisaku is also rightfully the property of Japan."

"The Japanese government would incur serious disadvantages by taking possession of this island, its people, and the Kamisaku, Mr. Onwani," DeVoss pointed out. "By doing this, Japan would be forced to assume all monetary responsibilities in regards to ransoms, murders, losses of ships, and the cost spent by the United States in discovering the perpetrators of these crimes."

"At this point in our conversation," Onwani said, "may I point out the fact that not all the people on Kakureta are guilty of these misdeeds. According to your information, there are many young people there. We would like to accept the responsibility for their transportation back to Japan, where we will provide good homes and the proper education necessary for them to find places in modern Japanese society."

"That is commendable, and I can assure you that my government would be very happy to concede that to you, Mr. Onwani," DeVoss said. "But those other matters must be negotiated. We must first invade Kakureta and bring the people under our authority and control. That could cost us many lives."

"A tragedy for all," Onwani said.

"Would the Japanese government be willing to participate in that invasion with us?" DeVoss asked.

"Unfortunately, Mr. DeVoss, our Self Defense Forces would not be authorized to fight against fellow Japanese, no matter how misguided they may be."

DeVoss expected that. "Then would it be reasonable for us to request diplomatic services, Mr. Onwani? By that, I mean assist us in making contact with the leadership on Kakureta Island."

"I have been authorized to offer you such aid," Onwani said.

"Accepted," DeVoss said. "I can arrange for a delegation to meet with your government to work out the details."

"That would be most agreeable," Onwani said. "I will make arrangements to summon our side of the table."

"Very well," DeVoss said, gathering up his papers. "I believe that concludes this morning's business between us."

"Indeed," Onwani said. He stood up, then suddenly remembered something. "Oh! Shinju wants me to invite you to supper this evening, Horace. She says she will prepare your favorite Japanese dish."

DeVoss smiled. "*Suimono* and *koi no furai*? Tell her I'll be there with bells on, Hajiri!"

"She is most sorry that your wife could not accompany you on this trip."

"I'm afraid Gretchen has gotten herself deeply involved with a children's center in Washington," DeVoss said. "But she'll see you when you and Shinju come to America in November. We want to have you over for Thanksgiving."

"Wonderful, Horace!" Onwani exclaimed. "Turkey and dressing. I cannot wait!"

The two diplomats shook hands, then left the room.

Kakureta Island
4 August
0700 Hours

The sight of the aircraft overhead, while rare, did not particularly alarm the island's population. Such events happened two or three times a year, and everyone knew the Kamisaku would keep them hidden from electronic observance. But this time, the airplane, instead of flying on to some unknown destination, began a wide, diving turn in a maneuver that encircled the island. Then it straightened out and came in fast, obviously with the intent of making a low-altitude pass over Kakureta.

The S-3B Viking was normally used for ASW, but its crew had been sent off the *USS Jefferson* that morning to fly to a specific longitude and latitude to see if an uncharted island did indeed exist at that particular point on the planet Earth. The TACCO kept looking from her radar to the outside view of what was a populated island that should have shown up on her scope.

"Good God!" she said to the pilot. "There's not a shimmer showing."

"Then this is definitely the place they wanted us to check out," the pilot said.

With the mission accomplished, the aircraft quickly gained altitude and turned onto the proper course for the return flight to the carrier.

Washington, D.C.
Morris Arms Apartments
5 August
0215 Hours

Mori Kawaguchi, the Japanese gentleman who identified himself as Kawaguchi-*san* when he delivered ransom demands for the Kaigun Samurai, had been closely monitored by agents of the FBI. This surveillance was begun almost from the moment he made his first call on the Norwegian embassy. An arrest and detainment could have easily occurred weeks before, but no real advantage would have been gained from doing so. The man undoubtedly had little information about the perpetrators of the crimes on the high seas and acted under orders from persons he did not personally know. Thus, it had been decided to keep him under constant observation until further action seemed feasible.

The revelations of Dr. Gomme Zunsuno made Kawaguchi's arrest and subsequent interrogation a necessity. The most important matter was learning when, where, and how he was informed of captured ships and crews.

The trio of agents had rented an apartment on the floor above Kawaguchi's residence in anticipation of that early morning's activities. When the orders came to take the man into custody, they simply walked down a flight of stairs to the third floor and went to the door. A couple of deft twists of a skeleton key popped the lock, and the insertion of a shaved plastic card finished the job by pushing back the dead bolt block against its holding spring and rotating cam.

The FBI men entered the apartment, crossed the living room, and turned into the bedroom. The slight figure of

Kawaguchi could easily be seen under the sheets. He gasped a snore, then came abruptly awake as he was hauled to his feet. It took a few moments for him to comprehend that he was completely helpless and in the firm grip of some very large visitors.

"FBI!" one snapped. "You're under arrest."

"Here," another said, pulling a sheet off the bed. "Wrap this around you."

"Please," Kawaguchi said. "May I get dressed?"

"There's a jumpsuit down at the federal lockup just waiting for you," the third said as he put the cuffs around the prisoner's small wrists.

Kawaguchi was taken downstairs to a waiting Ford van that immediately sped off as soon as everyone was settled in. The Japanese, now fully awake, angrily demanded to know what was going on. His captors remained silent, letting him rant for the few moments it took him to realize they had no intention of answering his questions or engaging him in any sort of conversation.

Kawaguchi recognized the FBI building when they pulled up to the curb. The vehicle's side doors opened, and everyone exited, taking him with them. He was hustled along in the middle of the small crowd, hanging on to the sheet as best he could with his cuffed hands. They went inside, passed reception, and went down a hall, then made a couple of turns before stopping in front of a single elevator door. The conveyance took them down to what was obviously a subbasement. The group followed another hallway to a room and went inside. Kawaguchi was pushed down onto a metal chair. A bright light came on, and his escorts stepped back out of the way to a position behind him.

Charlie Greenfield, a senior agent who had been impatiently directing what seemed a do-nothing operation for several months, entered the room. He walked in front of the prisoner, nodding to him.

Kawaguchi smiled politely and nodded back. "Good morning, sir."

"Good morning, Mori Kawaguchi," Greenfield said. "We have some questions to put to you. It will be to your definite and immediate advantage if you answer them as truthfully and completely as you can."

"I do not know anything," Kawaguchi said, knowing well what the subject of the interrogation would be. "I have explained this to the many people with whom I conducted negotiations."

"We know now of Kakureta Island," Greenfield said. "And of the Kaigun Samurai, along with many other things."

What he said meant nothing to Kawaguchi. He was a *hokannin,* one of the trusted ones who worked for the secret naval society, and who were purposely kept in the dark. All he knew was that he performed great patriotic services by doing his masters' bidding.

Kawaguchi sighed and smiled pleasantly. "I now recognize my disadvantage in this situation," he said. "May I have please a glass of water before I answer your questions? My mouth is most dry, and it is difficult to speak."

Greenfield looked at one of the men. "Bring him some water. There're some paper cups outside by the fountain in the hall."

Kawaguchi ran his tongue along his teeth, then went directly to the spot on a molar. A quick push, and the cyanide capsule dislodged. He bit down on it, gasped loudly, then fell to the floor, dead.

One of the men rushed to his body and knelt down, vainly trying to find a pulse or other sign of life. He stood up and shrugged.

"Now ain't this some shit?"

Kakureta Island
1600 Hours

Another aircraft appeared, but it was not the same one from the day before. This one was a helicopter, flying quite slowly though at a bit higher altitude than the airplane. This time the AA gunners on the destroyer *Isamashii* stood by their weapons, more than happy to shoot it down. The gunnery officer, holding his samurai sword, waited impatiently for the word to be passed down from the bridge that would authorize him to order the commencement of firing. But the only activity from the ship's captain was to stand on the signal deck and watch the chopper through his binoculars.

Hara-*sama,* shogun and supreme leader of the Kaigun Samurai, had issued strict orders that no hostile actions would be taken at the appearance of any aircraft unless it launched an attack. He instinctively knew that something consequential was in the making, and he did not want to rush into any rash action until he knew for sure how this developing situation would evolve. He'd had a nightlong discussion with the chief counselor, Sonkei Hanagawa, about the latest events and what they might mean.

Everyone on the ground watched the helicopter as it turned toward them, obviously going to make a run from one end of Kakureta to the other along the narrowest configuration of the island. Suddenly, leaflets began spilling out of the fuselage. When the last piece of paper was expelled, the aircraft turned seaward, gaining speed as it flew away.

In a rare display of spontaneous indiscipline, the people rushed to see what the visitor had left behind. What they found after the papers fluttered to the ground was a message in Japanese. They scanned the lines, then instinctively looked in the direction of the shogun's castle in a collective perplexed need for guidance.

People of Kakureta Island:
    Greetings from your friends and families in Japan. Since becoming aware of your existence, we have been looking forward to contacting you and bringing you back into the bosom of your nation and race.
    Tomorrow at noon a helicopter will visit you again. This time it will land. We urge you to greet it with open friendship. There will be two important officials aboard who wish to speak to your leaders. One is a representative of the Japanese Foreign Ministry, and the other is from the

Department of State of the United States of America. This
is the beginning of a process that will bring you great pros-
perity and happiness.

We weep with joy at the thought of bringing you into
our hearts to take your rightful places in our great nation.

The People of Japan

Commander Gentaro Oyama, holding a leaflet, ran as
fast as he could from the docks to the castle of Hara-*sama*.
He was quickly admitted into the inner sanctum of the
leader and escorted directly to the throne room. The officer
rushed into the chamber, then dropped to his knees in a
deep bow, touching his forehead to the floor. When he
straightened up, he handed the leaflet to the shogun.

Hara-*sama* read it carefully, then paused for a moment
to think. He glanced down at Oyama, painfully noting the
confusion and uncertainty in his young face. The shogun
carefully rolled the leaflet into a neat tube and stuck it into
the large sleeve of his kimono. This was something that he
and old Sonkei Hanagawa had been expecting.

"The helicopter will be allowed to land," he said. "The
visitors will be brought to me and shown every courtesy."

"Hei!" Oyama said.

Hara-*sama* remained alone for several moments after
Oyama left. The time of a great reckoning was upon him.
The actions he took in the next few days would either result
in victory or ignominious defeat for the Kaigun Samurai
and Imperial Japanese Navy.

6 August
Noon

A half-dozen SH-60 Seahawk helicopters hovered some
forty feet off the waves at a distance of five miles from the
coast of Kakureta Island. One of them carried the two-man
diplomatic delegation made up of Horace DeVoss of the
United States State Department, and Hajiri Onwani of the

Japanese Foreign Ministry. The other five contained the fully armed and ready attack-and-support elements commanded by the CIA's Martin Albright. At the first sign of treachery on the part of Kakureta's leadership, those five aircraft would sweep in for a violent rescue operation that would be conducted with full prejudice and deadly force.

At high noon the one chopper's nose dropped and began a swift run in toward the island. The pilot and copilot, working with a diagram of the destination supplied by Dr. Gomme Zunsuno, knew exactly where they were going. They flew past the breakwater, over the harbor where an old Soviet destroyer was moored, then inland to the location of the shogun's wooden castle. At that point, the Seahawk pulled back into a hover, then slowly descended to land.

DeVoss and Onwani, each carrying a briefcase, stepped carefully to the ground, then hurried out of the powerful downdraft generated by the Seahawk's four rotor blades. They were met at the rear entrance of the castle by a young, boyish officer. He saluted them without making any greetings, then turned and motioned them to follow him. After entering the building, they were led around the veranda of an inner courtyard to a pair of red doors. These were immediately opened, and the officer indicated they were to enter.

This was Hara-*sama*'s throne room, and he sat at the head of the chamber with Sonkei Hanagawa, his venerable chief adviser. The old man had advised the shogun not to mention the two prisoners held in the brig of the destroyer. He also counseled Hara-*sama* to stand firm and uncommitted to any demands made by the visitors.

The shogun and his adviser were seated on traditional curved, backless chairs. Two more examples of the furniture were to their front. DeVoss and Onwani walked up to the two men, bowing stiffly.

"*Konichiwa,*" Onwani said. "I am Hajiri Onwani of the Japanese Foreign Ministry. My companion is Horace DeVoss of the American State Department."

Old Hanagawa stood up and returned the bow. "I am Sonkei Hanagawa, the shogun's chief counsel. This is Hara-*sama*, the shogun of Kakureta Island."

"I am pleased to meet you," Hara-*sama* said. "I welcome you both to Kakureta Island. Please be seated."

The two sat down, placing their briefcases at their sides. Onwani studied the shogun's features. "I think we have met before, Hara-*sama*. Did you not serve in the Maritime Self Defense Forces?"

"I do not discuss my past," Hara-*sama* said.

"As you wish," Onwani said. "As the shogun of this island, am I to assume you are also the leader of the Kaigun Samurai?"

"I also refuse to discuss my present situation," Hara-*sama* said. He looked menacingly at Horace DeVoss. "Why are you here?"

"The United States of America is deeply involved in this situation because of acts committed on the high seas," DeVoss said in a firm tone. He would let the shogun know that America was a determined and influential player in the present situation. "However, at this juncture, I am only an observer. It has been agreed between the United States and Japan that the Japanese government will deal with you at this point. We reserve the right to step in when we think the moment is right."

Hara-*sama* turned his eyes back to Onwani. "Then have your say, Onwani-*san*."

"The Japanese government has sent me to urge you to step down from whatever authority you have here and return this island to Japan," Onwani said. "This will mean that whoever here desires to be repatriated to the mainland will be allowed to return."

"Many of our people have never been to Japan," Hara-*sama* said.

"This island *is* Japan," Onwani declared. "I said they would be allowed to return to the mainland."

"We of Kakureta do not recognize any authority of the present Japanese government over us," Hara-*sama* said. "This declaration most certainly includes America."

Horace DeVoss entered the conversation, saying, "You have stolen ships and cargo, sir. You have kidnapped crews. These were from many different countries, which desire restitution for those crimes. And that includes punishing the person or persons responsible for the murder of the crews of the *SS Dileas* and the *SS Buenaventura*."

"This meeting is over," Hara-*sama* announced.

"We have diplomatic documents to pass on to you," Onwani said.

"This meeting is over."

DeVoss and Onwani grabbed their briefcases and stood up. They purposely did not bow as they turned and walked from the throne room. The young officer waited for them and gestured they were to follow him. They retraced their steps back outside the building. The Seahawk, its rotors disengaged, waited. As they walked toward the aircraft, DeVoss glanced at Onwani.

"We are at war," he said.

"Unfortunately, you are right, my friend," Onwani said. "Beginning this moment, the Japanese government will step out of the situation until or if developments warrant our participation once again."

They entered the chopper fuselage just as the pilot engaged the rotors to lift the aircraft into the air.

CHAPTER TWENTY-FOUR

Kakureta Island
7 August
0630 Hours

The Avenger Flight had approximately twenty miles to fly from the *USS Jefferson* to their target on Kakureta. They had been catapulted off the carrier at 0623 hours and now had the objective in sight; it was the destroyer anchored at the docks in the warehouse district of the island. Commander Gene Erickson, leading the trail of four aircraft, alerted his people as he lined up for the now customary tactic of attacking from stern to bow on the warship.

The intelligence for the bombing raid was gotten from Horace DeVoss after he and Hajiri Onwani returned from the conference with the shogun, Hara-*sama*. Onwani, acting under strict orders from the Japanese government, made no contact with the aviators to give them any tactical information. DeVoss sketched out the layout of the wharf area, showing the destroyer's exact position where it was docked. It was decided that in order to avoid collateral casualties within the population, the attack would be conducted in such a manner that any bombs or machine gun rounds missing the vessel would strike in the harbor water rather than any occupied areas or buildings. DeVoss stated that he saw no AA emplacements anywhere on Kakureta but warned Erickson and his people that the destroyer seemed to be fully armed and capable of returning fire.

Now Erickson checked the Xerox of DeVoss's map, making sure he was coming in on the correct side to rake the destroyer. The bomb bay doors of the Avengers had been opened immediately after getting airborne off the carrier, and the four bombardiers sat at their stations ready to pull the levers that would ripple a total of twenty 500-pounders onto the unsuspecting ship and her crew.

Erickson came in at a thousand feet ASL and gave the execute order to James Warrenton when he was in the right position. The bombs came out a millisecond apart from *Avenger1,* striking the target just as Westy Fields began his run.

Destroyer **Isamashii**
The Brig

When the first four bombs hit the destroyer, Gerald Fagin and Lars Stensland were together belowdecks in a brig cell. The interrogations had unexpectedly ceased the day before, and they were given the khaki trousers of their merchant marine uniforms to cover their lower nakedness. The ship's physician had even applied a splint to the Norwegian's broken upper left arm.

The *Isamashii* rocked violently, causing the two prisoners to roll to one side of the steel compartment. At almost the exact instant they stood up, the pair was knocked off their feet by three more quick detonations. Both came to the same immediate conclusion: they had to get the hell off the ship, even though they didn't know the sources of the explosions.

The soon to be ex-prisoners pushed the cell door open, lurching out into the passageway. The lights were out, but a few shafts of faint illumination came down from above, indicating the route up the ladders was open all the way to the main deck.

When the second four bombs struck, the bulkheads buckled, causing steel plates to bend and pop open. By the time Fagin and Stensland reached the midpoint on the way to the deck above, the water was already swirling around their feet. They continued going up another deck. Now they saw corpses, including their tormentor Commander Gentaro Oyama. He lay sprawled in front of an open watertight door, almost cut in half by what appeared to be fragments of his metal desk. His mouth seemed open in a silent scream, and his eyes were swollen shut in his battered face that had been blanched by the loss of blood and other bodily fluids.

When Fagin and Stensland reached the next deck, they encountered nervous sailors rushing to their damage control stations. None, including officers and petty officers, paid any mind to the loose captives, and they were able to continue upward unimpeded. Now they could hear the angry roar of aircraft engines.

"That's got to be Erickson and his bunch!" Fagin yelled happily.

"Remember that they do not know we are aboard," Stensland reminded his companion.

"Whoops! Let's get the hell off this bucket!"

They instinctively threw themselves down when the next series of bombs struck the vessel. This time the attack resulted in a marked listing to starboard by the battered ship. Stensland had reinjured his fracture by then, but gritted his teeth against the pain as he got to his feet to follow Fagin up to the main deck. They went to the railing to leap overboard but had to duck back into the superstructure as the last quartet of bombs blasted the dying destroyer with thundering detonations and flying chunks of steel. Fagin gave Stensland a quick but careful look.

"Are you up to jumping overboard?"

Stensland shrugged weakly. "I don't think I have much choice."

"Follow me into the water, and I'll help you swim," Fagin said. "I saw a stretch of sandy beach straight head."

He went out, jumped over the rail into the harbor water feetfirst. When he broke the surface, he saw Stensland splash a couple of yards away. He swam over and grabbed his friend's good arm. They began paddling toward their destination just as the strafing runs began.

Stensland looked at the Avengers. "What a beautiful sight!"

Fagin spat out some water he'd taken into his mouth. "Yeah! If they don't kill us!"

They swam awkwardly, slowly getting closer to the opposite shore. Spent .50-caliber cartridges splattered around them as the Avengers whipped by, pouring fire bursts onto the *Isamashii*. Ten minutes later, the escapees were ashore, and they stumbled into the sparse scrub brush to get out of sight as quickly as possible.

Noon

Hara-*sama* stood on the roof of his castle, looking toward the wharf area. The aerial attack was over, and he could easily see the destroyer *Isamashii* lying on her side in the harbor. Several small craft were beside her, pulling both survivors and corpses from the water. The inadequate medical facilities of Kakureta would be strained to the ultimate by the number of casualties from the attack on the ship. Women and children lined the docks, looking desperately for the husbands, fathers, and brothers who had been aboard when the bombing and strafing started.

Hara-*sama* slowly turned and went to the trapdoor that offered entrance into the interior of the frame palace. He climbed down the steps and made his way through the maze of corridors until he reached his private quarters. His wife Hano seemed dazed as she sat on the floor in the corner of their bedroom. She was weeping, but without sobs or tears. Her body shook slightly as she stared straight ahead in shocked disbelief.

Hara-*sama* went to his weapons closet and withdrew the bow and quiver of arrows. This was a time when he must turn to *kyujutsu* for guidance in decision making. He slung the quiver over his shoulder and started to leave when Hano unexpectedly spoke aloud.

"Why did not the Kamisaku protect us, *shujin*?"

"We have been betrayed," he replied as calmly as if he were responding to a question about the weather. "Our enemies from within have told our enemies from without what they must do to destroy us."

"I am glad our children are at school in Japan," Hano said.

This was a thought that had swept unbidden through Hara-*sama*'s mind. He knew moments before as he gazed at the destroyed ship in the harbor that it was a selfish attitude in light of so many people dying that day. But he was still glad his oldest son had not been aboard the destroyer. Death in battle didn't seem so glorious when it involved one of his children.

Hano now noticed his bow and arrows. "What are you going to do, *shujin*?"

"I must contemplate and discover what the spirits of *Yamato Damashii* will command me to do," he replied.

"Have the war gods turned against us?" she asked.

"I do not know," Hara-*sama* replied sadly.

He walked from the room to the rear egress of the castle. After going outside, he continued out into the open countryside to the archery area. When he reached the spot, he sat down on the ground, placing the quiver and bow to his direct front. Then he closed his eyes and let his inner spirit carry his consciousness away to where the god *Sieshin-no-Kyujutsu* lived in that place where mortals could never physically visit. For more than an hour Hara-*sama* was unaware of not only his surroundings but of his own personal existence.

When he returned to full wakefulness it was a gradual process that was at first confusing before slowly evolving to absolute clarity. Now he had to continue the meditative ceremony in the proper manner to find out what he must do.

The shogun stood up and took his bow. After pulling the sacred long arrow with the white falcon feathers out of the quiver, he slipped its notch into the string. He drew it back, closing his eyes for a moment, then aimed at a leaf at the end of a limb. When the arrow was loosed, it streaked directly toward the target, then suddenly veered to one side and struck the tree trunk. The shaft shattered like it had been made of glass.

The message was clear.

1600 Hours

Carrier Battle Group Fourteen made its presence known on the watery horizon of the sea that surrounded Kakureta Island. An aircraft carrier, two guided missile cruisers, one guided missile destroyer, and a frigate could be seen by the now frightened and uncertain population.

Everyone—officers and *jun-i* alike—had always been filled with an optimistic confidence. Even if they faced a situation that would require that they fight to death, they believed the result would always be victorious. Their leader, the great shogun Hara-*sama,* had been put on Earth by the warrior spirits of Japan to bring back the grandeur of the ancient empire. The successful completion of this sacred goal was inevitable.

Or at least it used to be.

The Kamisaku had failed. Foreigners had shown up brazenly on the island, then bombed the ship *Isamashii* (the *Courageous*) into an obscene wreck that excreted oil like the carcass of a rotten whale washed up on a beach. The damage to the keel, however, had been self-inflicted when a preset explosive was detonated to obliterate the ship's Kamisaku.

Now a great enemy fleet floated nearby, obviously ready to deal out more fiery death and destruction to this holy place. The men of Kakureta were silent and glum, while their women trembled and wept with fear. The children stayed home from school, huddled in frightened little groups.

This was a situation that could well require that everyone—men, women, and children—fight to the death.

The old Admiral Sonkei Hanagawa was driven in a medical van from island headquarters to the castle of Hara-*sama*. When he went inside, a guard appeared and immediately escorted the ninety-year-old man to the throne room. He found the shogun sitting in the somber company of the other senior officers that were still on the island. Those missing included Hara-*sama's* best friend, Rear Admiral Heideki Tanaka, who was still at sea aboard the cruiser *Hayaken*.

Hanagawa bowed deeply and sadly. "Hara-*sama*," he said, "I have done your bidding exactly as you instructed me."

"Please give me a report, Hanagawa-*san*," the Shogun said.

"Hei!" Hanagawa said obediently. "All the Kamisaku have been destroyed along with the technical papers. Dr. Zunsuno's house has been searched thoroughly, and nothing was found pertaining to the sacred barriers."

"Very well," Hara-*sama* said. "Please continue."

"A message has been sent to the cruiser *Hayaken* to return to Kakureta," Hanagawa said. "Specific instructions were included that informed Admiral Tanaka of the coming occupation of Kakureta by enemy armed forces."

"I am glad I was not there to see my friend's face," Hara-*sama* said in sincere regret and sadness.

"Those instructions included your directive that he is to cooperate fully with the occupiers," Hanagawa said. "He was also told to destroy the Kakureta aboard his vessel. Thus, I have fulfilled my duties, Hara-*sama*."

"I have one more task for you," Hara-*sama* said. "You are to contact the American fleet that now stands off our shores. Pass on a message from me to the gentlemen from the Japanese Foreign Ministry and the American State Department that at oh six hundred hours on August eight, Kakureta Island will be surrendered to them."

The gasps from the assembled officers were loud in the room. Hanagawa felt exactly the same, but he remained passive. *"Hei*, Hara-*sama!"*

One of the young officers leaped to his feet. "We must give up our lives rather than suffer the disgrace of surrender. *Bushido* demands nothing less!"

Hara-*sama* scowled fiercely at the protester. "I have issued my orders! I will not tolerate disobedience!"

The young officer bowed respectfully, saying, "Forgive my impoliteness, Hara-*sama*."

"Thank you," the shogun said. "Now I would be alone."

The others stood up and looked at him, their faces twisted into expressions of grief and sorrow. After bowing, they turned and followed the old man from the chamber.

CHAPTER TWENTY-FIVE

Kakureta Island
8 August
2401 Hours

The fenced enclosure behind the shogun's castle was illuminated by flickering paper lanterns hooked to ten-foot-tall bamboo poles. A nine-meter square platform covered with white muslin stood to the front of the assembled guests. These were the senior officers of the Kaigun Samurai, and all were dressed in the garb of ancient Japanese noblemen. They carried the long *katana* and shorter *wakizashi* swords in their obis, sitting on *magari* chairs brought from the castle for the occasion. They were a silent group with heads bowed and eyes looking down at their feet.

Hara-*sama* walked onto the scene, followed by Sonkei Hanagawa. The old admiral was dressed in the same manner as the others, but the shogun wore a plain white kimono, and there was only a *wakizashi* in his obi. The pair walked up to the platform, and Hara-*sama* stepped up on it, then turned to face the audience for a long, solemn moment. Then he slowly lowered himself to his knees, obviously struggling for self-control. After a few moments he felt confident enough of his command over his emotions to speak.

"Hanagawa will be your leader," he announced. "The honorable admiral will lead you and the rest of the Kaigun Samurai through the negotiations of surrender to the foreigners who are even now waiting to come ashore on our sacred island. You will offer them no resistance, and you will order your men to follow your example. This is the end of our society. It was only through the deepest and most painful meditation that I reached this sad conclusion. This is our inevitable *Karma,* thus the lives of our followers must be preserved. We are not to vainly sacrifice them as was done the generation of young men of World War Two. There would be no honor in such an action, and at a time like this we must exhibit only the most civilized of behavior."

He paused to let the words impress his listeners. The Kaigun Samurai officers acknowledged their willingness to obey in silent homage.

Hara-*sama* then continued, "I further charge you to tell the story of the Kaigun Samurai to the Japanese people, so that they will know we were devoted fully to *Bushido* and followed its tenets to the end of our existence. They must fully realize that our final actions involved not only the preservation of life and civilization but the beginning of a new enlightenment."

The shogun was once again seized by strong emotion. He was forced to suppress himself from openly weeping. After a fitful couple of minutes, he was able to speak again.

"I have written a death *haiku* to mark this last act of mine. I do this to accept all the blame, the criticism, and the denouncements that outsiders may heap upon the Kaigun Samurai. I absolve you and the people from all responsibility and culpability through this last act of my mortal life. Therefore, you may start your own lives again as you follow a path that will lead you to a more peaceful existence in a modern Japan you must wholly embrace and revere."

The audience remained silent in their sorrow, looking up as Hara-*sama* pulled his death *haiku* from the sleeve of the white kimono. When he began to read it in a loud, firm voice, several wept audibly.

An honorable death
means eternal life
for the true samurai.

Hara-*sama* drew the *wakizashi* and held it out. Hana-gawa went to a bucket beside the platform that was filled with *chikara mizo* power water. He dipped a ladle into the sacred liquid, then poured it over the blade of the shogun's short sword. After doing the same to his long *katana,* he stepped up on the platform, taking up a position to the shogun's left rear.

Hara-*sama* picked up a piece of *chikara gami* power paper and wrapped it around the blade of the *wakizashi.* He grasped it, aiming the point of the weapon at his abdomen. Now Hanagawa raised his *katana* high in preparation to strike down at the back of the shogun's neck. Hara-*sama* plunged the *wakizashi* into his belly, drawing it across his body. At the exact moment that his entrails spilled out of the wound, Hanagawa swung down his sword, decapitating his master.

The head fell to the platform, then rolled off onto the ground. The nearest officer left his chair to rush forward and pick it up. After brushing away the dirt on the distorted features, he placed it reverently beside the body that had collapsed forward until the stump of the neck rested on the muslin cover.

0615 Hours

The senior officers of the Kaigun Samurai appreciated the fact that their sailors had been brought up under harsh, unrelenting discipline that stressed blind obedience and even a willingness to die for the cause. However, they also knew that young men could be emotional under certain circumstances, and the fact that they had been ordered to give up something they had been taught should be defended unto death could bring about radical and irrational reactions.

Thus, an order was issued that all personal armament such as rifles, pistols, submachine guns, and other hand- or shoulder-fired weaponry was to be turned in to the central armory and put under lock and key. Everyone was then ordered to the docks to hear an address by Sonkei Hanagawa. They assembled in an orderly manner, silent and respectful, knowing that this would be an occasion that would change their lives forever. After a quarter of an hour the old counselor and the most senior officers walked onto the scene with an escort of sailors.

"By order of the shogun Hara-*sama,* I take command of Kakureta Island and the Kaigun Samurai," Hanagawa announced. "It is in this new office that I inform you the shogun orders us to surrender to the forces that are now off our coast. No matter the pain, we are all obligated by our sacred and binding traditions to obey our leader's final orders to us."

Any uncertainty among the young hotheads was swept away by the demeanor of Hanagawa and the senior officers with him.

"Last night," Hanagawa continued, "our shogun committed *seppuku* so his blood might wash away any blame that outsiders would cast down on us." A sudden eruption of wails and gasps came from the crowd. "His sacrifice makes it unnecessary for anyone to end his own life for the shame of this surrender. He has taken that humiliation with him into the eternal life of all true and honorable samurai. This was his last gift to you." Hanagawa paused and gazed affectionately out at the people. "You are to now retire to your homes and await further instructions."

When the five Seahawk helicopters appeared out of the sky, approaching from the direction of the carrier, all women and children were inside their dwellings. A special honor guard detachment of sailors was formed up in the open area behind the shogun's castle. The choppers came in, landing in a circle around the assembled sailors.

Martin Albright's paramilitary commandos rushed from the fuselages and formed up a defensive perimeter backed up by machine guns and mortars. Their appearance seemed bizarre to the Kaigun Samurai officers and sailors who were used to the militant orderliness of the Imperial Navy. These strangers wore various camouflage-pattern uniforms, sported no insignia of organization or rank, and had head-gear that matched their individual preferences. Some wore field caps, others had wide-brimmed hats, and a few looked like pirates with bandanas on their heads.

Albright personally checked each individual's deploy-ment and field of fire after they were positioned for any po-tential trouble. Their mission that morning was to protect a sixth helicopter that would be coming in with Rear Admi-ral John Miskoski, Rear Admiral John Paulsen, Horace De-Voss, and Hajiri Onwani. Treachery was always possible, and any sneak attacks might decimate Albright's outfit, but the helicopter with the main players would be able to es-cape unharmed.

The paramilitary leader had just finished okaying the fields of fire of the third machine gun team when a warning shout from the perimeter got his attention. He turned to see two strange-looking individuals walking toward them. They were shirtless, wearing khaki trousers, and one had a sling on his left arm.

Albright took the rifle off his shoulder. "Hold it! Iden-tify yourselves."

One of the strangers hollered, "I'm Commander Gerald Fagin, and this is Lieutenant Lars Stensland. We're off the *Buenaventura.*"

Albright hadn't met them before, but he had been briefed on the decoy ship. He signaled them to come into the perimeter. When they joined him, he noticed they'd taken some rough treatment, particularly the blond guy named Stensland.

"Where the hell did you guys come from?" Albright asked.

"We were down in the brig on the destroyer that was bombed yesterday," Fagin explained. "We managed to get away during the attack and have been hiding over in the bushes on the other side of the harbor ever since. We spot-ted you guys coming in and decided to join you. We swam back to this side and walked over to where we saw you

land. There wasn't anybody on the streets." He looked
around. "What the hell's going on?"

"The island is surrendering," Albright explained.

"Ah!" Stensland said, gingerly holding his injured arm.
"That is why they stopped interrogating us."

"It looks like they put you guys through the mill," Albright said. "C'mon! I'll have my medic look at you before
we take you back to the *Jefferson.*"

"You guys don't happen to have any cold beer, do you?"
Fagin asked.

"Sorry," Albright said. "But I'm sure they'll be more
than happy to accommodate you once you're back on the
carrier."

0730 Hours

The sixth helicopter bearing the dignitaries came in and
landed with the others in the middle of the paramilitary
perimeter. As soon as Miskoski, Paulsen, and the two
diplomats deplaned, Albright and a half dozen of his riflemen escorted them over to the castle.

They were met by the naval honor guard of the Kaigun
Samurai. These joined the procession, leading the foreigners
into the castle and up to the door of the throne room. When
the delegation entered the chamber, they found some uniformed officers and one old man in traditional clothing
waiting for them. The oldster came forward and bowed respectfully. An English-speaking lieutenant stepped up beside him.

"I am Sonkei Hanagawa," the old one said, as the words
were translated into English. "Last night, a few minutes
past midnight, our shogun appointed me the commander of
the Kaigun Samurai. He authorized me to surrender our
property, weapons, and people to you."

Paulsen, who was the senior military officer present,
since he had time in grade over Miskoski, glanced around.
"And where is your shogun?"

The lieutenant put the question in Japanese for the old man.

"Last night he committed honorable suicide in a traditional manner to atone for whatever wrongdoing had been committed by those under his leadership," Hanagawa explained. "I wish to have this sacrifice noted in any documents generated by the surrender."

"I cannot make nor accept terms," Paulsen said. "You must do your negotiation with Mr. Horace DeVoss of the United States Department of State and Mr. Hajiri Onwani of the Japanese Foreign Ministry."

"There is a table in the room behind us," Hanagawa said. "I suggest we retire there to make the necessary arrangements for this affair."

He turned and walked toward the door with the strangers following him.

Cruiser **Hayaken**
East China Sea
1000 Hours

Rear Admiral Heideki Tanaka sipped small cups of sake as he watched his servant carefully prepare his full dress uniform. The young sailor had already pressed and brushed the garments, and now pinned the medals on the breast of the coat. When he finished, he laid it out on the admiral's bunk.

Tanaka looked over and gave it a quick glance. There was no reason to make a close scrutiny. The servant had been with him for ten years and had always been very dependable in his work.

"That is fine," Tanaka said. "You are dismissed."

The man, sensing an air of angry gloom in the admiral's presence, quickly left the cabin. Tanaka, slightly tipsy, downed another cupful of the rice wine. He had just poured some more when a knock at the door sounded.

"Kurumasu!" Tanaka said.

The ship's physician entered, his face streaked with tears. He bowed, and a moment passed before he could speak. "I have come as you ordered, *Shosho-san*."

Tanaka frowned at him. "Do not be so emotional! Above all else, you are a Japanese warrior."

"I cannot bear the heavy burden of the shogun's death and our surrender." The bad news had been received and announced aboard the ship only an hour before. "We are returning to our home to find a most unhappy situation."

"The shogun's honorable death is an event to celebrate," Tanaka said. "Whatever happens now is the *Karma* of the Kaigun Samurai. Accept it with dignity and courage." He knocked back the fresh cup of sake. "Did you bring what I told you?"

"Yes, *Shosho-san*," the physician said, still close to weeping. "I have an enema and a hypodermic needle filled with a quadruple dose of morphine."

"Let's get to it," Tanaka said. He stood up and stripped to the buff. Then he leaned across his desk, presenting his backside to the physician. "Do you remember my instructions?"

"Yes, *Shosho-san*," the physician answered as he pushed the enema insert into the admiral's rectum. "You are to be buried at sea in your dress uniform before the ship returns to Kakureta." He opened the clamp to allow the contents of the bag to flow down the hose. "There!"

Tanaka quickly went across the cabin to the small head. He barely reached the toilet before his bowels voided themselves in a loud rush of feces and flatulence. After finishing up the act, he came back to the cabin. "Now, when my sphincter muscle relaxes in death, I'll not soil myself."

He carefully dressed himself rather than have his servant help him. This was a special event in which he wished to humble himself before the souls of dead Japanese warriors. When he finished, he lay down on his rack.

"The hypodermic, if you please, Physician."

"Do you wish me to inject you, *Shosho-san*?"

"I prefer to do it myself."

Tanaka put the needle point over the large vein in his wrist and stuck it in. Then he pushed the plunger. The physician withdrew the empty hypodermic and glanced down at the admiral.

Tanaka was already dead.

USS Jefferson
9 August
1600 Hours

Pamela Drake's situation aboard the carrier seemed to grow steadily worse on a daily basis. Not only was Captain Myra Fontenac's supervisory escort growing more severe and smothering, but the photographer, Tommy Dawson, was terrified of the naval officer. He hadn't taken a single photo since coming aboard.

Pamela's requests for interviews with key people were summarily refused for what Fontenac said were security sensitivities. Fontenac, while not exactly gloating, was smug when she said, "All the information you will be allowed to access can be found in the official U.S. Navy press release. You will be given that and time enough to have it published in your newspaper before it is released to the general media."

Pamela, realizing she would get the same information given to the rest of the world, tried a different approach about the old aircraft she had seen coming and going off the flight deck. "How about the lowdown on those vintage airplanes? Surely those aren't classified material. It seems like a great human-interest story."

"There is nothing special about them," Fontenac said with a pleasant smile. "They were part of a program to test the feasibility of using slower aircraft in certain types of tactical operations." Then she quickly added, "The navy has no conclusive results to report as of yet."

When a helicopter brought two injured white men back from Kakureta Island, Pamela instinctively sensed an interesting situation that would look great in the *Washington Herald-Telegraph.* The two individuals were barefooted, wearing nothing but khaki trousers, and showed signs of having received some extremely rough treatment. One of them even had his left arm in a sling. But again Captain Fontenac stepped between her and an exclusive story.

"Those men were participants in a particularly sensitive operation," she told Pamela. "Their experiences are not for public knowledge."

"I see," Pamela said with a sarcastic smile. "Well, anyway, fuck you very much for all the help you've been giving me."

"My pleasure," Fontenac pleasantly replied. "And if there's anything else I can do to make your life miserable, don't hesitate to let me know."

A few hours later, Pamela was handed the official U.S. Navy press release about Operation Yesteryear. She was given written permission to publish it at any time she wished. But she was advised that it would be released to other journalists on 12 August.

The navy's version of the affair stated that a Japanese secret right-wing military society had purchased three old Soviet warships and used them to hijack merchant vessels and crews passing through the East China Sea. These were ransomed in order to raise money to finance a rebirth of Japanese militarism. Their objective was to overthrow the government and launch the campaigns of the 1930s and 1940s to gain control over prosperous Asian territory. The plot was discovered by U.S. naval intelligence, who coordinated an operation with the Japanese government to raid the secret society base and take the perpetrators into custody. The results of the mission—code named Operation Yesteryear—had been a resounding success.

Pamela read the release aloud to photographer Tommy Dawson as they sat in a wardroom used by visitors. Tommy noticed that when Pamela finished, she looked at him with a devious smile.

"Don't tell me this puts you in a good mood," he said confused.

Pamela lowered her voice. "I'm going to kick back at the fucking navy and hit 'em right in the balls. Or—as in the case of Myra Fontenac—straight in the cunt."

Tommy was confused. "What do you have on them?"

"Whoever wrote this press release has forgotten one very important thing," Pamela said. "It was me who turned them onto the who and what of the East China Sea raiders when I let them know about the old Zunsuno couple." She chuckled. "That will be in my lead paragraph when the article comes out in the *Herald-Telegraph*." She uttered a loud laugh. "Man! I'd love to see Fontenac's face when I shove naval intelligence into the toilet."

Tommy smiled weakly. He was beginning to have his fill of assertive women.

Osaka Naval Base
2200 Hours

The gray Ford van rolled across the concrete of the runway up to the MATS C-141 transport aircraft. When the vehicle came to a stop, INS agent Glen Fox got out, then turned to help Gomme and Hikui Zunsuno step to the ground. A sailor went around the back, getting a pair of suitcases. He carried them up the steps and into the aircraft.

Gomme and Hikui slowly ascended the steps with Fox behind them. When they went inside the fuselage, they were surprised to see comfortable airline seats. Gomme turned to their escort.

"Are we the only passengers?" he asked.

"You sure are," Fox replied with a smile. "The United States of America wants to provide you with the best in flight and travel accommodations."

"That is very kind," Gomme said, knowing this was part of an attempt to woo him into giving them information on the Kamisaku. "We thank you."

The two oldsters settled into seats near the front, and Fox sat across the aisle from them. "We'll be taking off in about twenty minutes," he said, checking his watch. "We'll go to San Francisco, then take a commercial flight to Boston. First class, of course."

"Thank you most kindly," Hikui said.

"You look a bit sad, Mrs. Zunsuno," Fox remarked.

"She is thinking of her special belongings we abandoned on Kakureta Island," Gomme interjected. "They are sentimental things like her paintings and poetry."

"Not to worry," Fox assured them. "We will make arrangements to have everything packed up and sent to your new home in Cambridge."

"We-are unworthy of such consideration," Hikui said.

The jet engines suddenly rumbled and began turning, sending a slight shaking through the passenger section. "We'll be taking off very quickly now," Fox said.

Gomme Zunsuno turned to the window and glanced out for the last view of his native land. But all he could see were the runway lights and the concrete damp from the night's dew.

EPILOGUE

Dealing with the final disposition of Kakureta Island put the Japanese government in a quandary. By rights it belonged to Japan because it was discovered and settled by members of that nation's armed forces a century earlier. On the other hand, since descendents of those founders had participated in organized piracy that cost foreign governments and commercial enterprises billions of dollars, Japan would be liable for those monies by claiming Kakureta as part of its sovereign territory. The billion dollars in the Kaigun Samurai's East African bank account barely put a dent in the gigantic debt. Fortunately for all concerned, the problem was solved when a consortium of Japanese businessmen pledged to repay ransoms and damages over a period of thirty years in exchange for sole ownership of the island. This group of entrepreneurs planned on building a large, luxury resort as an isolated getaway for wealthy vacationers who could afford the maximum in luxury accommodations and diversions. The entrepreneurs changed the name of Kakureta to Rakuen, the Japanese word for "Paradise." The designer of the golf course unknowingly placed the tee off for the thirty-six-hole course at the exact spot where the shogun Hara-*sama* committed *seppuku*.

Another sticky situation the Japanese Ministry of Justice had was figuring out a way to identify and then punish those persons responsible for crimes on the high seas. The outrageous murder of the *Dileas*'s crew and the sinking of the *Buenaventura* with heavy loss of life were two incidents that became the focus of world attention. These crimes overshadowed the hijacking of vessels and kidnapping of crews for ransom. It was here that the uniqueness of Japanese traditions came to the fore. Since Hara-*sama* had announced he would accept the responsibility for all acts and conducts of the Kaigun Samurai, then committed *seppuku* as a sincere atonement, the Japanese public clamored for clemency. After all, Hara had done the honorable thing, bravely accepting all blame, then killing himself to spare his people punishment. The only dissention came from left-wing elements who resented the return of former Kaigun Samurai officers to Japanese society. Consequently, they did their best to see that the leaders were prosecuted as villainous felons. But this proved impossible when the government eventually declared universal clemency for all concerned. However, a fund was set up to provide the families of the dead victims of the *Dileas* massacre a million U.S. dollars each in compensation for their losses. Unfortunately, the men who went down with the *Buenaventura* were not included in the payments. As members of the U.S. Armed Forces, their survivors received benefits from their GI insurance.

Meanwhile, a program was set up to bring former island residents to the mainland for reeducation, orientation, and introduction back into modern Japanese society. This was particularly appreciated by the *jun-i* families who had endured second-class citizenship over the decades. Now they would be able to seek higher education and meaningful professional opportunities in a Japan they had never really known before.

Commander Gene Erickson's VFAX Squadron was finally fleshed out with the addition of five each of F/A-18E and F/A-18F aircraft to the *USS Jefferson*. Among the pilots permanently assigned to this naval air organization were Lieutenants Westy Fields, Junior Stump, and Ariel Goldberg. Additionally, two of Erickson's old buddies who had flown with him against the North Koreans off the *USS Lincoln* were among the new personnel shipped in. These aviators were Lieutenant Commander Benny Lemmons, who would be the squadron executive officer; and Lieutenant Charlie Fredericks as a lead pilot in one of the fighter-attack teams.

All the ordnancemen and aviation machinists from Operation Yesteryear stayed with Erickson, acting as cadre for the new technical and maintenance specialists assigned to the unit. Chief Petty Officer Earl Monger headed up this side of operations.

The squadron took the name High Rollers and used an insignia of a winged pair of dice showing a natural seven as its symbol. This was superimposed over a diamond royal flush in a fanned five-card poker hand.

Dr. Gomme Zunsuno and his wife Hikui obtained official permanent residency in the United States. Numerous government agencies expedited the paperwork and firmed up arrangements for laboratory facilities at the Massachusetts Institute of Technology for the old scientist. He and his wife were afforded a nice condo in Cambridge, Massachusetts, to spend the remainder of their days. They also became the darlings of the community elite and enjoyed an exciting social life of dinner parties and invitations to local cultural events.

The only downside for Dr. Zunsuno came from pressure put on him by various scientific government agencies to reveal the secrets of the Kamisaku force field. But Gomme steadfastly refused to reveal any technical data of his invention. His experience with the Kaigun Samurai had left him hostile and distrustful of those people and bureaus who dealt in national defense. He found plenty of backing from the intellectual communities of Cambridge and Boston. They did not know about the Kamisaku but recognized that pressure was being put on the scientist to work

for the government rather than his own interests. This Ivy
League intelligentsia used their considerable political influence to make the government back off the scientific genius.

Gomme and Hikui settled into a quiet, comfortable life
as he spent his time at MIT working on his project of communicating into deep space to make contact with any other
civilizations out in that great void. Ironically, he actually
employed a bit of the Kamisaku technology in this scientific work.

Meanwhile, Dr. Harry Levinson was given all papers
about the Kamisaku by the U.S. Navy. He completely renovated his laboratory at the submarine base in San Diego
so he could devote all his energies to developing a working
Kamisaku prototype. The preliminary result of his efforts
was called the EBDS for Electronic Blocking Defense System. It was crude and inefficient when compared with the
original. The doctor had a long way to go.

Pamela Drake got back at the U.S. Navy big time for the
heavy-handed treatment she was given aboard the *USS Jefferson*. She broke the story that it was her contact with Dr.
and Mrs. Gomme Zunsuno that brought out the true facts
behind the piracy on the East China Sea. She wrote a series
of articles revealing that it was she and she alone who took
the information to the navy. She emphasized that naval intelligence had been struggling in the dark until she showed
up like a guiding beacon in a dense fog. A Pentagon
spokesperson issued a statement saying that Pamela Drake
was exaggerating her part in the discovery of the perpetrators and the location of their headquarters.

That was a big mistake.

Pamela came back strong, giving the entire story beginning with the accidental meeting with Gomme and Hikui
Zunsuno in the Osaka park. She also revealed that she
arranged for the Zunsunos to be allowed to immigrate to
America and live in Cambridge, Massachusetts, while the
doctor did research at MIT.

This revelation increased her celebrity status with the

American public. She made countless appearances on talk shows, while popular magazines featured articles on her career and freewheeling lifestyle. Additionally, a leading book publisher in New York City advanced her a million and a half dollars for her autobiography.

Pamela was eventually wooed away from the *Washington Herald-Telegraph* by billionaire Mort Sanderson, who owned the new but rapidly expanding International Satellite News Broadcasting Network. The deal was three million per annum along with generous stock options. Sanderson also agreed to give Pamela complete unsupervised license to produce any specials on any subject she wished, as well as unlimited travel to hot news spots anyplace in the world. Pamela assembled a large staff and launched this new phase of her career.

Commander Gerald Fagin returned to the OTSI office at Cape Canaveral, Florida. His attitude toward the organization had changed greatly since his perilous activities in Operation Yesteryear. Fagin decided he'd had about as much adventure as he could stand and took up new desk projects with an improved attitude. This change in his outlook pleased his U.S. Air Force boss more than anyone else.

Scotty Ross got his Avengers back. He, Paddy Paderewski, and Sparky spent all the next winter preparing the aircraft for the coming air show season. Unfortunately, because of the classified situation about the Kamisaku force field, they were to never learn about these great airplanes' final glories and service to the nation. The navy informed the old veteran that the Avengers were part of a training exercise to test how the slow, propeller-driven aircraft might be employed in certain tactical situations.

Lars Stensland returned to Norway, where he was released from active duty with the Royal Norwegian Navy. He was a national celebrity because of his adventures in Operation Yesteryear, and when he returned to his civilian job, he was appointed the captain of his old ship the *SS Edvard Grieg*. This meant an excellent paycheck every month and a chance to make voyages to some of the world's most important commercial ports. He bought a big house overlooking a picturesque *fjord* on the west coast of Norway just north of the town of Bøvagen.

During his absence from his native country, his former fiancée Kristina's marriage to her banker husband deteriorated, and the couple went through a bitter divorce. When Kristina heard of Stensland's new prestigious and well-paid position in the Norwegian Merchant Marine, she visited him during a break between voyages in hopes of renewing their relationship. He responded to her romantic overtures by going to bed with her prettier, younger sister.

GLOSSARY

0-3 LEVEL: The third deck above the main deck. Designations for decks above the main deck (also known as the damage control deck) begin with zero. The zero is pronounced as "oh" in conversation. Decks below the main deck do not have the initial zero and are numbered down from the main deck, e.g., Deck 11 is below Deck 3; Deck 0-7 is above deck 0-3.

AA: Antiaircraft.

ABAFT: Toward the stern or rear of a vessel.

ACLS: Automatic Carrier Landing System. System used to guide the aircraft to the deck automatically.

AGL: Above Ground Level.

AIR BOSS: A senior commander or captain assigned to the aircraft carrier, in charge of flight operations. The boss is assisted by the miniboss in Pri-Fly, located in the tower on board the carrier. The air boss is always in the tower during flight operations, overseeing the launch and recover cycles, declaring a green deck, and monitoring the safe approach of aircraft to the carrier.

AIR WING: Composed of the aircraft squadrons assigned to the battle group. The individual squadron commanding officers report to the air wing commander, who reports to the admiral.

AIRDALE: Slang for an officer or enlisted person in the aviation fields. Includes pilots, NFOs, aviation intelligence officers, maintenance officers, and the enlisted technicians who support aviation. The antithesis of an airdale is a "shoe."

AKA: Also known as.

AKULA: Late-model Russian-built nuclear attack submarine, an SSN. Fast, deadly, and deep diving.

ALR-67: Detects, analyzes, and evaluates electromagnetic signals; emits a warning signal if the parameters are compatible with an immediate threat to the aircraft, e.g., seeker head on an antiair missile. Can detect enemy radar in either a search or a targeting mode.

AMRAAM: Advanced Medium-Range Air-to-Air Missile.

ANGELS: Thousands of feet over ground. Angels twenty is twenty thousand feet.

APC: Speed-holding automatic throttle.

ASAP: As soon as possible.

ASL: Above Sea Level.

ASW: Antisubmarine Warfare.

ATCC: Air Traffic Control Center.

AVIONICS: Black boxes and systems that compose an aircraft's combat systems.

AW: Aviation antisubmarine warfare technician. The enlisted specialist flying in an S-3, P-3, or helo ASW aircraft.

AWACS: Advanced Warning Aviation Control System. Long-range command-and-control and electronic-intercept aircraft.

AWG-9: The primary search and fire control radar on a Tomcat. Pronounced *awg nine.*

BACKSEATER: Also know as the GIB, the Guy In Back. Nonpilot aviator available in several flavors: BN (Bomber/Navigator), RIO (Radio Intercept Operator), and TACCO (Tactical Control Officer), among others. Usually wears glasses and is smart.

BALL: Optical landing aid to keep the pilot on the proper glide path.

BAT TURN: Pilot talk for a very sharp turn.

BB STACKER: Nickname for ordnanceman, i.e., Red Shirt.

BEAR: Russian maritime patrol aircraft, the equivalent in rough terms of a U.S. P-3. Variants have primary missions in command and control, submarine hunting, and electronic intercepts. Big, slow, good targets.

BITCH BOX: One interior communications system on a ship. So named because it's normally used to bitch at another watch station.

BLUE ON BLUE: Fratricide. U.S. forces are normally indicated in blue on tactical displays, and this term refers to an attack on a friendly by another friendly.

BLUE WATER NAVY: Outside the unrefueled range of the air wing. When a carrier enters blue water ops, aircraft must get on board, i.e., land, and cannot divert to land if the pilot gets the shakes.

BOLTER: When an aircraft making a carrier landing misses all the wires, the aviator must speed up and fly off the carrier to try it again.

BOOMER: Slang for a ballistic missile submarine.

BOQ: Bachelor Officers' Quarters.

BUSTER: As fast as you can, i.e., immediately if not sooner.

BVR: Beyond visual range.

C-2 GREYHOUND: Also known as the COD, Carrier Onboard Delivery. The COD carries cargo and passengers from shore to ship. It is capable of carrier landings and also operated in coordination with CVBGs from a shore squadron.

CAG: Carrier Air Group Commander. This is an obsolete term, since an air wing rather than an air group is now deployed on carriers. However, everyone thought CAW sounded stupid, thus the original acronym is still employed.

CAP: Combat Air Patrol.

CARRIER BATTLE GROUP: A combination of ships, air wings, and submarines assigned under the command of a rear admiral. Also known by the acronym CVBG.

CCAFS: Cape Canaveral Air Force Station.

CDC: Combat Direction Center. This replaces the old term

CIC for Combat Information Center. All sensor information is fed into the CDC, and the battle is coordinated by a tactical action officer on watch there.

CHERUBS: Hundreds of feet above ground. Cherubs five is five hundred feet.

CHIEF: Term used to denote chief, senior chief, and master chief petty officers. On board ship the chiefs have separate eating and berthing facilities. They wear khakis as opposed to dungarees for lower enlisted ratings.

CHIEF OF STAFF: The COS in a battle group staff is normally a senior captain who acts as the admiral's executive officer or deputy.

CIA: The Central Intelligence Agency.

CIWS: Close-in Weapons System, pronounced *see-whiz*. Gatling gun with built-in radar that tracks and fires on inbound missiles. If you have to use it, you're dead.

CNO: Chief of Naval Operations.

CO: Commanding officer.

COD: (See *C-2 Greyhound.*)

COLLAR COUNT: Traditional method of determining the winner of a disagreement. A survey is taken of the opponent's collar rank devices. The senior person wins. Always.

COMMODORE: Formerly the junior-most flag rank, now used to designate a senior captain in charge of a bunch of like units. A destroyer commodore commands several destroyers, a sea control commodore commands the S-3 squadrons on that coast. Contrast with a CAG, who commands a number of dissimilar units.

COMPARTMENT: A room on a ship.

CONDITION TWO: One step down from general quarters, which is Condition One. Condition Five is tied up at the pier in a friendly country.

CPO: Chief Petty Officer.

CRYPTO: Short for *cryptological,* the magic set of codes that makes a circuit impossible for anyone else to understand.

CV, CVN: Abbreviation for an aircraft carrier, conventional and nuclear.

CVIC: Carrier Intelligence Center located down the passageway from the flag spaces.

DATA LINK, THE LINK: The secure circuit that links all units in a battle group or in an area. Targets and contacts are transmitted over the link to all ships. The data is processed by the ship designated as Net Control, and common contacts are correlated. The system also transmits data from each ship and aircraft's weapons systems, e.g., a missile firing. All services use the link.

DDG: Guided Missile Destroyer.

DDI: Digital Display Indicator.

DESK JOCKEY: Nonflyer who drives a computer instead of an aircraft.

DESRON: Destroyer commander.

DICASS: An active sonobuoy.

DICK STEPPING: Something to be avoided. While anatomically impossible in today's gender-integrated services, it has been decided that women can do this as well.

DOPPLER: Acoustic phenomenon caused by relative motion between a sound source and a receiver that results in an apparent change in frequency of the sound. The classic example is a train going past and the decrease in the pitch of its whistle. When a submarine changes its course or speed in relation to a sonobuoy, the event shows up as a change in the frequency of the sound source.

DOUBLE NUTS: Zero zero on the tail of an aircraft.

DSCS: Defense Satellite Communications System.

E-2 HAWKEYE: Command, control, and surveillance aircraft. Turboprop rather than jet, and unarmed. Smaller version of an AWACS, in practical terms, but carrier-based.

ECM: Electronic Counter Measure.

ELF: Extremely Low Frequency. A method of communicating with submarines at sea. Signals are transmitted via a miles-long antenna and are the only way of reaching a deeply submerged submarine.

ENVELOPE: What you're supposed to fly inside if you want to live to fly another day.

ETA: Estimated Time of Arrival.

ETS: Expiration of Term of Service.

EW: Electronic warfare technicians who man the devices that detect, analyze, and display electromagnetic signals.

F/A-18 HORNETS AND SUPER HORNETS: A combination fighter/attack aircraft.

FAMILYGRAM: Short messages from submarine sailors' families to their deployed sailors. Often the only contact with the outside world that a submarine sailor on deployment has.

FBC: Flag Battle Center.

FF/FFG: Fast frigate and guided-missile fast frigate.

FLAG OFFICERS: Admirals.

FLAG PASSAGEWAY: The portion of an aircraft carrier that houses the admiral's staff working spaces. Includes the flag mess and the admiral's cabin. Normally separated from the rest of the ship by heavy plastic curtains and designated by blue tile on the deck instead of white.

FLIGHT QUARTERS: A condition set on board a ship preparing to launch or recover aircraft. All unnecessary persons are required to stay inside the skin of the ship and remain clear of the flight deck area.

FLIGHT SUIT: The highest form of navy couture. The perfect choice of apparel for any occasion as far as pilots are concerned.

FLIR: Forward-Looking Infra Red.

FLTSATCOM: Fleet Satellite Communications System.

FOD: Foreign Object Damage, or loose gear or debris that can cause damage to an aircraft.

FOX: Tactical shorthand for a missile firing. Fox One indicates a head-seeking missile, Fox Two an infrared missile, and Fox Three a radar-guided missile.

FROG: A member of the catapult and arresting crew, i.e., green shirt.

GCI: Ground Control Intercept. This is a procedure used in the Soviet air forces. Primary control for vectoring the aircraft in on enemy targets and other fighters is vested in a guy on the ground rather than in the cockpit where it belongs.

GIB: (See *Backseater.*)

GMT: Greenwich Mean Time.

GRAPE: Member of aircraft refueling team, i.e., Purple Shirt.

GREEN SHIRTS: (See *Shirts.*)

HANDLER: Officer located on the flight deck level responsible for ensuring the aircraft are correctly positioned—"spotted"—on the flight deck. Coordinates the movements of aircraft with yellow gear (small tractors that tow aircraft and other related gear) from maintenance areas to catapults, and from the flight deck to the hangar bar via the elevators.

HARM: Antiradiation missile that homes in on radar sites.

HOT: Reference to a sonobuoy holding enemy contact.

HUFFER: Yellow gear located on the flight deck that generates compressed air to start jet engines.

HUD: Heads Up Display.

ICS: Inter Communications System. The private link between a pilot and a RIO or the telephone system internal to a ship.

ILS: Instrument Landing System.

IMC: The general announcing system on a ship or submarine. Every ship has many different interior communications systems, most of them linking parts of the ship for a specific purpose. Most operate off sound-powered phones. The circuit designators consist of a number followed by two letters that indicate the specific purpose of the circuit; 2AS, for instance, might be an antisubmarine warfare circuit that connects the sonar supervisor, the USW watch officer, and the sailor at the torpedo launch.

INCHOPPED: A ship entering a defined area of water, e.g., inchopped the Med.

IN RNG: When this appears on the HUD or DDI, it indicates that the selected target is in range.

INTELREP: Intelligence Report.

INS: Immigration and Naturalization Service.

IR: Infrared.

ISOTHERMAL: A layer of water that has a constant temperature with increasing depth. Located below the thermocline where increase in depth correlates to decrease in temperature. In the isothermal layer the primary factor affecting the speed of sound in water is the increase in pressure and depth.

JBD: Jet Blast Deflector. Panels that pop up from the flight deck to block the exhaust emitted by aircraft.

JTFEX: Joint Task Force Exercise.

KADETT: Cadet (Norwegian).

KAIGUNSHO: Admiralty.

KAMIKAZE: "Divine Wind"—name given to Japanese suicide air squadrons of World War II.

KAPTEIN: Captain (Norwegian).

KAPTEINLØTNANT: Norwegian naval rank equivalent to U.S. Navy lieutenant.

LEADING PETTY OFFICER: The senior petty officer in a work center, division, or department, responsible to the leading chief petty officer for the performance of the rest of the group.

LOFARGRAM: Low-Frequency Analyzing and Recording Display. Consists of lines arrayed by frequency on the horizontal axis and time on the vertical axis. Displays sound signals in the water in a graphic fashion for analysis by ASW technicians.

LONG GREEN TABLE: A formal inquiry board.

LØYNTNANT: Lieutenant (Norwegian).

LSO: Landing Signal Officer.

MACHINIST'S MATE: Enlisted technician who runs and repairs most engineering equipment on board a ship. Abbreviated as MM, e.g., an MM1 is a petty officer first machinist's mate.

MAD: Magnetic Anomaly Detection equipment.

MATS: Military Air Transport Service.

MCAS: Marine Corps Air Station.

MDI: Mess Decks Intelligence. The rumor mill aboard a ship.

MEZ: Missile Engagement Zone. Any hostile contacts in the MEZ are engaged only with missiles. Friendly aircraft must stay clear.

MIG: Russian Mikoyan line of aircraft designation.

MIT: Massachussettes Institute of Technology.

MRE: Meals Ready to Eat, i.e., field rations.

MWB: Motorized whaleboat. These are lifeboats and shipboard utility boats powered by diesel. They are usually around twenty-five feet in length and are steered by a tiller.

NAS: Naval Air Station.

NATIONAL ASSETS: Surveillance and reconnaissance resources of the most sensitive nature, e.g., satellites.

NATOP: The bible for operating a particular aircraft.

NFO: Naval Flight Officer.

NOMEX: Fire-resistant fabric used as material for shirts. (See *Shirts*.)

NSA: National Security Agency. Primarily responsible for evaluating electronic intercepts and sensitive intelligence.

NUGGET: Rookie aviator.

OER: Officer Evaluation Report.

OOD: Officer of the Deck. Responsible for the safe handling and maneuvering of the ship. Supervises the conning officer and other underway watchstanders. Ashore, the OOD may be responsible for a shore station after normal working hours.

OPLAN: Operations Plan. What is written before an OPORD.

OPORD: Operations Order.

OTH: Over the Horizon. Usually refers to shooting at something you can't see.

OTSI: Office of Technological and Scientific Intelligence.

P-3: Shore-based antisubmarine warfare and surface surveillance long-range aircraft.

PHOENIX: Long-range antiair missile carried by U.S. fighters.

PIPELINE: A series of training commands, schools, or necessary education for a particular specialty. The fighter pipeline, for example, includes basic flight, then fighter training at the RAG (Replacement Air Group), a training squadron.

PRIFLY: Primary Flight Control. (See Air Boss.)

PUNCHING OUT: Ejecting from an aircraft.

PURPLE SHIRTS: (See *Shirts*.)

PXO: Prospective Executive Officer. The officer ordered into a command as the relief for the current XO. In most squadrons, the XO eventually "fleets up" to become the commanding officer of the squadron, an excellent system that maintains continuity with an operational command. The surface navy does not use this system.

RACK: A bed or bunk.

REDCROWN: The ship in the CVBG that coordinates air defense.

REDOUT: This occurs when an aviator goes through a negative force field of gravity, and his vision reddens from blood forced into his head.

RED SHIRTS: (See *Shirts.*)

RHIP: Rank Has Its Privileges. (See *Collar Count.*)

RIO: Radar Intercept Officer.

RWR: Radar Warning Receiver.

RWS: Range While Searching radar.

S-3: Command and control aircraft. Redesignated as sea control aircraft with individual squadrons referred to as torpedo bombers.

SAM: Surface-to-Air Missile.

SAR: Sea-Air Rescue.

SCIF: Sensitive Compartmented Information Facility. On board a carrier, used to designate the highly classified compartment next to TFCC.

SEAWOLF: Newest version of the navy's fast-attack submarine.

SENSO: Sensor operator on board an S-3B Viking aircraft.

SERE: Survival, Evasion, Resistance, and Escape.

SHIRTS: Color-coded Nomex pullovers used by flight deck and aviation personnel for rapid identification of their functions. Green: maintenance divisions. Brown: plane captains. White: safety and medical. Red: ordnance. Purple: fuel. Yellow: flight deck supervisors and handlers.

SIDEWINDER: Antiair missile carried by U.S. fighters.

SIERRA: A subsurface contact.

SLR: Self-Loading Rifle.

SONOBUOYS: Acoustic listening devices dropped in the water by ASW or USW aircraft.

SOP: Standing Operational Procedures.

SPARROW: Antiair missile carried by U.S. fighters.

SPECOPS: Special operations.

SPETSNAZ: The Russian version of SEALs, although the term encompasses a number of difference specialties.

SPOOKS: Slang for intelligence officers and enlisted sailors working in highly classified areas.

SSN: Attack Submarine.

SUBANT: Administrative command of all Atlantic submarine forces.

SUBPAC: Administrative command of all Pacific submarine forces.

SWEET: When used in reference to a sonobuoy, it indicates that buoy is functioning properly.

TACCO: Tactical Coordinator; the NFO in an S-3.

TACTICAL CIRCUIT: A term that encompasses a wide range of actual circuits used on board a carrier.

TANKER: A fuel-carrying aircraft for in-air refueling.

TDY: Temporary Duty.

TEU: Twenty-foot Equivalent Unit. Capacity of cargo containers used on a container ship.

TFCC: Tactical Flag Command Center. A compartment in flag spaces from which the CVBG admiral controls the battle. Located immediately forward of the carrier's CDC.

TOP GUN: Advanced fighter training command.

UNDERSEA WARFARE COMMANDER: In a CVBG, normally the DESRON embarked on the carrier. Formerly called the ASW commander.

UNREP: Underway replenishment—the resupply and refueling of ships at sea.

VDL: Video downlink. Transmission of targeting data from an aircraft to a submarine with OTH capabilities.

VFAX: Experimental fighter-Attack squadron.

VIP: Very Important Person.

VJ DAY: Victory over Japan Day. The day the Japanese surrendered in World War II.

VX-1: Test pilot squadron that develops envelopes after Pax River evaluates aerodynamic characteristics of new aircraft. (See *Envelope*.)

WCTU: Woman's Christian Temperance Union—an organization that promoted prohibition of alcoholic beverages.
WHITE SHIRT: (See *Shirts.*)
WILCO: Will comply.
WINCHESTER: Out of weapons.
XO: Executive Officer. The second-in-command.
YELLOW SHIRT: (See *Shirts.*)

Armored Corps

by
Pete Callahan

West Point graduate Lieutenant Jack Hansen is
stationed near the 38th Parallel in South Korea with the
1st Tank Battalion. They haven't seen any action yet,
but that's about to change.

On Christmas day, North Korea's power-mad dictator
launches a surprise attack, and Hansen and his
battalion of untested warriors must charge into
battle to halt the invasion.

0-515-13932-7

Available wherever books are sold or at
penguin.com

b259